TO WHOM DO YOU TURN WHEN

a vicious and violent aristocrat has his head bashed
in? . . . a beautiful and high-born lady is charged
with the ugliest and lowest of crimes? . . . a great
scientist is found dead and papers that threaten the
peace of the world are missing? . . . a criminal genius
seems on the verge of mocking justice and getting
away with murder? . . . a tattered glove is the only
clue to the unknown hand that has killed and killed
again? . . . one of two brothers is a murderer, and
each seems more innocent than the other?

To whom do you turn when these and other heinous
acts chill the blood and leave the official forces of
law and order helpless and hopeless?

The answer is elementary, dear reader, elementary . . .

THE ADVENTURES OF CREIGHTON HOLMES

THE ADVENTURES
of
CREIGHTON
HOLMES

by Ned Hubbell

POPULAR LIBRARY • NEW YORK

THE ADVENTURES OF CREIGHTON HOLMES

Published by Popular Library, a unit of CBS Publications,
the Consumer Publishing Division of CBS Inc.

ISBN: 0-445-04350-4

Printed in the United States of America

10 9 8 7 6 5 4 3 2 1

Contents

"Elementary, my dear Watson, elementary."

The Mysterious Death at Wetherby Manor

I had not seen Creighton Holmes for eight years. I had first met him at Eton. When several of us had become known to each other, one of the group had asked young Holmes if he was related to the great criminal investigator, and with a quiet smile he had replied that we would not believe him if he said he was.

Later, when he and I had become better acquainted, he had confided in me that he was in fact the grandson of the celebrated Sherlock Holmes. Although Dr. Watson, biographer of the famous detector of crime, who confessed that he knew little of his subject's youth, had not been aware of the fact, Sherlock Holmes had been married when he was very young, but the union had ended in tragedy. Within a year the lovely bride had died while giving birth to a son. In the bitterness of his grief, Holmes had turned the child over to his mother's parents and thereafter had had little use for women.

Naturally the son, who had been virtually disowned, had cared little for his father; but early in life the grandson, Creighton, had conceived a great admiration for his remarkable ancestor and had followed his every accomplishment with avid interest. Moreover, fancying he had inherited something of his grandfather's unique talent, he had, when still quite young, attempted to copy his methods of observation and deduction.

Of course, as was inevitable, others at Eton had soon discovered young Creighton's true identity, and a few of us who were among his intimates had often amused ourselves and him by inducing him to display evidence of his peculiar gift—which was, indeed, much like that of his illustrious forebear.

After we left school, we had gone our separate ways. Though Holmes had secretly aspired to follow in his grandfather's footsteps, he had been possessed of little means and had therefore had small hope of realizing his ambition, as he might well starve to death while awaiting clients. Accordingly, he had undertaken the study of law, attending to a routine job to eke out an existence.

As for myself, I had embarked upon my chosen calling of journalism by getting a place on the *Manchester Guardian* where I had continued until now on my job as reporter.

But while he was still studying Blackstone, Holmes's career had taken an unexpected turn. The father of one of his former classmates, had become involved in a serious difficulty of some mysterious nature, and at his son's insistence had called upon Holmes to solve it. As fortune would have it, Holmes had been successful, with the result that the beneficiary of his efforts, a man of wealth and position, had been most grateful. To show his appreciation, he had assumed all expenses necessary to set up young Creighton in an office with some youthful barristers and stake him for a year as a private investigator.

However, in spite of these modern facilities, I was to learn later that, either because of the tradition of his fabled grandfather's doing business in his living quarters, or a compelling desire for secrecy, or the feeling of the urgent need for his services without delay, many of Creighton's clients came to his personal apartment on Baker Street, as they had come to that of the great Sherlock, according to the memoirs of the good Dr. Watson.

It should be noted that as a consequence of his change in fortune, Holmes had immediately given up his other activities and had devoted himself entirely to the unraveling of mysteries.

Moreover, thanks to the influence of his patron, he

had not been without clients from the very beginning, and in a short time was enjoying a lucrative practice.

As for myself, I was now back in London, having severed my connection with the *Guardian* to take a berth on the London *Times*. As I was not to assume my duties for another week, however, I was temporarily at loose ends. Giving way to an impulse to see my old-time schoolmate, I rang up Holmes and was pleased and not a little flattered to have him warmly invite me to come and spend a couple of days with him.

Interestingly enough, I found that his living quarters were at almost the same location on the famous Baker Street as had been those where Sherlock Holmes himself had hung out. We were delighted to see each other and quickly fell into the old intimacy. After a hearty meal outside, we returned to his diggings to spend a long evening talking over schooldays and catching up on the time in between, so that it was close to midnight before we finally retired.

I must have been in bed less than an hour when I heard the telephone bell insistently ringing and was aware of Holmes shuffling to it in dressing gown and slippers. He was at the phone for some time during which I lay awake, intrigued by such words of his as I happened to overhear. When at length he hung up, I could not forbear blurting out, "No bad news, I hope."

He came and stood in the doorway. "Nothing personal, as far as I'm concerned. But if a murdered man is bad news, then I fancy you might say there is."

"A murdered man!"

"Well, at least a dead one," he went on, "and it looks suspiciously like murder. The call was from a law-enforcement officer near Lesser Dalton. He says a wealthy old lord at Wetherby Manor near the village of Pippingate was found in a room of his home with his head bashed in, dead as a mackerel." Then his voice took on an apologetic tone. "I'm sorry, old man, but Dodson would very much like to have me come down to help him in the investigation. I am under an obligation to him, and it does sound a bit intriguing. I would ask you to go along, but my motorcar is laid up and I will have to be getting up about five of the clock to catch the five twenty-five train out of Waterloo Station. You are welcome to make yourself at home here, and I will probably be back before evening."

"But my car is available," I offered, "and I would be more than glad to drive you. That is," I added doubtfully, "if you are really serious about wishing me to go."

"Of course I'm serious!" he exclaimed. "That will be capital! And it will give me an extra hour in bed. Meanwhile, you'd better try to get back to sleep. I want to look up a bit of information before I turn in. I'll tell you more about the affair in the morning." We exchanged good-nights, and he turned away.

Next day, before we left, Holmes slipped a note under his landlady's door asking her to notify his office as to where he could be reached.

It was a cold, lowering day in November, fit weather for the somber journey upon which we were embarked. I glanced at my companion. He was middle-sized, pleasant, and unassuming—little like his noted ancestor in this respect. But I knew that he was shrewd and that, once on a scent, he was like a hound that would never let up until he had run down his quarry. I wondered if he would get on the scent of the unknown killer of the lord of Wetherby Manor.

"I may as well tell you what I know of this puzzling affair," he said as we rode along, "which isn't much. Dodson will have to fill us in on the details when we get there. I looked up Ambrose Wetherby, the victim of the killing, in the *Book of Peerage* last night, and found him to be the sixth lord of the line. At the time of his death he should have been some two and seventy years of age. In his youth he served in our military forces as a colonel abroad. He was a widower and lived on the ancestral estate that dates back almost to the time of the Tudors. That's about all that I can tell you about the man himself.

"As for the crime we are about to investigate, Dodson said that the lord and the granddaughter who has been making her home at the manor had been out for the evening and had just returned to the house shortly before midnight. The granddaughter went immediately to her room, but Lord Wetherby went to the library, in which a light was burning—an unusual circumstance for that time of night—which aroused his curiosity.

"Some ten minutes later, the entire household was alarmed by a series of terror-stricken shrieks from one of the maids, who had taken advantage of the lord's absence to go out with a local admirer. It seems that she had just come into a dimly lighted hallway through a rear entrance, and was attacked and severely beaten by the killer as he fled through the hall to make his escape. A few minutes later the lord was found dead in the library. He had been struck on the head and fatally injured after what appeared to be a violent struggle."

"No clues?"

"None whatever, as far as Dodson could discover. And no apparent motive, nor any suspects."

"Anything stolen?"

"Nothing."

"Sounds truly baffling. By the way, what is this man Dodson like?"

"A good sort, but a bit slow-witted and devoid of imagination. He is earnest and hard-working but is likely to overlook the most obvious clue and to fail to appreciate the significance of those he does discover. But he realizes his limitations and is quite willing to avail himself of help. On the whole, not a bad fellow to work with."

He lapsed into silence, and soon I saw his head nodding. Before long, because of his few hours in bed, he was fast asleep. He did not awaken until we reached Pippingate, when I roused him to get more precise directions as to our destination.

The house of Wetherby Manor, set in grounds surrounded entirely by a stone wall some four feet high, was a grey, gloomy structure built in the rambling style characteristic of its day. This morning, as we approached it with the bare, bleak trees about it and the drab November sky above it, the place seemed grim and forbidding. The air was chill and biting and the ground still damp from a drizzling rain the day before.

Dodson was awaiting us at the entrance with a long face. After introducing me, Holmes asked him how things were going. "It's a bad business and that's a fact. Nothing to get hold of," he replied. He told us that he had stayed all night there at the insistence of the women, who had been badly upset by the gruesome death of the lord. He explained that he had intercepted us because he wished to apprise Holmes of such details as he could before Holmes met the inmates of the place.

Ushering us into the house, he led us toward the room that had been the scene of the crime. "I thought that you would like to look it over first," he explained. "I tried to see that nothing was disturbed, as you directed."

The library, a room about sixteen by eighteen feet in dimensions, was in the west wing of the manor. It opened off the large withdrawing room and was entered through a door at the extreme northerly end of the wall separating the two rooms. To the south of this door, in the easterly or inner wall of the library, was the fireplace in front of which the dead body of the lord had been found. Near the southerly wall was a large, dark, flat-topped desk with a swivel chair behind it. Near the west or outer wall was a big easy chair with a footstool before it. Beside the chair and to the left of it was a good-sized stand, apparently of walnut, as presumably was the desk. Upon this stand there now rested an ashtray with some bits of tobacco ash and a partly used match folder in it. On the stand also lay a package some ten to twelve inches across and three or four inches thick, done up in brown wrapping paper and secured with a tarry-looking string. Two massive

14

armchairs on the northerly side of the room completed its furnishings.

All in all, it was an elegant if somewhat gloomy chamber with three of its walls lined with shelves of richly-bound books, its heavy leaded windows set deep in the thick stone walls, and with sumptuous ornamental drapes and, on the hearth, sturdy brass andirons. But just now it was in a sad state of disarray, with the andirons set at an odd angle, the footstool overturned and laying upside down on the well-worn but handsome oriental rug, and the rug itself badly rumpled and awry—and discolored by an ugly dark blotch where the dead man's blood had stained it, while the gruesome body itself still lay in a heap before the hearth.

"Everything is just as it was," Dodson assured us. "The local doctor did not even wipe the blood off the wound. In fact, he made the most cursory of examinations. He had been up all night and only stopped out of accommodation on his way to another call. He glanced at the body just long enough to say that the lord was dead, said it was a matter for the official authorities, and left. I think he had no great love for the late lord and was irked by the call."

Holmes squatted down over the corpse and carefully scrutinized it. There was an ugly gash just back of the right temple where the victim, a big man weighing fully fourteen stone, had evidently been struck by some heavy object. A few strands of brightly colored wool, apparently torn from the scarf of his assailant, were clutched in the dead man's hand. But the thing that struck me most forcibly was the look on the murdered man's face—a horrible grimace that might have been caused by fear or pain or anger.

The murky atmosphere of the room, its disturbed state indicative of the desperation with which the slain man had fought for his life, and the all-but-inhuman look on his face, all these gave me an eerie feeling. But Holmes seemed unaffected. "Just a few minutes while I go over the room," he said, getting up from his inspection of the body.

Thereupon, he took from a coat pocket a magnifying glass, such as had been used by his grandfather, and proceeded systematically to scrutinize the various parts of the room. Even as a boy I had been somewhat amused by employment of such a glass by the great Sherlock Holmes, being inclined to regard it as an interesting bit of stage property. But I was to learn that Creighton Holmes never did anything for mere effect, and in this instance the use of the glass was to have a vital part in the solution of this apparently insoluble problem.

Appearing to glance only casually at the tobacco ashes in the tray, he looked carefully at the partly used matchbook, then turned and pored long over the sills and locks of the windows. Finally he faced Dodson and said, "You found no marks indicating how the intruder made his way into the room?"

"None at all. And there were no footprints or broken shrubbery outside. I found that all the doors and windows were securely locked. How the fellow ever gained entrance is a mystery."

"Indeed!" said Holmes, in a tone, it seemed to me, almost of satisfaction. "This promises to be quite intriguing. Now I want to make a little further examination, and I fancy that we are through here."

He then got down, made a rather casual inspection of the rug, then turned and lingered a long time over the two heavy brass andirons. What he hoped to find there was beyond my comprehension.

At length he straightened up. As he did so, he turned toward the stand and lightly touched the package on it with one finger. "What's this?" he asked.

Dodson answered. "I don't know. I assumed it was something belonging to Lord Wetherby that he had not got round to opening."

Holmes grunted. "Possibly. But we'll learn about it later." He put the magnifying glass back in his pocket and turned to take a seat in the easy chair. "Well, I fancy that we can do no more here for the time being."

"Did you find anything?" I could not refrain from asking.

"Why, yes," he replied. "Three interesting circumstances, two of which are of considerable significance if I am not mistaken, not to mention this curious package." Then, turning to address our companion, he said, "Just now I would appreciate it, Dodson, if you could tell us something about the inmates of the house." As he spoke, he pulled out his tobacco pouch, filled his pipe, lighted it and leaned back to listen. "Suppose you tell us about the lord first. Did he have any enemies?"

"Well, not what you'd call enemies. He wasn't popular, but as far as I can learn, no one hated him—or at least not enough to kill him."

"How did he get along with his neighbors?"

"He didn't. They mostly let each other alone. He was said to be high-handed and short-tempered. Whenever some matter came up in the district, he always wanted to run things, and didn't like it if things didn't go his way. He was never very sociable and has been even less so since his wife died six years ago. I fancy you could say it was a case of live and let live." Then he added gloomily, "Only someone didn't let him live."

"How about the servants?"

"The same story. They got along, but I dare say they didn't worship him. Still, some of them have been here at the manor for some time: the gardener for thirty years, the butler for nineteen, the housekeeper and the cook for some ten years each.

"I understand that Lady Wetherby was different from her husband. Kind and agreeable. I fancy most of the servants have stayed partly out of loyalty to her and partly because it would be hard to catch on somewhere else at their time of life. And, likely, the younger ones are glad of any situation at all these days. The only one, as far as I know, who was really close to the lord was the butler. Of course, both the young and the old are fond of Miss Compton."

"Miss Compton?"

"She's the granddaughter."

"And what were the relations between her and the late lord?"

"That's just what I don't understand."

"What do you mean?"

"Well, I don't think she doted on him, if you get my meaning, sir. She had a mind of her own and wouldn't take kindly to having someone try to run her life, and I can't imagine the old lord keeping his hands out of her affairs. But she seems completely done in by his death. She's in her room now. She's taken to her bed and won't see anyone but her maid Peggy. She's the one person I haven't had a chance to talk to."

"Most interesting," commented Holmes. "Now tell me about the staff."

"Very good, sir. First, there's the housekeeper, a widow named Mrs. Wiggin, in her early fifties. She seems capable enough but inclined to talk a lot. I fancy she is your best bet for information, sir. Then there's the butler, Pawlings, around sixty, unmarried; the cook, Mrs. Fogarty, a middle-aged widow; the gardener, Binks, an old fellow over seventy, hard of hearing; his helper, a young fellow by the name of Joe Hendy— he's the one that drove Lord Wetherby and his granddaughter last night; and two maids. Peggy Morris, three or four and twenty, who acts as Miss Compton's personal maid; and Rose Brooks, about one and twenty, the one that the killer ran into in his getaway.

"As I said, I haven't talked with Miss Compton, and I did not get much out of the maid, Peggy. She and the housekeeper and the gardener were all in bed when Rose Brooks was attacked. The housekeeper and Peggy, along with Miss Compton, heard Rose scream and came downstairs at once. Joe Hardy heard her too, as he was putting the car away in the carriage house that serves as a garage. He and the old gardener sleep in the upper part of it, and the gardener heard nothing. The cook was away, spending the night with her sister in the village. And the butler was not available for questioning."

Holmes looked up sharply. "He wasn't? Why not?"

"Well, that's the funny thing. He wasn't here, sir."

"I don't think I understand."

"It's this way, sir. Pawlings left before this happened. At least from what he said, he did."

"From what he said. I thought—"

"What I mean to say is that he left a note. Here it is, sir, if you would like to see it." And he reached into his pocket and drew forth a folded scrap of paper, which Holmes unfolded and read, holding it so that I might read it too. It ran as follows:

Dear Lord Wetherby—Received a call from my sister in Brighton that mother was critically ill there. Am leaving for that city at once. Expect to return in a few days. Will telephone as soon as I know definitely. Respectfully, Paulings.

"Well, that seems clear enough."

"Yes, but we don't know if he ever went there, sir. Just as a matter of routine, I thought I should follow up the matter. But I found out next to nothing."

"How was that?"

"It's all very strange, sir," Dodson said, "I thought that he would naturally leave from Pippingate station and would probably call a cab to take him there. I learned that he did call a cab about ten of the clock, then called back half an hour later to say he would not need it."

"Yes? Go on."

"So then I called Pippingate station and had the police check at Lesser Dalton, five miles away, but there was no record of anyone of Pawlings's description leaving for Brighton from either place. We did not have the name of Pawlings's sister, so I could not get in touch with her, but I had the Brighton police call all the hospitals in that city and there was no patient by the name of Mrs. Pawlings registered in any of them. The truth is that Pawlings is gone but we don't know how or where. He just vanished into thin air, you might say. It looks sort of suspicious, but it seems stupid for him to have run away. Besides, there is no motive; or at least, none that anyone knows of. Then, too, there are the calls about the cab. Of course, they could be a blind. But it is all most peculiar, especially as he and the lord were supposed to be so friendly."

"It is, indeed," agreed Holmes. "This case grows more and more intriguing. Now tell me exactly what happened when Rose Brooks screamed."

"Well, when the three women rushed down they found Rose in a state bordering on hysteria. When they finally got the truth out of her, Mrs. Wiggin and the maids were all for getting the men servants before going to see what, if anything, had happened to the lord. But Miss Compton, who seems to have plenty of courage, said nonsense, she was going to find out. The others waited for Joe Hendy to come and then followed Miss Compton to the library, where they found her by the dead body of the old man as you see it now, sir. Later they found Pawlings's note—they had wondered where he was. Meanwhile, they got hold of the doctor, and young Hendy insisted upon calling the police. At first Miss Compton, for some reason, seemed to object, but the rest overruled her and I was called. I think that about covers it."

"Yes, and I would say very thoroughly," assented Holmes. "I think you are to be commended, Dodson. And now, I think that I would like to interview some of these people myself, if you have no objection."

"None at all, sir. I was hoping you would."

"Very well. I think for the time being we may dispense with questioning the men. Suppose we start with Mrs. Wiggin. Is there somewhere else—"

"There's the sewing room. That's private and cozy."

"Excellent. Suppose you show me where it is and then have them come to see me there, one at a time."

When Dodson had left to locate the housekeeper, I asked Holmes, "What do you make of it all?"

"A very pretty little problem. There is hardly enough evidence to form an opinion as to the whole case, but there are one or two conclusions that seem pretty clear. For instance, I think I can safely say how our unwelcome visitor gained entrance. As for Pawlings's unaccountable—but here comes Mrs. Wiggin now, if I am not mistaken." We heard the sound of approaching footsteps.

The housekeeper proved to be a solidly built, efficient-looking woman. She confirmed what Dodson had told us, including the fact that Miss Compton seemed all but prostrated by her grandfather's death.

Holmes innocently asked, "Were she and her grandfather so fond of each other?"

"Well, they were and they weren't. I mean they weren't what you would call close to each other," replied the housekeeper. "I don't think that Miss Mary ever wanted to come here too bad. But after she lost both her parents in a motor accident, it seems like she had nowhere else to go, and anyway, she thought it was her duty to come, as you might say. She's an independent body, and I wouldn't have thought she would have taken a thing like this so hard. Maybe it's the way that her grandfather went. But it don't seem like her, an' that's a fact. If I didn't have reason to think different, I would say that she was upset by more than just the lord's death."

"A very astute observation, Mrs. Wiggin, if you don't mind my saying so," commented Holmes. "By the way, I think that you are an unusually neat housekeeper. I noticed how bright and shiny you keep the fire-set in the library."

"We try to keep things looking fit," she responded, obviously flattered by Holmes's remark.

"How often do you polish those andirons?" Holmes pursued.

"Once a week. They was last polished day before yesterday."

"And they weren't wiped with a cloth or anything like that yesterday?"

"Nothing in the room was touched yesterday," she said.

"Remarkable! I will have to learn the brand of polish that you use." He seemed rather pleased with something, and I wondered what it was. Knowing him as I did, I did not think that he had brought up the subject of the andirons because of the housekeeping ability of Mrs. Wiggin.

"And I don't suppose that the ashtray was touched, either."

"No, sir. If you are a wondering about the litter on it, you can depend on it that the murderer left it there, though just why he should sit there smoking before a killing is beyond me."

Holmes nodded in assent. "It does seem a bit peculiar. But there are several peculiar aspects to this incident." Then he asked the housekeeper about the bundle on the desk in the library, and she said that she knew nothing about it, that she was sure it had not been there before the tragedy. When asked if it would be all right to open it, she said she didn't know why not.

Holmes thanked her and said that he had just one more question. "Was the butler, Pawlings, left-handed?"

She gave him a startled look, "Left-handed? Why, now that you mention it, he was."

"Thank you," he said. "And now, Mrs. Wiggin, I think that we can excuse you. You have been a great help."

When she had gone, he turned to Dodson. "Now I think that it would be well to talk to the granddaughter."

"But she said that she was not to be disturbed," the police officer demurred.

"Perhaps she did. But I'm afraid that she will have to be. We happen to be investigating a possible murder, and we must explore every avenue of potential information."

Accordingly we made our way upstairs to what we had been told was Miss Compton's room. It was a large, pleasant chamber on the east side of the manor house with a wide semihexagonal bay lighted by three many-mullioned windows. It was furnished with an old-fashioned mahogany four-poster bed by the south wall, a reading stand in the bay by the windows, several comfortable chairs, and an escritoire to the left of the door that opened from the hallway.

Miss Compton, a dark-haired beauty of some five and twenty years of age, was propped up in the bed. After what I had heard of her grief-stricken condition, she looked to me surprisingly well. The expression on her face was a combination of defiance and wariness. The maid, Peggy, a comely brown-haired girl of respectful demeanor, sitting near the head of the bed, seemed to share her mistress's attitude.

Both seemed strangely guarded in their answers to Holmes's questions. When he had apparently done interrogating them, he had merely succeeded in corroborating what we already knew. Then, just as we were about to go, he asked the granddaughter a final question: "When you went into the library ahead of the others and found your grandfather on the floor, did you get down on your knees, to his left by his head, with your back to the fireplace?"

"Why . . . why, yes, I did," she stammered. "But how did you know that? I could have sworn that I was standing when the others came in—I mean, I am sure I was."

Holmes ignored her question. "Perhaps you were," he said. He thanked her and the maid for telling what they knew, and we all rose to leave. I noticed that when we went out he managed to pass the reading stand and the escritoire and scan them closely as we went by.

When we returned to the sewing room, the last one to be interviewed was Rose Brooks, a rather flighty young person with blue eyes and yellow hair. She had a large lump on her forehead and a badly discolored area of considerable size about it. The account of her experience was hair-raising enough. Holmes listened

23

patiently to her recital, then asked, "Did you see how your attacker was dressed?"

"I can't say for certain, sir. The hall wasn't very light and it all happened so quick. I think he was dressed in some dark clothes, but—"

"I see. Are you able to give us any other information as to his appearance?"

"Well, I can't be positive 'cept he was uncommon big."

"How tall would you say? As much as six feet?"

"Oh, more nor that, sir. A precious sight more. Four or five inches. I'd take oath on it."

"And how heavy was he?"

"Well, I couldn't say exact. But he was monstrous big. Most like, he weighed fifteen stone or thereabout."

Holmes seemed impressed. "And did he carry a club?" he asked. "A big bludgeon something like a war club, larger at one end than at the other?"

Rose opened her eyes wide. "A club?" She appeared to consider. "Why, yes, he did. A big one like you say. I'm sure of it."

When she was gone, Holmes said, "I think now our next step is to open the mysterious package on the library stand."

"But don't you suppose that we should ask Miss Compton first?" Dodson temporized.

"And what if she says no?"

Dodson hesitated. "Why . . . er . . . in that case ... that is—"

"Precisely," remarked Holmes. "The housekeeper said that she saw no objection to our opening it, so we won't take the chance of Miss Compton's saying that we should not."

With that we repaired to the library, where he carefully untied the rather complicated knot and opened up the paper, taking pains to touch only the edges. We all gaped at the contents: a large roll of elegant brocaded silk of beautiful blue shade and exquisite pattern.

"Well, I say!" gasped Dodson. "That seems like a

rum thing for a murderer to be carrying around. I fancy this will complicate things more than ever."

But Holmes mildly shook his head. "I'm not so sure. I would not be surprised if this simplified our problem rather than otherwise." He left the package open, feasting his eyes on the lovely contents. "After we're through here, Dodson, it might be well for you to check this paper for fingerprints. And now I think I'd like to take a look around outside."

"Before you go, would it be out of place sir, to ask if you had come to any conclusions yet?" ventured Dodson.

"Not at all. As you have no doubt guessed, I am quite certain that the intruder was left-handed. I am also reasonably sure that he was a pipe smoker."

"A pipe smoker? But how—"

"Well, it is really quite obvious, and I am sure that you would have come to the same conclusion if your thoughts had not been distracted by so many other matters. The ashtray showed that the fellow smoked a pipe—if he was, in fact, the one who last used it."

"But there is hardly a trace of ash on the tray, and—"

"Precisely. If the man had been a cigar smoker, there would have been ashes in it, and if he had been a cigarette smoker there would have been cigarette butts in it. And the presence of so many match stubs argues the use of a pipe; a cigar or cigarettte doesn't need constant relighting."

Dodson nodded. "It does sound easy, now that you explain it. Makes me feel a bit of a chump not to have figured it out for myself. But how about the fellow being left-handed?"

"Oh, that?" said Holmes lightly. "That is even more simple. The used match folder tells us that. The missing matches were all taken from the left side."

"Of course!" Dodson ejaculated. Then his tone became more eager. "I say! The blow on Lord Wetherby's head! It's on the right side. That means that a left-handed man facing him must have struck the blow." Then he sounded even more excited. "And Pawlings was left-handed."

"That's true," assented Holmes. "But how about the package of brocaded silk? How are we going to account for that?"

"It could have been something that Lord Wetherby ordered himself."

Holmes appeared unconvinced. "It could have been, but I don't think that it was." He touched the rich fabric with his hand. "China and the seven seas," he murmured abstractedly. "Makes you think of pirates and cutlasses and pieces of eight." Then he roused himself. "Dodson, could you put a couple of questions to the maid, Rose, while I take a look outside?"

"Certainly, sir."

"I would like to have you ask her if the man who struck her had a heavy black beard and wore a patch over one eye."

Dodson's jaw dropped. "Are you serious, sir?"

"Entirely so. I have an idea that her answers will be of material help to us."

"Just as you say, sir." And the law officer, looking completely bewildered, left to seek the maid while Holmes went outdoors, alone. He was gone a full half hour, and when he got back he was breathing heavily.

By this time Dodson had returned. "Why, you've been running!" he cried.

"Yes, I have," Holmes answered.

"You don't mean you saw the scoundrel and took after him, sir?"

Holmes shook his head. "Nothing like that. I was only—"

But just then Rose Brooks came to the door of the room and said that Mr. Holmes was a wanted on the telephone. "Very well," Holmes said. "If you will show me where the phone is, I will answer it. And in the meantime I would like to have you ask the other servants to the sewing room. I wish to talk with them."

"Meaning the cook, too, sir?"

"All of them, if you please."

"And will you be needing me, too, sir? I was—"

"Thank you, but I think not. You have given us a great deal of information already. You can relieve Peggy at Miss Compton's bedside. And now I'd better answer that call."

When he returned to the library he explained to us that the call had been from a distinguished personage who had engaged Holmes to straighten out a very delicate government matter. There had been a very sudden turn in events and it was imperative that Holmes get back to London at once. "So I'll have to be getting out of here in a few minutes," he concluded.

"But this is important, too, Mr. Holmes. Are you going to just drop it? You've just begun—"

"On the contrary, my dear Dodson, I am about finished. I trust that we may conclude the matter shortly. But first, let me ask you what Rose Brooks had to say to your questions."

"Why, you could have bowled me over, sir. She said that the fellow who attacked her *did* have a black beard and a patch over one eye. What do you make of that, sir?"

"That the girl's testimony is wholly unreliable. I suspected as much when she gave me a positive answer to any question about the fellow's carrying a war club. She seemed a bit too anxious to play up her role in the affair. She is also too imaginative and too susceptible to suggestion. We can ignore what she has to say about the burly ruffian with the war club, which makes me feel more certain as to my own findings regarding his appearance. But we had better be adjourning to the other room."

When we got there, all the members of the staff but Joe Hendy were already there. Hendy had been dispatched to pick up the inquiring medical officer,* who had telephoned to Dodson while Holmes was outside that he was at liberty to examine the dead

---

* Sometimes also called "medical inquest officer," an English official similar to the American coroner.

body, but had no means of transportation as his motorcar was laid up.

"Perhaps it will help you," Holmes continued, "if I describe the prowler to you. Of course, I am not sure as to the smallest detail, but I am reasonably sure that he smoked a pipe and was left-handed. and also that he was moderately young—that is, not over thirty, probably, at the most. He was presumably about five feet nine in height, weighed some thirteen stone, and was unusually strong and agile."

This time they exchanged glances of even greater amazement.

"Why, that's young David Johnson, as ever was!" cried old Binks.

"That's right," agreed Mrs. Wiggin, "there be'nt any doubt about it. But Rose said—"

"I think that Rose's estimate of the man's size can be discounted," Holmes interrupted. "You will recall that it was rather dim in the hallway and she was naturally excited. Now, who is this David Johnson? A friend of Miss Compton's?"

"Why, yes—or leastways he was. Though I can't think as how he's a murderer," the housekeeper said.

"Nor me, neither," put in the cook, shaking her head.

"He never would, he's just not that kind," Peggy Morris blurted out, then suddenly reddened.

"I hope not," Holmes agreed, "and you may be right." Then he thanked them for coming and excused the cook and the gardener, but asked Mrs. Wiggin and Peggy to stay. Then he turned to the maid, "Peggy, do you know what dress Miss Compton was wearing last night when she came downstairs after hearing Rose scream?"

"Why, she wasn't wearing a dress at all, sir. I mean to say that she had started to get ready for bed and had put on a dressing gown over—" She broke off, reddening again.

Holmes said, "I see. I would very much like to look at the robe. Will you go and bring it down, please?"

The girl hesitated. "But Miss Mary . . . that is, maybe she wouldn't—"

"You'll bring it anyway," Holmes said, a little tartly. "And at once, please. We're in a hurry."

As the girl left, he faced the housekeeper. "Now, Mrs. Wiggin, what about this David Johnson? Just who is he and what were his relations with Miss Compton? You may as well speak out. We will find out sooner or later, anyway."

Mrs. Wiggin sighed. "Very well, sir. A real good sort, he was. I surely hope he had nothing to do with the killing of Lord Wetherby, though the good Lord knows he had no reason to love him."

"How's that?"

"Well, the young fellow was sweet on Miss Mary, and she was just as sweet on him. But he lived in the village and his folks weren't even gentry. Lord Wetherby would have none of it, said his granddaughter wasn't going to marry beneath her station; though if you ask me, there couldn't be a nicer young fellow than David Johnson—good-tempered and hard-working and all that. I'm sure that he would have made Miss Mary happy. But the lord made a monstrous fuss about it, told young David one time to leave and never show his face about the place again. Even said as how he and Miss Mary wasn't to write each other; though, between you and me, I'm not so sure but they do—and that was two years ago. Think maybe his letters come through a girl friend that Miss Mary is forever seeing."

"And where would you say that he is now?"

"No one knows. He just disappeared. That is, no one unless it's Miss Mary, and she's terrible close-mouthed. Keeps her own counsel, though I dare say she confides in Peggy more than either lets on."

Just then Peggy appeared with the robe, and the housekeeper left. Taking out his magnifying glass again, Holmes went over the robe minutely, looking particularly at the hem near the back. At length he gave an ejaculation of satisfaction, carefully folded the garment up, then handed it to Dodson. "You may possibly have use for this as evidence later," he said, "although I doubt it."

"But what—"

At this juncture Rose Brooks appeared with a paper in her hand. "It's a wire for you, sir, Mr. Holmes, what just come over the telephone. I writ it down so as you would have it just as it was phoned."

"Thank you," he said, taking the paper with its childish scrawl, which read as follows.

Your presence badly needed here. Request come at once. Signed, M.

Holmes handed it to Dodson, saying, "It is from Sir Arthur Madden, a member of the crown counsel. It is in regard to the same matter that I had the telephone call on. Evidently he did not know that I had already heard from my client." He turned toward Rose, who was standing by. "Will you please get our hats and coats for us, young lady?" he said, then addressed Dodson. "Well, this means that we must be off without further delay."

"But what am I to do?" Dodson asked.

"I suggest that you pick up this David Johnson."

"But where?"

At this point, Rose returned with our wraps and Holmes replied, "I fancy if you will go aboard the cruiser Victoria in the port of Liverpool, that they can tell you where to get your man."

"But I have no idea—" Dodson started to say; but seeing Holmes' impatience to get away, I left to get the car from the carriage house and speed our departure. When I drove it round to the front entrance, Holmes was waiting there, still talking with Dodson, who tried to detain him to answer a few last-minute questions, but Holmes tore himself away, turning at the last moment to say, "By the way, when do you expect the inquiring medical officer?"

"Within the hour, I hope, sir."

"Good. I think you'll find his report interesting."

"I suppose so, sir. Would you like a copy?"

"I would indeed. I am curious to see if he agrees with my findings."

As soon as we were in the car, Holmes took a little black notebook out of his pocket and began writing in it. "Excuse me," he said, "But I like to keep a detailed record of every case. I find that when I have another like it, it often is an advantage to have it to refer to."

He was busy for some time and when he finally stopped writing and put the book away, he leaned back and closed his eyes in an apparent fit of abstraction. I was sure that he was engrossed in contemplation of the new problem he was soon to be engaged in and knew better than to disturb him. Moreover, I knew it was useless to inquire further regarding the present case, for I had long since learned at Eton that, whether because of a reluctance to tell how he arrived at his deductions until he was sure they were correct or because of a love of the dramatic, Holmes seldom would reveal how he reached his conclusions until a case was successfully terminated.

When we reached London, he asked me to park near the House of Parliament, saying he was sure he could find where his client was there. As he eased himself out of the car he broke into an engaging smile.

"Thank you for driving me today, Harrington. And I'm sorry to have been such poor company on the way back. Also, I'm afraid that this cuts our visit short for the time—"

"I understand," I interrupted. "It was good to be with you as long as I have been. But I confess I would like to see you again and hear how this case comes out and how you solved it."

"And I will be more than glad to satisfy your curiosity. Dodson promised to call me up, and as soon as he does and I am at liberty, I will call you up and we will review the whole matter over a bird and a bottle."

And so it was that six days later found us in a cozy little pub where they served good food. After giving our order, I turned toward Holmes. "Well, I am all ears. Is the mystery of Wetherby Manor cleared up?"

He smiled at my eagerness. "Yes, it is. But perhaps you would find it more interesting if I took up its solution, step by step."

"There is nothing I would like better," I agreed.

"Well, then, in the solution of a problem of this kind, you have to sort out the circumstances that seem peculiar and try to get at their significance. In the Wetherby affair there were several such circumstances. First the seemingly unaccountable disappearance of the butler, Pawlings; second, the mystery as to how the intruder—if, indeed, there was an intruder—gained entrance; third, the singular presence of the package of Chinese silk; fourth, the rather suspicious behavior of the dead man's granddaughter—somehow, it just didn't ring true that a vital young woman of her apparent energy and spirit who had no good reason to be overfond of her dictatorial grandfather should be so seemingly prostrated by his death—and, finally, the nature of the wound on the victim's head and the strange expression on his face. All of these were unusual circumstances that called for an explanation.

"Now as to Pawlings. He is back and has already told his part in the episode to Dodson. He did indeed get a wire from his married sister that his mother was gravely ill and he had arranged for a cab to come out from the village for him so that he might take a train from there. Then, pulling up outside he heard the cab that brought David Johnson from Sudley, some ten miles away. Thinking that something had befallen Lord Wetherby or his granddaughter and that they were returning home unexpectedly early, he rushed outdoors. When he learned the facts from Johnson, he engaged the cab to take him back to Sudley, where he could get a train that would land him in Brighton at least an hour sooner than would the one from Pippingate. Then he went back inside, ushered Johnson—who had come to see Mary Compton but wished to talk to her grandfather first—into the library. After that he called and canceled his order for the cab from Pippingate, wrote the note to Lord Wetherby, and, as Dodson put it, vanished into thin air.

"The reason that the police at Brighton could not find Pawlings's mother registered as a patient at any hospital there was the fact that she was registered under another name, having married again after the death of Pawlings's father—a circumstance that Pawlings had never chanced to mention at the manor.

"This explanation as to Pawlings's disappearance also takes care of the second peculiar circumstance I mentioned—namely, how Johnson made his way into the house, a solution that I readily guessed when there appeared to be no other.

"Now as to the package. You will recall that from the first I suspected this to have been left by the supposed intruder. This was because the knot with which it was tied was plainly a sailor's knot and the string was the tarred sort that is usually available on shipboard. It turns out that Johnson bought two pieces of the silk as gifts, one for a sister and one for Mary Compton. Both pieces were done up together at the shop where he bought them, and later he separated them and put the one for Miss Compton in a separate package, which accounts for the string and knot.

"Next, to consider the peculiar behavior of Mary Compton, the reason for which is already apparent. She had been corresponding with David Johnson as Mrs. Wiggin suspected, and knew that he was to be in those parts, but not exactly when. When the death of her not-too-dearly-loved grandfather occurred she feared that her sweetheart might be involved and took to her bed so that she might not be questioned—a course of conduct, I might say, that was only calculated to stimulate surprise, but she was in no state to reason logically.

"This brings us to the seemingly superficial wound on the victim's head and the ghastly expression on his face. I have left this until the last; though, perhaps, I should have put it first, as it is the circumstance that struck me most forcibly from the beginning and really was the key to the whole mystery. If Dodson had been a little more experienced or more observing, he would have realized this fact. But the position of the body and the brief verdict of the local doctor could have thrown him off. You will recall that the doctor was in a hurry and rather resented the call, anyway. The body was lying on the right side and he did not even bother to turn the victim's head. So he may well have overlooked the drooping right eyelid and the sagging right side of the mouth—or, if he did notice them, he was not concerned, as he considered the cause of death a matter for the attention of the inquiring medical officer. He merely wanted to get away.

"But to me the superficial nature of the wound seemed insufficient to cause death. And the condition of the face indicated some sort of seizure. So I assumed that the injury on the head may have been the result rather than the cause of his fall. If so, what could his head have struck to bruise it so badly? The andirons, of course. So, with my magnifying glass, I examined the andirons and found a hair and the slightest trace of what might be blood on one of them. Evidence of contact with it might have been clearer except for the fact that the andiron base appeared to have been wiped by a cloth. But, you will recall, the housekeeper said it had not been touched since it had been polished a few days before. So what could have wiped it off? Obviously the hem of Mary Compton's garment as she knelt by the head of her dead grandfather.

"So I examined the hem of her robe and found more hairs and some evidence of dried blood. You will understand that the lord's head struck the brass andiron but an instant and then rolled away, so that there would be a minimum of blood on it. The real bleeding would not start until an instant after.

"Before we left and while I was waiting with Dodson for you to get the car, I gave Dodson a hint of what his interrogation of Johnson might show, and David Johnson's answers confirmed my version of what had happened. The young fellow had gone to the manor house hoping to make his peace with Mary's ill-tempered grandfather and surprise her with the brocaded silk, from which she could make a bathrobe or something of the sort. But he had no chance to affect a reconciliation with the testy lord. When Lord Wetherby strode into the library and found his granddaughter's sweetheart there, he flew into a fury and grabbed hold of young Johnson. Naturally, the young fellow resisted, released himself, and pushed the old man away. Then, to his horror, he saw the old lord's face grow purple with congestion, the features become wildly distorted, and the old man pitch forward at full length, striking his head with terrific impact against the metal andiron. As I indicated, I suspected that the lord had suffered a stroke, a fact which, I understand, was later confirmed by the inquiring medical officer.

"The boy stooped down, drew the body away from the fireplace and stared at the revolting face. The eyes of the dying man stared back at him with implacable hatred until gradually the sagging features became fixed in their horrible mask of death. Terrified, the boy lost his head and tore out of the house, forgetting the present that he had brought for the girl he loved, forgetting everything but the threat to his own safety. He fled through the dim hall, hurtling against Rose Brooks as he did so and bumping her violently against the wall. It was contact with the wall and not the savage beating which her ready imagination conjured up that caused her injuries. Leaving the house, the boy ran across the back yard and over the stone wall to a road behind it, where he caught a ride on a passing lorry and made good his escape."

"Well!" I exclaimed, "So that is what happened! And there was no murder at all."

"None. Unless you call the mean old lord's evil temper his own murderer."

"Something of an anticlimax," I said, almost disappointed. "But a happy alternative to the sanguinary crime we expected—the ogre of a grandfather dies a

35

natural death and the granddaughter is free to marry her sailor sweetheart and live happily ever after. But there are two or three questions I would like to ask."

"Yes?"

"First, how did you guess so exactly as to the description of David Johnson?"

"It wasn't a guess; it was pure deduction. You will remember that it had rained the day before we got there and the ground was still damp. This made it easy, with the aid of my glass, to follow the footprints of young Johnson as he ran from the rear door across the backyard. By running myself, I found that the length of my stride just about matched his, so I assumed that he was somewhere near my height. Then I found where he had gone over the four-foot wall. By looking at the top of the wall I discovered that he had not even put a hand on it to vault over it but had apparently cleared it in a single bound, showing that he was young and agile. Then I found the imprints of his feet where he had awaited the lorry that picked him up. They were much deeper than my feet would have made, which indicated that he was heavier than I. Of course, all these things were merely approximate, but, taken with the fact that he was left-handed and indulged in a pipe, they made it possible for the servants to recognize readily who he was."

"Very good," I said, "but how could you be so sure as to where Dodson could locate young Johnson?"

"Oh, that?" he said, and smiled. "That was more of a guess. The string and the knot on the package indicated that in all likelihood he was a sailor—and what would be more likely than that a young Englishman disappointed in love should go to sea? Then, when I was in Mary Compton's room I noticed that a letter lying on her escritoire had a Greek stamp on it—you will recollect I am something of a philatelist—and this probably meant that Johnson had been on a ship that had been in Greece. Finally, the silk brocade had the appearance of what is known as 'Hongkong silk.' I surmised that in all probability such an article would be available on the island of Rhodes, which is what is called a 'free port,' where no duty is charged on foreign goods, so that rare commodities can often be purchased at unusually low prices there. By the merest chance I happened to know that the cruiser Victoria had touched at the port of Rhodes. What more natural for a young fellow in love than to look up some rare object in such a place as a present for his lady love? Really, to quote my esteemed grandfather—"

"I know," I interrupted, and we chanted in unison that familiar saying of Sherlock Holmes:

"Elementary, my dear Watson, elementary."

The waiter brought our order and we started to eat.

The Case of the Scientific Recluse

One of the most fascinating cases in which I was privileged to observe the successful workings of my friend Creighton Holmes's remarkably keen mind was what I have chosen to call "The Case of the Scientific Recluse," a case that I have felt impelled to record, not altogether because of the unusual display of Holmes's talents, but also because of the peculiar circumstances attending the victim's death and the distinguished character of the family of which he was a member. Indeed, it was a family prominent for three generations in the operation of our government. There are still many who will recall that the dead man's brother, Sir Brockton Pell, narrowly missed being appointed First Lord of the Admiralty only a few months before the tragic happening that I am about to relate.

It is true that once the incident was recognized as a homicide there may have been many alert and intelligent investigators of crime who might have solved it. What is most remarkable is that at the very beginning Holmes did so recognize it, although at the time all outward signs seemed to indicate otherwise. But he was never one blindly to accept the seemingly obvious.

It was in the year 1938, when interest in the atomic bomb was just beginning to get scientific attention. At the time I was lodging with Holmes at his address on Baker Street, having been induced some months before to consent to share his quarters—a consent, I must confess, that took no great persuasion on his part, as I was only too glad to do so, not only because of a liking for his company but also because of the opportunity it offered to participate in his investigations and observe at first hand his ability to detect at the very outset what would be totally obscure to the average officer of criminal investigation.

It was a Sunday afternoon and we were back in our diggings, enjoying a quiet smoke following a leisurely dinner together, when he got the telephone call that was to take us to the scene of this singular occurrence.

On the way there, Holmes filled me in on the details. He told me that the call had come from one Jimpson Dobbs at his home at number 14 Whippoorwill Street. He further explained that the house in question was a rather large one that had seen better days but was now sadly deteriorated. Many of the once imposing abodes in the neighborhood about it had been converted into multiple dwellings, while their former spacious gardens had in many cases been taken over by smaller houses or petty trading shops, so that what at one time had been an upper-class residential district was now a crowded jumble of nondescript buildings.

The Dobbs residence, to which we were now going, Holmes explained, had been purchased at a ridiculously low figure by the father-in-law of Dobbs when Dobbs and his young bride had first taken up housekeeping, on the assumption that the taking in of lodgers would supplement the young married couple's income until Dobbs, who was in business for himself, got on his feet, while they started rearing a family.

The combined residence and lodging house had so well served its purpose that it had not only accommodated two lodgers but Dobbs and four children, two of whom had by now married and departed from the family domicile. Now, with only two children left at home (a boy, Irving, some four and twenty years of age, and a girl, Daisy, three years younger), and the enjoyment of a well-established though modest income by Dobbs, they had had but one lodger, the well-to-do and eccentric scientist whose unaccountable death was the occasion of our call.

"But you say he was found in his lodgings, stone dead, this afternoon when Dobbs and his family returned to the house after being away overnight, that the doors and windows of his quarters were all firmly locked and the gas in his unlighted fireplace turned on full blast?"

"That's correct."

"Why, then, it's nothing but a plain case of suicide!" I exclaimed.

"So it would seem."

"Then why the need of an investigation?"

Holmes smiled. "That was my reaction. But Dobbs is rather an odd sort. Reads a great many detective stories and likes, perhaps, to think there is some mystery where none exists. Still, though he is uneducated, he has a native shrewdness, and there is one decidedly peculiar circumstance connected with the case."

"What's that?"

"The dead man seems to have had no reason whatever for taking his own life. Was unmarried with no domestic problems, in apparently perfect health, and with no financial worries. On the contrary, lately he appears to have been in unusually good spirits because of the successful solution of some very important research problem he had been working on for some time."

"Humph, does sound deucedly odd," I agreed. "But why call you in? Why not the police?"

Again Holmes broke into that quiet smile. "Well, Dobbs seems to have acquired an exaggerated opinion of my abilities. You see, he is a cabinetmaker, and a few years ago, when I was looking for some one to construct something unique in which to store the notes of my grandfather on the various crimes he had investigated, I was directed to Dobbs. It happened that he had an admiration for my grandfather's talents that amounted almost to awe—had read all that he could get hold of about him—and so he became most enthusiastic in doing his best in the execution of the small commission on which I had engaged him. The result was a most exceptional piece of work. Anyway, to make a long story short, he found out that I was attempting to follow in my grandfather's footsteps, and through this chance meeting we came to conceive quite a liking for each other. Since then I have reason to believe he has followed my career rather closely and has acquired almost as great an admiration for me as for my celebrated ancestor. I know it sounds silly, but that's the way it is."

"But what can you find out now? Surely by this time Dobbs has broken into the dead man's apartments and more than likely destroyed or, at best, obscured all clues."

Holmes gave a low chuckle. "Not at all. You don't know Dobbs."

"You don't mean to say that this . . . this Addison Pell is lying there yet, in an unopened room full of gas!"

"Exactly. Dobbs says that after he found the doors of Pell's rooms all locked, instead of breaking into one of them—as the ordinary man would do—he got a ladder, put it up to a second-story window, peered in, satisfied himself that Pell was undeniably dead, and then called me."

"I see," I said. "By the way, what's this about Pell's solving a research problem? What was his business?"

"Well, you see, Pell was a scientist," Holmes responded, "an odd genius who had sort of broken away from the rest of the family. Not that there was ever any falling out or anything like that; in fact, he and his famous brother, Sir Brockton, seem to have been very fond of each other in a rather unusual way. But one went in one direction and one in another: Sir Brockton has always liked people and been devoted to public affairs; the more obscure Addison, on the other hand, has always shunned society and has been the dedicated scientist, deeply absorbed in his work in research and caring little about people—sort of a case of the mole and the peacock, you might say."

I nodded assent. This background of the dead man

gave a little more zest to the case. I might be able to put a little color into my story for the *Times*—if there should be a story. Still, I was only mildly interested as we reached number 14 Whippoorwill Street. I did not foresee then that the incident was to be one of the most intriguing and bizarre of all those to engage the peculiar talents of my companion, nor that in fact, before it was over it would involve a document that carried such a threat to safety if the knowledge of its contents fell into the wrong hands that it would cause a violent shudder through out the entire British Commonwealth and have serious repercussions in the farthest parts of the civilized world.

When we opened the gate and entered the premises, we discovered Dobbs standing there eagerly talking to a neighbor. The downstairs doors as well as the windows of the house all appeared to be open, and Holmes commented on the fact after we had exchanged greetings.

"Yes, we're still airing it out," Dobbs explained. "There was the smell o' gas pretty much all through the place. Had got through under the cracks o' Mr. Pell's doors, though it looks like he had tried to plug 'em up with blankets. But there's no need o' your standin' here, Mr. Holmes. You'll be wantin' to go up the ladder an' take a look at the death room yourself. Nothin' has been disturbed, as you might say," he added with some pride.

Holmes indicating agreement, Dobbs managed to get rid of the neighbor, and we went around to the west side of the house. Mrs. Dobbs was standing there talking to the daughter while the son stood somewhat apart from them, sullenly smoking a cigarette. Dobbs introduced us. The wife seemed like a quiet, rather fussy woman, and I was well enough impressed with the girl, who was agreeable in manner and frankly outspoken. But I took an instant dislike to her brother Irving, a young upstart with a rude and offensive demeanor.

As we stood there, Dobbs explained that when the eccentric but well-to-do scientist agreed to take lodgings, it was arranged that he would not only have the use of the loft of an old carriage house in the rear of the premises for a laboratory, but that the entire west side of the upstairs of the house, which faced north, would be made over to suit his convenience. So now, at the time of his death, he had had an apartment, with a space that served as dining-room and kitchen where he could provide himself with a snack if he became absorbed in his work and did not want to go out to eat, with a living room back of that, followed by a bathroom with a narrow hallway passing it and leading to a bedchamber in the extreme rear. It was in the living room that the body of the dead man was now lying, a room that was closed and still full of gas.

Dobbs led us to the west side of the house and, pointing to a ladder that reached up to a living-room window, he said, "There she is."

"Excellent!" said Holmes, "I'll just go up and take a look." And forthwith he ascended the ladder while we stood some distance away from the house, looking up at him. It seemed that he remained there an interminable time, peering into the window.

At length he descended, but did not immediately come toward us. Instead, he stood at the foot of the ladder, intently scanning the ground where some low shrubs grew by the foundation. Suddenly he drew an envelope out of an inside coat pocket, withdrew the letter from it, then took a knife from his trousers pocket and leaned over to scrape something off the ground and to pick up some small objects that looked like cigarette butts, which he carefully put in the envelope. Finally he came toward us.

"What did you find?" Dobbs asked. But Holmes affected not to hear him and queried, "Did it rain here yesterday?"

"Why, yes, it did," nodded Dobbs. "Yesterday an' the day afore that."

"Ah!" ejaculated Holmes in a tone of satisfaction. "And when did it stop?"

"Round about five in the a'ternoon, I would say.

Leastways, we had just had tea an' was about to start for my sister's, where we stayed the night."

"Better and better!" said Holmes, rubbing his hands together in a characteristic gesture. "Now, if you and Harrington can take the locked door leading into the apartment off its hinges, I'll go in and make a further investigation."

Dobbs readily consented and went and got the necessary tools, and after some difficulty, we had the door off and Holmes entered the apartment wearing a gas mask that he had picked up on our way at a fire station (where he was on good terms with the lieutenant), while we hurried down the stairs to escape the blast of polluted air that issued forth.

Holmes seemed occupied for some time, and when he finally came down, he said, "It's a good thing that you called me, I fancy."

"How's that?" Dobbs asked.

"Because, unless I am greatly mistaken, Addison Pell was murdered."

Dobbs asked, "But how kin that be, Mr. Holmes? All the doors—"

"It may interest you to know," Holmes interrupted, "that I found no fingerprints whatever on the inside handle of the door that you removed, nor anywhere else, including the kitchen cupboard doors. Rather peculiar that a man about to commit suicide would take such action, wouldn't you say?"

We readily agreed that it was.

"By the way, while I think of it, Dobbs, I noticed that the filing cabinet was locked. Did the deceased always keep it so?"

"Yes, as far as I knows of. Said he had what he called 'valuable data' in it. Had something to do with his experiments."

"Was there any experiment he was particularly interested in lately, do you know?"

"Yes, there was. Somethin' about nuclear energy."

"Very good. I'll have to get his keys—I presume I'll find them in his pocket—and see what I can find. And, by the way, I appropriated the key to the door that you removed. I fancy it will contribute some valuable information. And now, before we call the police, I would like to have you go with me to the dead man's quarters. I want to show you something I'm sure you'll find of interest. The air should be fairly endurable by now."

Accordingly, we all followed him upstairs, where Dobbs and I entered the apartment with him while Mrs. Dobbs and the son and daughter huddled in the doorway.

The room was a fair-sized one, some eighteen feet long by fourteen in width. To the right or north of the doorway was the gas fireplace from which the deadly fumes had escaped. It was located by the inner wall about midway between the entrance door and the door leading to the kitchen at the north end of the apartment. Before the fireplace were two comfortable chairs, one directly facing it and the other at a slight angle.

By the north wall of the room, between the kitchen door and the filing cabinet in the northeast corner, was a desk with a straight chair pulled up to it. The only other pieces of furniture of significance were a smoking stand with an empty pipe and an ashtray devoid of ashes, and the settee near the southwest corner of the room, where lay the inert form of the dead scientist, a man some six feet in height and apparently weighing close to thirteen stone.

There were no paintings on the wall and no knick-knacks of any kind; but the furniture, though somewhat sparse, was of good quality, substantial rather than elegant, as befitted the obviously Spartan tastes of the deceased.

"These are what I wished you to see before they were obliterated by the police," Holmes explained, indicating two parallel indentations in the plain deep-piled carpet, leading from a point near the cabinet to a spot close to the settee. The marks were an inch or two wide and about a foot apart—slight depressions apparently made by some heavy object or objects having been dragged over the carpet.

"What be they?" Dobbs asked.

"The marks of the heels of Pell's shoes as his body was dragged to the settee, if I am not mistaken," Holmes replied. Then, in an unusual burst of frankness, he added, "My guess is that Pell and his prospective murderer sat before the fire visiting and sipping drinks until Pell, made drowsy by some drug that his killer had slipped into his glass, got up from his chair for some reason, then toppled and fell unconscious in front of the cabinet. Then the killer, who probably wanted to get into the file, tugged the body away. I wanted you to observe the marks so that, if necessary, you could testify to their existence."

"Blimey if I don't think you're right!" exclaimed Dobbs as we examined the marks intently.

"I'm surprised that the murderer didn't move the chairs," Holmes went on. "But when you are about to kill a man, your mind doesn't always function at its best, I fancy. He apparently did think to wash and put away the incriminating glasses and to wipe away fingerprints—but I am wasting time. We should call the police. Dobbs, you had better ring them, and I suspect it would be just as well not to tell them of our preliminary investigation. They might not take kindly to what they would regard as an encroachment on their prerogatives."

"Righto," said Dobbs, who started downstairs with me close behind him. In a short time Holmes joined us, and hardly had he got there when he exclaimed, "Unless my eyes deceive me, here comes the law." And just as he spoke, a big shambling figure came around the corner of the house. When he spoke I got the impression that he was somewhat below the standard of the average English bobby, whom I have always considered a superior breed. He was clearly close to the age of retirement and I could not help but think that with its approach he had lost most of the zest for his job, if, indeed, he had ever had much of any. Perhaps I felt all this because just now he seemed to be in a particularly truculent mood.

46

"Hear you got a dead man here," he grunted.

"That's right," Dobbs spoke up, "You see—"

"Seems like everything comes at once," the man broke in surlily. "There's a woman as has been strangled a block an' a half away—third in the last two weeks in these parts. We've all been alerted to comb the area, a house-to-house questioning if you get my meaning. By the way, you haven't seen any suspicious characters around here lately, have you?"

We all assured him that we had not. "Didn't s'pose you had," he nodded grumpily. "Well, we better get on with it. Who found the dead man?"

"I did," Dobbs said, drawing himself up. "We smelled the fumes as soon as we got into the house. Had been away all night an' jus' got back this a'ternoon. Suspected something, broke into his room, an' there he was—dead. The name is Dobbs," he said, extending his hand.

The policeman, seemingly unimpressed, growled, "What's his first name?"

"His—? Oh. Addison. Addison Pell."

"Thought you said it was Dobbs."

With some embarrassment, Dobbs straightened the matter out, then introduced his family, an introduction which the policeman, who said his name was George Higgs, grudgingly acknowledged.

"And this is Mr. Creighton Holmes, private investigator, grandson of the great Sherlock Holmes," Dobbs continued. "He's . . . um . . . a friend o' mine."

"Glad to meet ya," Higgs said, though he didn't sound so. "Heard of ya. Well, lets hop to it. Got lots to do. Where's the body?"

"Upstairs."

"Very good. Let's have a look," and he followed Dobbs as the latter led the way. Holmes, Dobbs, the boy Irving, and I stood just inside the doorway of the living room as Higgs entered it. As we did so, I took occasion to more closely examine the room where the murder—if it had been a murder—had occurred. The first object to attract my attention was the settee with the body of the dead man on it by the south wall next the bathroom. Then there was a metal filing cabinet in the northeast corner of the room which, though I had no way of knowing it then, had figured prominently in the commission of the crime and was to figure as much so in its solution. Finally, I was struck by one peculiar and incongruous circumstance: two chairs were setting cozily in front of the hearth as if two friends not long before had been sitting there together enjoying the warmth of the fire while comfortably chatting in what was now a room of tragedy and death.

Higgs's investigation, if you could call it that, was a perfunctory one. Giving the room a cursory glance, he went to the settee and briefly examined the slack figure lying on it. "Dead, all right," he commented, and then took out a notebook and pencil. "A couple of questions an' then I'll be on my way." He turned toward Dobbs. "Away all night, you say?"

"That's right. Me an' the fam'ly left right a'ter tea yesterday, to visit my sister, Mrs. Cedric Meeks, at 42 Pudding Lane—that's about one an' a half hours ride from here. Got back around three to'day. Smelled gas, opened up the rest o' the house, went to Mr. Pell's room an' found 'im a-lyin' there, jus' like you see."

"Relative o' yours?"

"Just a lodger. Been with us about three year."

"Know any reason why he should commit suicide?—ill health, financial worries, anything like that?"

"None as we knows of. Fact, seemed in unusual good spirits lately."

"Know him well? I mean was you intimate with him?"

"Well, not what you might call intimate. He kep' pretty much to hisself. Kind of a loner, you might say. Had hardly any close friends."

"Humph. Well, you can never tell about these here quiet ones. Most likely got the cold shoulder from his lady friend. Somethin' like that." He started to put his

48

notebook away. "Well, I fancy that about does it. I'll—"

But just then he broke off. A roly-poly little man with a bustling manner stood in the doorway with a look of inquiry on his face. "I understood you wanted my services. I'm Dr. Gridley."

"Higgs o' the police," the bobby said. "Glad you got here. Like to have you look at the body. Matter o' routine."

The doctor put down his case, looked intently at the form of the dead scientist, turned back the lids of the dead man's eyes, put his ear to the dead man's chest, picked up one hand, felt of the pulse, examined the ends of the fingers, then turned toward Higgs. "Dead," he pronounced profoundly. "Been dead for some time."

"How long would you say?" Higgs asked.

The doctor pursed his lips. "Hard to tell. Several hours, I would say. Rigor mortis fairly pronounced. By the way, if I might have the circumstances—"

He was filled in on the facts regarding the discovery of Pell's body.

"I see." He got out a memorandum book of his own and noted down Pell's name, address, and approximate age. "Makes things a bit more clear." And he went on writing as he said: "Cause of death, total asphyxiation by ingestion of carbon monoxide due to escaping gas. Death presumably around midnight of October twenty-third. How's that sound, officer?"

"Well enough, I'd say. Suicide?"

"I would say so," the doctor responded, and added the words, "self-inflicted" in the notebook.

"Thanks, Doctor," Higgs said. "An' now, I'll have to be about my business."

As we stood aside to make way for them, Holmes said, "You're altogether sure it's a case of suicide, officer?"

Higgs stopped and gave him a blank look. "Any reason why not?"

"Well, there were one or two things," Holmes said tentatively.

"Such as?"

"Well, for one thing, the deceased doesn't seem to have left a note. In a case of suicide, isn't it rather usual—"

But Higgs interrupted him. He appeared to have trouble keeping a note of contempt out of his voice. "Usual maybe, but I don't know of any rule as says there has to be. Anything else?"

"Well, I was wondering about the blanket by the doorway to the kitchen—"

But Higgs could hold in no longer. "Look, Mr. Holmes, I ain't questioning you're a smart man an' all that. An' I admit I'm old-fashioned an' have probably made my share o' mistakes, but when I find a dead man in a room that is all locked up so as nobody can get in or out an' a report that the gas was turned on full blast an' the doctor says death's self-inflicted, that's enough fer me. I ain't got time fer any fine-spun theories. Jus' now I got to help find a killer as is on the loose. So, if you don't mind, you'll have to excuse me." And he and the doctor left, the latter giving Holmes a peculiar look and shaking his head as they went out.

Dobbs cast a glance of inquiry at Holmes. "Looks like they was pretty sure o' themselves, Mr. Holmes."

Holmes agreed, but said he thought Higgs would have done well to be a bit more thorough. Then, addressing Mrs. Dobbs, he asked, "What time did you reach your sister-in-law's yesterday?"

"Six-thirty or a little a'ter, I should say, sir."

"And I assume that all four of you remained in the house all evening until you went to bed?"

"Well, no, we didn't. Irv went out about eight-thirty or nine, a little a'ter we eat. He gets the fidgets a'ter bein' around older people about so long."

"If you don't mind my asking, did he have any particular reason for leaving?"

"None as I knows of. He's the restless sort, gits uneasy jest settin' around and visitin'. Seems like he said he was goin' out to play pool—somethin' like that. He knows some o' the young fellers in the neighborhood around there."

"I understand. Any idea when he got in?"

"Yes. It would be pretty late, but I don't know zackly when. I never sleeps very well when either of the children is out till I hears 'em come in. I laid awake till the clock struck twelve an' then I dropped off. Then I was woke when he come back an' I heard the clock strike once. But whether it was twelve-thirty or one of the clock er a'ter, I couldn't say."

"Well, it makes no great difference," Holmes said lightly. "But there is another rather important question I would like to ask."

"Yes sir. What is it?"

"When was the last time any of you oiled the lock to Mr. Pell's apartment?"

"Why, never, ez far ez I recollect. No occasion to."

"Very good," said Holmes in a highly gratified tone. Then he continued, "Oh, I'm sorry, but there is just one more thing. When you and your daughter dust Mr. Pell's desk, do you always put the articles on it back in the same position that they were?"

"Allus. Mr. Pell is—was—most partickaler about that. Made a powerful fuss if there was the least thing out o' place, so we never moves a thing."

"That's what I thought. Thank you very much. And now I would be pleased if you would have your son see me, please."

But the outcome of questioning young Irving was very unsatisfactory, not to say a little puzzling. The fellow readily admitted that he had gone out the previous evening to play pool, but claimed he did not know the names of any of those with whom he played, except for the given names of one or two, and he was quite indefinite as to the designation of the pool hall or its location.

"And about what time did you get back to your aunt's?" Holmes asked.

"Oh, about eleven or eleven-thirty—didn't pay much attention."

"I see," said Holmes, apparently satisfied with the answer. "By the way, I notice"—looking at the humidor of tobacco on the smoking stand near the chairs—"that Mr. Pell smoked a pipe. Did he ever smoke cigarettes?"

"Not as I knows of. Leastways I never seen him."

"And was he a heavy pipe smoker?"

"How would I know? I hardly ever seen the bloke. Kept mostly to his room. But he did have a pipe in his kisser 'bout every time I seen him. S'pose you might say he was a heavy smoker."

"And does it strike you as a bit odd that there are no ashes on his ashtray?"

I thought that the fellow gave a slight start at this query, but if so, he quickly recovered. "Don't know as it does. A blighter as was goin' to do hisself in likely wouldn't feel like settin' down fer a smoke afore he done it."

Holmes said, "Perhaps you're right." Then he asked, "By the way, I see that you smoke Players; ever smoke any other brand?"

"Not unless they're give to me."

"Never Pall Malls?"

The boy shrugged. "Too rich fer my blood. Leastways fer my purse."

It was at this point that we heard the sound of a motorcar and looked out to see a shiny Daimler with long, sleek bonnet stop at the kerb while a liveried chauffeur got out to open the door for a distinguished-looking personage, who proved to be the deceased's celebrated brother, Sir Brockton Pell.

After introductions had taken place, Holmes told the peer that all signs pointed to the fact that his brother was the victim of foul play, to which Sir Brockton replied: "I confess it hard to believe that my brother would have taken his own life. I can think of no reason that would impel him to such an action. But, much as I would like to accept your theory, I find it fantastic that any one could have caused his death and escaped from securely locked lodgings without leaving a trace."

"I fully sympathize with your doubts," Holmes replied. "But the possibility is not so fantastic as you think. There are at least six indications that someone was present in your brother's lodgings with him last evening, and at least three of these reveal the manner in which he made his escape. If you care to examine his quarters with me, I think I can convince you of the soundness of what you call my 'theory.'"

Sir Brockton replied, "I would be only too glad to make such examination. By all means let us do so at once." And he followed Holmes upstairs.

When they returned, Sir Brockton was shaking his head in amazement. "I wouldn't have believed it possible! But I have no doubt of the accuracy of your conclusions. Now there is nothing I would like so much as to apprehend the murderer and justify my brother's good name."

"If you feel that way, sir, I suggest that you get in touch with Scotland Yard at once."

Sir Brockton shook his head. "No, I don't want the publicity until we are sure that we can lay our hands on the guilty party."

"But if you please, sir, there will be little publicity. The Yard—"

Still the knight was obdurate. "No, I wish you to handle the entire matter."

"Me?"

"Yes. Your reputation and what you have just shown and told me convince me that you have exceptional talent."

"But you realize that this may involve considerable expense? Of course, I will charge nothing for my services unless we are successful, but there will be considerable collateral charges necessary which I would not be in a position to assume."

To this Sir Brockton rejoined, "I am ready to undertake any reasonable expense. As for your services, we will talk about them later. But just what will occasion these collateral charges?"

"Well, in the first place, there should be an autopsy, if you would consent to same."

"An autopsy?"

"Yes. I am not at all satisfied that the inhalation of gas was the sole cause of your brother's death."

The peer raised his eyebrows. "Indeed? But of course I consent. Anything else?"

"I may need the services of another man to help me shadow any suspects?"

"Do you have anyone in mind for such services?"

"There is a young policeman whom I have used before and who is very good at such sort of thing. He is just about to start his holiday and should be available. He hopes to get married soon and would no doubt welcome the additional income."

"Very good. But you speak of suspects. With no clues whatever, where are you to find them?"

"Anyone who was at all intimate with Mr. Addison Pell. As has been said, he kept much to himself. I would start with those who ever came to see him. There shouldn't be too many. How about it?" He turned toward Mr. and Mrs. Dobbs and the daughter Daisy, who had been sitting by, silent. The offish Irving had lounged apart in a doorway, sullenly picking his teeth.

At Holmes's question, Dobbs spoke, "There was never but one as come here, far as we knows, and we don't none of us know his name. He was a solid-built, steady-goin' sort o' chap 'bout middle age. Think maybe he was employed in summat the same business as Mr. Addison was, but ain't sure. But he was the only one as ever come here."

"No, he wasn't, Pa," Daisy spoke up. "There was another, a fella what come here a year er so ago. I seem 'im a couple o' times."

"Oh, come off it, sis," her brother objected in a surly tone, "I don't believe there was no such blighter. You're allus dreamin' up somethin'."

54

But the daughter stuck to her guns, and when her parents asked her if she was sure, she said she was, and described the man as younger and slighter than the other: "A sort o' fancy dresser with a slick way about 'im. Smooth-lookin', but not quite a gentleman, if you get my meaning."

Holmes got a more particular description of the two men mentioned and said, "There's a possibility that they will come to the funeral. If they do, perhaps Daisy here can help identify them; if they don't, we'll have to find some other way to locate them." He looked at his watch. "Dobbs, could I use your telephone to make a call?" Dobbs assenting, he turned toward me and said, "When I am through, I may have a little job for you and Irving, Harrington, after Sir Brockton and I have checked the private papers of Mr. Addison—they may possibly give us some clue as to motive. That is, of course, if you agree," he said, addressing the peer.

"Sir Brockton nodded his assent and Holmes went into an adjoining room to make his call. Soon he was back, and we all went upstairs while he and Sir Brockton went through the papers of the dead man, including such letters as there were. These were pitifully few, being for the most part friendly letters from relatives. But his one bankbook was more revealing. It showed that some months before he had withdrawn two thousand pounds.

"Now why would he do that?" Holmes asked.

"Blackmail?" I suggested.

"A possibility, but Mr. Pell hardly seems to have been the type who would lay himself open to blackmail. Besides, it usually is a continuing thing and there have been no subsequent withdrawals of consequence. Could he have withdrawn the two thousand pounds for some investment, do you think, Sir Brockton?"

"I hardly think so. I never knew him to do so. He just wasn't interested in such things. And if he had thought of it, it seems likely that he would have consulted me." He paused and appeared to think. "Wait a minute. He did seem remarkably interested in uranium at one time. It was the sort of thing that might capture his interest, and some time back he talked a lot about it. It's just possible that he took a flyer secretly. Maybe he wanted to show me that he could do something of the kind on his own."

"About how long ago was this?"

"I'm not sure, but it could have been about the time of this withdrawal. And another thing: Now that I think of it, it seems peculiar that all of a sudden he should have dropped the subject entirely. Perhaps he got his fingers burnt."

"Interesting, and it might be worth looking into," Holmes said reflectively, "but as to furnishing a motive for——" He broke off abruptly and clapped a hand to his forehead. "By Jove, I've been stupid. Dobbs, didn't you say that he had been in unusually high spirits lately? Has he by any chance mentioned some new discovery that——"

"Why, yes, he did," Dobbs said eagerly. "Only t'other day I was in his room talkin' about some trouble with the heatin' when he picked up a file in a manila folder about somethin' as he had been workin' on, an' he says, 'Dobbs, here's somethin' as may revolutionize things,' he says. 'It's a breakthrough that may change the whole course o' manufacturin' and maybe of armament!' He seemed real excited like, if you understands me."

"And did he say anything as to what this discovery was? Anything that might help us to find what file was missing if it had been taken?"

Dobbs face fell. "Can't say he did. No sir, not a word, as I recalls."

Our hopes were down. Then suddenly Holmes said, "There's just one chance. Undoubtedly Mr. Pell kept an index of his files. If he did, and the thief failed to destroy the index card——" He began opening one drawer of the desk after another until he came upon one containing the index cards. "Harrington, we'll check these against the folders. You read off the titles and I will run through the folders in the cabinet." He turned toward the cabinet, saying as he did so, "The fact that Mr. Pell was left-handed may help us to grab our man."

I didn't see how this could be so, nor could I imagine how Holmes arrived at the fact that the victim was not right-handed, as most people are. "How do you know he was left-handed?" I blurted.

"Elementary, old man. Mrs. Dobbs told us that neither she nor Daisy ever rearranged anything on his desk. And if you took notice, you observe that Mr. Pell kept his inkwell on the left-hand side." He drew a pencil from his pocket preparatory to turning the folders in the filing cabinet and said, "Well, let's start."

We were about halfway through the index cards when Holmes suddenly uttered an exclamation: "Nuclear energy! There's no such folder here." Carefully he went through all of the folders again to see that the one in question had not been filed out of place, but there was no trace of it.

"It's missing, all right," he said at length. "That could provide the motive."

Sir Brockton exclaimed in a tone of bafflement. "But why commit murder to get it? Why not just steal it?"

"If the thief took it and left your brother alive, it would become known that there had been such a file and that it was missing. The only assurance that the murderer could have that he would be able to sell the information in the file to advantage lay in the fact that no one but the purchaser of the information could know that it existed."

Sir Brockton said, "I see." And then, as there appeared to be nothing more that required his presence, he said that he had an urgent appointment that he should keep, excused himself, and took his leave.

After he had gone, Holmes consulted his watch again. "I ought to go, too, in about twenty minutes, but before I do so, I would appreciate it, Dobbs, if you would show me the laboratory of Mr. Pell. And, Harrington, as I said, there is a little chore that I would like to have you and Irving perform."

"What is that?"

"I would appreciate it very much if you two would take some careful measurements of the dead man's rooms."

"Measurements! Just what—"

"I am particularly concerned to know exactly the height and width of every door and window in Addison Pell's entire lodgings. And—if you can get them—the height of the ceilings and the floor dimensions of each room. You may need a stepladder for that. And then, if you still have time, you might get precise measurements of the stairway—its width, number of treads and width of each, together with the height of the risers—all that sort of thing. I know that this sounds a bit odd, but I assure you it is tremendously important. And Irving, here is something for your trouble." And he handed the boy a half-pound note.

A bit odd? It sounded positively idiotic to me, but I knew that Holmes never did anything without good reason, and so we went about the task, although with no very good grace on young Dobbs's part.

When the boy and I got through with the business of measuring, which I insisted that we complete to the last detail, we returned to the living room to find Holmes awaiting us. He thanked us, then said, "Just a minute, Harrington, and we'll be on our way," And he quickly mounted the stairs and returned in a few minutes with the boots of the dead man, which he had removed, in one hand. After saying our good-byes, he put these carefully on the rear seat of the car with the soles uppermost.

We drove for some time in silence, but at last I felt impelled to make an effort to sound him out: "Dobbs's house impresses me as very old. Probably built at a time when the flues were big enough to accommodate chimney sweeps. Do you suppose that the murderer—"

"My dear fellow," Holmes interrupted, "we are evidently dealing with a clever criminal, but I don't think that even he would be clever enough to start up the chimney, turn round and close the damper with the handles on the lower side, and then continue his climb."

"No, I fancy not," I agreed. But I made another attempt later. "How about young Dobbs? Did it seem to you that his attitude was, to say the least, peculiar?"

"Most peculiar," he readily assented. "He seemed overanxious to ridicule the fact that Pell's death was the result of murder, he differed with his sister about a second man ever having visited Pell's lodgings, and he lied about the time that he got in last night—or, rather, this morning. There's something decidedly suspicious about it all. Still, it's hard to picture him as the murderer. Even if he had the will, I doubt if he would have the courage. Then, too, the murderer was undoubtedly on good enough terms to seek Pell's company and spend some time visiting and drinking with him last evening before he put him out of the way—and this I can hardly imagine young Irving being capable of doing."

Again I agreed, then asked, "Did it seem to you that the boy was restless and seemed anxious to get away?"

"Indeed it did. That's why I had you and him make those fool measurements."

"You mean," I gasped in angry disgust, "that they were wholly unnecessary?"

Holmes chuckled. "I'm afraid so. But I had to contrive some way to keep the young scapegrace there until Joe Stringer could arrive to tail him. My telephone call was to Joe, who couldn't promise to be on hand before five o'clock. I was relieved when I looked out the window and saw him lounging across the street just before you came downstairs. Sorry," he said, glancing at me with amusement.

"You might at least have told me," I complained.

"And perhaps have you give the show away? No, I couldn't take the chance. I had to make it convincing."

The funeral took place two days later. I was unable to attend, but Holmes told me afterwards that he had been successful in learning the identity of at least one of the suspects. Sitting beside Daisy in the rear of the church where the services were held and where they were unlikely to be observed but would have a good view of the door, he had been rewarded when the girl nudged him excitedly and said, "There's one of 'em now, sir," and had indicated the older, more dependable-looking of Addison Pell's two visitors. Holmes had followed the man as he left the church, and had ascertained that he went by the name of Henry Watkins, lived in a cozy little house on Owl Court and worked in the laboratory of the same factory where Pell had been employed. "He has the reputation of being a respectable, law-abiding citizen, but there is one interesting circumstance that I unearthed," Holmes ended his recital.

"What is that?"

"About eight or ten months ago Watkins apparently came into a sizable bit of money. Sort of blossomed out—bought a new Morris car and did some fixing over of his home."

"Eight or ten months? Wouldn't that be about the time that Pell drew the two thousand pounds out of his bank account?"

"Just about," Holmes replied. "I am going to have Joe check on it. Just now he's working on a lead picked up from shadowing young Dobbs.

"He discovered the boy met with a fellow that meets the description of the second suspect described by his sister, whom he was so ready to contradict. The meeting took place shortly after we left Dobbs's house the day after the murder. His name is Gerald Tuppy and he lives in a rather swank apartment at Wimberly Mews. I have written him a note to call here tonight."

"Tonight! But why here instead of the office? And will he come?" I asked.

"He'll come," Holmes assured me. "Out of curiosity, if nothing else. Remember, as far as he knows, no crime is suspected. And I am asking him here because I wish to have the meeting appear altogether unofficial."

When Gerald Tuppy appeared, he bore out the description of Daisy Dobbs. Dressed a bit more loudly than good taste demanded, he had an air of sophistication and self-assurance combined with a ready tongue and an engaging manner. Holmes greeted him warmly, introduced me, and invited him cordially to sit down.

"I got your message, Mr. Holmes," he said easily, as he took the chair indicated and crossed his knees with an air of nonchalance, "and, knowing your reputation, I am all agog with curiosity. To what do I owe the honor of your note?"

Holmes smiled. "Nothing too exciting, I'm afraid. But I thought that knowing the late Addison Pell, it was barely possible that you could be of assistance."

Tuppy's eyebrows went up inquiringly, but his attitude betrayed no agitation such as might be expected if he were guilty of a man's death. "Oh? Well, I would be only too glad to oblige; but, after all, my acquaintance with Mr. Pell was rather on the casual side."

"I was afraid of that," Holmes said. "By the way, my friend Harrington and I were about to have a glass of Scotch and soda. Would you care to join us?" This was news to me, but I was only too ready to fall in with Holmes's plans, and upon Tuppy's genial assent Holmes served us with drinks and went on.

"You see, it's this way. There was an heirloom in the Pell family in the form of a metal shield bearing the family coat of arms and dating back to the twelfth century. I need not tell you that it was regarded by the Pell family with considerable veneration both for its intrinsic and its sentimental value. As far as is known, Addison Pell was the last one to have possession of it, but it seems to have entirely disappeared. Pardon me, but will you have a cigarette to go with your drink, Mr. Tuppy? I hope you don't object to Pall Malls." And he extended a newly opened pack toward our visitor.

61

"Not at all. My favorite brand," said Tuppy, helping himself. "Never smoke anything else. Pray go on."

"Well, to continue, Sir Brockton Pell has caused a search in every possible place he thinks the shield might be, without success. So now he is appealing to everyone who he has reason to think may have known his deceased brother even slightly in the hope that they may throw some light on the missing heirloom's whereabouts. I might add that he is willing to offer a substantial reward for its recovery—in fact, as much as a thousand pounds."

"Sorry," Tuppy said, sipping his drink and savoring his cigarette. "Sounds interesting. But I'm afraid I didn't know Mr. Pell that well. He never mentioned such a thing to me. And I could find use for that thousand pounds," he added with his engaging grin.

"I feared as much," Holmes said, and went on for a few minutes to talk in a rambling way about the deceased Pell and his unfortunate suicide. Then, as Tuppy was about to leave, he said, "There seem to have been none of the poor fellow's friends around at the time he took his life. By the way, you didn't happen to be anywhere in that vicinity that night?"

Tuppy shook his head. "Hardly. I spent the night with a friend."

"A lady, perhaps?" Holmes asked with a conspiratorial smile.

"You might call her that," Tuppy agreed with an answering smirk. Shortly he left.

"A cool customer," Holmes remarked as he carefully picked up our glasses and bore them away.

"He is," I agreed. "But what's all this about a missing shield? I never heard of such a thing before."

Holmes grinned. "Neither did I, but I thought it as good an excuse as any to get Mr. Tuppy here without arousing his suspicions."

I regarded him with renewed admiration for his resourcefulness. "Yes, I suppose it was. But didn't you risk rousing them when you asked where he was that night?"

"Quite. But by that time I had learned all that I had hoped. And I roused them with malice aforethought. By now he is no doubt headed toward the abode of some dubious 'lady' to make good his alibi. With Joe Stringer close on his heels, I might add. We want to know what that alibi is."

I looked at him with increased respect. "Sounds devilish shrewd of you. But I fancy your colloquy was not very profitable otherwise."

"Harrington, you astound me," he replied. "In addition to its giving us an opportunity to look Mr. Tuppy over, it furnished us with two important bits of information."

"How's that?"

"We have some very excellent fingerprints of our visitor on his glass, and the knowledge that he is addicted to Pall Mall cigarettes."

It was but two days later that Holmes got a report from Joe Stringer that seemed to me most satisfactory, as it appeared to demolish entirely the alleged alibi of the debonair Mr. Tuppy. Coming to our lodgings one evening, Joe recounted the results of his sleuthing.

"It wasn't too hard to follow the subject," the young bobby said, "as he apparently had no idea he was being followed. First thing after leaving here he headed for a rundown lodging house in a shady neighborhood. I lounged across the street for almost an hour before he came out; but, when he did, I decided from the cocky way he carried himself that he had been successful in persuading the lady in question to go along with him on a fake alibi.

"I thought it would be cutting it a bit thin to barge in on the dame on Tuppy's heels, and thought it best to wait till the next day to interview her, to keep from 'rousing her suspicions. Anyway, I had to think up the proper dodge to make my approach, as I had reason to think there was more than one female in the house, and I had to figure out which one Tuppy was cozy with, then find some way of getting her to change her story or to prove that she was lying.

"Sure enough, when I went to the place next morning I found that there were three rooms let out by the landlady, two occupied by a couple of dames each an' one held by a single. As luck would have it, the dame in the first room I tried, a brassy piece about thirty years old, with yellow hair, hard eyes, and a husky voice, seemed to be the one who was Tuppy's friend. She was in one of the double rooms, but at the time her lodging mate was out.

"When she came to the door she was in a highly colored dirty wrapper with her hair down. She opened the door a crack and rapped, 'What d'ya want?'

"I flashed my badge and told her that I had a few questions to ask her. She wasn't too warm about it but let me in. Odds and ends of clothing were scattered about the room, with a cheap, battered piece of luggage open on the bed. It was plain that she was getting ready to take off somewhere, whether to some other living quarters or just on a holiday she didn't say and I didn't ask. She was going by the name of Doryce—she spells it D-O-R-Y-C-E!—Montrose, though I doubt it is her real moniker. When I asked her where she worked, she told me, 'Here and there,' though I gathered that when she was employed, it was as a salesclerk, most likely in one of the cheaper chain department stores.

"To make her think that my investigation had nothing to do with Tuppy, I said that there had been a robbery in a store in the neighborhood on the night that Pell was killed—though of course I didn't mention the Pell case—and that we had information that one of the fellows implicated was a big, hulking chap, with shaggy black hair and a scar on the forehead. I said that we had been tipped off that he had spent the remainder of the night with one of the girls in this house, and asked her if she knew anything about it.

"At first, she clammed up, said she wasn't tellin' nothin' to no bobby, but when I told her that I would have to book her and take her to headquarters if she couldn't rightly account for her own whereabouts that night, she calmed down. It looked as if, after arranging with Tuppy for his alibi, she had wanted to get away for a while and not be interviewed. But now that I had caught her before she made her getaway, she must have thought it was as good a time as any to help Tuppy out. So she claimed that she had spent the night with a man all right, but it was another blighter than the one I described, and gave me Tuppy's name and description. 'It's a pity that an honest girl can't entertain her fiancy for a night without bein' bothered by the bobbies,' she said.

"I thanked her, said I was sorry to have troubled her, and as her luggage case was now packed, offered to take her wherever she was going in my motorcar. By now she was considerable softened up, but said she didn't want to bother me and would take a bus where she was going.

"I left, but watched the house until I was sure that she was on her way, an' then hurried back into the house to try to knock out the Montrose dame's story before she got things fixed with the other girls there. I found only one other girl in, but luck was with me again. This dame was a cut above the Montrose piece. When I gave her the same song and dance about the big, tough man with the shaggy beard and the scar, she said that she was sure that none of the girls had seen any such man that night."

" 'How can you be so sure?' I asked.

" 'Why, I know because that was the night of the fire.'

" 'What fire?' I asked. Then she told me that there had been a small fire in a shop about a block an' a half away around midnight, and that all the girls who were in had gone down to watch it.

" 'How about Miss Montrose?' I asked. 'Your land-lady says that she's gone away on a holiday, or I'd ask her myself.'

" 'Oh, Doryce wasn't here that night,' she said, and

then went on to tell me that this Montrose had spent the night with a friend. Then I got out of her the info that the friend's name was Gracie Pringle an' that she lodged somewhere on Minchin Street near Crabapple Lane. So I got this dame to sign a statement an' that night ambled out to Minchin, located the Pringle dame. She wasn't too bright and was only too glad to think she was helping out her friend Doryce when she said that Doryce had spent the night with her an' not with any man. So I got her to sign a statement to that effect, an' it looks as if we had Tuppy's alibi pretty well knocked out."

"But just to make things as watertight as possible, I went back to the Montrose dame's lodging house an' got statements from two other of the girls there. Only one refused to talk, an' the landlady said she wasn't signing anything, that she ran a good, clean place, that all her lodgers were decent an' respectable an' she didn't like bobbies snoopin' around. But I think if it came to a showdown she would swear that neither Tuppy nor any other man slept there that night."

Holmes said, "Splendid! It looks very much as if our friend Tuppy might be our man. At least he must have something quite serious that he wishes to hide."

"But how about Henry Watkins?" I inquired. "There's that money—"

Holmes nodded. "Very true. I agree it needs looking into, as do some of the activities of young Dobbs. I am not altogether satisfied the good-for-nothing does not fit into the picture somewhere. As for Watkins, I believe that he gave it out that the source of his sudden bit of affluence was a deceased aunt—which is, of course, about what he would say in any case. What we must do is try to find out if this supposed aunt had 'a local habitation and a name'—to quote our much-revered Shakespeare. Joe, I believe that you have about three days left of your holiday?"

"That is right, sir."

"How would you like looking into the matter? I have received a rather delicate commission to perform on behalf of Lady Luddington, which promises to occupy the major portion of my time just now."

"I will be very glad to, sir."

It was at this point in the investigation that I was compelled to leave London on a special assignment for the *Times* having to do with possible peculation by some of those high in our government. I was loath to go, as I was anxious to have knowledge of the day-to-day progress of Holmes in this most peculiar and interesting case. I was concerned, too, that it might come to a conclusion, before my return, and I was particularly eager to be in on its denouement.

I was therefore somewhat surprised and not a little pleased to discover that Holmes had not entirely solved the matter by the time of my return. I was still more surprised and somewhat taken aback to find that the case had apparently taken a new and wholly unexpected turn.

When Holmes and I were settled over a glass of port that evening, I made bold to ask him how things were proceeding, as he filled his pipe while I lit up a cigarette.

"Well," he replied, "I got the report from Stringer on Watkins, and it totally exonerated him, as I had rather expected. Stringer interviewed Watkins, who readily gave him the name and place of residence of the aunt who had left him the windfall, and upon looking up the court records at the capital of the shire, Stringer verified the truth of Watkins' story.

"With the evidence I now had in hand I was convinced it was time to call in the services of Scotland Yard, as the situation clearly called for more work than I could handle alone, especially now that I have taken on Lady Luddington's case. So I called up Sir Brockton and told him that our research now showed it plainly to be a case of murder and asked his permission to solicit the cooperation of the Yard, to which he reluctantly consented.

"For one thing, I desired a search of Tuppy's lodgings, an action that could not be taken without a warrant. I had some hope that such a search might turn up the bottle that had contained the drug that put Pell to sleep, and even, perhaps, of locating the missing file from Addison Pell's cabinet."

"And—?" I asked eagerly.

But he shook his head. "Men from the Yard made a secret search at a time when Tuppy was out, but the results were wholly negative. All they got was the name of the chemist from whom he had purchased other drugs, as shown by bottles in his medicine cabinet. But when they interviewed the chemist he had no recollection of such a man as Tuppy buying the drug used to put Pell to sleep at any time. Furthermore there was no trace whatever of the missing file. I admit it was something of a setback, although I must say that I rather thought Tuppy too clever not to cover up his tracks."

"So what will you do?"

"Why, tomorrow I am going to have what I hope will be a very persuasive talk with Daisy Dobbs's dubious brother. After that, I think that we'll call in the man that the Yard agrees is undoubtedly the culprit. At my suggestion they have been doing some very effective undercover work and have dug up some very incriminating material on our chief suspect. He is a figure familiar to the police, with a record of three arrests, though so far they have not been able to pin anything on him."

"And what's the name of this fellow?" I asked.

"According to Captain Gregg, he has gone by a string of aliases, but the one they know him best by is 'Slippery Sam.' If I am as successful in my interview with young Dobbs tomorrow as I hope, we are going to call in Slippery Sam, and I think that I can promise you a few surprises."

"You already have," I said, now thoroughly at sea. "I'll be on hand if at all possible. I wouldn't miss it for worlds."

So it was that two days later at 2:15 P.M. I was seated in Holmes's office along with him and Captain Gregg awaiting the arrival of the mysterious suspect.

While we were waiting, Holmes showed the captain a small photograph of our expected visitor, which an amateur photographer had managed with some ingenuity to secure for Holmes.

"That's him, all right," the captain nodded. "He's a smooth customer and a cool one. We've been trying to get something on him for a long time. If you can pin him down and fix this murder on him, it'll be a big relief to the force as well as a service to society. But it's hard to picture him as a killer. As far as we know, that has never been his line."

"I fancy that's so," Holmes agreed. "But I don't suppose that it has ever been conscience that held him back. Up to now it has never seemed necessary—or, perhaps, worth the chance. But this time he had a lot at stake and it seemed like a foolproof setup."

The appointment was for thirty minutes after two, but when it reached that time there was no sign of Slippery Sam. Five and forty minutes after two he still had not put in an appearance. Captain Gregg fiddled with his watch. At five minutes of the hour he got up, went to one of the office windows and looked out. "Do you fancy he could have given our men the slip?" he asked. "They are two of our best."

Holmes said confidently, "He'll be here. He just doesn't want to appear anxious. And when he comes he'll be as jaunty as ever. If he knows why he's being called in, he's pretty sure that we have nothing more than suspicions. And even if he weren't sure, he's the kind that would play out his hand to the end."

"I fancy you are right," Captain Gregg agreed, and resumed his seat.

Seven minutes more elapsed while the captain and I fidgeted and worried and Holmes remained calmly relaxed. Suddenly we heard steps outside and all sat up alertly. Then the door opened and there stood the suspect—Gerald Tuppy!

So Tuppy and Slippery Sam were the same, and Holmes, with his love of drama, had staged this little scene just to impress me.

For a moment the fellow stood in the doorway savoring the effect of his appearance. Seemingly he was as calm and collected as ever. "Sorry to be a little late," he said breezily.

"It doesn't matter," Holmes replied. "We could wait and we knew you'd come."

"Mind if I sit down?" Tuppy asked, at the same time helping himself to a chair.

Holmes said, "Just as you wish. By the way, this is Captain Gregg of Scotland Yard; I believe that you have already met Mr. Harrington."

"More than glad to know you," Tuppy said, taking the hand of Gregg as if greeting a long lost friend and nodding cheekily to me. "More conversation about the Pell coat of arms?" he went on, taking out a Pall Mall and crossing his legs comfortably as he lit it.

"No," Holmes replied, "it is about the Pell murder."

Tuppy raised his eyebrows. "Murder? You don't mean to tell me that the good Sir Brockton has been done in."

"No. His brother Addison."

"Oh, come now. I thought that was a case of suicide. If I remember rightly, he was found dead—asphyxiated—with the gas turned on and all the doors and windows locked."

"So he was."

"Then how did the killer get out? He must have been some sort of wizard and just faded through one of the doors."

"You would know as much about that as we do. We are charging you with his murder," Holmes said coldly.

"Well, really," Tuppy said, smiling, "Is this some kind of game or something?"

"No game. But perhaps you would like to know how we arrived at our conclusions."

"I would, indeed, Mr. Holmes. It promises to be most entertaining."

"I doubt if you will find it so entertaining by the time that I am through," Holmes said. "Well, to begin with, I looked from an upstairs window of the house where Addison Pell lodged into the room where he lay dead, and I was curious when I observed that the north and south doors leading out of the room had blankets tucked close against the bottoms of the doors to prevent the gas escaping, but the blanket at the east door leading into the hallway, though tight against the back of the door near the hinges, was a foot or more from the front. What does this indicate to you, Mr. Tuppy?"

"That our friend Pell was a bit careless in his hurry to get the thing over, wouldn't you say?"

Holmes shook his head. "No. I would suggest that Pell did not put the blankets there at all; but that you, the killer, did, and that although the blanket against the west door was originally laid as close to its bottom as the blankets by the other two doors were, it got shoved back when you opened it to go into the hall and make your getaway."

I thought that Tuppy gave an all but imperceptible start, but his only comment was a flippant "Very interesting."

But Holmes was going on. "Then when I went into the room and made further investigation, I found additional proof of your presence in the room with Pell immediately preceding the time of his death. These were the heel marks of Pell's boots, left on the floor when you dragged him away from in front of the filing cabinet where he fell from his chair when he succumbed to the drug that you slipped into his drink while you were drinking together. His body blocked the drawer of the cabinet and you had to get it out of the way."

"You make it sound more and more intriguing," Tuppy said, changing his position slightly. "Pray go on."

"I will," Holmes said grimly. "Outside on the ground at the foot of a window where you had thrown them—along with ashes and crumbs of tobacco from

Pell's pipe—were the butts of cigarettes that you had smoked when visiting with Pell while setting him up for the kill. You had to throw them out or they would have been damning evidence against you if found in the room, as Pell never smoked cigarettes—only a pipe. But you overlooked the time element, which was against you. It had rained that day, but had dried off late in the afternoon. If the cigarette butts had been there before the rain stopped, they would have been soaked. But they were perfectly dry, which shows that they had been thrown there that evening. Incidentally, they were Pall Mall cigarettes. Still entertained, Mr. Tuppy?"

"Just cut the comedy and get on with the fairy story." Tuppy's voice had lost its breezy air and had a nervous note in it.

"It is you who thought the matter so funny," Holmes pointed out.

"You can save the lecture," Tuppy retorted. "You keep saying 'you' all the time when you talk about this imaginary killer. Just why are you so sure I'm your patsy?"

"You had the motive. About a year ago Pell bought some stock in a uranium mine that had no uranium in it. We found the certificate in his strongbox. We have reason to think you sold it to him. Investigation shows you peddled the stuff."

"And so I killed him? That's a laugh."

"Not such a laugh. Pell finally concluded he had been bilked, no doubt. Then it is probable he ran you down or blundered into you and threatened you with exposure. You didn't want that. You had always slipped through the hands of the police before, probably because you bought off your accusers. But it would be different if the Pells, with all their prestige and influence, got after you. But you were too suave and clever for the unsophisticated and simple Addison Pell. You calmed him down and probably promised a big dividend. You may even have made an appointment to meet him in his rooms and give him a check for it. By

72

this time you may have got so far in his good graces that he confided in you his hopes of the results of a startling discovery in nuclear physics that he had made.

"Before this you had the motive of fear; now you also had the motive of greed. If you could only get your hands on the information regarding his discovery, you were set for life. No more dodging the police. You could just sit back and take it easy. All you had to do was do away with Addison Pell. And you thought you had a foolproof way of doing it."

"Most ingenious," Tuppy sneered. But he looked strained and his collar seemed too tight as he put one hand up to his throat. "And, I suppose, I knew exactly when the other folks in the house where he lodged would be away, so that everything would be nice and cozy?"

"Exactly," Holmes agreed. "Yesterday I had a heart-to-heart talk with Irving Dobbs."

"Irving Dobbs?" The sound of strain was more pronounced in Tuppy's voice.

"Yes. There's no use in your pretending you don't know him. My assistant saw you talking with him after the murder. He told you when his family would be away. Would you like to hear about it?"

"Go ahead with your pipe dreams. I couldn't stop you, anyway."

"Very well. Yesterday when I got hold of the boy, he tried to brazen it out; but he caved in when I threw the fear of God into him and told him that he might be charged as accessory to murder. It was a rather long story. He got into debt gambling. He was even out late on the night of the murder, gambling at cards. He had got in so deep that he had held out several pounds that he had collected from a customer in the garage where he works as a mechanic, when the proprietor was out. Since then he has done the same thing twice again, using the money last collected each time to pay up the bill collected before. But this couldn't go on. He was worried and scared and afraid of going to prison. Then he saw you again and thought he saw a way out. He thought you had plenty of money. He would get what he needed from you.

"He had first seen you when you started coming to Pell's, presumably trying to talk him into buying the uranium stock. When he ran into you lately, about the time Pell was making things uncomfortable for you, he told you the mess he was in and tried to borrow money from you. This was a lucky break, you thought. You saw how you could use him. You said you couldn't let him have the money just then because of a big deal you had pending, but you knew how he could get all he needed and more. You told him you knew a handy thief who would break into his father's furniture shop and steal the money there and share it with him, and all his troubles would be over. All he had to do was to find out some night when his family would be away and let you know—which he did.

"Then the night came—and Pell lost his life. Young Irving met you by appointment and wanted to know why the thief hadn't broken into his father's shop, and asked when he was going to get his money. He also told you about Pell's being dead and about my saying it was murder and that I listed you as a possible suspect. You told him that your friend, the thief, had had another job that night, but that you would pay him his blighting money if he would just quit pestering you about it. Only he would have to keep his mouth shut to 'that damned Holmes' about his ever seeing you or knowing you, because if I got after you on this murder business it might ruin your big deal. You even went so far as to tell him that if he did open his mouth to me you would damned well shut it so he would never open it again."

"Quite a neat story, Holmes. Why, you could get that bloody squealer to say anything for a couple of quid."

"I could buy him almost as cheaply as you could Doryce Montrose, I suppose," Holmes replied.

Tuppy gave a visible shudder and his eyes darted

74

first toward Holmes and then toward Gregg. "What are you talkin' about?"

"Your alibi, Tuppy, with your accommodating lady friend."

"You can't prove I wasn't at her room that night."

"Maybe not. But we can prove *she* wasn't. No, it's no good, Tuppy, you're all washed up. Look at these," and he threw photostatic copies of the statements that Joe Stringer had secured onto the desk in front of Tuppy. Tuppy did not say a word; just leaned over and read them, one after another. His head shook as he pushed one aside to read the next.

When he straightened up, his face was as grey as a dirty shirt. "A bunch of damned forgeries. They're all lying. Besides, what if I wasn't with Doryce, that doesn't prove I was at Pell's."

"No, but your fingerprints do," Holmes said.

This was the final blow. "My fingerprints? Why, I—" he stopped suddenly.

"You were going to say that you wiped them all off. But you didn't. You left one beautiful set of prints on the index card marked 'Nuclear energy.' You see, Pell was left-handed and you are right-handed. So when Pell thumbed through the cards, his prints were mostly on the left-hand side while the other side remained comparatively clean. When I handled the cards, I was careful to use tweezers so as not to destroy any possible prints. And there were yours, Tuppy, clear and distinct. You are shrewd; but, after all, you couldn't think of everything. No, Tuppy, you are finished. The jig is up."

For once Gerald Tuppy's ready tongue was silent. He just sat there and looked at one of us and then the other like a cornered animal, terrified and desperate.

Holmes said, "There's just one chance that you might escape the death penalty."

Tuppy licked his lips. "What's that?"

"One of the men from the Yard who has been shadowing you saw you in conference with a known enemy agent at a secluded street corner, presumably bargaining about the stolen file. But he saw no papers change hands. If you still have the stolen file and can produce it—"

"Produce—" Tuppy's voice was a despairing wail. "My God!" and he put his head in his hands.

"What's the matter?" Holmes asked.

"It's gone!"

"Gone."

Tuppy took away his hands, lifted his face, and nodded. He looked ghastly. Then he started to speak, but his voice was so low that we could hardly hear him. "When I found out that you were on the case, I had a feeling that sooner or later you would get me— you're . . . you're such a damned bloodhound . . . can't be shaken off. I had the file hidden safe enough in the room of one of the lodgers who was on his holiday. But yesterday, when I got the call from you telling me to come here, I panicked and I . . . I burned the file. Oh, my God, what a fool, what a damned, blithering, blighted fool!" And again he leaned forward and put his face in his hands, shaking his head from side to side. We all sat and watched him for a long moment. Then Holmes nodded at Captain Gregg.

Gregg got up and tapped Tuppy on the shoulder. "Come on, Slippery," he said. "We're on our way." Tuppy got up like a man walking in his sleep, Gregg snapped handcuffs on him, and they went out the door.

"Not a very nice sight," I said, looking after them.

"No," Holmes agreed. "But then, he wasn't a very nice man."

I said, "He was the one you really thought guilty almost from the first, wasn't he? Why?"

"Well, I think the answer is rather obvious. When there are two possible suspects and one is a respected citizen while the other—to quote our perceptive friend, Daisy Dobbs—is 'not quite a gentleman,' then, in case of murder, the one who is not quite a gentleman is the more likely prospect."

"Of course," I nodded in assent. "There's just one other question?"

"Yes?" he said, filling his pipe.

"How *did* Tuppy get out of Addison Pell's lodgings?"

Holmes smiled. "Through the door into the hallway. Here's the key to the mystery. I'm keeping it for evidence." And he tossed a small, old-fashioned, slate-grey key upon the desk. "Look at the end that goes into the lock," he directed.

I did and saw two bright indentations grooved into the greyish metal. I looked at Holmes inquiringly.

"Those are the marks of a pair of small, strong tweezers that Tuppy inserted into the keyhole to turn the key and lock the door after he had passed through it into the hall. That's the reason he oiled the lock—to be sure the key would turn. It was really very simple."

"Yes, wasn't it?" I said.

The Strange Death of Matthew Tidmore

"What are you reading?" I asked.

My question was addressed to Creighton Holmes. It was a grey Sunday afternoon in mid-September, with the rain beating down in a steady drizzle, so that we were confined to our rooms on Baker Street. As usual on such occasions, when he was not engrossed in one of his endless experiments, Holmes was immersed in a book. His reading was almost always related in some way to the work to which he was devoted with such passion: the methods employed by criminals, the ruses they resorted to, the tools they used, or some remoter phase of their nefarious doings. So now his answer to my question was something of a surprise.

"*Macbeth*," he said.

"Shakespeare's *Macbeth?*"

"Whose else?" he inquired.

"But you almost always . . . I mean Shakespeare . . . that is—" I floundered, feeling myself grow red in the face.

"I fancy that what you are trying to say is that I never read anything not connected with the business of crime detection," Holmes smiled.

"Er . . . something like that," I replied weakly.

"Perhaps you are right," he said. "But then, I find that sooner or later any knowledge that I gather may help in some way in my detection of crime. And, as for reading Shakespeare, I can see how it might be a very direct help."

"What do you mean?"

"Shakespeare knew human nature and he could portray one attribute essential to the perpetration of crime as no one else could."

"What attribute is that?"

"Motivation."

"Motivation?"

"Yes. You often hear that in trying to identify the perpetrator of a crime you must look for two things: motive and opportunity."

"And isn't that what you do look for?"

"Yes, but there is a third element that must be present before a crime is committed, and that is motivation: the drive that converts motive into action. There are plenty of people who have motive and opportunity who never commit crime."

"Yes, that's true, of course," I agreed.

"For instance," he went on, "Macbeth might never have killed Duncan if Lady Macbeth had not urged him on. Remember what she said when he lost his nerve and almost backed out—'Infirm of purpose, give me the daggers'? She may have cracked up later; but at the time she had the ruthless disregard of the rights and welfare of others that makes your true criminal."

I saw his point. And I was to see it much more clearly later when he came to solve the mystery of Matthew Tidmore's death; for it was the knowledge gained from reading of quite another sort that was to make possible the solution of this diabolically cunning crime.

The call that was to involve us quite fortuitously in this sinister affair came from no less a person than the distinguished Baron Tidmore, barely a month after the above-recorded conversation. It had been discovered that someone in the government office where the baron was engaged had been passing on information of a most confidential nature to an agent of an unfriendly power. It was imperative that the identity of the guilty party be determined at the earliest possible moment to forestall further treasonous revelations. For reasons not revealed, it was not desirable in this particular instance to call in Scotland Yard. Therefore Holmes's services were being enlisted, as he had once before executed a highly important commission for the baron with singular success.

The baron's elegant country seat was located some sixty miles from the environs of London, and as soon as the call came, early one morning, we got on our way. It was a beautiful October day, bright with sunshine and spiced with the invigorating tang of autumn air. The foliage had just started to change color, and I was eager to see Tidmore Manor, of which I had heard so much.

Nor was I disappointed when we came in view of this old and celebrated mansion. Employing the Norman style of architecture, its designer had achieved such a happy combination of line and proportion that the result was a harmonious whole of great warmth and beauty. Its charm was enhanced by the rich coloring of walls mellowed by age and softened by the English ivy that clung to their sides. Broad-leafed rhododendrons and laurel, interspersed with darker-hued holly and euonymus, sheltered the base, while strategically placed trees, some in clumps, some standing alone, studded the wide rolling acres on which the building stood, the high bronzes and dark cardinals of oaks being relieved by the lighter greens and yellows of birch, beech, and aspen. All in all, it was a scene sweetly restful and inviting. As I gazed upon it, little did I suspect the ugly secret that lay concealed behind its ivy-covered walls.

As we drew near the ornate gateway that gave entrance to the grounds, a motorcar came out and passed us. We went through the gates, proceeded some two hundred yards along a winding, tree-shaded drive, and alighted at the entrance to the manor. A butler answered our summons at the great oak door and conducted us to our host, a large man of some eight and sixty years, with iron-grey hair, strong, heavy features, and a sedately benevolent air. After the exchange of greetings, Holmes said, "I see you've already had guests this morning."

"They were here last night," the baron responded. "We had a party to celebrate the birthday of my younger brother Matthew, who lives here with my daughter and me—a quiet family affair but quite enjoyable. But pray sit down," he said as he led us into a bright, cozy library off the great, dark-beamed withdrawing room.

Then, when we were seated, he continued. "I fear that I have brought you here on a fruitless errand. The case is solved. By merest chance, an undersecretary was caught red-handed in the act of abstracting some top-secret papers and has made a full confession. I heard about it less than an hour ago. I tried to call you at once, but you had already started here. I'm sorry and will be more than glad to compensate you for your time. I hope this needless trip has not too seriously disrupted your schedule. I know you're a busy man."

Holmes's disclaimer was interrupted by the sudden appearance of the butler, who just then reentered the room with solemn face and agitated manner. "What is it, Parkins?" the baron asked.

"It's about Mr. Matthew, sir. I'm worried. I never knew him to stay abed till such an hour, and when I went to his chamber door and listened, I couldn't hear a sound. Maybe I'm foolish, sir, but I can't help thinking something's wrong. Anyway, I felt that you should know."

"Thank you, Parkins. It *is* unlike Matthew to sleep so late. You're quite right to be concerned. Did you tap at his door?"

"No. I did not like to do that, sir. I did try to open it just to glance in, being careful not to disturb him; but it was locked."

"I see. I'll just step up myself and try to rouse him." He excused himself, and the two of them left us.

In a few moments they were back, the Baron's face as sober as the butler's.

"I knocked loudly on the door and called to my

brother, but there was no response," he said gravely. "Something must be seriously amiss. We'll have to break in the door, I'm sorry this should happen just when you are here. If you don't mind, I'll just get hold of the gardener and have him see you round while we make an attempt to force the door."

"But you don't need do that," Holmes said. "I have a picklock with me. You can use that."

"Excellent! That's very kind of you. But perhaps you had better come along and use it yourself, if you will."

I was curious to see what was the matter, as I am sure Holmes was too, so we were only too ready to follow our host. After mounting the fine old stairway and passing through a long hall, we entered a door near the rear of the manor. This opened into what appeared to be a sort of lounging room, which proved to be part of a three-room suite occupied by the baron's brother. The door of the bedroom adjoining was locked, but after some manipulation Holmes succeeded in opening it.

The room we now viewed was a large chamber equipped with handsome furniture. There were three heavy straight-backed chairs, a large dresser or chiffonier to our right against the inner wall, a huge four-poster bed by the far wall, opposite us, and in the corner near us, to our left, what had at one time been a washstand with, no doubt, a washbowl and pitcher on it. Now, though, it no longer served its original purpose and was kept, I assumed, as a matter of sentiment or appearance only. On its top were two or three decorative objects, but it was so situated as to attract little attention.

The rest of us stood just inside the doorway while the baron went to the bed, where lay the form of Matthew Tidmore, almost fully clothed. Only his coat and waistcoat had been removed and his braces let down from the shoulders. He lay partly crosswise of the bed, and my first thought was that he was in a drunken stupor.

The baron said something and leaned over to shake the shoulder of the apparently sleeping man, then suddenly recoiled with a startled exclamation. "I . . . I think he's dead," he said.

We all pressed forward to look. It took but the most superficial examination to see that Matthew Tidmore was, indeed, no longer alive.

"I . . . I just don't understand it," the baron gasped, his lips compressed and his face dead white.

"He hadn't suffered lately from ill health?" Holmes asked.

"Not at all."

"And he was in no way depressed?"

"No more than usual. Matthew was not the happiest of men. He had had a rather tragic past. But if you're thinking that he might have taken his own life, I can assure you, that's out of the question. Can you make any guess as to the cause of his death, Mr. Holmes?"

"Well, yes, I might," replied Holmes, who had been observing the body of the dead man very closely. "But perhaps we had better look around," and he stepped into the bathroom. In a moment he was back with an empty bottle and a drinking glass in his hand. "I think here is your explanation," he said.

"What is it?" the Baron asked.

"The bottle's labeled 'chloral hydrate,' a very potent soporific. Was your brother accustomed to taking something to make him sleep?"

"Occasionally. He did complain somewhat of sleeplessness."

"Is this the drug he took?"

"I don't know. I never saw the bottle before. Of course, he might have got it without my knowledge."

"Could he have taken too much by mistake?"

"I very much doubt it."

"Could—I hope you'll excuse me for asking this— but could he have had a bit too much to drink last evening? Sometimes these birthday parties—"

The baron shook his head. "Nothing like that. We did serve some wine, but Matthew hardly touched it. He had suffered from stomach ulcers and was under doctor's orders to partake of no spirits. The strongest thing he drank lately was Coca Cola, for which he seemed to have acquired something of a taste."

"And you say it's not possible that he took his own life intentionally?"

"I can't conceive of it. But if he didn't, I don't understand how his door came to be locked."

"He could have locked it himself even after a lethal potion," Holmes responded. "It would not take effect instantly. It's possible he could have taken it and still have had control of his faculties long enough to lock the door but not long enough to get undressed. Yet I confess I find the circumstances most peculiar. Perhaps if we make a further search we may discover something to help us. Harrington, you might look again in the bathroom. I'll see if the lounging room can tell us anything, and, Baron, I suggest you look to see what may be here."

I went into the bathroom, but had discovered nothing that might serve as a clue when I heard the baron's startled voice cry, "Here's a note!"

"Don't touch it!" Holmes called as we both rushed back to the bedroom to see the baron standing before the washstand, gazing down at a paper from which he was drawing back his hands.

"I'm sorry," Holmes said. "I shouldn't have spoken so sharply. But there could be fingerprints on the paper."

"I know," the baron said. "But I barely touched it."

He moved aside and Holmes went to bend over the paper, at the same time drawing from his pocket the magnifying glass that he always carried with him. Parkins and I stood close to him, also peering at the paper. It was a plain bit of writing paper about half the size of a typesheet and lay flat on top of the stand, the other articles on it having been pushed back or to one side by Baron Tidmore. The note was brief, with a one-word signature at the bottom. I read as follows:

I am sorry, but this is the best thing that I can do—Matthew

Holmes scrutinized it long and intently, then

straightened up. "Well, well, a most interesting note. Rather cryptic, wouldn't you say? And it poses some interesting questions. First, if the dead man wrote it, would it not be likely that he would do so before taking the fatal draught and while his mind was clear? Second, if this is so, why would he not also wait until he was undressed before he drank it? Third, why did he leave it here instead of on the dresser, where it would be more quickly found? All of which leads one to wonder if he did write it at all. Baron, tell me, do you recognize this as the handwriting of your brother?"

The baron stepped forward to examine the note again as Parkins and I made way for him to do so. "I assumed of course it was," he said, "but now that you ask me, I really can't say. I can't recall when I've had occasion to see his writing except for the address on the envelope of some letter he was posting—which would be seldom, and I would give it but a glance. There does seem to be something familiar about the script; but I just can't tell."

"How about the signature? Can you say as to that?"

"Yes, that I can vouch for. It's Matthew's signature. I'm positive of that."

"I see," Holmes commented. "This grows more and more intriguing. I would say that it calls for a full-scale investigation. You must have a doctor certify as to the cause of death, and I suggest that you have the inquiring medical officer be the one to do it, as he will, no doubt, be called in sooner or later in any event. And you must also notify the police."

"*Must* the police be notified?"

"Without a doubt."

"Then I'd like you to work with them. In fact, I'd prefer you to take charge, if possible."

"Thank you, I'd be glad to, if you could arrange it. But the police—"

"Are jealous of their authority and slow to give it up," the baron broke in. "I know. And of course they have a duty to perform. But I know the young constable at Wibberly—the village near us. He is under some obligation to me, and I'm sure that he'll cooperate when I tell him who you are."

"Capital!" Holmes exclaimed. "Perhaps you should make these calls at once."

Accordingly, the baron left us to use a telephone that I had noticed on a stand in the adjoining room.

When he returned, Holmes said, "Assuming that your brother did not kill himself, someone else who was in the manor last night did. Therefore, our first task is to narrow the field of possible suspects, if we can do so. So let me ask you, Baron, didn't your brother have a rather unusual pride of family and social position?"

"Why, yes, he did—most unusual," the baron said with a start of surprise.

"And—I don't like to ask this, but we *are* investigating a possible murder—was he somewhat sharp-tongued and given to making remarks that might hurt or offend people?"

"Yes, I'm sorry to say that he was. But how could you know? You never met him."

"I deduced his possession of these traits from his handwriting."

"But I thought you said he may not have written the note."

"That's true, but you said the signature was genuine."

"And you drew your conclusions from the way a single word was written? Really, Mr. Holmes, I respect your talents; but isn't it taxing our credulity a little too much to think that you can do this?"

"Perhaps," Holmes smiled. "I confess it was somewhat a shot in the dark. But the evidence, to me, was quite convincing. The first high stroke in the letter 'M' as he writes it is an almost infallible sign of inordinate pride of family and position. And the lancelike stroke across the *t*'s denotes quite definitely that the writer has a tendency toward sarcasm."

"I see," said the baron, shaking his head. "And I can't deny the accuracy of your conclusions. Still, it seems like pure fantasy to me. But why bring these things up? How are they going to help in the solving of his death?"

"Well, I was just wondering, if your brother were so conscious of his superior status and so caustic of tongue, if possibly he might have incurred the enmity of one of the servants."

"To the point where that servant would seek his death? Not a chance. Whatever other faults he may have had, Matthew never treated any servant scurvily. He always said that anyone who would abuse a person in an inferior position was nothing but a cad. He had a way with servants—just the right degree of reserve combined with intimacy. The truth is he was a sort of favorite with them. The caustic remarks that he made in their presence were not directed at them but at someone else, and only amused them. They liked him better than the rest of us."

"Good. That reduces the number of our suspects to your guests who were here last night. How many were there?"

"Five."

"Only five?" And the handwriting on the note is quite definitely that of a man. How many were women?"

"Two."

"Better and better. That lightens our task still more. I would like to get them all together soon. As close relatives, it is only natural that they should be notified promptly. But it is important that you arouse no suspicion. Forewarned is forearmed. I suggest you invite them to come here this evening—say, eight of the clock. I would further suggest that you be vague as to details. Say nothing of my presence here nor of the possibility of Matthew's taking his own life. We'll let the guilty party—if there is one—think you have not yet found the 'suicide note.' Simply say that Matthew was found dead in his bed, that the doctor is not certain as to the cause, and you would like to talk over the advisability of an autopsy."

"Very well."

"But there are several things I'd like to do to prepare for the meeting before you call them. It seems likely that the murderer, if there was one, drank with his victim and slipped the fatal dosage into his glass. If so, we should find another glass and probably a bottle, and we should also have these tested for fingerprints. Baron, didn't I see a liquor cabinet in your brother's lounging room?"

"Yes. He used to keep some spirits there when he was drinking, and he still keeps some for the entertainment of occasional guests."

"I thought so. Well, I want to get these things together and have Harrington take them to London as quickly as possible. I, myself, have some work that I wish to do here."

"But why London?"

"Because I wish to have another important call made there."

"I see. But it's not necessary that Mr. Harrington go. No doubt he'd like to stay at the manor and look around. My chauffeur Burrows is an excellent driver, highly intelligent, and knows London like a book. He can take care of the matter for you if you tell him what you want."

"Fine. Thank you. And he should be notified at once. It's urgent that he get back here before our meeting tonight. By the way, we'll need a carton and some packing so that we can pack any further glasses or bottles that we may find. I'd also like an envelope that we can slip this note into to protect it, and some small tweezers."

"Tweezers?"

"If you please."

"Very well. Parkins——"

"I'll see to it at once. I'll also get hold of Burrows and see that the cook gets him a bit of lunch." And the butler left.

Our search of the liquor cabinet netted an empty Coca Cola bottle, a partially empty claret flask, and three more tumblers, all of which we placed beside the note. Holmes had also located a fountain pen in an escritoire of the dead man's apartment. Carrying it gingerly by one tip-end, he asked Baron Tidmore if it was his brother Matthew's.

It was an elegant maroon-colored pen with the gold initials *M.L.T.* on the cap. The baron glanced at it and nodded. "Yes. I gave identical pens to all the close male relatives a year ago last Christmas. They were the best pens that I could get, and I had the donee's initials embossed on the cap of each."

Having recourse to his small magnifying glass again and using his kerchief to remove the cap from the pen, Holmes minutely examined the nib, turning it this way and that.

I noticed the baron giving him a skeptical look, as if he might think this extended scrutiny just so much dumb show to impress us; but, knowing Holmes as I did, I knew that he did nothing without a purpose, though I could not imagine now what that purpose might be. Little did I realize how important that seemingly senseless action was to prove.

Shortly Parkins was back with the articles Holmes had requested. Taking the tweezers he had brought, Holmes carefully got hold of one edge of the paper on which the note was written and turned it over. Then, once more using the magnifying glass, he closely inspected the blank side of the paper. As he did so, I caught a gleam of excitement in his eye as he exclaimed, "Aha, just as I expected."

The baron apparently noticed it too, for he asked, "What have you found?"

"For one thing, unless I am greatly mistaken, I have found that the note bears the handwriting of three different persons," Holmes responded.

"Three! But that's incredible!" the baron exclaimed. "Do you mean to say that three people conspired to take my brother's life?"

But with seeming abstraction, Holmes appeared not to hear. "There is just one word in the note that may be the key to the whole riddle. If we can find out who wrote that word, I think we'll know who killed your brother." He put the glass back into his pocket and said, "Just now speed is imperative, so if you will kindly pack this stuff, I'll step into the other room and make a couple of calls to London. Then we can see your chauffeur and I'll give him his instructions and he can be off."

When we emerged from the bedroom with the carton all packed, Holmes was saying over the telephone, "Thank you, Willie." He then hung up the receiver. I waited behind while he made his second call, to the fingerprint man, and as we started to join the others I asked, "That first call of yours couldn't have been to Willie Roberts, by any chance, could it?"

"Oh, but it was, my boy. I'm planning a little surprise for at least one of our guests tonight."

I knew better than to ask what that surprise was, for I realized it would do no good; but I could not help but wonder what Holmes was planning for this meeting that he clearly considered so vital. And I wondered what possible part could be played by Willie Roberts, a former criminal once called "Willie the Writer" because of his skill in forgery, but now leading a law-abiding life thanks to the good offices of Holmes, who had got him a job after his release from prison (where Holmes had helped to put him).

When we got downstairs, the chauffeur Burrows was soon on his way, instructed by Holmes as to where to go and charged with the absolute necessity of getting back before the meeting that evening.

Burrows had scarcely left before Dr. Cheevers, a long, cadaverous person with a no-nonsense air, appeared from the inquiring medical officer's headquarters, to be followed shortly by the young constable from Wibberly. After mutual introductions, the baron told them that Holmes would take them to the body of the deceased and acquaint them with the circumstances attending its discovery, then excused himself to communicate with the previous night's guests as arranged.

The two officials were there for some time, and it must have been close to two of the clock before we finally sat down to a savory lunch in the sumptuous dining room of the old manor. By common consent we made no attempt at idle chatter; we were all too full of the matter in hand. All our conversation during the meal, and afterward, while Holmes smoked his pipe and I enjoyed the rare cigar the baron had given me, had to do with the strange death that had occurred so suddenly a few hours before.

"*You* spoke of your brother's tragic past, Baron—what did you mean?" Holmes asked.

"There were four children in our family," the baron replied. "The oldest one was my brother John, three years older than I, then myself, then my sister Dorothea, four years younger, and finally Matthew, who was born fifteen years later. John was very able and had the gift of making money; my interest always lay in government; Dorothea was warm-hearted, lovable, and affectionate, and became happily married; and Matthew was the spoiled darling, handsome and gifted and temperamental.

"Our mother had been an actress in her youth, and a rather superior one, and the lure of the footlights has been in the family more or less ever since. Matthew took to the stage early and seemed to have a natural flare for acting. He was a success from the very start, and almost all were united in the belief that he was on the way to being one of the truly great actors of our time. He was not only talented and handsome but intelligent, witty, and, when he wished to be, winning and genial. Sometimes his love of applause led him to make remarks that were more diverting than kind, and he made some enemies, but with the general public he was immensely popular. He seemed to have the world at his feet; then, when he was only two and thirty, he suffered an accident that was to blight his whole life.

"One day in the off-season, when he was on a fox hunt, his mount stepped into a hole and went down. The fall was so sudden that Matthew was wholly unprepared for it and pitched out of the saddle with the most disastrous results. As fate would have it, the ground where the fall took place was exceedingly rough, with rocks strewn about, and Matthew suffered a hideous compound fracture of one leg and a gash on one temple that left a lasting scar. The scar might not have been so bad, for it could have been covered with makeup; but the limp that the broken leg left was fatal; it ruined him for lead parts, which were his forte, and for all but a very few character roles.

"He quit the stage, disheartened and embittered. Being what he was, he could not adapt himself to any other pursuit. Then, after some two years, John died and left Matthew enough to make him financially independent, which may have been a fatal mistake, for now, with all incentive to make something of himself gone, he surrendered himself to a life of ease and frivolity. To make matters worse, John, for all his financial acumen, made a grievous error in the way he left the legacy."

"How was that?"

"He set up a trust fund for Matthew, and should have left all of the legacy in trust. Instead of that, he left twenty thousand pounds of it outright to Matthew. Matthew seemed to have no sense of the value of money and lived as if the twenty thousand pounds would last forever; indulged in high living, went to London in the theatrical season, put up at the Savoy Hotel, and gave lavish dinners and parties. Needless to say, in almost no time it was gone and now he had only the income from the trust fund. For most people that would have been ample, but to Matthew, after indulging himself so freely, it seemed all but penurious. So now, after being the object of envy and adulation, he was only an ordinary person and felt cheated and abused. To make matters worse, his fair-weather friends, who had been the objects of his bounty when he was throwing his money around, were no longer interested in him, and instead of blaming himself he railed at them. There was only one thing that could have reconciled him to his lot and that was an unlimited amount of money. I sometimes think that he would have done almost anything to get it."

Holmes said, "I see. Was everything left to Matthew by your brother John?"

"No. He left the manor to me, as the oldest survivor."

"And what about your sister Dorothea?"

"She died before John did. Incidentally, she was then a widow."

"Did she leave any children?"

"Yes, two—both boys. Their names are James and Richard."

"And they got nothing from your brother's estate?"

"Nothing at the time. But they are the beneficiaries of the trust fund, now that Matthew's dead."

"Humph," Holmes said thoughtfully. I knew what he was thinking. These two were in a position to gain greatly from Matthew Tidmore's death. That fact could lay either or both open to suspicion. "And who were the others who were here last night? You said that there were five."

"Jim's wife—Rickey is unmarried—and a cousin named Carter Ives and his wife."

"I understand. Now suppose you tell me what you can about these five. I'd like to know what kind of people they are."

"Very well. I'll start with Carter. His mother and I were first cousins and her family and ours were always very close. Carter is about Jim's age, and from childhood for many years they were nearly inseparable. As a boy Carter seemed almost to live at Jim and Rickey's. He always excelled in any sort of athletic games they played—he was strong and stocky while the other two were less rugged—but I could never see that Jim or Rickey resented it; and, of course, Carter was happy, as any boy would be, as long as he was kingpin.

"Well, anyway, the friendship continued. He and Jim went to Cambridge together, and then both attended the Inns of Court at the same time. It was expected that they would set up practice together when they got out, and I think that that was their intention, but somehow it didn't come off. I don't know which one may have backed away from the idea or if it was dropped by mutual consent. Nothing much was ever said about it, and I have always been curious as to why it never went through. Perhaps the fact that they both fell in love with the same girl had something to do with it."

"Oh? How's that?"

"Well, it seems that they were both attracted by the same girl—her name was Louise Towne, a forthright, genuine sort of girl, and very attractive—a commoner, but with a fine, cultured family background. For a long time she gave little indication as to which she liked the better; but she finally chose Jim."

"And how did that affect the friendship between the two boys?"

"I really don't know. I do know that the idea of a law partnership was no longer mentioned from then on. But apparently they all continued friends. Of course, with households of their own now, they are not as close as they once were."

"You mean this Carter Ives is also married now? What kind of girl did he get and what sort of person is he?"

"Well, a couple of years after Jim and Lou became engaged, Carter married Roberta Hobman, a stunning beauty, but quite different from Lou Towne."

"Different in what way?"

"Well, I don't like to criticize; but I know you want the facts. Lou, as I said, is simple and genuine; Roberta seems quite the opposite—cool and not a little lofty. Rickey once had the presumption to address her as 'Robbie' and she set him down properly with ice in her voice, saying, 'The name is Roberta.' Her father is the wealthy Jacob Hobman. A few years ago he was granted a peerage—I suspect he actively sought it— and Roberta is exceedingly class-conscious. She and

94

Carter move a great deal in what is called high society, a thing that Jim and Lou do very little of and care very little for, and she looks down on Lou."

"And what's this Carter's attitude toward his one-time sweetheart?"

"Toward Lou? I'd say he's still as much taken with her as ever. Takes every opportunity to address her, follows her with his eyes—that sort of thing. But he tries to be careful to stay on the good side of Roberta. I suspect she has a temper and she helps him get what he craves: recognition and acclaim. He's very ambitious, a successful trial lawyer who fights every inch of the way. He's sort of a bulldog—never gives up. He's the kind that will do anything within the law to win and can't bear to be beaten. Some say he never forgives an opponent who gets the better of him and never rests until he 'gets even.' But outwardly he's always affable, with a vigorous, vital personality and a cocksure manner."

"I see. What was his attitude toward Matthew? Did they like each other?"

"Oh, they got along, though I doubt if they really cared for one another. I suspect they were too much alike—both rather selfish egoists. But I can't conceive of his killing Matthew. He would have no reason to."

"None that's apparent, I confess," Holmes agreed. "But coming back to Jim, you don't really know what his true feeling toward Jim is? You say he's a hard loser."

"No, I can't say that I do. But is it important?"

"I would say it's highly important if that note we found is what I think it is."

"Yet how—" the baron started to say.

But Holmes appeared not to notice the interruption and went on. "You say Carter Ives would have no reason to kill your brother. But how about your nephews? Didn't they?"

"Jim or Rickey?" The baron gave him a shocked look and his jaw almost dropped open. "Why, why—" Then he stopped with a startled expression. "I . . . I see what you mean. Now they'll inherit the money. And you think they had a motive. Well, perhaps they had. But they never could commit murder—neither one of Dorothea's boys."

"Perhaps not. Still, the chance to get hold of a great deal of money can do strange things to people. But tell me about these two. Did they like your brother Matthew? Were they the grasping sort or need money badly?"

"They both liked Matthew. Rickey remembers what a talented and popular actor he was when he saw him as a little boy. He was quite blind to his faults and had only admiration for him. Rickey has the family love of the stage and is pursuing a dramatic career himself. He would like nothing better than to follow in Matthew's footsteps and become a famous actor."

"And what about his attitude toward money? Does he overspend? Is he deeply in debt?"

"I doubt it. He's rather happy-go-lucky, has a gay, lighthearted temperament. When he has money, he spends it; when he doesn't, he goes without."

"Hardly sounds like one to plan a cold-blooded murder," Holmes said.

"Indeed, he's not."

"Now what can you tell me about James?"

"Jim's a much more serious type. He recognized Matthew's shortcomings, but liked him nevertheless. But his liking was more one of pity than admiration."

"Sounds like a sound sort of person."

"He is. A real gentleman. Has high principles. He's quiet but likes people—warm-hearted and outgoing like his mother."

"Is he successful?"

"Yes. But in a different way from Carter. His practice is altogether of another sort: mostly probate and corporation work. Seldom goes into court, and when he does, he is quietly logical, not spectacular or dramatic."

"Then he has no financial worries, is in no urgent need of money?"

The baron's expression became very sober and his

voice held a note of deep concern. "Must say that question troubles me. I fear of late he has been hard-pressed. Through no fault of judgment on his part, he invested in a company that is in serious financial straits. It seemed perfectly sound: made a good product, had a capable management and a good sales force; but one of the officers embezzled a huge sum, and now it's in dire trouble. Then Lou's mother, who is old and alone, has been very sick and has incurred terrific doctor's bills, which Jim has assumed. Yes, I'm afraid he needs money badly."

"I see. So he could have had a motive. But you don't think he'd kill to get it?"

Baron Tidmore firmly shook his head. "No. Not Jim. Not ever."

"Let's hope you're right," Holmes said. "Now another question; do you know whether any two of these ever discussed a business deal of any kind?"

"A business deal? Let me think." He paused, then said, "No, I don't think so."

"Are you sure? It could have been a tentative deal that didn't go through. One between Carter Ives and James, for instance."

"A tentative—" Again he paused and seemed to reflect, then suddenly said, "Why, yes, there was such a deal. Jim bought a beautiful piece of land somewhat similar to this—a plot of about ten acres. He always had an admiration for Tidmore Manor and probably had secretly nursed the idea of someday having a setting rather like it. He built an attractive home on half of it and kept the other half as an investment. I understand that Carter tried to buy this other half. He apparently wanted to be near Jim and Lou—especially Lou, I suspect. But the sale never went through. Jim may have been too wise to consummate it. If not, the women would have undoubtedly vetoed it, anyway. I can't fancy Lou relishing the idea, nor can I imagine the elegant Roberta consenting to such an arrangement. But isn't this going rather far afield?"

"Not at all. I'll be surprised if the negotiations for such a purchase do not play a large part in the solution of this crime. Now one thing more: something I probably should have asked before; but I assumed that at least one of the three men was assigned last night to a bedroom that was near enough to Matthew's suite so that he could have slipped into it unobserved, particularly if he were expected by Matthew, as I have reason to think he was. Can you say—did one of the men have such a room?"

"Why, yes—in fact, all were so located. Carter and Roberta had two rooms opposite Matthew's suite (Roberta says that it disturbs her to have someone else in the room where she sleeps). These rooms have a common bathroom shared by both occupants. Rickey was in the bedroom next to them, and Jim and Lou were in the room opposite Rickey's and just this side of Matthew's suite."

Holmes stroked his chin in thought. Seemingly this explanation of the baron's, showing the easy access to Matthew's rooms by all the guests of the previous evening, did nothing to simplify matters. Finally he said, "Well, I must be on my way. I have things to do. Tell me, though, Baron, what is the surname of your sister's sons, and where are the five who were here located?"

"Landreth. Rickey lives in Cambridge and Jim has his business there and lives just outside. The Iveses live in Bury St. Edmunds."

"And did James and Ives live in different cities when Ives tried to buy the property from James?" Holmes asked.

"Yes."

"So that the negotiations for it might have been carried on by mail?"

"Yes. Quite probably they were."

Holmes rubbed his hands together and mused. "Ah, very good. Very good, indeed! Now if we can only get hold of this correspondence—"

Shortly he excused himself, saying he wished to

leave us for the afternoon to make some inquiries after he had used the phone.

It was half after six before he was back, with a confident air and a pleased look on his face.

"You look as if your inquiries were successful," the baron remarked.

"Yes, I feel that they were. If all goes well, I expect us to unmask the killer this evening."

"Surely you're not serious!" the baron cried.

"Never more so, I assure you." Then his face assumed a more somber expression. "But is Burrows back?"

"No. Not yet."

"I hope nothing holds him up," Holmes said soberly, then left us to wash up for dinner, which was scheduled for seven of the clock.

When he came down, Burrows, had not yet appeared and he looked still more serious. "Not yet! He's got to get here. If he doesn't—" And he shook his head.

The meal was a spiritless one in spite of the fact that Barbara, the baron's widowed daughter, who made her home at the manor, was one of our number. She had not been at the party the night before, but she had returned upon news of her uncle's death from the baron that day. Though I understood that she had not been too patient with her uncle's aimless life, she was still depressed by the manner of his leaving it and could add little to our feeble efforts at conversation. Holmes's all-too-obvious anxiety affected us all. He was more ill-at-ease than I had ever known him to be. I caught him surreptitiously looking at his timepiece more than once. He volunteered almost no remarks, and his replies to ours were often aimless and abstracted. By half after seven gloom had settled over us all.

"You're quite sure this man Burrows is dependable, Baron?" he asked. "I don't know what—"

But just then we heard the sound of a motorcar arriving and he heaved a great sigh of relief. He was out of his chair at once and making for the door before the car had come to a stop. The driver was, indeed, the chauffeur, and in a moment we could hear them talking, Burrows no doubt explaining the reason for his tardiness, which, it proved, was due to numerous unforeseen delays, among them a tedious detour and a tyre that had had to be changed.

But with his arrival, Holmes's assurance was fully restored and he was all smiles. He took the carton with its contents from Burrows and carried it away. In a moment he was back. "I saw Constable Barney again this afternoon," he announced, "and told him what I'd found out. He's to come here tonight shortly after eight of the clock. Parkins will let him in at the servants' entrance, if that's agreeable. If we have need of his services, as I hope we will, we have only to tug at the bellpull."

The guests arrived close to the appointed time. James Landreth and his wife, together with Rickey, were the first to come. I was impressed most favorably with the first two. Jim, tall and trim with serious manner and low-pitched voice, seemed like a man of breeding and culture, and Lou was quietly attractive in a dark blue dress of soft wool. Rickey, who was obviously younger and less mature, seemed of a naturally high-spirited disposition; but now he was sadly subdued. It was plain that he was deeply affected by the death of the uncle whom he had adored.

It was not long before the other two came. Carter was a bluff, hearty man some five feet ten inches tall, with a barrel-like chest. It was evident that he had his full share of self-esteem. Roberta, wearing a sheathlike dress of some shiny greenish material that revealed every line of her tall, stately figure, had an air half of boredom, half of disdain, as she acknowledged the introduction of Holmes and me.

I felt that almost all of them were curious and not a little piqued by our presence there, until the baron told them why we had first come and explained that

100

Holmes was an old friend and that he had prevailed upon us to stay partly because he wished to have us as his guests and partly because he thought that Holmes might help in accounting for some peculiar circumstances surrounding Matthew Tidmore's death.

"What circumstances?" Carter Ives asked.

The baron then told them for the first time about the finding of the note with Matthew Tidmore's signature on it. Then he produced the note, which Holmes now handed him, and passed it around the group for all to see.

The reactions of the various ones were interesting. James Landreth was absolutely silent, and it almost seemed to me that he was expecting the intelligence. Lou, too was silent, but appeared disturbed and shocked. Roberta seemed almost indifferent, as if she were little concerned. Ives burst out in what I thought a characteristic manner: "Great grief, but this is terrible. What could have induced the poor fellow to take such an action?"

But the effect upon Rickey seemed the most violent. "I don't believe it!" he said in a voice choked with emotion, an emotion that seemed more of anger than of grief. "Uncle Matt would never do such a thing. There's something wrong here! Something fearfully wrong!"

"You really believe that?" the baron asked in a kindly voice.

"Of course I do. And you do, too. And so does everybody else here, unless—" Then suddenly he was silent and looking around with startled eyes.

"Unless what?" Carter Ives inquired with what appeared to be honest curiosity.

"I won't say it. But . . . but Uncle John knows what I mean. It . . . it's just too awful!" And the distress in his face was painful to see.

The baron shook his head. "I know how you feel, Rickey. And I know what you mean. I was inclined to agree with Carter that it was a clear case of suicide;

but Mr. Holmes here, who is a specialist in crime detection, felt the same as you."

"Oh, come now," Carter said in a tone of disbelief, "You're not saying that some one did poor Matthew in?"

"I'm afraid so."

"But who would want to do a thing like that? Surely—"

"That's what we're here to find out," the Baron said rather grimly.

Carter's face took on a shocked expression. "You mean—!"

"I'll be frank with you. Mr. Holmes thinks there has been some sort of wrongdoing here, and at my request has consented to try to find out what it is."

"In other words, you mean he suspects one of us here of murder? Jim would never be guilty of such a damnable action. And Rickey never would. And I know I wouldn't; I'd have no reason to."

"What you say sounds reasonable; but Mr. Holmes seems quite convinced that one of us here had something to do with Matthew's death, and he has an experiment he wants to try. Of course, the only possible suspects can be we men, so I assume that the ladies will wish to be excused."

Barbara and Lou got up at once, but Roberta stayed in her seat. "This sounds like nothing but nonsense to me," she said in a throaty voice, shrugging her shoulders. "If it's all the same to you, I think I'll stay and see what goes on."

We all stared at her while Barbara and Lou stopped in their tracks. Then Carter Ives spoke. "My dear, I'm inclined to agree with you. But if Uncle John wants to go through with it, I, for one, am perfectly willing to go along. And I think if Lou and Barbara are leaving, you'd better go, too."

Roberta gave him a haughty look. "Oh, very well," she said, then slowly gathered up the gloves and handbag from her lap and swept out of the room ahead of the other two.

"Now, just what kind of test are you proposing?" Ives asked, looking at Holmes with skeptical eyes.

"I'll explain in a moment. But first I'd like to ask a question," said Holmes. "Have any of you ever seen this note before?"

All present shook their heads.

"Very well," proceeded Holmes. "In that case, none of you can object to saying so in writing, I assume."

They all gazed at him with a questioning look, wondering what this was all about. "I'll just pass out paper and you will write as I dictate, if you please. You can use your own pens," he went on. Then, when all were supplied with sheets of writing paper, he continued, "This is what I want you to write: First, the words contained in the note"—which he then repeated. "Then, please add these words." And, pausing between phrases to give them time to write, he dictated as follows: "I have carefully scrutinized . . . the foregoing note . . . and I truthfully say . . . that I have never seen it heretofore."

They all wrote with puzzled expressions on their faces. Then Ives said, rather derisively, "Is that all?"

"That's all."

"Oh, I say!" Rickey exclaimed, his tone one of disgust.

"Yes?" queried Holmes.

"Do you really mean that this sort of thing is going to help us find who murdered Uncle Matt?"

"I think so," replied Holmes calmly as he gathered up the papers. Then he stood and studied them closely, one after another. Finally he turned toward Carter Ives, near whom he was standing.

"Mr. Ives, would you mind letting me look at your pen? You seemed to have some difficulty writing with it."

"The pen's all right. You needn't bother," Ives answered. "Your imagination is working overtime."

"Perhaps. But I'd still like to look at it."

"Oh, forget the act. I told you the pen's all right."

"Is there some reason why you don't want me to see it?" Holmes persisted.

"Of course not. It's just—"

"Then your pen, if you please," and Holmes held out his hand while Ives pulled it from his pocket and handed it over with ill grace.

Holmes then drew out the familiar magnifying glass and looked closely at the point of the pen after removing the cap, while Ives stared at him with an expression I could not fathom; but it seemed to me that he was not so cocksure as he had seemed up to now. Finally, looking up, Holmes said, "Are you sure this is your pen?"

"Certainly it's my pen. What in thunder are you getting at?"

"I'm trying to get at the truth. I think you are mistaken. This is Matthew Tidmore's pen."

"Why, you damned mountebank! Are you crazy?"

"No, Mr. Ives, but I think you were, to suppose you could get away with your harebrained scheme. Baron, if you please." And as he nodded, the baron promptly jerked the bellpull and almost instantly Constable Barney and a deputy entered the room.

"What's the meaning of this?" demanded Ives with an assumption of outrage.

"It means that you are being arrested for the murder of Matthew Tidmore," Holmes informed him.

"Give me that pen!" Ives shouted, and made a lunge for Holmes. But Holmes stepped back and by that time Barney and the other officer had seized Ives, who raged and struggled in their grasp.

"Easy does it. Just come along peaceable an' you'll save yourself trouble," Barney said calmly. "Best slip the nipper on 'im, Joe." And in a moment Ives was handcuffed and being led from the room still struggling and cursing.

The uproar had been considerable, so that it had penetrated the nearby room where the women had gone, and just as Ives was being hustled out of one door, the women entered at another. Roberta just caught a glimpse of Ives in the hands of the police and demanded to know why her husband was being treated like a common criminal. Upon being apprised by Holmes that he was being arrested for murder, she completely lost her pose of studied indifference and flew into a fury. She railed at Holmes, at Baron Tidmore, at ignorant country bumpkins in uniform who thought that they were officers of the law, at Ives himself, who plainly had no regard for his station or for the disgrace he might inflict upon others.

After some time, the baron, with the help of Jim and Lou, pacified her sufficiently so that they could prevail upon her to leave. When finally she was gone and we were once more settled with Barbara and Lou among us, the baron turned toward Holmes. "I assume that you are certain that Carter is responsible for my brother's death," he said. "But we would be interested to know how you came to that conclusion. I, for one, am all at sea."

"Very well," replied Holmes. "And when I'm through I think you'll all agree that Ives is the guilty party. First, then, I should explain that graphology, or the art of determining the character of a person by the form of his handwriting, has been something of a study of mine for a long time. At first I looked into it simply because it fascinated me. Then, as I came to believe more in its significance, I saw that on occasion it might be of material help to me as a criminologist. I read every book about it that I could get hold of and have made it a practice through the years to analyze every bit of handwriting that came into my hands, so that I think I have gradually developed some degree of skill in the art.

"It goes without saying that in the course of time you acquire a sort of second sense so that you usually can detect the slightest variation from the general pattern in a bit of writing almost instantly. So when I first looked at the pretended suicide note, reading, 'I'm sorry, but this is the best thing that I can do,' one word in the text stood out as being peculiar. This was the word 'thing.' It seemed unnaturally spaced, being a bit too near the words 'that I can do' which immediately followed. Moreover, these following words were not exactly on a line with the other words in the note.

"These variations led me to believe that the word 'thing' had been inserted into a phrase that originally did not contain it. This suspicion was confirmed when I turned over the paper on which the note was written and examined the other side with my magnifying glass. When I did this, I discovered the imprint of all the words in the note except the one word 'thing.' This meant that the writer of the note had taken the phrase 'I'm sorry, but this is the best that I can do' from some writing in his possession and had put it on top of the blank sheet that was to bear the note and traced the letters with some implement like an empty ball-point pen, so that the imprint of the words could be written over with ink and an exact copy of the words as originally written could be made. But to insert an extra word without a change in the spacing and alignment of the text would be well-nigh impossible.

"Then I began to wonder what the original text, 'I'm sorry, but this is the best that I can do,' meant; and the obvious answer was that it was a part of some correspondence relating to a business deal in which a prospective buyer protested that the price set by the seller was too high and the seller replied that he was sorry but it was the best that he could do. As you know, it is a familiar phrase often used between parties to a proposed business transaction.

"So then it seemed clear to me that what we had in the note was not the handwriting of one person, but of three: that of the writer of the word 'thing,' that of the writer of the other words in the note, and that of the signature—who, of course, was Matthew.

"Then I examined the handwriting in the note to try to determine the characters of the writers. I was interested to find that the letters in the body of the note had a decided slant to the right, which clearly indicated that the writer was of an open, friendly disposition.

The long loops in the *h*'s denoted an idealistic person, while the rounded loop in the *y* in the word 'sorry' pointed to a person of culture and the moderately rounded *m*'s and *n*'s showed the writer to be one who was trusting and sympathetic. All these features combined certainly did not point to one who had the temperament to plan a deliberate, cold-blooded murder such as this appeared to be.

"I then turned my attention to the word 'thing.' It is risky and unreasonable to try to estimate the character of an individual by the way he writes a single word. In this case it was probable, too, that the writer had tried to disguise his hand to conform to the other writing in the note. Nevertheless there are always some telltale marks that the average person cannot conceal when he writes, and even this one word seemed somewhat revealing. Unlike the other words, it slanted almost imperceptibly to the left, the mark of an untrustworthy nature. The *t* was pointed and not looped at the top, which indicated a lack of frankness. It was also wide open at the bottom, another mark of deception and evasion. Finally, the crossmark on the *t* had an upward hook, a rather sure sign of a vindictive nature.

"So, it seemed, I had before me a fake suicide note writ by a deceitful, vindictive person with the intention of throwing suspicion upon a person of a generous, open-hearted nature in case it became suspected that it was not a genuine suicide note.

"Of course those involved had to be two of the three men who were among last night's guests, and when I came to talk to the baron about them he told of the attempt of Ives to buy the building spot next to Jim. Accordingly, I went to Cambridge this afternoon and saw Jim—and, as I had suspected, found out that he had at one time written a letter to Ives containing the phrase in the pretended suicide note. The letter was handwritten instead of typed because it was written by Jim from his home. Ives had been at Jim for a long time to put a price on the property he wanted to buy; but Jim had steadfastly refused, not wanting to sell to Ives under any circumstances.

"But Ives, unaccustomed to not getting what he wished, had been so insistent that, to discourage him, Jim had finally mailed Ives a letter fixing an exorbitant price (at least three times its actual value) on the land; and then had gone on a vacation with Lou, supposing that would be an end of the matter, only to find on his return a communication from Ives wanting Jim to reduce the price. It was then that Jim, now thoroughly out of patience, sat down and wrote a handwritten letter saying that the price quoted was the best that he could do. And luckily he had kept a carbon copy of same, which showed that it corresponded with the handwriting that Ives had imitated in the suicide note.

"So now you all see that Ives is undoubtedly the murderer of Matthew."

"But why would he try to implicate Jim?" Rickey asked.

"Probably because he hated Jim and he knew that Jim would be the primary suspect, because he was supposedly hard-pressed financially and as beneficiary of half the trust fund that pressure would be relieved."

"But he was a friend of Jim's," Rickey said.

"He pretended to be. And no doubt he was when you were all young and he bested you in sports. But when he and Jim grew up, things became different. At college it became clear Jim had the better brain. And when Ives wanted them to become partners, Jim, who by then knew him better, turned him down. Then Jim beat him out with Lou. And, finally, Jim refused to sell him the building site he tried so hard to get. So Ives has been a loser all around. And so his ill will against Jim has piled up and up. And now he's completely overcome with resentment and jealousy."

Rickey looked at him and dumbly nodded. Then the baron said, "I think you have made your point. But how about that business with the pen? What did that all mean?"

"Oh yes, the pen. Well, as perhaps you know, after

long use a pen is sometimes likely to become somewhat more worn on one side of the tip than the other—usually the right side. But I found out from Jim that he discovered in college that Ives had a tendency to wear down the left side of the point. You will recall that I carefully examined the point of the pen in Matthew's apartment, and *it* was worn on the left side. So I deduced that before he left Matthew's rooms he switched the points of their pens, which outwardly looked the same, so that it would appear that it was Matthew's pen that wrote the note.

"So the net of evidence is pretty closely drawn about Ives, and I fancy it'll be drawn still tighter when they find his fingerprints on the suicide note. It would take considerable skill to go through the manipulations that he did and not leave any mark on the paper. You can't trace indentations on blank paper with a pen held in a gloved hand. And Burrows tells me that a faint print was found on the note."

"But the prints of all the rest of us are on it, too. We all handled it tonight," the Baron said.

Holmes smiled. "You thought you did, and Ives thought so, too. But you didn't. What you handled tonight was a duplicate I had made in London this afternoon by Willie the Writer. It never pays to underestimate your adversary—a thing that I wished Ives to do. I thought if he considered me stupid enough to let you all handle the note, he would be less on his guard. I could then more readily get him to give me a specimen of his handwriting when I asked you all to copy the note and deny former knowledge of it. I wanted such a specimen and I wanted it tonight before he got suspicious and got rid of his pen. That is why I was so anxious for Burrows to get back. Incidentally, his writing confirmed the fact that he could be capable of murder—ruthlessly selfish, egotistical, and vindictive. I might add that he probably would have preferred copying some words of his victim for a more authentic-looking suicide note; but since that was not possible, he wanted to fix it so that if murder were suspected, Jim, his successful rival in love, would appear to be the guilty party.

"So now we know why he is guilty. But there is one thing we don't know."

"What is that?" Jim asked.

"*Why* he killed your uncle."

"You mean you don't know!"

"No. But I can guess. And I'm sure the police will find the reason when they start digging."

"Just what is your guess?"

"Blackmail."

"Blackmail?"

"Yes. It's likely that Matthew found out that Ives was short in his accounts with some client or was playing round with some woman and thought it a good idea to cash in on the knowledge."

"But Uncle Matt would never do such a thing!" Rickey cried indignantly.

"Possibly not. But what other explanation can there be? And you have to recollect that your uncle's nature very probably had changed. His misfortunes, real and fancied, may very well have warped his outlook. He felt himself ill-used and probably came to think that he was entitled to unlimited wealth to satisfy his extravagant desires. Then he saw Ives—whom he may have looked upon as a coarse, pushing sort of fellow—successful, with plenty of money, and thought it no great crime to relieve him of some of it."

"I suppose that's right," Rickey said glumly, shocked by the fall of his idol.

"But I don't understand how Carter managed it. If Matthew was blackmailing him, how did he ever succeed in setting up a secret meeting with Matthew? Wouldn't Matthew suspect something?" the baron asked.

"I would be inclined to think that the blackmail was only contemplated, and not yet really put into effect," Holmes answered. "I rather fancy that the rendezvous was set up by Matthew himself, that when he got wind of Ives's misdoing he got in touch with him perhaps a week or two ago and proposed a meeting. Very likely it would have been a highly polite communication as between two gentlemen, advising Ives that he, Matthew, had some interesting information to impart and it might be to Ives's interest to drop into Matthew's rooms after the birthday party and have a confidential chat over a bottle. And Ives may well have answered in the same vein—all very friendly and proper. I can picture them sitting there: Matthew filled with contempt and itching for money and Ives ugly with fear and anger and hate, but both pretending to be nice jolly good fellows. It would have been something to see."

The baron nodded. "Yes, I suppose it could have happened that way. But it is hard to see how Carter managed it, how he slipped the drug into Matthew's drink—all that sort of thing."

"I know. And we can only guess at a number of things, unless Ives breaks down and makes a full confession. But I think I could attempt a reconstruction of the crime."

"I wish you would."

"Very well. In the first place, then, we can assume that because of his habitual air of bluff good nature, Ives would not appear to Matthew as at all dangerous. No doubt he considered him a fairly able, somewhat tricky lawyer, but basically rather shallow and not at all brilliant. It is safe to say that it did not enter his head that Ives could be a cool, calculating killer.

"But Ives knew the peril of blackmail, that once you started paying, it might never end. And he was prepared to go to any length rather than be subjected to the alternative of constant extortion or having his reputation and his advantageous marriage with the socially prominent Roberta irrevocably ruined.

"So he laid his plans carefully. Much of his practice, Jim tells me, was the defending of criminals, and so he probably had knowledge of contacts not possessed by the average man. He probably had means of getting a prescription for poison from some shady doctor who was a client. The doctor may have told him, too, that the taste of the stuff could be concealed in such a highly-flavored drink as Coca Cola. And it's conceivable that Ives put some in a bottle of 'Coke' and took it with him to present to Matthew as a friendly gesture.

"The drinking and the conversation between the two, of course, would have been in the lounging room. And it would have been quite natural for Ives to excuse himself and go to the bathroom, at which time he could have left the empty chloral bottle there and slipped the fake suicide note, which he had previously prepared, onto the top of the washstand where Matthew would be least likely to notice it.

"When Matthew showed signs of sleepiness, Ives could have very easily ushered him into the bedroom and told him to get to bed and that he, Ives, would clean the glasses and put the bottles away. Matthew, heavily drugged, would be too befogged to realize what was going on or to protest. He would just have wits enough to follow orders, stagger through the door, lock it, and start undressing before falling onto the bed. Ives could then have taken the glasses across the hall to his own bathroom, rinsed them out, and returned them and the bottles to the cabinet after wiping off all fingerprints."

The next day we left Tidmore Manor.

Of course Holmes had been right. About two weeks later he got a long-distance call. It was a long conversation. When it was over he turned to me. "That was from Constable Barney," he said. "The police in Scotland Yard have turned up the fact that Ives was keeping a flashy music-hall girl in rooms in London where he frequently went, supposedly on business."

"I wonder how her highness Roberta is taking it?" I mused.

"She isn't. She has washed her hands of him. I understand from the constable that she is not so much outraged by the unfaithfulness itself as by the nature of it. If he had been having an affair with a countess or other female of high title she might have been able to condone it; but to pass up her exalted favors for the embraces of a cheap third-rate actress was just too much."

"So Ives has reached the end of his rope," I observed. "And he probably never would have been caught except for you." I lapsed into thought, recalling the masterly way in which Holmes had unraveled the bewildering tangle surrounding Matthew Tidmore's death. "Your solving of that case was one of your greater triumphs," I said. "It's astounding how you figured out that the bumptious, good-natured Ives was the guilty one."

He shrugged. "It was not so astounding. It had to be Ives. He had the potential of a killer; Jim and Rickey did not. He had the motivation. You should read your Shakespeare, old chap. Not all murderers are ugly, hulking brutes like Dickens's Bill Sykes. Except for Judas Iscariot, the classic villain of all time is the suave, treacherous Iago. And do you remember what Hamlet said about his royal uncle?"

"No. What was it?"

" 'One may smile, and smile, and be a villain.' "

The Kohinoor Gem Shop Burglary

The great Sherlock Holmes did not suffer fools gladly. According to his biographer, the good Dr. Watson, he was arrogantly intolerant of those of lesser abilities than himself. On the other hand, his scarcely less talented grandson, Creighton Holmes, was almost uniformily characterized by tact and courtesy in his dealings with others. Indeed, it was because of the possession of these qualities that he was able to solve the mystery of the Kohinoor Gem Shop burglary. Had it been otherwise, there is every reason to believe that the mystery never would have been solved and the criminal not only would have gone unapprehended but would have been able to lead a comfortable and respected life for the rest of his days on his ill-gotten gains.

However, it is not only because of the exercise of diplomacy and, I might also say, of blatant flattery on Holmes's part that this particular case is worthy of recording; but also because these traits were exercised at a time when he was presumed to be recuperating from a severe illness and was under strict orders from his doctor to have a complete rest. This illness, I might add, was brought on by his long and arduous efforts to forestall a most grievous scandal in government circles. Unfortunately the details of the case are of such a delicate nature that I am not permitted to divulge them. Suffice it to say that they implicated an official close to the prime minister himself and, before it was over, involved blackmail and attempted murder.

Fortunately Holmes had been able to bring his investigation to a successful conclusion; but the tax on his energies, unusual as they were, had been such as to leave him completely exhausted. As a result he contracted pneumonia, almost lost his life, and suffered such a nervous strain that for a time his very reason was thought endangered.

So it was that the tenth day after he had left the hospital found us at Blythestown with every intention on his part of doing nothing of a professional nature for another three or four weeks. Blythestown, as everyone knows, is an exclusive watering place not too far from the thriving city of Middington. Originally little more than a fishing village, the place now boasts two smart summer hotels and a fair-sized shopping district that caters not only to trippers but to the more than twelve thousand inhabitants that live farther inland.

We had been in the place only two days, but already it seemed to me that there was more color in Holmes's cheeks and a livelier spring in his step; and I reflected that in another fortnight he might well be his old self. Then, on the third morning, just as we had finished breakfast in our hotel room and were preparing to go out for a stroll, there came an insistent knocking at our door. When Holmes opened it, there stood a uniformed boots who asked: "Be you Mr. 'Olmes, sir?"

Upon Holmes' answering in the affirmative, the boy held out a card, saying, "There's a gentleman in the lobby as said I should give you this and h'ask for a h'answer."

Holmes took the proferred card with an air of irritation, glanced at it impatiently, and handed it to me. It bore the legend *Richard B. Granby, Special Representative of The Anglo-Fidelity Insurance Co.*, and a notation on the reverse side to the effect that the person in question was "exceedingly anxious" to see Mr. Holmes "on a matter of the greatest urgency."

"Now what the devil do you suppose the fellow wants?" Holmes exclaimed in an uncharacteristic tone of disgust. "I suppose I'll have to see him just as a matter of decency. But I propose to get rid of him in

115

jig time. I want to get out of here and soak up a little of that warm sunshine." Thereupon, turning toward the boots, he said, somewhat more graciously, "All right, lad, send the gentleman up, but you may as well tell him that my time is limited."

Then, when the boy had gone, he stood holding the card in one hand and flipping it nervously against the other as he muttered, "Matter of the greatest urgency, bah!"

When the sender of the card appeared, obviously somewhat apprehensive as to the nature of his reception, he proved to be a lean, angular man a little above middle height, of some eight and forty years of age. His rather sallow, deep-lined face was surmounted by a shock of unruly dark hair beginning to be streaked with grey at the temples. He gave the impression of being of a more than normally serious temperament and just now seemed in a particularly somber mood. His first utterance, however, was an effusive expression of gratitude to Holmes for granting him a hearing. His gratitude, moreover, was so patently sincere that Holmes, exasperated as he was, seemed frankly ashamed of the abrupt manner in which he had greeted the man and made a noticeable effort to appear more cordial.

"I am sure you came here to relax," Granby was saying after the preliminaries of introduction were completed, "and I would not presume to intrude upon you in a professional capacity if it weren't that our company is threatened with a very severe loss and you, with your exceptional abilities, are the only one who can help us."

"Oh, come now," Holmes said in a tone of obvious skepticism, "it can't be so bad as all of that."

"Oh, but it is," Granby asserted. "I assure you that I do not say this to flatter you, but merely to state a sober fact."

Holmes gave an impatient shrug. "Just what is this

116

unusual problem that requires my remarkable services?" he asked with heavy sarcasm.

But Granby refused to be ruffled. "It's the theft of a quantity of valuable jewels from a concern that we insure here. It occurred last night."

"You mean the place was burglarized?"

"That's right. You see—"

"But what is there about that to require services such as mine? It's a matter for the local police, not a private investigator."

"But that's just the point. The local police aren't up to it."

"Just what makes you think so?"

"Everything; but mostly their chief constable—a bounder if there ever was one. Gubb is his name—Ed Gubb. The very name is enough—but let that go. It's not only that he's young—he can't be over seven or eight and twenty—but I'm satisfied that he's utterly unfit to cope with a situation of this kind."

"What's wrong with him?"

"What's wrong with him! Why . . . why, everything. It's obvious he has next to no training, a minimum of perception, and unmitigated conceit. He owes his appointment, I'm told, solely to political connections and not at all to merit. I understand that the local weekly praises his every move but that the thinking people consider him a monstrous fraud."

Holmes smiled sardonically. "And you expect me to work with him? No, thank you."

"I'm afraid you don't understand, Mr. Holmes," Granby said in a tone of desperation. "We've got to recover those jewels if at all possible."

"But my dear sir, how can it be possible in the circumstances? Do you expect such a fellow to cooperate with anyone who he thinks might share in the credit? No, I'm sorry, Mr. Granby, but it's out of the question." Upon which he turned rudely away and moved to pick up that morning's *Middington News-Journal* as if the matter were disposed of.

But Granby was not one to give up easily. "I understand how you feel," he said placatingly, "but from a monetary standpoint you are passing up a very unusual opportunity. Our company is prepared to pay one thousand pounds in case the jewels are recovered."

"Oh," Holmes returned in a disinterested air as he picked up the paper.

"Yes," said Granby, by no means disturbed by Holmes's baldly indifferent manner. "And that isn't all. Contrary to the policy followed by most insurance companies, which are satisfied with the return of stolen goods and no questions asked, we believe it important to apprehend and punish the criminal to discourage future crime. So we make it a practice to double the stipend we give if the guilty party is brought to justice. You might well make two thousand pounds in a matter of a few days, Mr. Holmes. I know that you must be accustomed to receiving exceptionally generous fees, but surely—"

Holmes slapped the folded newspaper sharply against his thigh and turned to face the persistent claim agent. "I'm sorry, but I don't seem to be able to make myself clear. I'd like to have you understand, once and for all, that I am not going to consider your offer. I'm simply not interested."

"Not even if we guaranteed a liberal drawing account and—"

"Not under any circumstances," Holmes said shortly.

"Very well," said Granby, who evidently was one who could recognize defeat and accept it graciously. "I don't mind saying that I am deeply disappointed, because I feel that you are the one person who could probably deal with this odious Gubb successfully. But I respect your feelings in the matter. I apologize for being so insistent. I never should have intruded on your much-needed rest."

"That's all right," Holmes replied, somewhat shamefacedly. "I fear that I have been rather short with you. But . . . well, the truth is I've not been quite myself lately."

118

"I understand," Granby returned. "And I don't think I'd care so much, badly as I would like to recover the gems, if it were not for this fellow Gubb. When I think what he said about you—" Then he clamped his lips tightly together as if regretting that he had already said too much.

Holmes's nostrils seemed to flare perceptibly and a cold glint came into his eyes. "Said about me?" he asked sharply.

But Granby shook his head. "Oh, it's really not worth talking about. I shouldn't have mentioned—"

"But I take it that his remarks were not flattering," Holmes persisted.

"Well, not exactly. Still—"

"Just what did he say?" Holmes prodded.

"I'm sorry, Mr. Holmes, but I'd really rather—"

"Still, I would like to hear it."

"Well, if you insist. But I hope that you will discount it, coming from such a source."

He paused, and Holmes said impatiently, "Yes?"

Granby cleared his throat. "Well, the truth is that I told him that I assumed he might welcome some help and said that I understood you were in town and might be available. His reply was a nasty sneer and a remark to the effect, 'A big shot, eh? From the big city. Well, let me tell you something, my boy. We ain't such hicks here as you think we are. We know a thing or two about investigating crime ourselves. All this Holmes bloke can do is get the evidence like anybody else. We ain't having no headline-grabber like him come in and claim all the credit for solving a case we can handle easy as not ourselves.' "

"So that's what he said?" Holmes asked.

"That's it."

"Interesting," Holmes commented drily, then turned to pace restlessly a moment about the room. Then he faced toward Granby and I caught a new note in his voice—a note that sounded more like the old Holmes that I knew, eager and challenging. "It might be entertaining to hear about this simple little crime that Mr.

Gubb is going to solve so easily. Suppose you tell me something about it." And he motioned Granby to a seat as he reached for a chair himself.

"Certainly," Granby replied, but I broke in:

"Now, just a moment, Holmes, you aren't seriously considering—"

But he shut me off. "Oh, don't be such an old woman, Harrington. I'm just going to listen. Now, Mr. Granby?"

Taking his seat in the chair indicated, the claim agent said, "Well, there is not much to tell. I am located in our claim office at Middington. This morning, about nine of the clock, I got a call from the agent who wrote the business here saying that this place that we insured had been broken into and a quantity of jewels—mostly fine diamonds—worth at least fifty thousand pounds had been stolen and urging me to get over here immediately."

"What is the name of the place?"

"It is called the Kohinoor Gem Shop and is operated by a man named Rucker—Ambrose Rucker. It is located on Shore Street near Queen's Lane."

"Humph, yes," Holmes said reflectively, "I seem to recall seeing the place. Kind of a showy little spot with souvenirs in the window as well as jewels."

"That's the place," Granby nodded. "Carries curios as well as jewelry and caters to trippers more than the local trade. Does quite a bit of business. And lately the fellow has apparently put in some pretty high-class merchandise along with his less expensive stuff. As a matter of fact, he got in a particularly large shipment of exceptionally fine diamonds some four months ago, and they appear to be mostly what was taken. He showed me the invoices listing the stones; there seems to be no question about the validity of the loss."

"I see. And how was entry gained?"

"The thieves apparently broke a window and got into the basement, then forced a door at the head of the basement stairs into a rear utility room that it opened into, and from there made their way into the office and opened the safe."

"Was the safe forced open?"

"No. The lock had been manipulated. Gubb is of the opinion that it was the work of professionals from out of town."

"And just why does he come to that conclusion?"

"Well, when Rucker made the purchase of these diamonds of particularly high quality, he made quite a play of it in some special advertising. Gubb figures that these professionals learned about the purchase and decided to cash in."

"Anything to support this theory?"

"Yes, there is. Rucker says that about a week ago he noticed a fellow loitering across the street opposite the shop. He did not think much about it at the time, but now that he looks back he realizes that the fellow's actions were highly suspicious and is sure he was 'casing the joint'—I believe that's the term in criminal parlance."

"I see. And did Gubb get a description of the fellow?"

He tried to. But it was rather vague. Could fit any one of a thousand people. You know how it is—Rucker 'paid no special notice to the fellow at the time.' "

"Well, well," Holmes said, a note of keen relish in his voice. "I am beginning to think that this case has possibilities. Tell me, Mr. Granby, what day of the week is it?"

"Why—er—Tuesday. But I don't see—"

But Holmes was rubbing his hands contentedly together in that characteristic manner that he had. "Better and better!" he exclaimed. "I confess I find some aspects of this affair most intriguing. If you could arrange it with your friend Gubb, I might wander over with you and glance at the premises."

"Splendid! I'll make arrangements—"

"Holmes, are you out of your mind?" I interposed. "You know the doctor said—"

Holmes snorted. "Drat the doctor. Besides, he said I should find something to take my mind off myself. It isn't as if I'd committed myself to anything. I just want to look things over."

I didn't like it. And I liked it even less when, after a call from Granby about an hour later, we found ourselves at the Kohinoor Gem Shop with the fellow Gubb, who proved to be every bit as obnoxious as Granby had represented him to be: disgustingly officious, crudely patronizing, and given to much use of American slang. I wondered at the time, how the claim agent had persuaded the young coxcomb to agree to Holmes's participation in the case, and did not learn until later that he had accomplished it not only by assuring the fellow that he would get the lion's share of the credit in the event that the case was successfully solved, but also by slipping him a not inconsiderable sum, which he was not above accepting, as the price of Holmes's entry into the case.

We found the Kohinoor Gem Shop to be a one-storey building of some twenty feet frontage facing north on Shore Street with the rear backing onto an alley. At the back of the salesroom, which was fairly deep, was a tiny office on the left and a small utility room or hallway on the right. It was into this latter room that the thieves presumably had gained entrance through a door on the right that led to the basement. The room itself was devoid of furniture and had no covering on its bare wooden floor. On the rear wall were some hooks where the employees of the shop could hang their wraps on cold or rainy days, while on the east side of the room, immediately back of the office, was a small toilet equipped with washbowl and mirror. To get from the utility room to the office one had to pass through the rear of the salesroom and thence to the office itself.

The office, which was cramped for space, contained a desk, two chairs, a filing case, and the burglarized safe. It was enclosed with solid walls on three sides, with a glass front containing the door through which entrance might be gained.

Once we were in the shop, Gubb took over, introducing us to the proprietor, a stubby, greying man in his middle fifties, who just now, quite understandably, was visibly nervous and seemingly uncertain as how to take Holmes's appearance on the scene. This aspect of unease was accentuated by the fact that he appeared to be the victim of some respiratory disorder and was given to constantly clearing his throat.

"This is Mr. Holmes, high mogul from London," the bumptious chief constable said, half sneeringly, half condescendingly. "Mr. Granby wants him to look things over. Not that he's likely to find out anything we don't already know. But if he wants to play around with the case, it's all right with us. An' I can't say as I blame 'im fer wantin' to pick up a little easy money if the insurance company is sucker enough to give it to 'im."

Holmes took no notice of these uncomplimentary remarks, other than to say to the jittery proprietor that he was confident that Mr. Gubb and his associates were amply able to handle the matter but that it was common practice in a case involving a loss of such magnitude for an insurance company to call in outside help. Then he said if it was all right with the chief constable he would like to make a routine check of the premises.

"Sure thing," Gubb agreed, clapping him familiarly on the back. "Anything to oblige. After all, my boy, you've got to do something to earn that juicy little fee. So let's go through the motions. Where do you want to start?"

"Well, we may as well start at the beginning, I fancy," Holmes said. "Suppose we look at the basement window first."

So we made our way to the cellar: Gubb, Rucker, Granby, Holmes, myself, and a young uniformed fellow who attended the chief constable much as the man

Friday must have trailed Robinson Crusoe. Holmes inspected the basement window through which the thieves had supposedly gained entrance, asked two or three questions, which Gubb answered in a supercilious, off-hand manner while the rest of us looked on.

"Not much here," Holmes said as he shook his head. "I suppose, of course, that you have tested everything for prints?"

"Surest thing you know," Gubb answered glibly. "We're way ahead o' ya. Nary a print. These blokes wasn't any amateurs. They know their stuff."

"Well, we may as well take a look at the door," Holmes said noncommittally, and we went to the utility room above, where he took considerable time looking at the door that the thieves apparently had forced to get into the rear of the shop itself. He even got out his familiar magnifying glass to scrutinize it more closely. The basement side of the door showed a deep indentation where a jimmy of some sort had been inserted to pry the door open. The inner side showed a bolt still attached to the door but pulled loose from the frame where it had been attached. Holmes took some time examining the loosened bolt and the door frame while Gubb regarded him with a look of superior amusement.

Finally, his inspection apparently completed, Holmes turned to Gubb and said, "Was this the only lock to the door? I notice a keyhole."

I thought I saw the chief constable give a slight start and suspected that the possibility of another lock had not occurred to him. But if he were at all discomposed, he speedily recovered. "A good point," he said. "I was just about to ask about it myself. How about it, Rucker? I suppose there was a key."

Rucker cleared his throat. "Well, as a matter of fact, there was, but it got lost or mislaid somehow. I don't know just how it happened."

Holmes gave him a sharp look. "How long ago was that?"

"How long? Well, I can't say exactly. Maybe a

week, ten days. I been expecting it'd turn up. That's why I didn't replace it."

"I see. Do any of the help know where it may have gone to?"

"Well, to tell the truth, I haven't asked them. As I said, I kept thinking it'd turn up. Besides, they don't have anything to do with locking up at night. I always take care of that myself."

"So that you are the only one that has a key to this door? Now, how about the front door—who opens up in the morning?"

"Well, we all have keys to that, and to the rear outside door here, too—that is, the three of us: myself, Mr. Peskind, the older salesclerk, who has been with me for some time, and Michael McCall, a young fellow that I took on about three years ago."

"And who opens up in the morning? Do you?"

"No. Usually young Michael does. Occasionally, if for some reason he is off, Reuben or I do it."

"And who cleans the place at night? Do you have a porter or charwoman?"

"No. There's not very much to do. The place is not too large and we try to keep it neat. Michael opens early and gives it a sweeping-out as soon as he gets here."

While this questioning went on I could see Gubb shrug in a bored way and look at his confederate in a superior manner, as much as to say he considered all these queries as so much nonsense. But I, who knew Holmes better, knew that he had a purpose in everything he asked.

At length he left off this line of questioning and said, "Now, another thing. What's become of one of the screws that fastened the end of this bolt to the door frame? I see it's disappeared."

"Disappeared?" Gubb said in a jeering tone, at the same time giving a broad wink to his subordinate. "That's really too bad."

"Yes, it is," Holmes agreed. "I suppose that you've examined it. But I would like to see it. It must have dropped out." And forthwith he was down on the floor while the rest of us started looking near our feet; but it was Holmes himself who discovered it in a corner into which it had rolled. Picking it up, he scanned it closely by means of the glass. "Ah," he muttered to himself in a tone of satisfaction, as if to say, "Just as I expected."

At length, apparently through with his inspection of the rooms, he slipped the screw negligently into his pocket. "Well, I think we're through here," he said. "Suppose we glance at the safe a minute or two."

So we adjourned to the office, where a prim-looking female of some thirty-odd years of age appeared to be working on the books. The man Rucker did not trouble to introduce her, and Holmes began at once to examine the safe. But evidently the safe revealed no clues, and after a brief look about the rest of the room, which disclosed nothing unusual, Holmes asked one or two routine inquiries, then dusted off his hands and said, "Well, I fancy that is all."

"What, no more questions?" Gubb jibed.

"Not at this time," Holmes rejoined, ignoring the sarcasm. "And by the way, Chief Constable, I wish to congratulate you on the way you're handling this. I want a few words with Mr. Granby, and then, if you don't mind, I'd like to discuss the case with you. I find it pays to pick up pointers wherever I can."

"Sure thing," the chief constable said, puffing out his chest. "I gotta get back to headquarters, but I'll be in my office if you want to see me. If there's anything I can do to fill you in, I'll be glad to oblige." And he strutted off with the other young constable hurrying to keep up with him.

After they had gone, the proprietor excused himself to go to the front of the shop where his two salesclerks were, while Holmes turned back to the claim agent."

"Of all the blundering idiots!" he exploded. "I never saw such a stupid ass."

"You mean you found out something?" Granby inquired eagerly.

"I most certainly did. If this is the work of out-of-town professionals, I'll turn in my license as a criminal investigator."

"Are you sure?"

"I couldn't be more positive. The evidence is as plain as the nose on your face."

"Then you'll take the case?"

"You couldn't keep me out of it. I would be an accessory to the crime if I stood by and watched this insufferable upstart manhandle the case."

"But you understand that Gubb will want to take all of the credit if you are successful in apprehending the criminals?"

"I understand it. But I think that my reputation will speak for itself. Anyway, I am not so concerned about that as I am about the possibility of the criminal escaping justice."

"And, of course, Gubb is going to be very difficult to work with," Granby went on, seeming now almost as anxious to discourage Holmes as he had been to persuade him at the beginning.

Holmes gave a wry grin. "I think that I can handle our friend Gubb. I've dealt with his kind before. And it's going to be a real pleasure to put the fellow in his place." His vibrant voice sounded little like that of a sick man recovering from a near nervous breakdown.

A few moments later we had opened the door to the chief constable's office, where he let us stand for a time while he made a show of poring over some papers on his desk that I suspected he had just put there for that purpose. At length, looking up, he said, "Well, well, if it isn't the big-city sleuth and his pal. Help yourselves to chairs."

When we were seated, he finally bothered to present for the first time the young constable who had been with him at the shop and who now was sitting near the desk. "This here is Barney Keenan," he said. Then, when we had acknowledged the introduction, "Now, what can I do fer ya?"

Holmes said, "I just wanted to chat about the case with you. It is going to be a pleasure to collaborate with so keen a man, Chief Constable. From your conduct of the case so far I have reason to think that you know your way around."

"Well, we ain't got the training an' facilities o' Scotland Yard exactly," the fellow said with something of a swagger. "But we get by."

"Quite," said Holmes. "That story that you gave out about this being a professional job by outside yeggmen was deucedly clever."

Gubb shifted uneasily. "Well, now . . . I mean, the evidence—"

"Precisely," Holmes broke in smoothly. "You and I both know that the evidence clearly shows that this is an 'inside job' and a rankly amateurish one, at that."

Gubb's face flushed. It was plain that he was all at sea. But he was not going to admit it. To save time and get his bearings he pulled out a package of Player cigarettes and deliberately lit one. At length, after two or three heavy draws, he appeared to pull himself together and tried to assume a knowing grin. "So you saw it too, eh?"

"Naturally. No one who pretends to know anything about crime detection could possibly miss it. Of course, it was the fact that the safe was not blown that would first put you on your guard."

"Yeah. Sure it would—er—that is, I mean it did."

"Then, too, there was the day of the week—or rather, the night—that the burglary was committed. You would realize at once that that tended to confirm your suspicion."

"The night? Oh, yes, the night," Gubb tried not to look bewildered.

"As a skilled criminologist, you would perceive immediately that out-of-town professionals would be highly unlikely to pull such a job in a place like this on any night but a Saturday, when they would have ample time to get a long distance away and make good their

128

escape before the crime was discovered. And, finally, there was the nature of the damage."

He paused, but, for once, the chief constable seemed at a loss for words and dumbly nodded while Constable Keenan, in a mild case of shock, stared first at his seemingly confused superior and then at Holmes.

"I'm speaking, as you know, of the damage to the door and the door frame at the top of the basement stairs, which are constructed of soft pine. Anybody with half an eye could see that the screws holding the bolt had been loosened before it was ever jimmied. Otherwise the woodwork would have been badly splintered, and it wasn't. Besides, the heads of the screws showed clearly that they had been recently tampered with. I know that you must have detected it as soon as you looked."

"Sure," Gubb, who had finally realized what was going on and had regained some of his composure, said loftily. "But I thought it wouldn't hurt anything not to tell all I knew."

"Not a bad idea," Holmes agreed. "In fact, I would call it a very shrewd move on your part. It should throw the real culprit off his guard."

Gubb nodded sagely. Then noticing an odd expression on his young aide's face, he said, "Barney boy, you better go out and check on the parked cars." But just then a serious-faced, hard-bitten man of some five and forty wearing a sergeant's stripes entered, saying, "There's no need, I just checked them."

"Okay, Yates," grated Gubb, not bothering to address him by his title. "Barney, forget it. Yates, meet Mr. Holmes, the famous London dick, who is goin' to work with us on this Kohinoor Gem job."

"But I thought you had that all figured out as a job by out-o'-town professionals."

"Well, ya thought wrong."

"Wrong?"

"Yeah. That was all an act. It was an inside job."

"Oh?" Yates glanced curiously at Barney Keenan, but Keenan avoided his eyes. I had a feeling that the older policeman was not as enamoured of the chief constable as young Barney was.

Gubb noticed the glance and his face reddened again. "An' by the way, Yates, you an' Barney better run out to Kipp's junkyard an' tell him he's gotta watch his step: There's been more complaints about his gettin' onto adjoinin' property."

"But I was just out there yesterday," Yates said. "If it's all the same to you, I think Barney and I should stay here. It seems to me more important—"

Gubb gave him an ugly look. "Okay, okay. Only, just—" But whatever he had in mind to say, he seemed to think better of it, cleared his throat, and turned toward Holmes as if the other two weren't there. "Now, old man, what can I do for ya?"

"Well, if it's not too much trouble, I'd be glad if you could fill me in on the backgrounds of all who might possibly be considered suspects. First, how about the older salesclerk?"

"Rube Peskind? He's a bachelor, fifty or thereabouts. Lives with his mother in a two-by-four cottage in the southeast part o' town."

"How long has he worked for Rucker?"

"Ever since Rucker started, far as I know. Heard once that he thought he oughta been taken in as partner. Probably saw all the dough Rucker was makin' an' wanted a slice of it. But old Amby ain't lettin' go o' nothin'."

"Interesting. And does he work hard at his job?"

"You can bet he does, or Rucker wouldn't keep 'im on."

"I see. What's he like, would you say?"

"Average sort o' bloke. Quiet, steady-goin'. Never heard nothin' against 'im."

"Any expensive tastes?"

"Not as I know of. Dresses modest. Don't own a car. Never goes out much."

"Doesn't gamble or chase women?"

Gubb gave a laugh that was partly a sneer. "Rube? Hardly. At least, if he does, it's news to me. What do

130

you chaps say?" And he turned to the two policemen, both of whom shook their heads.

"Not the free-spending type, I take it?" Holmes continued.

"I wouldn't say so. Lives fairly conservative."

"Humph," Holmes commented. "That seems to dispose of him. Now how about the younger clerk?"

"Young Mike McCall? Decent sort, as far as I ever heard. How about it?" And again he turned toward the two others.

Barney nodded agreement and Yates said, "Straight as a string, I'd say. I'll swear young Mike's all right."

"How old is he?" Holmes asked, turning to Gubb.

"Three or four and twenty. Lives with his parents at a little place called Chiddlesby about three miles from Blythestown. Pedals in on his bicycle every morning."

"And how long has he worked for Mr. Rucker?"

"Three years or thereabouts. Hear he was always crazy about jewels. Picked up all he could about 'em 'n' one day walked in cold turkey and braced Rucker fer a job. Hear that the old boy was so impressed with the kid's nerve that he took 'im on straight off."

"Was the business growing enough to need the services of another man?"

"I don't know about that. But Rucker's not the type to stick 'is neck out. Pretty cagey when it comes to lettin' go of the ready. Old Ambrose has probably got the first sixpence he ever earned. Piles one on top o' t'other. But anyway, business has been lively enough so Rucker kept 'im on. Think probably young Mike helped it to grow—he's a wide-awake, up-an'-comin' chap."

"I see. How about his habits? Any reason to think he might be wanting a great sum of money?"

Again Gubb turned toward the two others. "Yates, I fancy you know the kid best, what d'ya say?"

"Well, like I said, I think he's altogether honest. O' course, he's pretty fond o' Molly O'Rourke; but she's the steady, sensible type. Think she'd help 'im save rather than the other way round."

"So he seems about as free from suspicion as Peskind," Holmes said. "Doesn't seem to be too much to go on, does there? Now, what of the young woman I saw in the office?"

"Young?" Again the chief constable gave that unpleasant laugh. "Stacy's no spring chicken."

"Stacy?"

"That's what they call 'er. Her real name's Anastasia Simms. An' that's what she likes to be called. Sounds more swanky. She don't like to be called Stacy; but she's stuck with it."

"What can you tell me about her?"

"Not much to tell. Somewhere in her thirties, I'd say. She ain't a regular employee. Just comes in two or three days at the end o' the month to balance the books. Lives with her mother. Colorless sort o' dame if you ask me."

"Expensive taste? Like fine clothes? Anything like that?"

"I wouldn't say so. Just an ordinary plain-livin' old maid."

"No boy friends?"

"Well, they ain't exactly breakin' down the doors."

"No attention at all?"

"Well, there is one toff by the name o' Lewis—Snarky Lewis, they call 'im—that goes to see 'er once in a while, mostly Sunday evenin's fer dinner or some such thing. He's a commercial salesman—travels fer a chemist house er somethin' like that."

"Does he take her out much?"

"Never takes 'er out as far as I know. If he wants to spend money on a dame he gets some one younger an' flashier. If he wants a good meal he goes to see Stacy."

"I understand. And what kind of fellow is this Lewis?"

"Quite a lady's man, if you ask me. Likes to put on the dog."

"A free spender?"

"That depends."

"Oh?"

132

"Yeah. When it comes to himself, I fancy he's free enough with his money. Likes good clothes, good eatin'—that sort o' thing. Tries to make people think he's a big shot."

"And is he? I mean does he make real money?"

Again that sneering note came into Gubb's voice. "I doubt it. Though he'd like to have people think so."

"Humph," said Holmes meditatively. "Likes money . . . By the way, how much do you think this Miss Simms cares for the fellow?"

"Couldn't say, but I think she's pretty sweet on 'im . . . Hey, wait a minute, I see what you're drivin' at. Stacy girl could have loosened up those screws and made it easy for Snarky to pick up a little easy boodle. An' he's just the boy as might do it. I'll just get little Snarky up here an' give 'im the third degree. I'll—"

"You're not serious?" Holmes said.

"Serious?"

"Yes. I'm sure that you must be putting us on the way you did about saying this was a professional job. Because, of course, you know that if we do that and it turns out that this Lewis is not the thief, then it'll be more than a bit harder to find who the real culprit is."

Again that telltale flush came into Gubb's face and I saw young Keenan glance quickly at Yates, then glance quickly away. As for the older policeman, I found him gazing with a cold, questioning look at the chief constable.

After a moment in which Gubb pulled at his collar as if he found it uncomfortably tight, he spoke. "I mighta known you'd catch on," he said to Holmes. "You're not so slow." And again he tried to assume a knowing grin.

"What you really have in mind," Holmes said suavely, "is to put a tail on all these possible suspects—Peskind, McCall, the Simms woman, Lewis—and keep them under a four-and-twenty-hour surveillance."

"Sure, that's what we gotta do," Gubb said.

Then the two of them, Gubb and Holmes, with a

suggestion or two from Yates, worked out a schedule for an oversight of all the movements of the suspected parties. Just before we parted, Holmes said, "Perhaps it would be just as well to try to make sure of the whereabouts of this fellow Lewis on the night of the burglary. If he's a commercial traveler, it's possible that he was out of town at the time."

"Just what I was comin' to," Gubb announced. "Now—"

But before he could finish, Yates volunteered. "I think I might be able to find out for you. Lewis works out of the Middington office of his company. I know a chap in the sales department over there that can get the low-down for us."

"Okay," Gubb agreed, and with an understanding that we meet the next morning to check on results, we parted.

When he and I were out of hearing, Holmes gave a snort of disgust. "God give me patience," he growled.

"Gubb??" I asked.

"Exactly. Why, the veriest tyro ought to know who the guilty party is."

"Surely you're jesting!" I exclaimed.

"Not at all, there are at least half a dozen distinct clues pointing to his identity."

"Then why don't you have Gubb arrest him?"

"I said 'clues,' Harrington, and, unfortunately, clues are not proof. Proof is what we have to have and what I mean to get if I can keep this blundering idiot occupied long enough for me to do a little investigating on my own. What troubles me right now is determining the motive."

"But surely any one of the parties in question had plenty of reason to want the money the stolen jewels would bring."

"Wanting money, my dear fellow," said Holmes, "is one thing. Wanting it badly enough to commit a crime for it is something else."

"I see what you mean," I murmured, feeling rather foolish.

Because of the shortage of policemen in Blythestown and the comparative inexperience of some of them in the art of surveillance, I had been pressed into service, at Holmes's suggestion, inasmuch as I had acted in a like capacity for him on previous occasions. Thus it was that evening that it fell to my lot to check on the movements of the salesclerk Peskind, that same day, after he left the gem shop.

Shadowing a suspect can be a weary business, particularly if there is little reason to think that the actions of the person under observation are of significance. So I was prepared to spend a dull and boring evening as I loitered across the street in the shadow of a tree opposite the unpretentious cottage occupied by the salesclerk and his mother.

It was therefore with surprise and some measure of excitement that I saw Peskind emerge from the house about eight of the clock. As he came out of the front door I thought I saw him pause and peer furtively about before proceeding on his way. I could not be sure of this, and it may be that my imagination was overactive on account of the circumstances.

At any rate, because of my previous experience, I had no difficulty in following the clerk without arousing his suspicion, although two or three times I fancied that he glanced warily behind him. I wondered where he was going, and my curiosity was roused all the more when he finally turned in at the staid residence that I now knew to be the home of Ambrose Rucker, proprietor of the burglarized jewelry shop. What, I wondered, could be the object of this visit? Could Peskind be the one who had stolen the jewels, and had fear or conscience driven him here to confess? Or had he and the asthmatic Rucker planned and committed the theft together? Either explanation seemed highly fantastic; but, for that matter, everything connected with this incredible, crudely committed crime seemed strangely unreal.

I had glanced at my watch when Peskind went into the house, and I continued to glance at it at intervals while he remained there; for time can pass slowly when you are alone in the dark and have nothing to do but wait. I need hardly say that it was with considerable relief that I finally saw the object of my watch come out of his employer's house almost a full hour later. I followed him back to his cottage, which he did not leave again up to the time I was relieved by the bobby who took over my duty at midnight.

When I reached our hotel I was tempted to awaken Holmes and apprise him of the outcome of my vigil. But I did not. He needed the sleep and might not welcome being disturbed. Besides he might regard Peskind's trip to his employer's house as a matter of small import.

When I awoke next morning he had already risen, breakfasted, and left the hotel, so that I had no chance to see him till we met in Gubb's office, where I found him with Gubb and Gubb's man Friday. The chief constable was in a surly mood, the reports submitted by the constables who had shadowed young McCall and Miss Simms all being negative, and Sergeant Yates, who was to have checked on her friend Snarky Lewis, not having yet arrived. And when I came to make my report regarding Peskind, I was just as well satisfied that I had said nothing about it beforehand to Holmes, because of the reception it now received.

Gubb gave it only the scantest of attention. "Probably just went there to play chess," he said disinterestedly. "Understand they're both chess hounds and play regular once or twice a week, though they ain't crazy about each other."

"Are they good chess players?" Holmes asked offhandedly.

Gubb gave him a look of thinly veiled disgust, as

136

much as to say, "What if they are?" but managed to answer with a fair show of politeness. "That's what I hear. Been playing together for years, anyway. As fer me, I think it's a silly game. Give me somethin' I can get my teeth into like soccer or rugby. Even cricket ain't so bad."

Holmes turned toward me to ask one or two casual questions, then drop the matter. "Who met Peskind at the door?" he asked.

"Rucker himself."

"And did he seem surprised, or did he act as if he expected him?"

"I couldn't be sure," I answered. "I was too far away. But if I were to guess, I'd say he had not been looking for him."

"And how long would you say he stayed?"

"Close to an hour."

And that was the end of it. Obviously it was the report to be given by Yates regarding the whereabouts of Snarky Lewis on the night of the theft that was awaited with most interest. But when it came, it too was disappointing.

It was fully thirty minutes before the sergeant finally appeared.

"You're late," Gubb snapped.

"That's right," Yates answered calmly, then proceeded to make it plain the delay was no fault of his, as he had been held up in getting some last-minute information. Thereupon he gave his report and ended up by saying, "So it looks as if we had been barking up the wrong tree. Lewis couldn't have committed the burglary because he was miles away in Twickenham on the night it happened."

"You mean that's where he was supposed to be," Gubb said. "But how do we know he was? How do we know it ain't just a nice alibi?"

"Because I checked," said Yates. "I checked at the hotel where he puts up in Twickenham and he was registered there that night. And I had the boys at the police department check with concerns he was supposed

137

to call on and they found he was there the day before and the day after the crime. He's got an alibi, all right." Yates's tone was belligerent.

Gubb gave him an ugly look, but there was nothing he could do about it. Clearly the suspect that he had been so sure of had not been the right one.

"Now what—" he began in a frustrated tone, when young Keenan said:

"There's somethin' that seems to me could bear lookin' into."

"Yeah? What's that?"

"It's about Michael McCall."

"McCall? From what Yates said, I thought he was in the clear."

"Well, maybe he is, an' maybe he ain't."

"What d'ya mean?"

"Well, it seems he claims somethin' happened that sounds as if it could be a little fishy."

"Yeah? What?"

"It's this way. Leastways, this is the way it come to me. I got it from Bert Hanks, an' he got it straight from Rucker. Seems that some time last summer a poor-grade diamond ring showed up in place of a good one in one o' the showcases under what looked like suspicious circumstances."

"How d'ya mean?"

"Well, young Mike was the only one in the shop one noon when—accordin' to him—a slick-lookin' cove come in, claimin' he wanted to look at a solitaire ring fer his girl. Said he couldn't buy right then 'cause he didn't have the ready with 'im at the time, but he'd like to pick one out, have it put aside, an' then later he'd come in an' pay fer it.

"So—at least, this is young Mike's story—he showed the fellow several rings, all pretty high-grade stuff, 'cause the fellow said he didn't want nothin' but the best. Mike said he was a smooth talker an' he felt suspicious of 'im, so he didn't never take a whole tray o' rings out o' the case, but took care to show 'im just
138

one at a time, bein' sure to put one ring back before drawin' out another.

"Anyhow, this smoothie had just about decided on a ring when a classy-lookin' dame, about eight an' twenty years old, come in all dolled up, sayin' as she had lost 'er compact an' just had to have one right away 'cause she was on her way to a party an' was late already.

"So the cove as had been lookin' at rings gets real polite, says he don't want to hold the lady up, an' anyhow, he had already decided he wanted the ring he had just been lookin' at. So he gives Mike his name an' address, shoves the ring at 'im, an' leaves.

"Meanwhile this dame had been waitin', all of a flutter, an' makin' it plain as she oughta be waited on straight off so she could get away fer her party. So Mike puts the ring aside an' sells 'er a compact an' she leaves.

"After she's gone, it strikes Mike suddenly that these two might have been in cahoots, an' he looks at the ring he'd just put aside an' finds that the cove has switched rings on 'im, leavin' a cheap substitute for the good one while the dame distracted Mike's attention.

"So he rushes outside, but neither sharpie is in sight. Then he sees Scottie McCrae, who is on the force then, across the street an' tells 'im about it. Scottie takes a description of the crooks an' says he'll follow it up."

Gubb asked, "What are you gittin' at?"

"Just this. How do we know this really happened, or if young Mike switched the rings hisself? Scottie ain't on the force no more an' don't even live here, so how we goin' to check?"

Gubb pursed his lips with a knowing air. "Maybe you got somethin' there, Barney boy," he said.

"Righto. Nothin' more was heard about these supposed crooks, an' I understand that when Rucker found out about the phony ring the slicker had supposedly left, he an' Mike had a regular set-to. The way Bert Hanks tells it, Rucker claimed not to believe Mike, tried to get Mike to pay the difference between the two rings, and threatened to fire 'im. But Mike stood 'is ground an' wouldn't pay fer it, an' they finally patched it up. Bert says he fancies Rucker knew Mike was too valuable a chap to lose fer what he was payin' 'im. But the point 'is: if Mike did pull a fast one like that, maybe he would try fer bigger game, 'specially after he'd got away with it the first time. Everybody knows that Rucker, bein' what you'd call more than a bit thrifty, probably don't pay Mike no fortune. An' Mike's devilish sweet on Molly an' achin' to get married, an' could use an extra bit o' money."

"Well now," the chief constable said, beaming at his toady, "maybe you got somethin' there, my boy. We'll just pick up—" Then, catching the appraising eye of Holmes upon him, he came to an abrupt stop, cleared his throat, and said, "We'll—er—pick up some information about our boy Michael. As you say, he could use the money. An' he's a smooth-actin' customer. Looks innocent as Mary's little lamb. He might just be our man."

"If you don't mind, Chief, I'd like to check on young Mike," Yates said.

"You?" Gubb said. "You're a friend o' the bloke."

"I'm a friend, yes. But I'm the one that can ask around about him without arousing suspicion. And you want to find out the facts about him, don't you?"

"You bet I do. Okay, Yates, you can handle it. But I don't want no whitewashin' job. I want the truth. Just remember that."

"You'll get the truth."

Gubb growled, "You can make all the inquiries you want, but I'm havin' somebody else trail young McCall."

"Suits me," answered Yates.

"How about you takin' im' on?" Gubb asked me, to which I agreed.

"Okay, you trail 'im at noon; an' Barney, you can follow Peskind. Then you can switch in the evenin'."

Shortly the meeting broke up.

As we left the office, I could not help thinking to myself that maybe Holmes had not been up to his

140

usual form when he had seemed so sure of the identity of the thief. I was therefore more than a little surprised at his response when I tried to sound him out by saying, "Well, this case gets more baffling all the time. Yesterday it looked certain that it was the fellow Lewis. Now we get this story about young McCall and we're more at sea than ever."

"Not at all, my dear fellow," he said. "On the contrary, it becomes increasingly clear that there can be but one explanation of the case."

"Oh?"

"Precisely. One very valuable bit of information was received this morning points to a situation that should make our task much easier. I have felt all along that if we waited long enough without showing our hand, one of our parties would make a fatal move that would incriminate him. Now it looks as if he had."

"I hope you're right," I said.

He said, "I'm sure I am, and I shall be very much surprised if within a day or two we can't lay our hands on the guilty party. Just now I am still somewhat at a loss to fix the motive, but I'm confident it will come out. Today I intend to do a little investigating of my own to that end. I rather think it may take me to the neighboring city of Middington. And, by the way, Harrington, you provided us with some very valuable information this morning."

"I? I don't see—"

"Exactly. There's just one point I would like to be certain of. Are you quite sure that the salesclerk Peskind was not at Rucker's more than an hour?"

"There's no doubt about it. In fact, it was rather less. I looked at my watch when he went in and again when he came out. It showed that he was there just fifty-three minutes."

"Good," Holmes said, rubbing his hands gloatingly together. "Very good indeed."

"You think it important?"

"Highly important, my dear fellow, I would say."

This, of course, left me more confused than ever.

Try as I would, I could not see how the length of time that his clerk had been with Rucker could be of significance.

My shadowing of young McCall that noon and of Peskind in the evening brought no results. At noon the youthful Mike did not even leave the shop, having presumably carried his lunch and eaten it there in the shop itself, quite probably in the utility room where was located the basement door that Holmes had scrutinized so carefully. As for Peskind, when I took over the duty of shadowing him as he left the shop, nothing of interest occurred. He went straight home and stayed there all evening.

Moreover, the surveillance of these two by the constables who trailed them the rest of the day had proved equally fruitless. Peskind had had a brief lunch of fish and chips at a small eating spot called Kate's Korner Kitchen, then had gone idly window-shopping, spending considerable time looking into the show windows of the two motorcar dealers of the town. In the evening Michael McCall had cycled directly to his home in nearby Chiddlesby, gone out briefly on a routine errand, then remained in the house until bedtime.

The report of Yates was even less encouraging. In fact, it seemed entirely to eliminate the younger salesclerk as a possible suspect.

"Well, here's what I found out," the sergeant said. "This incident that Mike reported about the switch of diamond rings occurred on the sixth of last September. I looked up our records and found that that was the last day that Scottie McCrae worked as constable. If you remember, it was late that afternoon that Scottie got word that his father was seriously sick at his home on a little farm in northern Scotland. The next day Scottie left and was gone two weeks. While he was up there his father died. When he came back he immediately resigned from the force to go up there and run the farm. I understand that he had always wanted to go

142

back there some time—particularly as there was a girl up there that he liked pretty well.

"Anyway, I called Scottie on long distance last night, and he distinctly recalls that Mike reported the ring incident to him that afternoon before he left, but in the worry and confusion of getting the news about his father and going away, Scottie completely forgot to make any report of it, especially as it didn't seem too important to him at the time."

Gubb said unpleasantly, "So that leaves us where we was before. When we come right down to it, all we got is young McCall's word fer it. Fer all we know, he still coulda made the whole thing up."

"But it isn't all we've got," Yates said.

"What d'ya mean?"

"Just this. I called up the police departments of several places, thinking that one of them might have had a similar report on this pair of slickers, and I found that they had—in Twickenham."

"Yeah. But what does that prove? Just a report!"

"But it wasn't just a report. Three weeks after this caper was pulled here by these two, a couple tried the same thing there and got picked up. They're in jail right now. And their description tallies with the one given by Mike. If you have any doubt about it, you can call Twickenham and talk with the officer at the desk. His name is O'Leary."

Gubb glowered. "Okay. I'll take yer word fer it. But we ain't lettin' young McCall off the hook. I'm suspicious of these pretty boys that act like butter wouldn't melt in their mouth. We'll get 'im next time."

"There won't be any next time," Yates retorted. "There hasn't been a first time yet."

"Okay, okay, stow it," grunted Gubb, who plainly was at a loss as to what to do next. "So where does that leave us? I'm commencin' to think that we was right in the first place an' that this was an outside job."

"Surely you don't mean that," Holmes said.

"An' why not?" Gubb said, nettled. "You got somethin' to suggest?"

"Only that we keep up our surveillance another day and you'll have your man."

"Are ya kiddin'?"

"I was never more serious in my life."

"Well, ya better be," Gubb growled. "Because if you ain't, things are goin' to happen around here—an' fast. Meetin's adjourned."

A moment after we had got out of the room, Yates overtook us. "You really meant what you said, didn't you, Mr. Holmes?"

"Yes, I did. I have every reason to think that the case will be cleared up and the guilty party arrested tomorrow at the latest."

"That being the case, would you mind if I tipped off Charley Dalton, the Blythestown representative of the *Middington News-Journal*? The local weekly paper isn't due to come out for another three days; and, anyway, it's all for Gubb. Whatever report it gives is bound to be slanted in his favor. Almost every one in town takes the Middington paper; I'd like to see it come out first with a true account."

Holmes nodded. "Tip the Middington reporter off. I promise you he'll have a story that'll be worthwhile."

As we turned away, I said to Holmes, "You seem pretty sure of yourself."

"I am," he rejoined. "And I think you know me well enough to know that I would not be so without reason. I picked up some very valuable information at Middington today, information that firmly establishes a motive and confirms my suspicions as to the identity of the thief. Moreover, some evidence came out at our meeting this morning that should make our task much easier."

"Evidence? This morning?"

"Precisely. And Harrington—"

"Yes?"

"I want you to do something for me."

"Very well. What is it?"

"You have the assignment of shadowing Peskind at noon today. I want you to be very careful that he does

144

not notice you. And I want you to observe his every action very closely. And, if you don't mind, I'd be pleased to have you report the results of your surveillance to me as soon as possible. Suppose you meet me for a hot cup at that little tea shop on Regency near Tottem Street—Lydia's Tea Room, I think it's called—about four of the clock."

"I'll be glad to," I said.

"And one more thing, Harrington."

"Yes?"

"Keep it confidential. Tomorrow I plan a little surprise for our friend Gubb."

So it was that at the appointed place and hour we met later over some well-brewed tea and hot, tasty scones. When we did, Holmes could scarcely restrain his eagerness to question me. Hardly were we seated when he asked, "What happened? Did Peskind visit either of the motorcar dealers today?"

I looked at him in surprise and answered, "Why, yes, he did." Then I went on to tell him how, after an apparently hurried lunch of kidney stew at his usual eating place, the clerk had made his way directly to the salesroom of the local Morris dealer where, from my lounging place across the street, I saw him look up one whom I took to be the proprietor. Then, in the other man's company, I saw him look over quite thoroughly the model of an attractive runabout. Peskind had appeared to be asking questions while the other man had seemed to point out particular features of the small, smart-looking car.

After that, they had gone into what appeared to be an office, and when they came out the other man held some papers in his hand while Peskind appeared to be returning his wallet or a checkbook to his pocket. Then they had stood together and talked a few minutes, until finally they shook hands and Peskind departed.

"Capital! Capital!" Holmes exclaimed. "I will get in touch with this proprietor or sales manager or whoever he may be, and if I verify the fact, as I expect to, that our friend Peskind has purchased a car, I'll make a call

145

on that gentleman this evening. If this call results as I anticipate, I think we will have everything in readiness for the chief constable tomorrow."

"You mean the case will be solved?"

"My good chap, thanks largely to you, it is solved right now. The information I expect to get from Peskind tonight will merely add the finishing touch to our case. I think, Harrington, that you are going to enjoy our morning conclave with the chief constable tomorrow."

The next morning when we met in Gubb's office, there was an air of tension. Whatever he may have felt inside, Holmes was the only one seeming outwardly relaxed. I had a feeling of heightened interest I found it hard to conceal. The chief constable was on edge. Young Keenan was plainly uneasy and kept casting furtive glances at his onetime idol. Yates, for some reason, was not there.

"Well?" said Gubb, glaring at Holmes. There was no attempt at the air of easy good nature that he had at first tried to assume. He knew that he had been outmaneuvered. He realized that he had been led on by this hated big-time detective who then, free from interference, had conducted his own investigation to an apparently successful conclusion. His face was a dull red. At best, the relationship between the two had been an armed truce. Now the truce was over.

"What is it?" Holmes blandly asked.

"You promised you'd have everything ready for an arrest today. It's about time you told us about it. And it better be good."

"So I did," replied Holmes, "and I'm ready to make good on that promise. I suggest that you arrest Reuben Peskind."

"Peskind! You mean he stole the jewels?"

"Not at all. You should arrest him for blackmail."

"Blackmail, eh? Now this *is* gettin' good. An' what's it got to do with stealin' the jewels?"

"Just this. Rucker committed the theft. Peskind caught him at it and has been blackmailing him."

"So Rucker stole his own stuff? That's a good one. What did he do it for—just tell us that."

"To collect on the insurance."

"To collect on the insurance? An' when did you figure all o' this out, *Mister* Holmes?"

"Oh, it was quite simple. There were at least seven distinct clues that pointed to his guilt. Six were evident the first day. The seventh followed inevitably. It had to be there. It just took a little time to ferret out."

"Seven clues! That's really somethin'. Did you hear that, Barney boy?" but Barney did not reply.

"Yes," Holmes went on as if there had been no interruption. "Surely you did not overlook them. They were there for any one to see. That is, any one at all versed in criminology."

"Oh, is that so? Suppose you tell us just what these seven clues was that stuck out so plain. An' if you're tryin' to pull my leg—"

"Not at all. And I'll be glad to enumerate them. Of course, some were not so important nor so obvious as others, but taken all together—"

"Okay, okay. You can cut the guff. Just name the clues."

"Quite. First, there was the fact that it was an inside job. Of course, any one of four people—Rucker himself, the Simms woman, or either of the salesclerks—had access to the utility room and the basement door and therefore was a possible suspect; but it's clearly evident that Rucker stood to profit more than anyone else. These others would have had to dispose of the stolen gems for a small fraction of their real value through a fence; Rucker, on the other hand, would think he was in a position to sell them for their full retail value by using a little finesse and slipping them back into his regular stock after a reasonable length of time and at discreet intervals."

"So that's one clue. How about—"

"Second," Holmes proceeded, "there was Rucker's

story about a 'suspicious character' casing the place. But it is interesting to note that no one else observed such an individual anywhere at any time, that Rucker did not think it worthwhile to call anyone's attention to the fellow or even mention him, and that the description of him that he gave was so vague and shadowy as to lead to the conclusion that he was wholly a figment of the shopkeeper's imagination."

"Yeah. What—"

"Third, there was the very convenient loss of the key to the basement door, making it so much easier to force same. Had the key been in the lock it would have required considerable strength and ingenuity to force the door. It is worthy of note that the key disappeared at such a strategic time and that Rucker was not concerned enough about its disappearance to mention it to any of his help, although he'd have us think that it had been gone for more than a week."

He paused to give the chief constable time to make a comment, and when none was forthcoming, he went on. "Fourth, there was the nature of the damage to the lock and door. You will recall that this was held to a minimum. Only one person would have been interested to have this the case, and that would be the owner of the property. And the owner was Rucker."

"Sounds goofy to me," Gubb sneered.

"I agree. But people of penurious natures such as his find it hard to commit any sort of seemingly useless damage, no matter how trifling. Besides, Rucker was not an experienced criminal, was highly nervous and not thinking too clearly. I admit it is a minor point; still, taken in conjunction with the other incriminating pieces of evidence, I believe it has significance."

"So you think it's important," Gubb said, "but it still sounds like bunk to me. Are these other clues that you're talkin' about any better?"

"I think so. The last three are related to each other, and in my opinion are so convincing as to leave no doubt as to the accuracy of my original hypothesis. The first of these last three and the fifth of the entire seven clues was the purchase of this lot of especially fine diamond rings. This was highly out of character and a most suspicious circumstance.

"Here was Rucker with a brisk and growing business in cheap jewelry and knickknacks. He was making money on quick sales and small profits. Suddenly he decides to take a different tack: to stock an entirely different type of goods that would appeal to an entirely different clientele. Why?

"No doubt he had the hope that the sale of one of these rings would net him as much profit as he would make in a whole month of routine business. But he wasn't thinking straight. Had he done so, he would have realized that people who buy expensive jewels—even people of taste and discrimination—do not trust their own judgment but go to a jewelry shop with an established reputation and a name that they can trust, and not to a second- or third-rate shop like Rucker's.

"But he wasn't thinking straight because he was desperate, and he was desperate because he needed money and needed it quickly."

"Oh, come off it, Holmes," Gubb rasped. "What's this about Rucker needin' money?"

"I'll come to that in a moment," Holmes replied. "Just now I want to take up the next clue—the fact that his gamble did not pay off, the fact that the rings he'd banked on didn't sell. From Michael McCall—a shrewd young man who has his eyes and ears open and suspicions of his own—I learned that in the four months that they'd had them they had sold but one of these rings, and that one was sold 'on time.' I also found out from McCall that through one thing and another he had reason to believe that Rucker was having trouble meeting his obligations and his credit was getting shaky, so that, instead of bettering his situation, the purchase of these high-class diamond rings had only made it worse. He had to get rid of the rings and there was but one way to do it: sell them to the insurance company, and this meant staging the fake burglary. Perhaps he'd had the burglary in the back of his

149

mind as a desperate last resort and only needed to get sufficiently worked up to do it."

"But this business of Rucker bein' hard up fer money just don't make sense," Gubb said. "Everybody knows that old Amby had plenty salted away."

"Maybe he did at one time," Holmes responded. "But people lose money, you know."

Gubb gave a sneering laugh. "But not old Amby. He ain't no high flyer. How could he ever lose dough?"

"That's what I set out to discover, Chief Constable, and that brings me to the seventh and last clue and the motive for the crime.

"I knew from the beginning that Rucker was the thief. And I knew that the only logical reason for it could be that he was hard-pressed for money. It took a little digging, but in the end it was clear that there could be but one reason for his precarious financial condition.

"He did not gamble or chase women or indulge in riotous living, which meant that there was only one way that he could have dissipated his resources, and that would be through poor investments. My first thought was that he might have spread himself too thin in the accumulation of real estate, as that is the commodity in which most people who are unused to handling much money are inclined to invest. But an investigation along that line revealed the fact that instead of acquiring real estate lately, he had sold and taken a substantial loss on two parcels that promised future high profits, if he had but held on to them. This was, no doubt, to pay some of his more pressing debts, and confirmed young McCall's suspicion that his credit was fast becoming impaired.

"So, to avoid going into too much detail, I may state that the elimination of all other causes for his financial reverses left but one alternative: speculation in stocks."

"Wait a minute!" Gubb cried. "Are ya tryin' to tell us that tight-fisted old Amby played the stock market?"

"Yes," Holmes said. "I know that it does not sound

150

true to form, but no doubt it was the old story. Probably at some unlucky moment when he had money available, some friend recommended a speculative stock reputed to promise fabulous profits and he took a small 'flyer.' The venture paid off beyond his wildest dreams, and before he knew it he was bitten with the speculative bug. Then the inevitable happened: he scented bigger and bigger profits and took greater and greater chances. Being totally lacking in judgment and experience in such matters, it was not long before he started to lose money, and the more he lost, the more desperately he plunged. I know it sounds contrary to the character of the man, who was by nature niggardly and cautious; but we have to remember that he had one fatal weakness—an inordinate love of money and that was inevitably his undoing."

"A pretty theory," Gubb said, "but how do we know it's true?"

"I don't know all the details, but I have little doubt that they can be rather easily filled in," Holmes replied. "What I do know is that he went to his brokers' in Middington day before yesterday, where I followed him and where he sold some of his holdings and then went to a bank, as I expected him to do."

"Expected him to do? Now just why—"

"He went to get money to pay Peskind off—some two thousand pounds in small bills. Two thousand pounds is quite a bit of money, particularly in cash, I think you'll agree."

"Sure I will. But this payin' off Peskind . . . Are ya tryin' to make us think—"

"I'm not trying to make you think anything, Chief Constable. But when Peskind called at Rucker's two nights ago, it was plain for anyone to see that it was not to play chess. Nor was it at all likely that he went there secretly at night to talk about the weather. It was much more likely that it had something to do with the fraudulent burglary. And the natural assumption is that some way or other Peskind had learned that Rucker was the guilty party and aimed to profit by the knowledge."

"And just why was it so plain that they wasn't playin' chess?" Gubb asked.

"Why, it was all but self-evident, my dear fellow. It is highly improbable that Peskind would have walked all that distance from his house to Rucker's just to play a single game. The reasonable assumption is that they would have played at least three. But that would have taken the whole evening. You will recall that you said that they were both good players, and good chess players play slowly. The chances are that one game would last the better part of an hour, and Peskind was there less than that time. You pride yourself on the fact that you care nothing for chess, Chief Constable, and I won't quarrel with you about that, although personally I think it has its points. But I do find that the more things you are informed about, the better job you can do as a criminal investigator—or anything else."

"Okay, okay," Gubb growled, "just save the lecture. What's all this about arrestin' the bloke for blackmail? What evidence we got?"

"I have his written confession."

"His—his—?" For once the self-assured chief constable could do nothing but stammer.

"That's right. Last evening, after Peskind had bought a new Morris car with the money Rucker had given him, I made it a point to see him. At first he tried to brazen it out and say he'd made it on the horses; but when I got him confused with questions and told him what I knew, he capitulated and acknowledged everything.

"The confession shows that the weather was inclement on the morning of the day preceding the supposed burglary, and Peskind carried a showercoat with him when he left home for the shop. He hung the coat in the utility room and forgot to take it with him when he knocked off that evening, as the weather had cleared up. But he scarcely had started away when he remembered the coat and went back. As it was the more con-

152

venient route, he went along the alley at the back of the shop to enter the rear door. You may remember that he and young McCall both had keys to the front and rear doors of the shop.

"When he got back and was about to unlock the door, he thought he heard a sound inside and hesitated. He was uncertain as to what to do. He suspected it might be thieves and was afraid to go in alone—and was reluctant to leave to call the police for fear the thieves would get away while he did so. At that point he heard a familiar clearing of the throat and was sure the person inside was the asthmatic proprietor. Then he glanced across the alley at a vacant space and saw Rucker's motorcar where he was accustomed to park it.

"His first impulse was to go in; but then he had a second thought. Why was his employer in the shop at such an hour, and, why, particularly, in the utility room? It might not hurt to find out. So he slipped back to the end of the alley, which was only a short distance away, then went across the street into the shadow of a doorway and waited for Rucker to come out. After a little time Rucker's car came out of the alley and turned toward his home. Then Peskind slipped quietly back, found the basement door as we found it, and later drew his own conclusions.

"After that, putting the bite on Rucker was easy— he was a worried man with a guilty conscience. Peskind admitted that at first he tried to hold the shopkeeper up for five thousand pounds as the price of his silence, but Rucker made it plain that the two thousand would take all but his last sixpence."

"An' ya got all that in black an' white?"

"Exactly."

"An' where is Peskind now?"

"He's at the shop. I told him to go to work as usual, as if nothing had happened. I wished to report to you so you could make the arrests."

"An' what's to prevent him from makin' a break fer it?"

"He won't. I told him that we'd keep him under observation. I asked Yates to set a watch on the shop."

"*You* asked Yates? Just who—"

"I consider Yates a very reliable officer," Holmes returned coolly. "And I suggest that you have these two picked up at once. I don't want the stolen jewels spirited away where we can't find them. Just now I think it more than likely that you will find them tucked away in Rucker's strong box in the bank at Middington where I saw him cash the check."

"Just a minute, my fine friend. Don't be in such a hurry. This is goin' to be done my way. A little neat publicity—"

"But, Ed," young Barney broke in, "you can't stall around. Don't you see—"

"You just keep your little mouth buttoned up, my boy," Gubb said, shutting him off. "I'll handle this. An' remember, *Mister* Holmes, I'm callin' the shots."

"Not altogether. I think you've overlooked one thing," Holmes said.

"Yeah?"

"Yes. It's true you have jurisdiction in criminal matters here in Blythestown. But I wish to call to your attention the fact that that jurisdiction is not exclusive. The county constabulary of this shire shares the authority with you. I have a duty to recover the stolen jewels and I intend to do it. If you do not act and act at once, I shall consider it my duty to call Officer Reams at Twickenham."

"Okay, stow it. Barney, you can take care of the office. I'm goin' out to nab these birds."

Holmes said, "If you'd like the name of Rucker's bank—"

"I don't need it," the chief constable rasped as he started to open the door. "I'll sweat it out o' Rucker. He'll find out I ain't no pink-tea papa."

As he started through the hall outside, where there were several hangers-on, a man of smart appearance and keen manner, some five years Gubb's senior, grasped him by the arm and asked, "How about a story, Chief Constable?"

"Not now, Charley boy," Gubb said, pulling unceremoniously away. "I'm busy. See me in about an hour in my office. I'll have somethin' fer ya then—somethin' big."

Holmes and I had followed Gubb, and now Holmes stopped to speak to the man who had tried to detain the chief constable. "Do you represent the *Middington News-Journal*?" he asked.

"Why, yes," he replied.

"Then I think I can save you some time. If you just step into the chief constable's office now, I fancy that policeman Keenan will be glad to give you your story."

"Thanks," the man said, and immediately went in.

"You're sure young Keenan won't give him a slanted version of this thing?" I asked.

Holmes smiled. "If he does, I rather suspect that it will be slanted against the chief constable. It's my opinion that just now Constable Keenan is a sadly disillusioned young man, and the merciless snubbing he got just now from Gubb is not going to make him feel any more friendly. No, I think that the story that the *News-Journal* reporter gets won't paint too favorable a picture of brother Gubb."

Of course Holmes proved to be right. Thanks to some previous priming by Yates, the newspaperman got a surprisingly detailed account from Barney Keenan giving all the credit for the solution of the Kohinoor Gem Shop burglary to Holmes and putting the bumptious chief constable in a most unflattering light.

Some three weeks later, when we had been back in our rooms on Baker Street in London about a fortnight, Holmes got a note from Granby repeating the thanks which he had already heartily expressed for the recovery of the jewels and enclosing a clipping from the *Middington News-Journal*. The clipping stated that Edward P. Gubb had resigned as chief constable of the

Blythestown police force and that "Brandon B. Yates, an experienced officer of recognized integrity, intelligence and initiative" was expected to be appointed in his place.

"A good man, Yates," said Holmes—a Holmes who was now as fit and alert as ever. "I did not think it wise to say so at the time, but it was Yates who secured important information for me from young Michael McCall about the fellow Rucker. I put in a good word for him where I thought it would do the most good before we left Blythestown."

He stirred in his chair and rubbed his hands together in that eager, energetic gesture that was so familiar. Then he spoke again. "Looking back, the solution of the Kohinoor Gem Shop burglary was quite a stimulating experience, wasn't it, Harrington? Granby's coming into our hotel room that morning was a most fortunate circumstance, wouldn't you say?"

The Incriminating Glove

Creighton Holmes, grandson of the great detective, and I were sitting rather late one Sunday morning in our lodging on Baker Street. I was absorbed in an amusing satire in *Punch* while Holmes was engaged in reading a work on criminology entitled *Crimes and Clues*, by the distinguished Archibald Treadway Joslyn, onetime King's Counsellor. At length he finished it.

"An interesting book," he commented as he closed its covers and laid it aside. "A bit superficial at times, but it has some solid meat in it, nevertheless."

I grunted an assent.

"By the way, Harrington, the book has given me an idea. I have a mind to do a monograph which might be called "The Art of Misdirection in the Commission of Crime." It should furnish me an opportunity to record some of my more interesting successes, don't you think?"

"No doubt of it," I observed absently.

"And a few examples like that of the 'Case of the Scientific Recluse' should make rather entertaining reading, wouldn't you say?"

"Of course," I mumbled, as I still tried to follow the article in *Punch*.

Holmes got up and strolled toward the front of the room. As he did so, he said, "Harrington, old man, don't you ever get bored?"

"Bored?" I repeated mechanically. "Can't say I ever really thought much about it."

"My dear fellow, surely there are times when you

157

get weary of the daily routine and long for something exciting and unusual to happen."

I gave up and let the copy of *Punch* drop into my lap. I might have known that when Holmes got to talking it was useless to ignore him.

"Well, now that you put it that way, old chap, I suppose maybe I do. But don't tell me that you find anything boring about crime detection and tracking down criminals."

Holmes was now standing at one of the front windows with his hands clasped behind him, looking down into the street. "Of course I do," he responded irritably. "The average criminal is so stupid and unimaginative as to make the feat of bringing him to justice a mere humdrum matter. Now, if just once in a while some wily rascal could conceive an original way to accomplish his skulduggery, it might—" Then he broke off to exclaim, "By Jove, what's this?"

"What's what?" I asked.

"It looks as if we were about to have a client, Harrington, my boy, and a devilish pretty one at that, or I miss my guess."

He turned away from the window with the well-known sparkle of anticipation in his eye and unconsciously rubbed his hands together with a subdued air of excitement. As he did so, we heard a light step upon the stair followed by a peremptory knock on the door.

"Come in," Holmes called, and the door swung open to reveal a young lady of some three or four and twenty of slightly less than medium height, with a neat figure, a mass of dark, curly hair, bright hazel eyes, and a look of animation that gave the impression of unusual intelligence and force of character.

"Are you Mr. Creighton Holmes?" she asked, staring at him and totally ignoring me.

"Yes," he smiled, "and this is my friend and colleague, Mr. Harrington."

She acknowledged the introduction and said, "My name is Ann Winter. I came to—to consult you on a professional matter."

"Very well," said Holmes. "Please have a seat." And he motioned her toward a chair. "By the way, I assume that this is a matter of some urgency, to have brought you here from out of town and, if I am not mistaken, from rather a considerable distance, on a Sunday morning. I also take it that you have made the journey on your own responsibility and possibly with some secrecy. Moreover, it is obvious that you decided on the step largely on impulse and prepared for it in no little haste; although, of course, you may have contemplated such a move for a considerable time."

The girl gave him a look of incredulity. "I—I did have to slip away," she said, "And though I've been worried for quite a while and planned to do something about it, this was the first chance that offered, and I hurried up and took it. But how could you know that I was from out of town and . . . and all the rest?"

Holmes smiled. "Well, it's really quite simple, Miss Winter. That you come from out of town is a natural deduction since you arrive by cab and not in a private motorcar or public conveyance as you would most likely do were you a resident of the city. The presumption, of course, is further strengthened by the fact that you come from the direction of Waterloo Station, which is not too many blocks away.

"That you come from a more rural setting is evidenced by the fact that there is a bit of clay on the inner portion of the heel of your right shoe which by no stretch of the imagination could come from London—but would, in all likelihood, come from some place in the Midlands, if I am accurate in my recollection of our English soils.

"As for your coming here on impulse, the fact that you did not write or telephone to make an appointment argues such action, as you look to be an intelligent young lady who would ordinarily take such a precaution if not impelled by some strong emotion or sudden sense of impending crisis. And—if you'll pardon me— that you prepared to depart in haste is attested by the circumstance that your right stocking is of a slightly lighter hue than the left, indicating that you dressed in some precipitation.

"Finally, that you took this action upon your own responsibility and without taking anyone into your confidence is sheer assumption based upon the foregoing circumstances and upon the general impression that you convey of suppressed excitement and ill-concealed anxiety."

"I see," Miss Winter nodded. "I *am* from out of the city. I come from the little village of Wembling, midway between Watley and Midgwick. And I don't see how you could guess right about so many things. No wonder people credit you with almost occult powers."

Holmes gave a gesture of modest denial. "Oh, that!" he said. "But I encroach upon your time, which, I assume, is of some consequence. May I ask what brings you here? I hope no crime has been committed."

"No, there hasn't," Miss Winter replied, coloring with embarrassment. "And I—I know it sounds foolish, but I'm afraid there *will* be. And . . . and I had heard all these wonderful things about you and . . . well, I didn't know where to turn."

"I see. And just what is this crime that you fear?"

"That's just it. I don't know. And I'm not sure whether it's being plotted against my guardian or against David. David's his grandson," she said, reddening again. I suspected that she might have more than a passing interest in this young fellow.

"Oh?" Holmes said. "Well, suppose you tell us who your guardian is and who is plotting this crime, and why—if you know."

"Well, my guardian is Sir John Rumford."

"Of course," I blurted out. "He was the old member who was called—"

But Miss Winter did not seem to notice. "Yes, he was the one who was called 'Old Rummy' and 'the contentious earl' because he was always feuding with someone, even with members of his own party. I wouldn't have a home if it weren't for him, and perhaps I shouldn't say it, but I guess he deserves the title
160

because he—well, to be truthful about it, he's plain contrary, seems to be *for* all the wrong things and the wrong people and against all the right ones."

She paused as if wondering how to proceed. "I'm afraid I'm not making myself very clear. You would think he had mistreated me or at least treated me unjustly; but that's not true. I really owe him a lot. He took me in when I was only eight at my mother's dying request. It's a long story . . . She was the daughter of his dearest friend years ago, I'm told, and that's the way it worked out.

"But to get back to the point, As you say the earl is very wealthy. By every rule of blood and common sense David—David Rowe, that is—should be his heir. David is an orphan. When he was a little boy he lived with his grandfather; in fact, we were brought up together, you might say." Again her face had that telltale flush. "Uncle John—that's what I call him—was very fond of him, or, at least as fond of him as he could be of anybody. But then David got older and got to thinking for himself and things were different. Uncle John had it all mapped out that he should follow in his forefathers' footsteps and go into public life—the earl is the fourth of the line to sit in the House of Lords—but David had his mind set on being a doctor and wouldn't give in. Luckily his parents had left him a slight legacy when he came of age, and with that and all sorts of economy and hard work he has gone to medical school. Now the earl threatens to disinherit him, and now that the Plunkets have come, I think that that may happen, or maybe even worse."

"The Plunkets? Who are they?"

"Some kind of distant cousins of Uncle John's. About a month ago Uncle had a slight stroke and the happening got considerable publicity—he being who he was. There was even some hint of the attack being nearly fatal, though that was all nonsense. At any rate, about a month later the Plunkets showed up—Horatio and Rafe, or Rafael. Horatio must be about five or six and thirty and Rafe four or five years younger. I have

161

heard that Uncle had a sentimental attachment for their grandmother when he was young. He seems to have been warmer-hearted years ago than he is now. Maybe things went wrong and soured him. Anyway, the mother of these Plunkets was a great favorite of his, and he has always spoken of them as if they were something special.

"Up to four months ago I had never set eyes on them. Then, all of a sudden, they appear. Where they had been or what they had been doing in the meantime, I don't know. To me there is something decidedly fishy about them. But Uncle John is just too blind or too stubborn to see through them. And now there they are, hanging around—and poisoning his mind against David and plotting to get his property, or I miss my guess."

"You mean that they are living at your uncle's house?"

"Well, not exactly, though they might as well be—at least, Horatio might. He's there most of the time, though they live at the lodge-house and not at Rumford Grange, as it's still called. You see, the Grange is still quite a big estate, though not so extensive as it once was. The house is a great greystone pile of a building over two hundred years old. It sets on a slight elevation facing south to a road some distance away at the end of a long winding drive that comes up to the west side of the house and swings round to the back, where what was once the carriage house and stables are. To the west beyond the driveway the property slopes down to fields of cultivated land that used to belong to the Grange but was gradually sold off. But there is still a great yard dotted with trees and shrubs in the haphazard English fashion, while to the east there is a woods, mostly of oak and beech with some larch trees. The lodge-house is beyond the woods, some half-mile from the house."

"I see," Holmes said. "And how do you get from the Grange to the lodge-house?"

"Well, there's a narrow gravel road that leads from

162

the rear of the Grange and curves round to the north along the foot of the slope, then swings south to the lodge. Or you can go by a footpath that leads almost directly east from the house through the narrower part of the woods."

"Do the Plunkets live there alone?"

"I understand that they have a housekeeper who does the cooking for them."

"And what are these fellows like?"

"Horatio—or Horrie as Rafe and Uncle call him—is tall and rugged-looking and . . . and graceful. Every move he makes is like a cat. He has dark wavy hair and dark eyes and skin—looks almost foreign in a way. He has a low, purring voice and an insinuating manner—in fact, there's something compelling about him; almost mesmeric, you might say. Rafe is built along much the same lines, though not quite so tall and a bit heavier. And he's blond instead of dark, with rough, tousled hair. He has the same catlike way of moving, but he doesn't put himself out to get into people's good graces the way Horatio does. He has a more swaggering, devil-may-care way about him, but a kind of fatal charm, just the same. Oh, they're a smooth pair all right!" And she shook her head, though whether in reluctant admiration or disgust, it would be hard to say.

"As to how they get around Uncle . . . well, it's mostly little things. And it's not altogether what they do, but the way they do it. They're so . . . so adroit about it; or, at least Horatio is. He doesn't seem to toady, but he's always flattering Uncle in some subtle way, or doing something for him—running an errand or taking him for a stroll or a ride—incidentally, in one of Uncle's cars. They don't have one of their own; that is, they claim to have one but say that it's laid up just now.

"And Horatio never says anything outright against David. He's much too shrewd for that. But he's always making some sly remark; saying how too bad it is that David isn't a little more understanding—or commiserating with Uncle, saying how fair and generous he is,

163

and how with just a little more compliance on David's part everything could be so pleasant and agreeable. Oh, he's a slick one!" And again she shook her head in the same gesture.

Holmes said, "I understand how you feel, Miss Winter, and I feel sure that there are good grounds for your apprehensions; but do you have anything concrete to bear out your suspicions of criminal intent?"

"I see what you mean," said Ann Winter, biting her lip. "And that's just it. It all seems so . . . so sort of nebulous. But I am sure that they would go to any lengths to gain their ends. There's something so . . . so sinister about them. But anything really criminal . . . oh, I have heard Horatio making roundabout suggestions to influence Uncle to remake his will—saying that a man never knows what the future may hold, that he should always have his house in order—that sort of thing. But . . ." She paused, knitting her brows. Then she said, "Of course, there's Hawkins."

"Hawkins?"

"Yes. At least, that's what he calls himself, though I doubt it's his real name. The truth is, I doubt everything about him. You see, he's the new butler, though I question if he ever had a job as butler before. He doesn't act like it. But he came to the Grange about six weeks ago, after Horatio had persuaded Uncle to get rid of Hanks, who had been with us for almost eighteen years. I don't know how he did it, but he did. And then he got this . . . this slimy fellow in his place. On Horatio's recommendation, I am sure. He's a long, lean, horse-faced, sanctimonious creature—a regular Uriah Heep if there ever was one.

"He's continually slipping about, as silent as a ghost, and I have the feeling that he's always snooping. Once I caught him going through some papers on Uncle's desk. When I asked him what he was doing, he said he was looking for a pen for 'Mr. Horatio.' And two or three times I have seen him talking in low tones with Horatio. That seems like a strange thing for a guest to be doing with a servant."

"Yes, it does. Is that all?"

"Well, once I heard—or rather overheard—a conversation between Horatio and Rafe that made me prick up my ears. Evidently Rafe had made improper advances to the maid, Lizzie, a dim-witted, tempting piece, and had been caught at it by the housekeeper. Horatio was furious and was giving Rafe a dressing down. Then Rafe said. 'Don't be so damned pious,' or something like that, and Horatio said, 'Piety's got nothing to do with it. Just remember, you've got just as much at stake as I have, and remember what happened at Melbourne that time.' I didn't want to get caught eavesdropping, so I slipped away and didn't hear any more."

"I understand. You speak of a maid and a housekeeper. Are there any other servants at the Grange?"

"Yes. There's a cook that Horatio tried to have Uncle replace too, I don't know why unless he intended to poison my uncle or something like that. But Uncle balked and Horatio had the sense to drop it. He seems to know just how far he dares to go. Then there's the chauffeur, an uncouth, youngish fellow that Uncle still calls the carriage man, who also doubles as gardener. And, finally, there's Will Fairlee."

"Who's he?"

"He acts as Uncle's secretary. You see, Uncle is writing his memoirs—or trying to. And Will is helping him. They work at it two or three hours a day, each morning in the library, which is a wing all by itself on the east side of the house—the side toward the lodge. Uncle goes there about nine o'clock to go over the manuscript that Will has transcribed from the previous day's notes and which he has turned over to Uncle for correction. Then a half hour or so later Will joins him and they work together."

"I see. And what is the attitude of these different people toward the Plunkets?"

"Well, the cook, Hannah, as you might expect, has no love for them. And neither has the housekeeper, Mrs. Jennings, who is rather old and slightly deaf. Will

Fairlee feels as I do. He speaks to Horatio and Rafe when he has to and is polite about it, but he has talked to me about them. The maid is too shallow-pated to see through them or to care if she did. As for Hicks, the chauffeur, he's rather a worthless fellow with no great sense of loyalty. Neither of the brothers has the instincts of a gentleman, and they are the kind that treat those in a subordinate position with contempt unless they can get to use one of the cars. Once they even went out together in the Daimler, got drunk, and nearly wrecked it."

She paused and thought a bit. "Well, I guess that's about it," she said. Then, in a more disturbed tone, she added, "I know, Mr. Holmes, that this may sound fanciful. But I assure you that I am not given to foolish fancies. And I have an awful foreboding that some dreadful thing will happen unless something can be done to stop it."

"I agree," Holmes said warmly. "And I do not think that you are imagining things. You have convinced me that these distant cousins of your guardian are a pair of scoundrels. The question is how we are to circumvent them."

"Oh, I do hope that you can do something!" the old earl's ward exclaimed, clasping her hands in desperation.

"Well, we'll try. The first thing, it seems to me, is to find out something, if we can, about this pair and the fellow calling himself Hawkins. If we could get some really convincing evidence, your guardian might listen to reason. Now, could you get hold of a photograph of these Plunket brothers, by any chance?"

"I thought you might want that," she replied with amazing promptness, "and I have a snapshot here. I snatched it off Uncle's chiffonier just before I left. It's a pretty good likeness. I don't know what Uncle John will say when he finds it gone." And, taking the snapshot from her purse as she talked, she handed it to Holmes.

"Capital!" he exclaimed. "You'll just have to think

up some plausible explanation for its disappearance. It *is* a good picture. I'll have enlargements made immediately and return the original to you as soon as I can. Then I'll set about making inquiries at once." He paused a moment as he thought, then added, "Do you know *anything* specific about either of them—anything that might give us a lead?"

"Just one thing. I'm sure I heard at some time that Horatio had been in some kind of show business. Though when or where or just what it was, I don't know. I'm afraid it isn't much," she ended apologetically.

"It's a start, at least," Holmes assured her. "And I think from what you've said about him, it may well be a good one. He seems like one who might very well have what we call 'stage presence'—good looks, a good voice, a compelling manner, plenty of self-assurance. But I doubt if he went under the name of Horatio Plunket; I can hardly imagine a man getting by on the stage with such a name. Now, how about the spurious butler?"

"Hawkins? I have no photograph. But I think I have given you a fair description of him."

Holmes smiled. "Yes, you have, except for his age and personal appearance."

"Oh, yes. Well, he's about six or eight and forty, I would judge, though he might pass for as much as ten years older with that solemn face of his. As for his personal appearance, I would say that he is at least six feet or slightly taller, lean and cadaverous, and somewhat stooped, with a kind of peering expression as if he might be rather shortsighted. He has blackish hair beginning to get grey and thinning on top. He has shifty eyes, slightly sagging jowls, and this soapy, mealymouthed manner."

Holmes said, "That should pretty well identify him, I would say. Now I wonder if you could do something else for me."

"Anything you say."

"Please try to get hold of a water glass with his fingerprints on it. That shouldn't be too hard. And if the opportunity presents itself, do the same in regard to the Plunkets. Then, when you can, get them to the police chief at Midgwick. I'll get in touch with him and he'll take care of the rest."

Ann Winter nodded, then asked, "Is there anything else?"

Holmes said, "I think not. Only keep me advised of any happening you think may have significance. We are dealing with some very crafty rogues, or I'm badly mistaken, and we can't overlook any lead, no matter how trivial."

"I'll keep my eyes open," said Miss Winter, getting up. "And I'll attend to the glasses with the fingerprints as soon as I get a chance. And thank you *so much* for all your help," she added, holding out her hand.

After she had gone, Holmes turned toward me. "Well, what do you think?" he asked.

"I think she's a very observant young lady," I said.

"Exactly," Holmes returned. "And not one likely to conjure up goblins when there are no goblins there. Now let's hope that she succeeds in getting these fingerprints. I have a feeling that tracking down the history of these two pretty rascals may not be at all easy."

This was the state of things when, unfortunately for the affairs at Rumford Grange, the services of Holmes were engaged to solve the mysterious disappearance of some valuable papers from the office of the Chancellor of the Exchequer, an account of which is to be found in the story of "The Pigeon-Toed Man." As a consequence of this commission, Holmes's mind was so absorbed for some time that he had little opportunity to give thought to anything else. Had it been otherwise, a serious delay in the investigation of the dubious past of Horatio Plunket and his swashbuckling brother might have been avoided and the tragic happenings which were to take place at Rumford Grange might never have occurred.

Confirming our opinion of Ann Winter's practicality, in less than two weeks' time some excellent fingerprints of all three suspects at the Grange were in Holmes hands. Nor was it many days later that Holmes greeted me one evening with the remark, "Harrington, old man, we have some enlightening news regarding the scurvy scamp posing as butler at Rumford Grange."

"Oh? What is it?" I replied.

"As we suspected, he has a decidedly unsavory record. His real name is Willie Fink. He is also called 'Fingers' Fink. The title of 'Fingers' refers to his skill in opening locks. He had been in and out of prison several times, but dropped out of sight when he was being sought after one of his more pretentious efforts some four years ago. Where he has been since, the police don't know."

"Well, that fits in with Miss Winter's suspicions. What about the Plunkets?"

He shook his head. "Nothing at all. There is no record of the fingerprints of either, and, so far, all inquiries through the theatrical channels have led to a dead end."

"That's bad," I said.

"Yes. Without some definite information against them, there would be little use in trying to convince 'the contentious earl' of their evil intentions. We'll just have to keep on trying."

Then, only about a week later, came a letter from Ann Winter bringing the ominous news that her guardian had made a new will.

"There was something funny about it," she wrote, "as if in some way the stage had all been set. We were all called into the library—at least, Will Fairlee and the housekeeper and I. Horatio and Rafe were already there with Uncle John. Will and Mrs. Jennings were to act as witnesses. Just why I was there I don't know, unless it was to convince me that everything was fair and aboveboard. I am sure there was some purpose in it and that the whole thing was carefully planned by Horatio, who was hovering around Uncle while Rafe sat at one side near Uncle's flat-top desk with a sardonic look, almost like a sneer, on his face.

"When the rest of us were seated, Uncle got the will out of the wall safe. Almost as soon as he did so, Horatio took it from him and helped seat Uncle at the desk as if he were a helpless old man. Had anyone else treated him that way, he would probably have flown into a rage. But Horatio seems to cast a spell over him. At least he will endure petty attentions from him that he wouldn't tolerate in anyone else. Then, just as Uncle was seated, Horatio picked up a pen, cleared his throat, and said, 'Now I fancy we're all ready.'

"He had no sooner spoken the words than Hawkins came through the door carrying a tray with a decanter of wine and some glasses. Just as he did so, he stumbled and said something like, 'Oh, I say. I beg your pardon!' It all happened very suddenly and I thought he was going to fall down, tray and all; but eventually he regained his balance with no worse result than spilling a little of the wine. But for a few moments it caused quite a commotion and we all had our eyes on him, wondering what would happen. But after things had quieted down, Uncle signed the will that Horatio spread on the desk before him, it was witnessed, and nothing further of an untoward nature happened. Do you think, Mr. Holmes, that all of this could have been prearranged—and if so, why?"

"Ah!" said Holmes, "The plot thickens, Harrington. And Miss Winter is a very astute young lady, wouldn't you say? As for the redoubtable Horatio, my respect for that gentleman's evil genius increases by the minute. But I do wish we could get some information about him. If he ever was on the stage, it is deuced strange that we can find out nothing about him even if he did appear under another name. But his photograph has been distributed and inquiry has been made concerning the most obscure actors on the legitimate stage and in the music halls, not only here in London and other large cities, but in the outlying districts, with absolutely no results. If only—" He broke off suddenly. "Harrington, old man, I've been a fool!"

"A fool! What are you talking about?"

"Melbourne!"

"Melbourne?" I said blankly.

"To be sure. Don't you remember that Horatio Plunket said something indicating Rafe has been in some trouble over a girl in Melbourne? *Melbourne, Australia!* Why didn't I think of it before? It all makes sense. The tricky 'Hawkins' dropping out of sight, the mystery of the past of these two sainted brothers. They've been out of the country, all three of them! It's probably in Australia that the Plunkets met Hawkins and arranged to take him on in their scheme here. Yes, by Jove, it all fits! We'll push our inquiries there at once, and let's hope we hear from them quickly."

It was some ten days after this that Holmes greeted me one evening when I reached our quarters with the information that he had had a telephone call from Ann Winter that morning.

He said, "She seemed very much upset, and you will admit that she does not seem the type of young lady to get unduly concerned over trifles. She had contrived to get away from the Grange on some pretext and was making the call secretly from some friend's house in the nearby village of Watley."

"What was it all about?" I asked.

"She thinks things are coming to a head. She says that David Rowe, the earl's grandson, is coming to the Grange tomorrow for a visit over the weekend, and she is sure that in some way Horatio has been instrumental in getting him there. Just why it should be at this particular time she is not sure; but she thinks it has something to do with it's being the time of the annual fair at the neighboring town of Midgwick. She admits that her fears seem to have no basis in fact, but says she has a presentiment that something dire is being plotted

171

against her guardian or David or both. And the worst of it is, I think she's right!"

"But what? And how——"

"I don't know," he said. "I do know I wish we had some results from our inquiries in Australia. I would like to go to Rumford Grange tomorrow, but this matter of the Chancellor of the Exchequer requires my attention here one more day. But Saturday we're going, whether or no. Let's pray we'll be in time."

But when I reached our lodgings the next evening, he was in better spirits. That very afternoon word about the older Plunket had come through from the Melbourne police, confirming the fact that a fellow of Horatio Plunket's description had appeared in the music halls of various cities in Australia under the name of Raoul Romaine, evidently posing as a Frenchman.

"I don't think there is any doubt about it's being our man," Holmes said. "They seem very sure he is, and the facts seem to bear them out. They even mention his being seen in the company of a blond man with a family resemblance, who could be none other than his swaggering brother. Moreover, our friend Horatio seems to have put on quite an act as a sleight-of-hand man, with a novel twist to the performance that he may well try to employ in his present nefarious scheming. Tomorrow, Harrington, we're off to Rumford Grange."

The next morning when we left at an early hour, the day seemed dark and forbidding. Ugly rain clouds lowered near the horizon and there was a raw chill in the air. Holmes, with face grimly set, pressed the motorcar on at a dangerously fast speed. Neither of us had much to say. Something of Ann Winter's vague foreboding gripped us both. Nor was this sense of unease lessened when we left the main road to go up the long driveway, with its darkly overarching trees, and came in sight of the ancient seat of Rumford Grange, looming grey and bleak before us. We swung around the west side of the house and brought our car to a stop on the graveled space behind. Then it was that our fears seemed all too well founded, for standing there already was another motorcar marked *Wembling Police!*

We got out, wondering what had happened, when Ann Winter, who apparently had been awaiting our arrival with anxious impatience, came running out of the great rear oaken door and down the deeply worn stone steps. "Oh, Mr. Holmes," she gasped, "I'm so relieved you've come. It . . . it's horrible! Uncle John's been shot and killed!"

"Killed!" Holmes echoed.

"Yes, and the police are here. And David is being blamed for it. They just—" Then her voice dropped. "Here they come now. Watch out, Horatio—"

And she broke off as a tall, dark saturnine-looking fellow, obviously the older of the two Plunket brothers, came out of the door followed by a man in uniform and a third man of some five and thirty years of age, of medium build. This man had a good-looking face and an intelligent expression, although just now, like everyone else, he seemed in a state of mingled surprise and shock. He stopped near the top of the steps while Plunket came down with a lithe, self-assured stride and the man in uniform followed close behind.

Plunket, who apparently had assumed direction of affairs, was the first to speak. "What's going on, Ann? Who are these men?" he asked sharply.

"Mr. Holmes and Mr. Harrington."

I thought I saw a wary look flash into the fellow's eyes and as quickly pass away. "Mr. Holmes, the detective?" he asked.

"That's right," Holmes answered.

"Well, well, if this isn't a coincidence!" His tone was brisk, almost insolent. "What brings you here?"

"I had business in these parts," Holmes replied. "Perhaps you'd like to introduce us to these men."

"Certainly, I was just about to do so," Plunket said

glibly, presenting the man in uniform as Chief Bilkins of the local police and the man on the steps as Mr. Fairlee, his cousin's private secretary.

"You're the officer in charge here?" Holmes asked the former.

"Well," the man said rather uncertainly, "I suppose you might say so." He was tall, with a somewhat full figure, though not fat, and a round, serious face. Just now it bore a harried expression, as if he were not too sure of himself.

Before he could say more, Horatio Plunket spoke again: "This morning, a little after nine of the clock and about fifteen minutes before he was to join Cousin John in the library, Mr. Fairlee thought he heard a shot in the direction of that room and immediately ran down, only to find him at the desk dead—shot through the head.

"He notified Chief Bilkins right away, then got in touch with me by telephone down at the lodge. My brother and Ann—Miss Winter here—were there with me at the time. Ann and I hurried up here. The servants are all away at the fair in Midgwick. Will and my cousin's grandson, David Rowe, were the only ones in the house with Cousin John. In spite of all the commotion, David failed to make an appearance. When Chief Bilkins and his deputy got here, we went up to rouse him. He was locked in his room, and when we finally got him to the door, he claimed he had been asleep. But there was a pint whiskey bottle on the stand in his room, almost empty, and his gun—the one that probably shot Cousin John—was missing and just now has been found in some bushes in the woods, not far away, where apparently the foolish fellow had tossed it. Of course it had been wiped clean of prints."

"I see," Holmes commented, then turned toward Ann. "Is Mr. Rowe accustomed to drinking whiskey to excess?"

"I never knew him to take any at all. Beer and ale, or wine, yes—at least at times. But never any hard liquor."

174

"That's right," Plunket put in quickly. "Evidently, though, he had worked himself up to where he was reckless. Unfortunately, he and his grandfather hadn't got along too well lately. Apparently he thought himself abused. The butler told me just this morning that he had heard high words between them only last night."

"Sounds quite damning," Holmes said drily. "Miss Winter, how did the boy happen to have a gun?"

"In a way it wasn't his," she answered.

"Oh, come now, Ann," Horatio Plunket interposed. "I know how you feel. But you know better than that."

"Well, it's true," the girl persisted. "He never bought it. It belonged to his father. It was a souvenir. His father took it off a German soldier during the war."

"Was it in working condition? Did you ever know him to shoot it?" Holmes asked.

"No, I didn't."

Plunket interjected again. "I'm sorry, but it would shoot all right. I used to see David oiling and polishing it plenty of times."

"Humph," grunted Holmes. "By the way, couldn't the killer have been a burglar? Was nothing taken?"

"Not a thing. And the wall safe had not been touched," Plunket replied. "No, Mr. Holmes, it's a great pity, but there seems to be no doubt about the boy's guilt. One of his gloves was discovered near the top of a back stairway that leads almost directly from the door of his room to the yard outside, and a window in the library where Cousin John was shot was found open. It would have taken David but a moment to leap out the window, run around the corner of the house, and dash upstairs. I'm afraid it looks pretty dark for the poor fellow."

Holmes said, "I know what a shock it must be to you to think such can be the case; but there may be another explanation to your cousin's tragic death. Tell me, Chief Bilkins, is your investigation complete?"

"I would like to talk to you about that," the chief said in reply. "I don't mind saying that this thing is out

175

of my line. I don't know when we've had a murder round here. Any help that you can give will be most welcome."

"Good. I'll be glad to do anything I can. I think we might begin by looking over the scene of the crime. But, first, you may wish to have Mr. Plunket and these others stay someplace where they will be available."

I thought that Plunket was about to protest, but before he could say anything, Ann Winter spoke up and said, "We'll go into the east room," and started up the steps to go into the house. If Plunket had intended to speak, he evidently thought better of it, and we all followed her inside.

As we did so, Holmes remarked, "Perhaps I should go with you so that we may know where you are," and he went with Ann, Plunket, and the secretary, Fairlee, to a room at the front of the house while Bilkins and I awaited his return in the dim old hall. Before he came back to join us, Holmes stopped at the door of the room that they had entered, and I could hear him say, "I suggest that none of you use the telephone. *None of you.* I hope you all understand." And I suspected that for some reason he wished to forestall Horatio Plunket's trying to communicate with his brother.

When he had rejoined us, Bilkins led us to the library, a room that constituted a wing all by itself on the side of the house looking east over the lawn toward the woods through which the path led to the lodge. Holmes looked at the body of the dead earl, examined the room and the sill of the open window, through which a breeze was blowing and gently stirring the curtains on either side. He found there the mark of what appeared to be the sole of a shoe, but it was too faint to identify. "Not much here to help us," he said. "Suppose we look outside." But an inspection of the hard, dry ground beneath the window failed also to reveal any identifiable prints.

He shook his head. "Nothing here either. Where was the gun found?"

Bilkins led us to a patch of alder near the edge of

the woods just to the south of the path, but again an inspection of the spot yielded no helpful clue.

"Well, I fancy there's no more that we can do here," Holmes commented. "By the way, you brought a deputy with you?"

"Yes," replied the police chief. "He's upstairs in the room with the suspect."

"Very good. Let us go up, shall we?"

In the upstairs bedroom we found the deputy, a well-set-up fellow of something over thirty, sitting in a chair grimly facing the bed, on which young David Rowe lay in his pajamas. He seemed in a half stupor and barely stirred as we entered the room.

"Has he said anything yet, since we first questioned him?" Bilkins asked, after introducing us to the deputy, whose name proved to be Hodges.

"Not a peep since them words he said when we first got 'im up out o' bed. He must have really tied one on."

Holmes glanced over the room and noticed the whiskey bottle on a stand near the bed, with a very little of its contents in the bottom.

"Has any one handled that bottle?" he asked.

"Not since we first found it," Bilkins replied. "This fellow Plunket was about to pick it up, but I told him it was best to leave it alone."

Holmes gave him a look of approval, and I began to have a greater respect for this stodgy-looking country policeman.

"May I ask why?" Holmes queried.

"Well, I don't know as I can say, except I've always been told in a case of a crime like this to leave things as they were, and I thought it would do no harm to follow the rules. Then, too, it seemed to me that Plunket was a bit too ready to run things and I just didn't cater to it."

Holmes nodded. "You did quite right. I'll be much surprised if the bottle shows any fingerprints."

Bilkins gave him a questioning look, but made no

comment, and said, "Did you want to try to question the boy?"

Holmes answered, "Not unless you feel I should." Then when Bilkins said he did not, he inquired, "Has the doctor been here yet?"

"Not yet. We had trouble getting hold of one, it being Fair Day and all. But we finally reached Dr. Petley. He should be here before too long."

"Good," Holmes replied. "Suppose we go to some room downstairs, where we can see him when he comes, and talk things over."

When we were seated about a table in what was called the breakfast room, where we could look onto the graveled space in the rear, Holmes went on. "First I think I should explain my presence here. I fancy you've been wondering about it."

"Well, I did think it a bit more than coincidence, you might say. But I thought it was your own business, and if you wanted me to know, you would tell me."

"That's good of you," Holmes said, then proceeded to tell the police chief about Ann Winter's visit to us and what he'd found out about the two Plunkets and Hawkins.

When he got through, Bilkins slowly nodded his big head. "So that's the way it is. I thought there was something bloody odd about this case."

"You did?"

"Yes. As I told you, murders ain't in my line, but it seemed to me that Plunket wasn't feeling so bad about this grandson being blamed for the killing as he would have us think. Then I thought it a bit peculiar that this boy who is smart enough to study for a doctor should use his own gun, throw it where it was sure to be found, likely wear gloves so that his fingerprints wouldn't be on the gun, then drop one of the gloves near his own bedroom door. It didn't make sense. Still, with no signs of burglary, it looks like an inside job, and with every one else around with airtight alibis, there seems to be no way to pin it on anyone but the grandson."

"I know," Holmes said, "but I think that we will do it. For one thing, I would like to find out from Miss Winter just how she happened to be at the lodge-house on this particular morning at just the time she was. Her being there at all strikes me as a little unusual. When I have heard the explanation of her presence there, I have an idea that I may be able to form a pretty good guess as to how this whole affair was planned. But before we call her in, I would like to ask that you do one thing yourself. How well do you know the chief of police at Midgwick?"

"Why, pretty well. Well enough so that we work all right together, if that is what you mean."

"It is," Holmes nodded. "Now, if you are willing to trust my judgment, I wish you'd call the Midgwick chief and ask that he have Hawkins picked up and brought back here. It ought not to be too hard to find him. He should be at one of the pubs if he's not attending the fair."

"And what charge will we make against him?"

"I think it as well that he be not told. It won't hurt to have him do a little wondering. When we get him here, I fancy we may find a way to get some valuable information out of him. And I suggest that two men bring him here. It will impress him more with the gravity of his position, and we may need their services before this is over."

"Very well, whatever you say," Bilkins agreed. "I'll call the Midgwick chief, then bring back Miss Winter for you to question, sir."

When he returned with the dead earl's ward, Holmes said, "Now, Miss Winter, I want you to tell us exactly how you happened to be at the lodge-house this morning and what occurred there. But first, perhaps you'd better let us know if you have been accustomed to go there often."

Ann Winter gave a vigorous shake of the head. "I

certainly haven't. I've never been there but once or twice before since those . . . those scum came there. Then this morning Horatio called and said he badly needed some help about roasting a joint and would I come down. He said their housekeeper had left for a day off at the fair, that Rafe was laid up and they had this joint of beef to cook but didn't know just how to do it."

"All right, go on. But what's this about Rafe being laid up?"

"Well, he had had a bad felon on the third finger of his left hand. We all knew about it—he had cursed enough about the pain. Then, day before yesterday, the doctor lanced it. Meanwhile, it seems, Rafe had caught a cold and the doctor had told him to stay in bed. Otherwise, he might get pneumonia with his vitality so low from all the infection in him."

"I see. And who gave you this information?"

Ann Winter opened her eyes wide. "Why—why, Horatio."

"Very well. Please continue."

"Well, when I got there, I rapped at the door and Horatio called to me to come in and I did. He was in the kitchen with a hot toddy of whiskey in his hand and he was calling out, 'Take it easy, I'll be there in a minute.' "

"Yes? And to whom was he calling?"

"Why, Rafe, of course."

"And had you heard Rafe call first?"

"No. But there was no one else in the house. As I told you, their housekeeper was at the fair."

"All right. Then what happened?"

"Well, Horatio excused himself, took the toddy on a tray down the hall, and went into the bedroom where Rafe was."

"And you stayed in the kitchen?"

"Yes."

"So, of course, you didn't see Rafe?"

"No, but I could hear them talking."

"I see. What did they say, as near as you can tell?"

"Well, I didn't pay too much attention. But it went something like this: Horatio said, 'Here's your toddy you've been yelling about,' and Rafe said, 'Thanks.' Then Horatio asked Rafe how his finger felt and Rafe said, 'What do you think—it hurts like hell.' Then Horatio told him that I was out here and he should watch his language, and Rafe said, 'Oh, don't be so damned sanctimonious, Horrie, she's heard worse than that plenty of times. Besides, I'm going to get up, I'm tired of lying in this damned bed.' Then they argued about that for a while, and after some more words Horatio came back."

"And how long would you say this conversation lasted?"

"Oh, I don't know. As I said, I didn't pay much attention. Maybe three or four minutes. Maybe longer. I know it seemed longer than necessary, considering that Horatio had called me down there to do them a favor, and then was keeping me waiting. Besides, it seemed to me like just talk—they weren't really saying anything."

"Could you hear them both distinctly?"

"Well enough, considering I wasn't listening particularly."

"And could you hear Rafe just as well as you could Horatio?"

"Well, no, not quite, I suppose. He sounded farther away. But of course he would, he being in bed and Horatio standing near the door, I suppose."

"Naturally," Holmes agreed. "But there's no question in your mind that it was Rafe to whom Horatio was speaking?"

"Oh, no, not at all. It was Rafe's voice, I am sure. And anyway, it sounded the way Rafe would talk—rough and reckless."

"And the conversation all took place in the bedroom?"

"Well, yes. Except just at the end. Horatio stood in the open doorway of the room as he was about to go. I

181

could see him speaking from there and hear Rafe answering from inside."

Holmes said, "Very good. Now, what happened when Horatio came back to you?"

"Well, he apologized for keeping me so long. Said Rafe had to be humored, that I knew how he was. Then explained that they had had nothing but pan meat for quite a spell and that Rafe was tired of it— and that he was, too, for that matter; their housekeeper was not much of a cook. So they had got a joint, but the housekeeper had gone off to the fair without telling him how to roast it, that they had a new-fangled electric stove that he had never operated and he didn't know what temperature to have the oven or how long the joint should be in, and so on."

"And was the stove so complicated?"

She shrugged and laughed a little. "Well, I didn't think so. But you know how men are. And I do suppose he wouldn't know just how a joint should be cooked."

"But couldn't he have asked you over the telephone?"

"Why, yes, I suppose he could."

"In any event, didn't it seem a little strange to you that he would call you down to the lodge on such a pretext? Especially considering the fact he must have known that you weren't too enthusiastic about him or his brother?"

"Well, it did seem a bit odd, but the fact that we weren't buddies wouldn't stop Horrie from asking me to do something he wanted. He thinks he has so much charm that he's irresistible."

"Perhaps so. Now, when he came back to you and asked about how to operate the stove and cook the joint, what happened?"

"I started to tell him, when, all at once, the telephone rang and Will Fairlee told him that . . . that Uncle John had been shot."

"So you hurried right back up here?"

182

"Well, yes. That is, as soon as Horatio had gone back toward Rafe's room to tell him what had happened."

"You say *toward* the room. Didn't he go in?"

"No . . . no, he didn't. He called out to Rafe as he went back, saying Uncle had been shot, and Rafe opened the bedroom door and stood there in a lounging robe."

"And what did Rafe say?"

"He said that David had probably done it, that he had been making a fool of himself, and that it was just what you might expect him to do sooner or later."

"Sounds true to form. Now something else: when Horatio first requested you to go to the lodge, didn't he ask you to tell the earl that you were going there and ask you to deliver a message to the earl that he, Horatio, would see him later in the day or something like that?"

Ann opened her eyes wide. "Why—why, yes he did. But how did you know?"

"An inevitable assumption, my dear Miss Winter. He wanted you to know, without the slightest doubt, that your guardian was alive when you left the Grange."

She gave him a stricken look. "And he was! And Horatio and Rafe were at the lodge all the time I was there, and neither could possibly have done the killing. And that means that David . . . Oh, you don't think that David did it, do you, Mr. Holmes? You will save him, won't you?"

Holmes replied, "I'm confident we will. I think Horatio is a very clever blackguard, but that this is once that he has overreached himself." He got up from his chair and took a turn about the room, rubbing his hands together in that peculiar way he had when things were going well. I wondered why he seemed so pleased. Then he turned back toward Ann and said, "And now I want to ask about another thing, if I may. Has David Rowe always slept in the room where he is now, when he's been here at the Grange?"

She gave him a puzzled look, then said, "Why, no. That is, he had a different room farther up the hall when he was a boy, and later always slept there when he came back here to visit. But recently he started sleeping in the room that he is in now—at the head of the rear stairs."

"How did he happen to do that? Did he ask to have a different room?"

"No, I'm sure he didn't. I only know that a month or so ago when he last came home for a visit, that Uncle John told Mrs. Jennings to prepare this room where he now is for him."

"And what reason did he give?"

"That it was a little more convenient if David should want to come and go without disturbing the rest in the house."

"And does he go out so much when he is home?"

"Hardly at all. In fact, I don't remember when he has. He comes here to visit."

"Interesting!" Holmes said. "Very interesting, indeed. It seems to me that I detect the delicate touch of the charming Horatio—" Then he suddenly broke off as we heard the sound of tyres on the gravelway outside, and Bilkins exclaimed, "Look, here's Dr. Petley now."

"Dr. Petley?" Ann echoed. "Why, he's the one that's been taking care of Rafe."

"Good!" exclaimed Holmes. "I have a question or two to ask the gentleman before he leaves." As he ceased speaking, a Ford runabout drew up behind the Grange and the doctor, a little, balding man, got out and came up the rear steps as we all went out to meet him. Bilkins told him what had happened and asked him to examine the old earl's body. Whereupon Holmes spoke up and said he thought it would be well if he looked at David Rowe as well, and give his opinion as to why the boy was in such a stupor, to which the doctor agreed.

"We are also somewhat concerned about Rafael

Plunket," Holmes said. "I understand you lanced a felon on his left hand day before yesterday. Was it very serious?"

"Oh, not too much so. Just a flesh felon, a common inflammation. Of course, these things are always painful, but once they are excised, they clear up fairly soon."

"So there's no danger of pneumonia because of poison in his system?"

"Pneumonia? Scarcely any at all. You see, there *is* no poison in the system. It's all localized."

"So there's no need for Rafael to be in bed?"

"In bed! A strong young fellow like him? Say, what's this about? He hasn't taken a turn for the worse, has he?"

"Oh, no, not at all. We're just interested. With this tragic death of the earl, I fancy we are all a bit upset."

When the doctor had gone, Holmes said, "Miss Winter, if you will kindly help, I would like to do a little investigating of my own. I want to look through our friend Hawkins's room if you can show me where it is."

"But the housekeeper has the keys," Ann demurred.

"Don't worry, there'll be no difficulty about that," Holmes said, drawing a skeleton key from his pocket. "Harrington, you had better stay here, if you don't mind, in case the Midgwick police should bring Hawkins in before we return."

After a time Holmes was back with Miss Winter, a look of satisfaction on his face; and shortly, Bilkins and the doctor joined us. The doctor made a routine report as to the time and cause of the earl's death, then announced that he had also examined young David Rowe.

"And did you find evidence that he had been drinking?" Holmes asked.

"Drinking!" The doctor's tone was one of amazement. "None whatever. But I did find indication that he had been administered a strong sedative."

"Would you be able to give an opinion as to what the sedative was?"

The doctor shook his head. "I wouldn't even hazard a guess. It could be one of any number of things. I can only say it must have been quite potent. The young fellow doesn't look as if he would be himself for several hours yet."

Holmes pulled a small vial out of his pocket and handed it to the physician. "Could the knockout drops have come out of this bottle?" he inquired. The doctor took it, glanced at the label, sniffed the few drops remaining and nodded. "They certainly could."

After a few more words, he left and we were discussing the result of his findings when a car drove up behind the Grange and parked. Two men in uniform got out, followed by Hawkins, whom they took by the arms and led into the room where we were. Chief Bilkins introduced them as members Digby and Jones of the Midgwick police force.

"Well, here's your bird o' paradise," said Jones, the younger and more aggressive of the two. "We picked 'im up at a pub and it looked as if he had already got a good start of making a day of it. Fair insulted he was when we clapped our nippers on 'im. Said the Hawkinses had been 'in service' ever since the time of Queen Victoria an' there had never been a breath o' scandal against any on 'em yet."

"Well, this time there's going to be more than a breath," Holmes said. Then he turned toward Ann Winter. "Miss Winter, do you suppose that you could find some refreshment for these men while we ask a few questions of Mr. Hawkins?" Then, addressing the two policemen, he said, "I'm afraid that we may be needing your services later, if you can stay here for a time." They assured him that they could and left to follow Ann while the rest of us adjourned to the library, from which the body of the late earl had now been removed.

As we entered the room where the mysterious murder of the old Grange's owner had so recently taken place, I thought that the pseudo-butler looked about him in a puzzled manner. I don't know what he had expected to see, but it was obvious that he had been imbibing too freely and was rather the worse for it. His long face was preternaturally solemn and his steps were exaggeratedly careful as he worked his way to the chair that Holmes indicated.

"What is the meaning of thish . . . er . . . outrage?" he demanded with heavy dignity, after he had laboriously taken his seat.

"I think you know," Holmes said smoothly. "You're being held for the murder of your employer, the late Earl of Glossmere."

"Why, thass . . . thass preposhterous," he said, having difficulty with the words.

"I think not, Mr. Fink."

"What'd you call me?" he asked, with the hint of fear in his eye.

" 'Fingers' Fink. Now, would you like to tell us just how you got the job here and what you were to get for putting the earl out of the way?"

A wary look came into the fellow's eyes, which were not focusing too well. "I don't know wha' you're talkin' about," he slurred. "An' I ain't . . . I'm not sayin' anything."

But Holmes seemed sure of himself. "I think that you will talk before we're through, Mr. Fink, if you want to save your hide. Now, do you want to tell what happened, or shall I?"

"It's like I said, I ain't talkin'," he said owlishly.

"Very well, then. About four years ago, after one of your more ambitious operations, you had to get out of the country and you went 'Down Under.' There you met Plunket and his brother, and it was eventually arranged for you to come here. After you came, Plunket persuaded his uncle, the earl, to make a new will, which the earl did, and locked it in his wall safe in the library here. To be sure that the new will left all the earl's property to him and his brother, he had you, with your well-known skill at manipulating locks, secretly open the safe and extract the will. Then, when he found that the new will did not quite conform to his wishes, he drew up another will that was the same in outward appearance as that of the earl and had you return the authentic one to the safe.

"Now the stage was all set, and he got the earl to arrange that touchingly effective ceremony of signing and witnessing the will. Then, on the day that this ceremony was to take place he had his accommodating brother Rafe sit close to the desk with the fraudulent will concealed in his pocket. Finally, at the proper time, at a signal from him, you stumbled into the room and put on the act that diverted attention so that the deft-handed Horatio was able to substitute the false will for the true one. By this neat bit of hocus-pocus he was able to get the signatures of the earl and the witnesses on the will that left all his earthly goods to the two Plunkets while Miss Winter looked guilelessly on . . . Shall I continue?"

But Hawkins—or rather, Fink—sat, with bleary eyes and long, lean face drained of all color, staring terror-stricken at him and said not a word.

"Very well, I will go on. After getting the fake will executed, it was necessary, of course, to dispose of the earl, and again Horatio called on you, the willing stooge, to do the dirty work."

Fink stirred uneasily in his chair and swabbed away the sweat that was now all but streaming down his elongated countenance. The beer and ale that he had consumed so copiously were doing their work. As he put away the great handkerchief with which he had mopped his cheeks and brow, he looked as if he were about to speak, but licked his loose, rubbery lips and kept silent.

"Not speaking yet? Oh, I know that you were going to say—that you have an alibi, that you have witnesses to prove that you were in Midgwick all morning; but it just won't wash. Witnesses can be bought. You could have easily started for the fair and then come back. The evidence is just too strong against you, Mr. Fink. Plunket, who has pretended to be your friend, has played you for a sucker and will throw you to the wolves while he and his worthless brother live it up on the money that you helped them get."

The erstwhile Hawkins squirmed and had recourse to the big handkerchief again, but still said nothing as he stared with that dull, spellbound look in his blurry eyes.

"Yes, you took orders from your real employer, Plunket. While he lay back and played it safe, you took all the risk. You went to Watley and got some knock-out drops day before yesterday. Here is the bottle. I called up the chemist where you got it and he remembers that long, sober face of yours and your sleek, plausible manner. You slipped the knockout drops into a drink you gave young Rowe last evening. During the night you unlocked his room—you're an expert in locks, remember?—left the near-empty bottle of whiskey there, stole his gun, dropped one of his gloves on the stairway to implicate him, and later shot the earl."

He leaned suddenly forward and shook his finger in the face of the trembling, perspiring Fink. "But you made one mistake, Fink. One terrible, fatal mistake." And his voice rose to an ominous shout as he said, "You forgot to wipe your fingerprints from the bottle of whiskey."

"I . . . I didn't. It's a lie. I . . . I . . ." Then the wretch's jaw went slack and a look that was a mixture of sheer terror and chagrin came into his fuzzy eyes.

Holmes leaned back, a look of satisfaction on his face. "It's no use, Willie," he said, almost pityingly. "You just aren't cut out for murder. You should have stuck to safe-cracking. It's more in your line."

"All right," Fink said in a desperate, whining tone.

"It happened just like you said, only I didn't kill 'im. I even got the gun, but I didn't shoot it."

"Who did?"

"I . . . I don' know. I swear I don'. I gave the gun to Horrie. I . . . I didn' even know they meant to kill 'im."

"All right," said Holmes, knowing the last was a lie, but not caring since he had got what he wanted. "Now we want the whole truth. It's either that and turn Queen's evidence, or let Plunket make you take the whole rap. How long do you think he would hesitate to throw you over if it would save his own skin? Are you ready to give a full statement and sign it?"

Fink nodded and mumbled an assent. He could hardly speak. We got out pen and paper from the desk and I took down the fellow's words as he poured out a full confession. Then he signed it, and Bilkins took him away and locked him in his room. When the chief returned, he said, "Good work, Mr. Holmes. But won't Fink be able to prove that he really was in Midgwick at the time of the killing?"

"Yes, I'm sure he will," Holmes replied calmly.

"Then what—"

"That was just a little by-play to get Hawkins—or Fink—to admit that he was working with the Plunkets. Now all we have to do is unmask the real killer, and he will help convict him."

Bilkins stared at him in stupefaction. "All we have to do! Are you serious?"

"Never more so. If you and the Midgwick policemen will pick up Rafe Plunket while Harrington tips off Hodges to take Horatio into custody, I hope we'll soon wrap up the case."

"But what charge—"

"For the present, make it 'conspiracy to defraud.' But if I succeed in getting the evidence I soon hope for, we will change the charge to 'murder.' "

"Very well, Mr. Holmes. I don't understand it, but I'm certain that you know what you are doing," said

Bilkins, looking as if he were not so certain as he said.

Holmes returned, "I assure you that I do. And, by the way, please drive down to the lodge by the back road. Miss Winter and I will be taking the path through the woods."

When the police chief had gone, Holmes turned toward me. "I'm going to need Miss Winter's help in my search. Please have her come to me. And another thing. You had better warn Hodges to watch his step when he apprehends Horatio. These Plunkets are a dangerous pair and may put up a fight."

But Horatio Plunket gave no trouble whatever when Hodges announced he was under arrest; just acted grandly unconcerned.

"You poor dumb oaf," he sneered, "you won't feel quite so cocky when I sue you and that country yokel that calls himself a chief for false arrest."

With the hotheaded Rafe, however, it had been a different story. When, some twenty minutes later, he was brought in, manacled, between the two policemen with Bilkins plodding behind, it was apparent that he had put up a stiff resistance before he had been subdued. The man called Digby had a badly discolored eye, Jones was nursing a swollen jaw, and Bilkins's moon face, though unmarked, was red and angry. As for Rafe himself, he showed no damage beyond a button missing from his coat and skinned and bloodstained knuckles on one hand.

The two brothers did not exchange a word as the quartet entered the room; but I saw Horatio throw a glance of fury and contempt at the younger brother while the latter glowered back with brash defiance. After that one flash they did not look at each other. Nor was a word spoken by any of the rest of us; we just sat there, grimly silent. Will Fairlee seemed the most relaxed of all, gazing curiously from one person to another with a look of quiet satisfaction on his face.

I do not know how long we sat there. It seemed a long time, although it probably was less than half an hour. At last the door opened and Ann Winter said that Holmes wished to see me and Chief Bilkins in the library.

When we were all seated, Holmes handed Bilkins a pair of black kid leather gloves and said, "There, Chief, is the evidence, I think, that concludes this case. Handle them carefully. They're covered with dirt and we don't want too much of it to come off. We may need it for evidence."

The police chief took the gloves and examined them gingerly. "But there's a finger missing!" he exclaimed.

"Precisely," Holmes answered. "To accommodate the bandaged finger on the killer's left hand. If you smell the glove, you will detect a slight odor of formaldehyde."

Bilkins sniffed at the glove and stared incredulously at Holmes. "Rafe?" he asked.

Holmes nodded. "Exactly."

"But how could he?"

"Very simple. He lay in hiding close to the Grange and near to the path till Miss Winter had passed him on her way to the lodge in response to Horatio's call. He gave her about ten minutes' time to reach the lodge, then slipped into the library, where he knew he would find the earl, shot him, leaped out of the window and ran back to the lodge, stopping to bury these gloves that had held the gun in a hole not far from the path. He was taking next to no risk of discovery; all the servants were away, young David Rowe was doped, Will Fairlee was almost sure to be in his room on the far west side of the house, and when Rafe returned to the lodge he would not be seen by Miss Winter, as his first-floor bedroom is so located as not to be visible from the part of the house that she would be in."

"But he couldn't have done it," Ann said. "He was in the lodge all the time that I was there. I heard him and I saw him. He just wouldn't have had time."

Holmes smiled and shook his head. "But he wasn't in the lodge all the time that you were there. He wasn't there when you got there. You saw him the second time that Horatio spoke to him, but not the first."

"But I don't understand. Who was it that Horatio talked to the first time?"

"Nobody at all."

"Nobody?"

"That's right. Do you remember, Harrington, that I told you that Horatio had an extra twist to his sleight-of-hand performance? It was a gimmick that would have been particularly effective when he had a confederate and staged a disappearing act or something of that kind. Horatio is a ventriloquist."

"So that's the way they worked it!" Bilkins exclaimed.

"Exactly. The timbre of the Plunkets' voices is much the same, as is often the case with brothers. So it was easy for Miss Winter to deceive herself and think that she was hearing Rafe when it was really Horatio simulating Rafe's voice, particularly as it was Rafe's voice she expected to hear. Then, too, you will recall, Horatio was some distance away when he put on his act, and she was not in a position to distinguish voices too clearly. Add to that the fact that when a ventriloquist exercises his talent his tones are somewhat muffled, it became quite easy for her to think that she heard Rafe speaking from inside the bedroom while Horatio stood near the door."

"But how could Rafe possibly appear at his bedroom door just before we left? I hadn't been there much more than ten minutes at the most."

"Ten minutes would have been ample," Holmes explained. "If Rafe were hidden near the Grange, it would not have taken him over five minutes to enter the library, which is on the east side next to the woods, and carry out the killing. And it would not have taken over five minutes more to get back to the lodge. It is no great feat for an athletic young fellow to run half a mile in two and a half or three minutes, even fully dressed and over ordinary ground. Remember, the path is well-traveled and smooth. As for burying the gloves, that would need but a few seconds—he had only to throw them into a shallow hole already prepared, drag a little of the loose dirt back over them with his shoe, tamp it down an instant, pick up some twigs and leaves already at hand and scatter them on top. Then back and through the bedroom window at the lodge."

"But how would he get through the window?" I asked. "It must be at least three or four feet above the ground."

Holmes nodded. "Yes, it is. But they provided for that, too. There was a box about the size of an orange crate that they could place beneath the window. I found it in some shrubbery in the woods, where Rafe had evidently hidden it after Horatio and Miss Winter left the lodge and before Chief Bilkins and the Midgwick policemen picked him up."

Bilkins said, "You haven't told us how you found the gloves. It's reasonable to expect that the killer would wear them not only to handle the gun—he would have wiped his prints off that—but to get in and out of the room. But how could you figure out where they were hidden and recover them so soon?"

"A matter of simple deduction," Holmes answered. "Rafe had to hide them quickly. But he could not throw them in the bushes the way he had the gun, and he would hardly take them back to the lodge, which might be searched in the remote chance that he and his brother were suspected. That left but one other alternative: burial somewhere in the woods.

"It was also logical to think that they would be buried near the path—remember that time was a vital element. If the Plunkets were to mislead Miss Winter into believing that Rafe was in the lodge all the time that she was there, he must get back there in time to appear to her in person before she left. It seemed probable, too, that the gloves would be buried nearer the lodge than the Grange: when they scooped out the hole where they were to hide them, they would be less likely to be seen, or if seen, they could have a plausible excuse such as preparing a place to bury garbage or something like that. Finally, I thought it more likely that the spot they chose would be near a spinney than in some open space.

"So we started at the other end, with Miss Winter on one side of the path and me on the other, looking for such a spot where the dirt had recently been disturbed. Actually Miss Winter found it. Her task was made somewhat easier by the fact that Rafe, in his haste, had left a heel mark in the soft, moldy woods soil. His shrewder and less heedless brother would have taken more care to cover up his tracks and make discovery more difficult. All in all, in the circumstances it was not too much of a feat."

Bilkins said, "I think it was. And I think it took more than a bit of doing to figure out the whole setup and solve the case so quickly." Then he gravely shook his head. "It was a fiendishly clever scheme. And it might have worked except for the glove. Even with Fink's confession a jury might have found grounds for reasonable doubt."

"Well, you can't think of everything," Holmes said. "And Horatio made one big mistake."

"What do you mean?" Bilkins asked.

"He didn't plan on Rafe's having a felon just at fair time."

"He made another bigger mistake," Ann Winter said.

"What was that?"

"He didn't plan on Creighton Holmes," she said with a smile.

As we were driving back to London from the Grange, I remarked, "Well, Holmes, old chap, you have another good illustration for that monograph you're going to write."

"What monograph is that?"

"The one on 'The art of Misdirection in the Commission of Crime,' " I replied.

The Murder of the Enigmatic Husband

Creighton Holmes and I were sitting together one evening in our lodgings on Baker Street. We had been discussing the circumstances of a startingly bizarre crime and its equally sensational solution when I asked, "What *is* the difference between a merely good detective and a great one, Holmes?"

"An interesting question," Holmes replied, "but one I think that I can answer. Imagination."

"Imagination?"

"Yes. Your really great detector of crime has the faculty of imagination highly developed. It is this that differentiates him from the merely good detective. But perhaps I had better explain."

"Please do," I said.

"Well, the good but not great detective has two outstanding qualities or he would not be good. He has the ability to observe and he has stubborn persistence—you know, the perseverance that impels him to look into every aspect of a case and to pursue every avenue of inquiry: to wear out shoe leather ringing doorbells, interviewing every potential witness, and running down every clue. But while your truly great detective also has these same qualities of observation and persistence, he must have something else."

"Meaning imagination?"

"Exactly. For instance, your run-of-mine detective goes into a room where a crime has been committed and sees some article out of place for no apparent reason. He may wonder about it but does not have the imagination that enables him to determine why the article is not in its accustomed place.

"But your great detective not only notices and wonders, but his mind will not rest until he comes to a conclusion as to why things are not as they should be. Are they as they are by design or chance? And if by design, what was the reason, to facilitate escape, to mislead or confuse the investigator, or what?"

"I think I see what you mean."

"Of course you do. It's the ability of the great criminologist not only to notice every detail that exists, but to analyze and correlate and interpret, that makes him more effective than his less gifted confrere. In short, after seeking out and sifting all the evidence he must be able to put himself into the criminal's shoes—even to enter his very mind—and thus reconstruct the crime."

It was this faculty of imagination, which Holmes possessed to a high degree, that enabled him to solve what I have chosen to call "The Murder of the Enigmatic Husband." It is also the only case on record in which his investigation earned him his fee but did not lead to the apprehension of the criminal, a fact most worthy of note.

We first got the word that led him to become involved in this unusual case on a dismal afternoon in mid-September. I had been confined to our quarters, recovering from a cold. I was desultorily reading and Holmes was busying himself with one of those everlasting experiments that took up his time when he was not actively engaged on a case, when a ring came at the door at the bottom of the stair and shortly a boy appeared with a telegram.

He took the wire, handed the boy a sixpence, and then read it. When he had glanced it over, he gave a short laugh and handed the paper to me. I looked at it and read as follows:

Need your services to solve serious problem stop come at once. G. Rumford

Holmes is quiet and not too self-assertive. But he is his own man, not given to toadying to anyone, no matter how rich or famous. I could hardly imagine that his reaction to this summary command—it could not be termed a request—would be anything but a blunt refusal.

"Well, of all the brazen cheek," I said. "He just cracks the whip and you jump. Of course you're not going."

His response to my heated inquiry was wholly unexpected. "On the other hand, my dear fellow, I think I shall."

I looked at him aghast. "You . . . you can't mean it?" I stammered.

"Oh, but I do," he said.

"Who is this G. Rumford?" I gasped.

"Sir Guy Rumford."

"Don't tell me—" I sputtered.

"That I've fallen for a title? Not at all. But it just happens that I like Sir Guy. He knew and admired my grandfather, and we have a mutual understanding that is quite comfortable. He may be a little dictatorial, but in the main he's not unreasonable. And if he says a problem is serious, it is. And incidentally," he added, grinning, "he's not niggardly with his fees."

"Where is this temperamental lord?" I asked, feeling deflated.

"Cosborough," he answered.

"And when do you propose to go?"

"Within the hour. It's about ninety miles from here. We should get there in time for dinner, with a stop along the way for tea."

"We?" I asked.

"Of course. I assume you're free to go?"

"Yes. I've no pressing literary deadline; but this cold—"

"Is too trifling to consider," he interrupted. "So I suggest that you start getting ready, unless you really don't want—"

"Oh, all right," I said, and began packing.

Cosborough, as you no doubt know, is a city of some forty thousand. We got there about seven of the clock and had no trouble securing accommodations at the Royal Lion, a comfortable old hostelry where, Holmes informed me, he had been accustomed to put up before.

We had no sooner got settled in than Holmes telephoned Lord Rumford of our arrival. The latter was quite put out that we had not come to Greystun, his huge, castlelike home located on the outskirts of the town, with a lowering windbreak of dark pine trees, and he insisted that we check out and move at once. But Holmes, who made it a rule never to mix social with business affairs, was steadfast in his refusal and the old lord finally grudgingly gave in.

He declared, however, that it was imperative that we get to the matter at once and all but ordered us to visit him that evening and acquaint ourselves with the facts of the case. Holmes, who was always impatient to get started on a new assignment, readily consented.

So it was that after a plain but substantial meal consisting of a joint and sundry vegetables together with a tasty pudding washed down with a bit of claret, we found ourselves at the ancient and gloomy pile known as Greystun. A melancholy butler with a long horselike face met us at the door and led us into the cavernous, dark-beamed room where the master of the forbidding old mansion sat huddled before a flickering fire with a shawl over his knees.

The ceremony of introductions being over, Sir Guy proceeded at once to enlighten us as to the occasion of his peremptory wire to Holmes.

"It's my niece and sole heir, Beatrix," he said. "She's all but accused of murder by a dumb oaf of a constable."

"Murder!" Holmes echoed. "Who was the victim and where did it take place?"

"Her husband, and good riddance, too, if you ask me," Sir Guy answered bluntly. "And it took place at The Larches, her home in New Midden, a village of three or four thousand about fifteen miles from here.

You may have heard of it. It is supposed to be something of a health resort because of its springs."

"Yes, I believe I have. What are the details as to the husband's death?"

"Well, about three years ago Beatrix, who is the only child of my deceased sister Isabelle, who was married to the Earl of Kernsey, met this fellow and married him. His name was Horace Dodd—at least that's the one he went by. But I'd not be surprised to find it was as bogus as everything else about him."

"Oh? Why do you say that?"

"There was something damnably mysterious about him. From all I ever heard, nobody seems to know where he came from or what he ever did."

"Sounds highly peculiar. How did your niece happen to marry him?"

"That's just it. She wasn't one of your sheltered females, inexperienced and naïve. She had traveled more than a bit and had met plenty of people. And always seemed to know her own mind—self-willed, you might say, though I don't imagine where she got it from."

I glanced at Holmes, but he did not change expression.

"Well, to go on," Sir Guy continued, "those of us who knew her best had about given up the idea that she ever *would* marry, though the Lord knows she was attractive enough and had had plenty of offers. Then this bounder came along and swept her off her feet. Fact of the matter is, I fancy, that she met him at a peculiarly vulnerable time. Her mother had been dead for some years, then her father, to whom she had been unusually close, suddenly died. She was nearing thirty years of age and not getting any younger. Anyway, it happened. I tried to warn her against the fellow, but it did no good."

"What was he like? He must have been a dashing sort to cause a woman like your niece to lose her head so completely."

Sir Guy shook his head. "He wasn't dashing. Few men near forty are, and he must have been close to that. But he had a fascination about him. Didn't talk too much and had an air of hidden depths and broad experiences. Didn't seem to put himself out to be particularly agreeable. Just the type to intrigue a woman like Beatrix."

"I see. Sounds like a calculating fortune hunter. Did your niece have much money?"

"Enough. And seemed to have much more than she did, living in that ancestral home with its aura of luxury and grandeur."

"What about his finances?"

"To tell the truth, I don't know. Seemed to have enough. Didn't spread it on. Too smart for that. But somehow gave the impression he had money. Dressed like a country squire—affected tweeds and a rough sort of golf cap and smoked a bulldog pipe. Didn't seem to have any definite business, but talked obscurely of weighty investments and big business deals, never anything specific. As I said, there was a kind of mystery about him. I think it was this that attracted my niece—at first."

"At first? You mean she became disillusioned?"

"I'm sure she did, although she never said anything about it. But there were unmistakable signs. When you saw her she never talked about him anymore, and they weren't ever seen out together. Things like that. And then, there was plenty of gossip. Matters like that become known—through the servants if by no other way. They were married for three years, but I suspect for at least two they had not lived as man and wife."

"I see. What were the circumstances of the fellow's death?"

"He was shot in their house—or, rather, hers—about ten minutes after nine of the clock night before last."

"How?"

"He was sitting in what he called his office or study—a room that had a desk where he could retire and pretend to be occupied with business affairs. But I fancy it was only an excuse to get by himself and read sporting magazines and sip a bit of brandy."

"And who discovered his body?"

"Beatrix. It was the servants' night out. She had been to a meeting of some kind of ladies' literary club that met once a month—it was thirty or forty years old, her mother had belonged to it before her—anyway, she got home earlier than expected; the speaker had failed to appear or something like that. At any rate, just as she stepped into the front hall, she heard a shot. It sounded as if it had come from the direction of the so-called study. She called out her husband's name, rushed to the room, and found Dodd in a chair with a bullet in his chest and the window open as if the killer had just made his escape through it."

"Was he dead?"

"Not quite."

"Did he say anything?"

"Yes. Beatrix went to him and he managed to say, 'Get Tom,' or something like that. She said, 'What?' and he roused a little and said 'Tom' again, then gasped and choked up blood and in a moment was dead."

"And does your niece know who this Tom was?"

"She hasn't the least idea. She thinks Dodd may have been semidelirious and was calling for some one intimate he had known—it may have been a friend or brother or even a son. Nobody knows."

"And why is your niece suspected of the murder?"

"It's this McCready, the fool constable at New Midden. He's never had a major crime to solve in twenty years. Doesn't know the first thing about modern detection methods except to get fingerprints."

"But there must be some reason for him to—"

"Oh, there was. But no reasonable man knowing the character of Beatrix would have given the possibility of her doing it a second thought."

"Nevertheless, my lord, perhaps you should explain. If I am to—"

"Very well," Sir Guy snorted. "There was a gun lay-ing on the floor. Beatrix saw it and picked it up. Just as she did, a dull-witted old fellow by the name of Joe Simkins, who acts as gardener and caretaker for the place, and who had not gone out that evening, heard the shot and came into the room and saw Beatrix standing near her dead husband holding the gun. When he told this to McCready, whom she had notified along with a doctor as soon as she had got her wits together, McCready promptly jumped to the conclusion that she had done it."

"A rather natural conclusion you'll have to admit," Holmes said. "Particularly in view of the talk that your niece and her husband were at odds. At any rate, didn't your niece tell him how she'd just got home and heard the shot?"

"To be sure, she did. But the stubborn ass wouldn't listen."

"But how about the open window? Surely this Joe Simkins could testify to that."

"Of course he could. But McCready brushed it off. Said Beatrix could have opened it herself to divert sus-picion. A likely thing to do!" he growled. Then he seemed to grow more calm and said in a different tone, "Of course, there *was* the gun."

"What about the gun?"

"Well, there were no prints on it except those of Beatrix. And I admit it did look a bit odd for the mur-derer to leave the murder weapon at the scene of the crime."

"But surely your niece could show that it did not be-long to her."

Sir Guy compressed his lips and shook his head. "That's just it. She can't."

"Can't?"

"No. You see, her father had quite a collection at one time of small arms of all makes—foreign as well as English. The murder gun was a big Colt .45. Simkins and one of the other servants think there was such a gun in the collection, and Beatrix herself says she isn't sure."

"But wouldn't an inspection of the collection—"

"It wouldn't do any good. When her father died, Beatrix sold off most of the guns, and the Colt .45—if that's what it was—must have been one of them. At least, there's no such gun now."

"But the buyer could tell—"

"If they could locate the buyer. But they can't. She sold the lot off piecemeal to different parties—most of them strangers. And she didn't keep a list of the names."

Holmes looked earnestly at the old lord. "This *is* serious. You're quite sure that your niece has told the exact facts? You don't know how much reason she may have had to get rid of her husband. And anyone driven to desperation—"

"That'll do!" the old lord thundered. "I know my niece, she's the most forthright person you ever saw. And she's warm-hearted. She'd never kill anyone. And if she did, she'd be the first to admit it. Now, do you want to undertake to clear her name or not? I'll have no shilly-shallying. You've got to believe she's innocent or I've no use for your services, much as I respect your talents."

He was glaring grimly at Holmes, who looked steadfastly back. Holmes's lips tightened and his voice was low but firm. "If your niece is innocent, you have nothing to fear. Besides, I would not be working for the police, I'd be working for you, and I would report the results of my findings to you and you alone. But I think you know me well enough to know that I cannot undertake an investigation with anything but an open mind. If you want to engage my services with that understanding, well and good; if not—"

"Oh, very well," the old man broke in irritably. "But you've got to make it clear to McCready that he can't railroad any niece of mine without sufficient evidence or I'll have his hide."

"I'll take care of McCready," Holmes said.

But when we met the constable the next day at his office about nine of the clock, I wondered if Holmes had not spoken too soon. McCready was a big man in his late sixties, with a huge torso and perceptible paunch, a full red face with mutton-chop whiskers, and a truculent, suspicious manner.

When we were seated, Holmes said, "We are here at Lord Rumford's instance to look into the death of this man Dodd."

"Aye," McCready said shortly. The mention of Sir Guy's name seemed to command wholesome respect; but the constable's reception of Holmes's news made it plain that he was not going to welcome what he considered the interference of an outsider.

"Have you completed your investigation?" Holmes went on.

"Aye."

"Perhaps you'd like to tell us what you found."

"There's naething to tell. The Leddy Beatrix kilt her hoosban' an' thot's aw there is to it."

"Would you mind explaining how you came to that conclusion?"

" 'Tis as plain as a pikestaff. She an' her mon didna' get along taegether an' she shot 'im. She was foon' standin' over him with the pistil in her hend. It couldna ha' been ony ither pairson."

"I see. And have you arrested her?"

"Nae. Not yit. But I be plannin' to."

"Are you sure that such a step is wise at this time?"

"An' why the no? I'm spearin' ye."

"Well, of course you know your own business; but, as you are well aware, sometimes it is one thing to be morally certain of a matter and another thing to prove it. And it could be awkward to be sued for false arrest."

"Fawse arreest?" the constable repeated, getting even redder in the face.

"Yes. As you know, of course, if a person is taken into custody without justifiable cause, he can sue for false arrest and recover damages. And Lady Beatrix, being the spirited young woman that she is, would be likely to do so. So, unless you are very sure of the facts—"

"Weel, noo," the constable said, his ruddy face puffed near to bursting, "well, noo, I'm thinkin' as she's the verra yin as would." He wiped his perspiring face with a great handkerchief. "But, mind ye, I ha'na arreested her yit. As I was tellin' ye, I was on'y thinkin' aboot it."

"Of course," Holmes nodded.

"Thot's no to say but she's as guilty as the de'il himsel', I'd ha' ye ken."

"Perhaps," Holmes agreed. "But it might be just as well not to express yourself too strongly to the effect just yet, either."

"Och, an' why—"

"It might lay you open to a slander suit," Holmes said.

"A slander suit! Why of aw the skelpin'—" the constable sputtered and then fizzled out like a firecracker that had failed to explode.

"The Lady Beatrix is highly respected in these parts and is likely to resent any reflection on her reputation," Holmes went on. "Being in the class of society that she is, it would not be surprising if she would claim damages for as much as a hundred thousand pounds."

"A hunnerd thou—" McCready stared at him in outraged disbelief, as he pawed at his collar. "Why thot's downright thievery. A hunnerd thousan' poon', did you say?"

"Yes. Of course, it is not likely that she would be awarded that much. Barristers always sue for more than they expect to get. Still, even a fourth of that is quite a sum—unless, of course, you are very wealthy. Then, too, there is your reputation to be thought of, not to mention your position, which naturally you might lose, if she were successful."

The constable sat and looked at him aghast. For once, he seemed at a loss for words. He had recourse again to the great handkerchief, at the same time shaking his huge head like a wounded bull as his jaws silently worked.

At length he said, "If a body canna arreest her an' canna accuse her, what's a body to do, I'm spearin' ye?"

"Well," said Holmes, relenting a little, "for the present you might be noncommital. I don't suppose the inquest has been held yet?"

"Not till the morrow."

"Very well. So long as you do not declare yourself publicly, there'll probably be no trouble."

"Weel, I ha'na, nor ha' I ony intention o' doin' sae," the constable said, and then added, "—under the saircumstances."

"A very wise decision," Holmes said. "Now I wonder if we might go into the matter of your investigation a little more in detail."

"Aye?"

"First, exactly what was Lady Beatrix's reaction when you questioned her?"

"Weel, noo, she didna greet as muckle as ye'd expect a lovin' wife to do."

"But that might be taken as an evidence of innocence, not guilt."

McCready gave him a puzzled look. "An' why wad ye be sayin' thot?"

"Well, she's a smart woman, and if she had really killed her husband, wouldn't she be likely to pretend to be overcome with grief, rather than otherwise?"

"Aye, mayhap she would." The constable nodded. "She's no sae doomb."

"Very well. Now, did she say anything that would bear out the fact that someone else might have been the killer?"

"Weel, she did say thot her mon had been actin' a bit str-range lately, as if he was afeared o' someone or something, but I wasna believin' ony sicka nonsinse."

"Oh. Anything else?"

"Aye, she do be tellin' some scrumly tale aboot a

208

meesterious aud mon coomin' to see her hoosban'; but 'twas just so muckle haver-claver an' I paid it nae heed."

"You mean you did not take it seriously?"

"Thot's right."

"I see. Now what do you know about the dead man?"

"We ken thot his name was Horace Dodd, thot he was the hoosban' o' Leddy Beatrix, 'n' thot he was murthered. What mair was there to ken?"

"It might be well to know something of his background: what he had done, who his friends had been—and who his enemies—things like that. I fancy that these are questions that Lord Rumford will expect to be answered before he accepts your—"

"Aye. The laird! The laird! The auld—" McCready said in a kind of yelp, then suddenly stopped.

"Yes?" said Holmes.

"The auld gentleman is verra pairticular," the constable finished weakly, and glared fiercely at Holmes as if daring him to deny it.

"I agree," said Holmes. "Now, just one more thing. How much of an inspection of the premises did you make, and did you find anything whatever to support the theory of Lady Beatrix that the attack was made by an outsider?"

"We lookit ower the room thor-roughly an' we examined the gun an' inter-rogated Leddy Beatrix an' the mon Simkins. An' we foon' naething to confir-rm ony sicka wierd theo-ry."

"Did you look over the grounds outside?"

"We didna. There wasna ony need."

"I see. I assume you have no objection to my seeing Lady Beatrix and looking over the scene of the crime? Sir Guy can be a little difficult at times, and I am sure he is going to demand a complete report from me."

"Aye. Thot's true enouch. I've no objaiction."

We bade good-bye to the constable, who absently grunted a response. I thought I heard him muttering something about "a hunnerd thousan' poon'" as we left.

The home of Sir Guy's niece, called The Larches, was an impressive-looking manor built in the Tudor style and located at the edge of New Midden on pleasant, rolling land amid larches, oaks, and beech trees. It seemed a place designed for happiness, not misery and sorrow.

The butler who admitted us, a youngish, wide-awake-looking fellow quite in contrast with Sir Guy's rusty old retainer, led us to a large, comfortable withdrawing room equipped with rich old furniture. He told us that his mistress was expecting us and that he would notify her.

Shortly Lady Beatrix appeared. She was in her early thirties, somewhat above middle height, with an attractive figure, dark hair and striking features, and an aristocratic air of self-assurance. I fancied that her intelligent-looking face was usually keenly animated, but now it was sober and subdued.

After we had exchanged greetings, she said, "I'm very glad you've come. I won't pretend that I am broken-hearted over the loss of my husband, because I'm not, though I *am* upset by the manner of his death. And I won't deny that I'm deeply concerned about my status as a primary suspect of his murder. The facts seem all against me, and while I try to think that Constable McCready is a well-meaning official, I find it hard to accept his arbitrary attitude regarding my guilt."

Holmes nodded. "I appreciate your position. But I think I've convinced him for the present that it would be unwise to take any immediate action against you."

Lady Beatrix's face brightened. "That's a relief," she said. "Now, what would you like to know?"

Holmes replied, "I know most of the facts about the actual killing, I believe; but I *would* like to find out as much about your husband as I can."

She gave a shake of the head. "I'm afraid it isn't much. I really knew next to nothing about him when I married him, and I haven't learned much since. Now that I look back, I realize that he never actually said anything about his past—just spoke in vague generalities. I'm sorry, but that's the way it is."

"I understand. Did he depend on you for money?"

"Not exactly. He never seemed to want for ready cash. I think he had money coming through the mail. He never opened his mail in my presence, but he did receive envelopes rather regularly by post which he implied to me were dividend checks. But I doubt if they were."

"Why?"

"Well, I have investments myself and I know what an envelope bearing a dividend check looks like, and the ones he got did not look that way."

"What do you mean?"

"Well, I don't mind telling you it did not take me long to wake up to the fact that I'd been foolish and headstrong in falling for his blandishments, and I soon had reason to think he'd married me for my money, because he began to throw out hints about how he could double or triple my income if I'd just let him handle my affairs. But I had too much sense for that and from that time on I became suspicious of him. I did not say anything, but I noticed that these envelopes coming to him had no company or bank name on them, did not come at exact intervals, and were mailed from different places."

"Very interesting," Holmes said, rubbing his hands together in that characteristic way of his when he was particularly aroused. "Did you happen to notice what these places were?"

"Yes, I made it a point to. They were from various cities, all fairly large: Binghamton, Brighton, Liverpool, Manchester—places like that."

"Did he have a bank account?"

"No. Not so far as I know—at least, no savings account. But a friend of mine at the bank in Cosborough

211

where I do business said that he had a safety deposit box there."

"Did the man at the bank have any idea what might be in it?"

"He thought it might be cash."

"Well, well," said Holmes, "this grows more and more intriguing. Now, something else. I understand that your husband said, 'Get Tom,' or something like that, just before he died. Lord Rumford said that you had no idea who this Tom might be. Is that correct?"

She answered that it was.

"Constable McCready said you thought your husband was afraid of something or somebody. Why did you think that?"

"Well, he got little mail, and, as I said, the little that he did get he never opened before me. But one day he received the mail when I was out of the room; then when I entered he was standing with an opened envelope in one hand and a newspaper clipping that he had evidently just taken from the envelope in the other. I came in just in time to hear him mutter a curse under his breath; then he heard me and turned. His face was white as chalk and his hands were trembling. He walked by me without a word and left the room. After that he seemed constantly in fear: always on edge, continually looking about him, and starting nervously at the slightest sound."

"But you never said anything to him nor he to you about it?"

"No. We were scarcely on speaking terms and he was very close-mouthed."

"And you have no suspicion as to what the clipping was?"

"None whatever."

"Nor where it came from?"

"Why, yes, I do know that. I am not usually the kind to pry into other folks' affairs; but, as I say, by this time I did not trust him and felt that I should know what was going on for my own protection. So, after the foregoing incident, I made it a point to look

212

into the wastebasket in the room he called his study, when he was out, and found the envelope that the clipping had come in. It had no return address, but was postmarked from Manchester."

"Good. Did you keep the envelope?"

"Unfortunately, no."

"Never mind. Did you notice how it was addressed?"

"'Mr. Horace Dodd, Esq.' in a man's handwriting. It appeared coarse and crude, but I'm not sure it wasn't disguised."

"And that's all you know about it?"

"Yes."

"Very well. The constable also spoke about a strange old man coming to see your husband. What can you tell me about that?"

"There was something very peculiar about that. But Reynolds was the one who talked to him, and I think he's the one who should tell you." And she summoned the butler.

"Yes, sir, I remember the incident very well, it was so odd," the butler replied in response to Holmes's query. "It was late in the afternoon when there came this ring at the door. I answered it and there stood this old man. He asked if Mr. Dodd was in, and when I answered 'no,' I asked if I could deliver a message. He gave a peculiar laugh—more like a jeer, it was—and said 'Tell him I owe him something and I'll see he gets what's coming to him.'"

"You're quite sure of the words?"

"Quite."

"Very well, go on."

"Then I asked him if he would leave his name and he said it wasn't necessary, that Mr. Dodd would know who it was. Then, of a sudden, he was gone. Just turned and hobbled away. I feel now that I should have done something about it. But it all happened so quickly that I was rather not myself, sir."

"Don't blame yourself. What could you have done?

You had very little to go on. What was the appearance of this old man?"

"It's hard to say, sir. It was almost dark and the lights were not on yet. He was somewhat above middle height and well-proportioned—leastways not too thin nor too fat. Would weigh something like twelve stone, I would say. Had grey hair and scraggly chin whiskers."

"What about his hands?"

"His hands? It's strange that you should ask about that, sir, because, oddly enough, I didn't see them. He was wearing gloves."

"Was it cold?"

"Not that evening. In fact, it was unusually mild for that time of year, and it was close to the first of the month, I mean September."

"And his neck—was he wearing a scarf?"

"Yes, he was. But how did you guess that, sir?"

"Intuition." Holmes smiled. "Now another question: what about this old man's voice?"

"His voice, sir?"

"Yes. Was it husky or clear?"

"Clear, or very near it, I would say. Oh, it was somewhat quavery—'cracked,' I believe, is the word used—but unusually mellow for so old a man. I remember thinking about it at the time."

"How old would you say he was?"

"Quite old. In the neighborhood of eighty, I would think. I judge partly by the way he walked when he went away—bent over and with a slow, shuffling gait."

"And did you tell Mr. Dodd when he came home?"

"Why, yes, I did, sir. But it was such an odd circumstance that I thought best to consult her ladyship first. She thought Mr. Dodd should be told, so I told him."

"And what was his reaction? Tell it exactly as it happened as near as you can."

"Very well, sir. Well, when I told him he seemed very upset and out of temper. Quite out of character, you might say. He said, 'I don't believe a word of it. You're making the whole thing up!' "

"I assured him that I was not accustomed to 'making things up,' as he called it. Then he asked if I had told anyone about it and I told him I had not. I didn't think it necessary to say that I had informed her ladyship.

"Then he said, 'See that you don't. I don't care to have my affairs blabbed all over the place. Besides, it doesn't amount to anything. This old gaffer was probably just a crackpot—if there was any old man.'

"I asked him if he thought the police should be notified, and he said, 'Don't be a fool, Reynolds. Why should the police be notified? And when I need any suggestions from you, I'll let you know. Is that clear?' "

"Interesting," said Holmes. "Tell me, was Mr. Dodd in the habit of addressing you so cavalierly?"

"Why, no, sir, not exactly. But it was plain that he was not used to dealing with those of us in service. He was not quite of the gentry, if you understand me, sir."

"I think I do. And you have been most helpful. Now, just one more question before you go. Do you know anything about what happened here on the night of the murder?"

"Nothing at all, sir. I was out all evening."

Holmes thanked him and, when he had gone, asked Lady Beatrix how many servants she had.

"Only three besides Reynolds and Simkins; a cook and two maids. In fact, only two now. The second maid is gone—left to get married on the night Mr. Dodd was killed. Would you like to interview them?"

Holmes said he would; but, as anticipated, when they were questioned, the two women only confirmed the fact that they had been away at the time of the murder and could contribute nothing, while Simkins only repeated what we already knew.

When the questioning was over, Lady Beatrix said, "It isn't very encouraging, is it? Do you think there is any chance that you can find the one who's really guilty, Mr. Holmes?"

"I think there's every chance in the world," Holmes replied.

"Do you really mean that?" she asked, in a tone in which eagerness was tinged with anxiety.

"I do, indeed. I'm hopeful that we will have a solution in a fortnight at most. Meanwhile, just to be on the safe side, I suggest that you renew your efforts to locate that gun of your father's, and also give me now the name and address of the second maid, who's now left you."

"Very well. I'll try again to locate the buyer of the gun. The maid's name is Josie Tuttle—or was—her married name is Ricket. They live in a little town named Plimpton. But I fear that she'll be of no more help than the others."

"Very likely not," Holmes agreed, "but I like to tidy things up. And now, with your permission, we'll inspect the grounds."

But this inspection held out little promise. A cement driveway passed under the window of the room where the killing had occurred so that there were no marks there; and, although it had rained on the day of the murder so that the ground was still somewhat damp, the grass to the rear of the house was so lush that when we did find footprints to bear out the fact that the murderer had made his escape that way, the prints were too indistinct to be of any use.

Then suddenly I heard Holmes call excitedly, "I say, Harrington, look here!"

I turned and saw him squatting some fifty feet away, looking intently at the ground. As I went toward him, I saw him straighten up and then step back. Then, just as I reached him, he held out a warning hand and said, "Be careful, don't spoil it!"

I came up and stood beside him and looked down. He was gazing at a roughly circular spot six or seven feet in diameter where a tree or bush had apparently been dug up and the ground leveled off and seeded. The seed, however, had not germinated very well, so that the spot was still almost bare. Now, almost in the middle of this spot, were the marks where a man had apparently fallen forward on his hands and knees.

"Isn't it beautiful—absolutely beautiful, old chap?" Holmes was saying.

I looked and saw two dents, presumably caused by the falling man's knees, and, farther forward, the imprints of his hands where he had slid forward. I admit that I did not see much of anything to appeal to my aesthetic sense in this muddy display and found it hard to share in Holmes's obvious rapture. All I could say was "Oh?"

But he appeared not to notice my lack of enthusiasm and said, "We'll have to arrange for a cast and a photograph of this. Then I fancy we'd better call on the constable and acquaint him with our findings." So, after warning Simkins to set stakes about the area and see that nothing was disturbed, we left in Holmes's motorcar.

On our way I asked him if he really considered the marks left by the falling man so important, he answered, "No doubt of it. When the killer left those imprints of his hands he might as well have signed his own death warrant. Now all we have to do is to find the man who fits the prints."

"But how can you hope to do that?" I asked. "You couldn't have been really serious when you spoke so reassuringly to Lord Rumford's niece. It's not like you to hold out false hopes, but I'm sorry to say that you seem to be doing so now. I can't say I blame you. Lady Beatrix is a very attractive woman and her plight would excite anyone's sympathy. But you have nothing to go on, just a jumble of facts that have no connection with each other."

"Oh, but they do, my boy. The fake dividend envelopes and the leering old man have a very definite connection, as does the newspaper clipping, I suspect. And if the dying words of the murdered man mean what I think they do, it should be quite a simple matter to find the man who made those prints, provided my surmise about Dodd is correct."

217

"What surmise is that?"

"That he was an actor at one time."

"An actor! But how could that help?"

"My dear fellow, it could be the key to the whole thing. But here we are at the constable's. Let us hope he's in."

Fortunately he was. But when Holmes told him of our discovery and suggested that he go to The Larches to examine the prints for himself, his reaction was what might have been expected.

"Och, ye be makin' a muckle oot o' a mickle, I'm thinkin'. 'Twas probably caused by soom bairn runnin' ower the proppity."

"Some child?" Holmes exclaimed, hard put to it to keep his temper. "But what would any youngster be doing there? Lady Beatrix's house has no other dwellings near it. Besides, the prints are much too big to have been made by any child."

"Mayhap and mayhap not. Who's to ken where a bairn will run? An' as for the size, you say yoursel' that the yin who did it slippit, so who can tell aboot the size? Nae, I see neething to git sae fashed aboot, ma laddie."

I could see Holmes take a firm grip on himself as he said, "You mean you're not going to examine the marks at all?"

"Hoot mon, I didna say thot. But just the noo I have soom verra important matters I'll be lookin' awfter."

"Murder is important, too," said Holmes with an effort to keep his composure. "And if it should come out at the inquest that you had failed to consider important evidence, I fear that Lord Rumford—"

"Och!" said McCready in a tone that was half whimper and half growl, "there ye go talkin' aboot the laird again. It do be eneuch to drive a mon daft."

"Then you will look at the prints?"

"Aye."

"Today?"

"Aye."

And we left, Holmes to go to the morgue in Cosbor-

218

ough where he proposed to get fingerprints of the dead man, and I to return to our rooms at the Royal Lion.

When he joined me there later, he said, "I'm going to get these prints off to Graham at Scotland Yard and see if the Yard has a record on Dodd, as I suspect it has. Then I'm going to write some lines to be inserted in the paper asking that the purchaser of the Earl of Kernsey's Colt .45 identify himself. After that I'll get a note off to Lady Beatrix's second maid. Then we'll just have to mark time until the inquest is over tomorrow."

The inquest brought out nothing we did not already know. It was apparent from the atmosphere that prevailed that Lady Beatrix was still under a cloud of suspicion, although there was little mention of her name. But if those present hoped to hear incriminating testimony from McCready, they were disappointed. Evidently the words of Holmes and the presence of Sir Guy at the hearing had their effect. The verdict was death at the hand of a person or persons unknown.

When we got back to the hotel Holmes said, "Sir Guy is going to London on some business connected with the House of Lords and will be back in about ten days, at which time we are to make a report to him. I'm going to Manchester tomorrow to find out what I can about that newspaper clipping. I've asked Graham to write to me there, and if I have anything to go on I'll look into Dodd's murky past. It'll be all rather routine and not too interesting, I fear. Would you prefer to go back to London? You may be of service to me there."

I suspected that this was Holmes's tactful way of saying he could work more effectively on his own, and I said, "Yes, I would. I've been thinking of an article I'd like to write and will be glad to get at it. Of course, if I can be of any help to you there, I'll do what I can."

"Good," he said. "You'll probably hear from me in four or five days."

But it was a full week before I heard, and when I

did, the content of his letter was quite unexpected. I had thought that his statement that I might be of service to him in London had been a polite fiction to salve my feelings, and was therefore surprised to read, in part, as follows:

> If your business will permit, I'd like you to ascertain the names of all those who ever played with actor Rupert Carstairs. As near as I can learn, the stage career of Carstairs started sixteen or eighteen years ago and lasted only four or five seasons. The securing of this information, therefore, should not be too difficult, but is vital to the solution of the Dodd murder.

Then followed a list of the names of London producers whom I was to interrogate and word that he would meet me at the Royal Lion two days hence.

This meant that I should drop everything else and comply with Holmes's request, which I was quite willing to do as I was master of my own time as a free-lance writer. I had helped Holmes before in a similar fashion and had no trouble pursuing my inquiries. At the first three producers whom I consulted I drew a blank. But the fourth proved more helpful. I found out from him that Carstairs's stage career had indeed been short: two years in the case of one play and three in another. He furnished me with the names of the cast of the first play and thought that a producer by the name of Max Steuer had staged the second.

But when I finally got by the secretary of Steuer to see him, he was not so cooperative. "I have been in business thirty-five years. I should remember every actor of every play I ever produced? Besides, I do not have time to look up the names of every one who has two-bit parts to accommodate somebody's friend. I am a busy man."

"I am sure you are," I said. "But this is in the interest of justice. A crime has been committed. Surely you want to help out."

"Justice? What is justice? I go to much expense—scenery, costumes, publicity, everything—to stage an A-One show and it's a flop. A snide producer puts on a lousy show, spends a few sixpence, and makes a bundle. Justice, phooey!"

"I'm sorry, Mr. Steuer, and I hate to encroach on your time, but we badly need this information. I'd be glad to pay ten pounds or any reasonable sum to get it. Now, can't—"

"Now you are talking business. That is a language I understand. Now let me see . . . Carstairs? Carstairs? . . . Just a minute. . . . Ah, that would be the part of the two-timing lover in *Young Widow Malone*. I'll have it for you most immediately."

When I reached the Royal Lion on the day that Holmes had designated, he was already there. As soon as we had exchanged greetings, he asked eagerly, "Did you get the information about Carstairs' fellow actors?"

"Yes," I answered.

"Good! And is there an actor on the list named Tom?"

"Tom? I don't think so. No. I'm sure there's not," I said.

His face fell. "The devil! But there's got to be. Otherwise this whole thing makes no sense. Let me see those names."

I handed him the programs with their two casts. He looked at them with a puzzled frown. Then suddenly his face brightened and he exclaimed, "Here he is! And very near the top of his profession. A shining mark—for blackmail. Reginald Thompson! He's our man! We've done it, Harrington, we've done it!" And he thumped me on the back.

"But I don't see—"

"No? Perhaps I should explain. I felt right away that those dying words of Dodd did not mean what they seemed; that, as a matter of fact, they were not the pleading words of a delirious man calling for some loved one. People don't get delirious from an injury to the chest. And it was entirely out of character—a fellow who preyed on society and thought only of himself—to call out for one he loved under such conditions. No, he had recognized his killer, and his last cry was one of vengeance, a cry to get that killer. What he was trying to say was 'Get Thompson,' but he was too weak to quite complete the name and so it came out 'Tom.' "

"All right. But how could you know that you were looking for an actor? I can understand—"

"It was really rather simple," he broke in. "In the first place, it seemed obvious that the pretended dividends Dodd was receiving were really blackmail payments. And secondly, inasmuch as these were posted from different places, it appeared equally obvious that they were mailed by some one whose calling required that he move from place to place. This at once suggested a commercial traveler or an actor. Then, when that mysterious old man appeared on the scene, I was sure it was an actor."

"But why?" I asked.

"Because it's quite clear that this singular individual with the chin whiskers and hobbling gait was not old at all."

"What are you talking about?"

"My dear fellow, people, even when they are old, don't ordinarily wear gloves and scarves on warm summer nights. You can fake an old man's face with a few lines and some whiskers, and you can counterfeit an old man's walk; but you can't make a young man's hands look old and you can't duplicate an old man's scrawny neck. And do you recall what Reynolds said about the strange caller's voice? Apparently it was really clear and resonant, although its owner tried to assume a 'cracked voice.' Actually an old man's voice almost always becomes thin and husky, characteristics that are difficult to simulate."

"But why would Thompson—assuming that it *was*

Thompson—want to call and have Dodd see him? He couldn't kill Dodd then."

"He had no intention of Dodd's seeing him. He had undoubtedly scouted the house and knew that Dodd was out. His primary purpose was to leave his threatening message so that Dodd would suffer some of the misery and torture that Dodd had caused *him*. He may also have hoped that his masquerade would throw the police off in their investigation of the murder when it was committed."

"I see. And I understand how we ran down Thompson through this fellow Carstairs. But who was Carstairs?"

"Carstairs is—or was—Dodd. But maybe you would like the whole story. Perhaps I should start at the beginning."

"I wish you would."

"Very well. To find the killer it seemed necessary to me to know about Dodd's past so that we might determine the motive for his murder. So, as you know, I wrote my friend Graham at Scotland Yard enclosing Dodd's fingerprints. As I anticipated, he had a record. It seems he was a thorough rascal engaged in all sorts of skulduggery. But he had a plausible front and a persuasive tongue, and his principal role was that of a con man with a little blackmail on the side.

"He had been arrested more than once, but never convicted—always managed somehow to beat the rap. Then he stepped out of character, which was his near downfall. Two old hands at safe-cracking named Gunner Blodgett and Jocko Skaggs planned a job in Manchester. A third member of their gang was 'doing time,' and they pressed Dodd into service.

"The job was pulled off successfully at the Empire Bank and they made their getaway with about fifty thousand pounds. But they were under suspicion, and when the heat was on, Dodd ratted on his pals. The police had very little to go on, so Dodd was promised complete immunity for turning Queen's evidence because the police were extremely anxious to nail Blodgett and Skaggs, whom they had been trying to get for a long time. So Dodd got off scot-free and his two pals were sent up for long stretches.

"The result, of course, was that Blodgett and Skaggs had no use for Dodd, cursed him up and down and said they'd get even with him if they ever got out of prison. It was also reported that Skaggs's father, an old ex-con with a long record of his own, vowed that sooner or later he was going to see that Dodd got what was coming to him—which was taken as no idle threat as the old man was a vicious criminal with a reputation for violence.

"Most of the money that was stolen was recovered, thanks to Dodd, but there was some five thousand pounds that was not. Dodd said that the missing money had been lost in the escape; but the police suspected he was holding this sum out and had it stashed away somewhere. So they kept an eye on Dodd, partly to protect him from old Peter Skaggs and partly in the hope of tracing the missing money.

"Then suddenly Dodd disappeared—dropped completely out of sight. The guess is that he holed up somewhere with a relative or friend in some isolated spot. Maybe Dodd cut him in on part of the stolen money he'd held out—if he did hold out any. At any rate, while in hiding he changed his whole personality, thanks partly to the fact that he was a natural actor. It should be noted that his real name was not Horace Dodd but Al Mudge, although he had other aliases as well. But by tracing him down to his home town I found that at one time he'd been an actor under the name of Rupert Carstairs, until some shenanigans drove him out of the profession.

"Well, to bring you up to date, as I said, he changed his entire outward appearance during the two years he is supposed to have been in hiding. He went in as Al Mudge, a glib talker with a trim figure who wore form-fitting suits and a snap-brim hat and smoked cigarettes; he came out as Horace Dodd, a sedate and deliberate talker who wore loose-fitting tweeds and a flat cap and sported a bulldog pipe. Add to this the fact that he grew a sweeping Dundreary moustache and you have a shorter, stockier, older, more dignified Dodd who would be hard to identify with the young, slick, cocky Mudge.

"There's just one more thing. I went to the offices of the *Manchester Guardian* and examined their files covering several days for a period about two weeks back, and I found the article that was probably in the clipping that was sent to Dodd. It told of the death of Jocko Skaggs in prison and then went on to tell how the Queen's evidence by Al Mudge—whom we know as Dodd—had put him there, and how old Peter Skaggs had vowed vengeance against Mudge, hinting that now the elder Skaggs might be moved to carry his threat out if given a chance."

"Do you think that Skaggs's father sent Dodd the clipping?" I asked.

"I doubt it. I think it quite unlikely that he would advertise his intention if he really meant to kill Dodd. It's more reasonable to think that Thompson sent it to scare Dodd. He wanted his tormentor to suffer some of the torment he had endured."

"I suppose you're right," I said. "There's just one question I'd like to ask about the murder itself. The gun used was a most unusual gun. How would Thompson get hold of such a weapon?"

"He made an American tour last year, if you recall. He could have picked it up then. Its dramatic potential might well appeal to him. Its formidable size and the thunderous sound of its report would make it a wonderful 'prop' for a shooting scene on the stage. And it was ideal as a weapon against Dodd. If Thompson had told no one he had it, it would never lead to him as a suspect, if found."

"But why would he abandon it at the scene of the crime?"

"He probably didn't intend to. He thought he was alone in the house that night with his victim. Then, when he heard the front door open and Lady Beatrix call out her husband's name, he panicked—remember, he was not a hardened criminal. He hastily wiped the gun off and dropped it, opened the window, and sprang out. If he should be caught he didn't want to have the gun found on him."

"I see, and I confess you make Thompson sound like the logical suspect; but can you *prove* his guilt?"

"I have the proof right here," he said, tapping his briefcase.

I asked, "What do you do now?"

"Well, Sir Guy returns tomorrow. We'll make our report to him and then see McCready. I fancy that even he cannot refuse to act on the evidence we shall give him. But just now I suggest that we see Lady Beatrix. She should be relieved when she gets our news."

But when we saw her ladyship, her reaction was far from one of rejoicing, and we encountered an unforeseen obstacle in our path. She listened to Holmes's recital with absorbed interest, her expression changing from one of attentive curiosity to doubt and concern and then to shocked disbelief.

When he finished, her face was white. "I don't believe a word of it," she said.

"Why not?" Holmes asked, stunned.

"Reggie would never do such a thing."

"Do you know him?"

"Of course I do. I have not seen him for years; but he used to come here with his folks every summer. His mother wasn't well and thought the springs helped her. He still has an aunt here now. She's a sort of recluse—never goes anywhere and no one hardly ever sees her."

"But how well did you know him?"

"Very well. He's been in this house dozens of times. I knew him as a boy, but he was stagestruck even then—always was bent on being an actor. When he was here for the last time he was barely grown up."

226

"What makes you so sure he wasn't the murderer?"

"He was not the killing type. He was . . . well, kind and gentle. And he is not the philandering type—always having an affair with a different woman like so many actors. No, he just couldn't have done it. And are you trying to say that my hus— that Horace Dodd blackmailed him for fifteen years? It doesn't make sense."

"No, it doesn't. And I'm not saying that. It probably started just lately."

"But after all this time?" she asked fiercely. "How do you explain that?"

"There might be several explanations. He would hardly have been a subject for blackmail when he was a poor and struggling actor; but he would be now that he is rich and famous. Besides, it may have just occurred to Dodd lately that he would be a likely source of income, and I fancy Dodd was not one to turn down a chance to make a dishonest penny wherever he found it. Or something might have happened recently to make Thompson more than usually vulnerable. Tell me, your ladyship, do you know of anything in your friend's life that might make this the case?"

For the first time, it seemed to me, I saw a look of doubt come into the eyes of Lady Beatrix. "Well, I did hear that he'd recently become engaged to a very nice woman. But I still can't believe—"

"That could well be it. Don't you see, your ladyship, that a man could become desperate if he thought the revelation of something shady in his past would lose him the woman he loved? Almost anyone will kill under—der certain circumstances. There are times when it seems almost justified. And we don't know what misery and torture Thompson may have gone through. You can get pretty distraught when you are at the mercy of a bloodsucker like Dodd."

"But why would Reggie have to kill him? Why couldn't he just have threatened to expose Horace Dodd for what he really was and silence him that way?"

"Because Dodd would have merely laughed at him. Told him to go ahead, and then he, Dodd, would tell what he knew about Reggie. Don't forget that Dodd was an experienced rascal who could not be easily scared. No, Thompson could see only one way out, and that was the death of Dodd.

"I'm sorry, your ladyship, but it all fits together. Reginald Thompson had an impelling motive and he had the perfect setting for his crime. He could come here and stay with his aunt—tell her he was here for a rest and wanted absolute privacy—and she would not betray his presence. He had not been here for years, and the townspeople were used to strangers coming here for the springs, so with a very slight disguise he could go about unnoticed. What's more, he was familiar with your house and the habits of your household. With a little discreet checking he could be sure that you and the servants would be out on the night of the killing. But one thing went wrong: you came home earlier than expected and ruined what might otherwise have been a perfect crime."

"You mean you have proof of his guilt?" Lady Beatrix asked.

"Yes," Holmes replied. "I do. Tell me, your ladyship, had Reginald Thompson lost the greater part of his left little finger?"

She gave him a worried look. "Why, yes, he had," she replied.

"Look at this," Holmes said, opening his briefcase and pulling out a photograph of the handprints we had discovered in the backyard of The Larches.

Lady Beatrix looked at it and gasped. "I . . . I fear you're right," she said. Then she gave Holmes a stricken look and said, "But Dodd was such a beast and Reggie such a nice boy. Do you have to punish him?"

Holmes replied, "I have nothing to do with his punishment. That's up to the courts. I don't even have to arrest him, and couldn't if I would. I'm not an officer of the law; I'm a private investigator."

228

"Who else knows about this?" she asked.

"No one but Harrington and me—and yourself."

"And do you have to tell it?"

"I'm afraid we do. Just now it seems the only way to clear your name."

"Then you'll kindly keep this information to yourself."

"But your uncle hired me to free you from suspicion. He's paying me a fee and—"

Lady Beatrix turned on him with flashing eyes. "Mr. Holmes, is a fee worth more to you than the life or liberty of a decent man? If it's money you're worried about, I'll pay—"

Holmes flushed. "Pardon me, your ladyship, but I'm afraid you don't understand. Money is not the point. I have a duty to perform. I promised your uncle that I would see that you—"

"Oh, fiddle-faddle!" She cut him short with disgust. "How does my good name compare with the shame and ruin of someone who's been victimized? Besides, this supposedly scandalous act of Reggie's may not have been so awful, after all. He wasn't low and vicious. His parents were dead and he was young and poor and alone. Whatever it was, Horace Dodd probably cooked it up and got him into it. No, Mr. Holmes, if you think I'll stand by and sacrifice a . . . a person like Reggie for the sake of my own reputation, you're mistaken."

I never saw anyone more angry, and I could see that Holmes was visibly moved. "If we do not expose Reginald Thompson, do you have an alternative to offer?" he asked.

"I can't say that I do," she said.

"I never got any results from my advertising for the purchaser of your father's Colt .45 gun; have you had any better success?"

"No."

"I've written twice to your second maid without any reply. Have you heard from her?"

"No, and it would do no good if I had. She was out that night, as the other servants were."

"Which rather leaves us at an impasse," Holmes commented. "Do you realize what will happen if we do not expose Thompson?"

"I think I do."

"It means you might be charged with murder, to be followed by the anxiety and uncertainty you'd have to undergo while awaiting trial. After that there would be the ordeal of the trial itself, with the badgering of lawyers, the vulgar stares of spectators, and the ugly whispered comments. Then, if you were found guilty, there would be the punishment to follow, which I'll not dwell upon. And even if you were declared innocent, things could never be the same. There would still be those who thought you guilty, and you'd always be shunned and vilified."

"I know all that. I think I could live with it."

"I believe you could," agreed Holmes. "And I respect your attitude. But what am I to say to your uncle?"

"You'll say whatever you think best; and it's for you to decide whether you bring Reggie's name into it or not. But I would like one thing clear. If Uncle Guy so much as breathes the name of Reginald Thompson in connection with this thing, I'll never speak to him again. Never! Is that clearly understood?"

"It is, your ladyship. And I regret to say that at present I see no way out of this situation."

"I'm sorry, too—for your sake as well as mine, Mr. Holmes. But I could never live with myself if I took any other course."

When we left, I had never seen Holmes so depressed. He stared straight ahead with grimly compressed lips and drove on in silence.

"What are you going to do?" I finally asked.

"Tomorrow I'll go to Plimpton to interview the second maid. After that, I don't know."

I said, "But you know yourself it'll be useless to see that maid. Lady Beatrix said—"

He gave me a withering look and I subsided.

From then on, not a word was spoken. When we reached Cosborough it was a little after four of the clock and we stopped at a gay little tea shop where they had crisp, tasty scones and well-brewed tea and where we had stopped before. But it did nothing to cheer us. Today the atmosphere seemed drab and the food dull and tasteless. We made no attempt at conversation and we left as gloomy as we had entered.

We reached the Royal Lion and went up to our rooms. Holmes started to look up the best route to Plimpton while I made a pretense of reading. All at once there was a rap at the door, and when Holmes opened it, the boots standing there said, "There's a Mr. and Mrs. Rickert in the lobby to see you, sir."

"Send them up," Holmes said, handing the lad a tip.

The couple, when they appeared, were unimpressive-looking, undersized, and cheaply dressed. The girl was scarcely over five feet tall, with a pretty, characterless face and jittery manner. The boy, who was only five or six inches taller, with sturdy, compact build, was somewhat more composed, but still ill-at-ease.

"I'm Lady Dodd's second maid—or was," the girl said in a nervous, high-pitched voice, "and this is my husband Ernie."

Holmes introduced us, and when we were seated, the girl said, "We got your letters when we come back from our . . . our honeymoon, an' we come right here soon as we could. We was in the country, didn't see no newspapers nor nothin', an' didn't know nothin' about Mr. Dodd being killed till we got back. I couldn't see no sense in seein' you, but Ernie says as how we should, so we come."

"You did just right," Holmes assured her. "And we'll see that you do not lose by it. Your expenses will all be paid."

Ernie said, "That isn't necessary sir, we—"

But Lizzie was breaking in. "I always tried to be a good maid to Lady Dodd an' she never complained about my work. I don't see how she can think I had anything to do with Mr. Dodd's bein' kilt. I'm sure—"

"It isn't that," said Holmes placatingly. "There's no reason to suspect you. We just want some information."

"Well, we can't tell nothin'. We didn't do nothin' an' we didn't see nothin'. O'course, we did use the front stairway, an' I told Ernie at the time as we shouldn't 'a done it. But he said it couldn't make no difference an' it did save a mort o' time not to go down the backstairs an' out the service door, an' my bag was awful heavy an' we was in a hurry 'cause we was late. I says to Ernie—"

"Yes, I can see," Holmes interrupted, trying to dam the flood, "and I realize it was a great accommodation for you to come here. We didn't expect that. We really meant to go to you; but now that you are here, I'd like to ask some questions. It may not help us much, but a man's been murdered and we need all the information we can get, if we are to find the murderer. So now, if you don't mind, I'd like to put a few queries."

"I wish you would, sir," said the boy, rather taking over. "I told Josie that was all you'd want. But she was scairt and 'fraid someways we'd done wrong. It'll be all right, honey," he reassured her, placing his hand on hers. "Now, what is it you want?" And he turned back toward Holmes.

"Just tell us what time you and Josie left that night and the circumstances of your leaving."

"Well, it was this way. I was in Cosborough that day an' a friend o' mine was to drive me over to Lady Dodd's an' we was to pick up Josie in time to catch the train for Plimpton at nine twenty-seven—Plimpton's where me an' Josie's folks live. We was goin' to be married two days later an' then we was goin' fer a week's honeymoon at a cabin on the Wye River, where I was goin' to do some fishin'.

"We was to pick up Josie about forty-five minutes

after eight of the clock; but we didn't get there till after nine an' so had to hurry. That's how it happened that we was goin' out by the way o' the front stairs 'stead o' the back ones. I couldn't see how it would do no harm; anyways, we didn't have no choice if we was to catch the train, an' if we didn't, everythin' would be ruint— all our 'rangements to get married an' everythin'.

"Anyways, that's what we done, an' jest as we was onto the upper landin' o' the stairs, the front door opened an' in come Lady Dodd. We was scairt 'cause we knowed we shouldn't 'a been there. There was a little light in the lower hall but none on the landin', an' we was kind o' in a shadow an' couldn't be seen. So we stopped dead in our tracks an' kep' quiet, hopin' Lady Dodd wouldn't see us.

"Then, all of a sudden, there was what sounded like a shot an' Lady Dodd yelled 'Horace' er somethin' an run through the downstairs hall toward the back o' the house, an' we run down the stairs an' out the front door.

"That's all we know, Mr. Holmes, honest it is. Then we was married an' we went on our honeymoon an' we didn't see no paper er know nothin' about this here Mr. Dodd bein' murdered till we got back to Plimpton. Then we found these letters from you sayin' you wanted to question Josie an' we didn't know what to do. Josie was scairt an' said we shouldn't see you, but I said there wasn't nothin' to be afraid of an' that we should.

"So we wanted to come to Cosborough to buy some things anyways, an' the first chanct we got, we come—an' that's all we can tell you, an' that's the truth."

"I'm sure it is, and thank you very much," Holmes said. "I have just one question or two I'd like to ask."

"What's that, sir?"

"From what direction did this shot that you heard come?"

"We wasn't even sure then it was a shot. An' I couldn't say zackly where it did come from. But it

233

sounded like it was somewhere below us an' toward the back."

"In the house or out?"

"We couldn't say, but seemed like it was inside er clost to it."

Holmes got up, and the rest of us arose, too. He drew a banknote from his wallet and handed it to the boy. "Thank you both for coming here. You have been a great help. Here's something to help out with your expenses."

Ernie looked at the note and gasped. "But this is too much, sir! Our expenses wasn't near this much—an' we was comin' here, anyways."

"Keep it," Holmes smiled. "It's worth much more than that to me. Now, just one thing more. I'd like to write out your statement and have both of you sign it." He glanced at his watch. "It's now twenty minutes after six of the clock. If you'd care to eat here at the hotel at my expense, I'll get the statement ready. You may order anything you like."

"Oh!" Josie ejaculated with round eyes. Then, her face all aglow, she turned and said, "Ernie, do you think we could?"

"Yes," said Ernie as he seized Holmes's hand and shook it. "Thank you, sir! I say, this is jolly good of you!" Then he took Josie's hand and the two of them left for the dining room like two children about to open their stockings Christmas morning.

As we looked after them, I exclaimed, "Well, that was lucky!"

"Perhaps," assented Holmes. "But I wonder how lucky we would have been if we hadn't followed through and written that we wished to question her." To this I made no reply.

The next day we saw Lord Rumford, and Holmes made his report. First, to relieve Sir Guy's mind, he told him of the information we had received from the

Rickets, confirming the fact that Lady Beatrix had reached her home just as the fatal shot was fired.

Then he told in detail his investigation of the background of Horace Dodd and the various villainies in which Dodd had indulged, ending with an account of the burglary of the Manchester Bank, the ratting of Dodd on his accomplices, the threat of the elder Skaggs to "get" Dodd, and the receipt by Dodd of the newspaper clipping that presumably told of Jocko Skagg's death. I noticed that throughout the recital he studiously avoided any reference to the fact that Dodd had ever been an actor and made no mention whatever of Reginald Thompson.

"Excellent!" Sir Guy said when he was through. "That clears Beatrix of any hint of implication that she was involved in her husband's murder. Now I'll give this information to McCready and see that he runs down the real culprit. It's that Skaggs fellow, no doubt."

"I don't know as I would do that," said Holmes in a dubious tone.

Sir Guy looked at him in amazement. "Why not?" he demanded.

"For Lady Beatrix's sake. She has endured three years of torment and humiliation in the company of this fellow, not to mention the suffering that comes from the calumny and suspicion that she is guilty of her husband's death. She is a brave and wonderful woman; but I doubt if she can take much more. I am very sure that the sooner all this can be forgotten, the better for her. And is it really so important that Dodd's murderer be apprehended? He's well out of the way. And as for McCready, what do you owe him? If he had had his way, your niece might now be on her way to prison or even to her death."

"By Jove, Holmes, you're right! I'll let him stew in his own juice."

When we left, I said, "It looks now as if Lady Beatrix would not have to worry about her friend Reggie Thompson."

Holmes shook his head. "I'm afraid that I have to disagree. The English police have an aversion to murder and they have a way of tracking murderers down if at all possible. I fancy that we'll find that there'll be further action when the newspapers start to clamor for results. Which suggests to me that I'd better call Lady Beatrix and warn her that it would be just as well for her butler to forget about the gloves and scarf when he's questioned again about that mysterious 'old man.'"

As usual, Holmes was right. It was not long after we returned to London that we heard that the matter of the murder investigation had been taken out of McCready's hands by Richard Radnor, Chief Constable for the shire, while Sir Wilfred Amberly, Queen's Counsellor, was announcing that solution of the crime would be "pursued with the utmost vigor."

I am not one to condone murder, but I must confess that my sympathies were all with the "nice boy" whom Lady Beatrix had known in her youth. He had resorted to extreme means only when driven to it through sheer desperation. Why should he be punished? Society did not need to be protected against him. He would never kill again. And after all, what harm had he done? Getting rid of Dodd had been a public service. It would have been better for the world if he had been disposed of long before.

Then we heard that Dodd's strongbox at the Cosborough Bank had been opened by the police authorities and had been found to contain some two thousand pounds in cash. It was further reported that, after diligent inquiry, this had been identified as part of the money stolen from the Empire Bank of Manchester, and the so-called Dodd was now known to be Al Mudge, con man, extortionist, and member of the Skagg-Blodgett gang.

A few days later came word that the police had a

definite suspect under surveillance and it was only a question of time until the murderer would be apprehended. Did this mean that they had at last ferreted out Al Mudge's connection with the stage and that this would lead them, as it had Holmes, to Reginald Thompson? I could not help but wonder how he was feeling now, of the worry and tension he was undergoing, the sleepless nights he was enduring, the nervous meals choked down . . . Clearly the hunt was on and the chase was getting hotter.

Then one day came the end. Holmes got a letter with a newspaper clipping enclosed. He looked them over, then tossed them to me. "From Lady Beatrix," he said. The letter was a polite note of transmittal. The clipping was from the previous day's issue of the *Cosborough Daily Journal*. I read it with eager interest.

It stated that Peter Skaggs, ex-convict and father of Jocko Skaggs, had died suddenly at his home in Hoddersgate on the foregoing afternoon. It then went on to tell about the Manchester Bank burglary, the ratting of Al Mudge on his accomplices, and Peter Skaggs's vow of vengeance.

Then, after a reference to the marriage of Mudge, under the alias of Dodd, to Lady Beatrix Kernsey, beautiful and talented niece of Sir Guy Rumford, one of the first lords of the realm, and his subsequent murder, it ended as follows:

Since Mudge's death the police have relentlessly sought his killer. Now it can be revealed that Skaggs was about to be taken into custody as the guilty party. Thus death has evidently saved Skaggs another conviction in a long career of crime. Today Chief Constable Radnor announced that all further investigation would be discontinued and the file on the case marked 'closed.' So ends the most puzzling and celebrated crime that ever disturbed the peace of the quiet little village of New Midden.

"Well, this means that at last the case is definitely over and Lady Beatrix can breathe freely again," I said.

"Yes," nodded Holmes. "And she deserves to. She is a very admirable person. Too bad she couldn't have married the boy she really loved. Let's hope that the 'nice woman' he's engaged to loves him as much."

The Case of the Bewildering Alibi

Some of the criminal problems that my friend Creighton Holmes was called upon to solve were intricate and involved, requiring not only the exertion of all of his keen powers of observation and deduction but long and painstaking investigation before he arrived at a solution. Others, while seemingly quite baffling to the average individual engaged in the detection and apprehension of criminals, were solved immediately by Holmes with no investigation whatever. Such was the incident that I have chosen to record as "The Case of the Bewildering Alibi." Yet, simple as it appeared to him, to me it was one of the most fascinating and bizarre of all the varied cases in which this talented grandson of the illustrious Sherlock Holmes was ever involved. Moreover, eventually it was to take us across thousands of miles of ocean to witness its dramatic denouement.

At the time that Holmes was first consulted about the matter he was at loose ends and, as usual in his periods of inactivity, was fretting like a spirited horse long penned in a stable. Only the week before, he had brought about the successful recovery of some indiscreet letters of the Viscountess Pemberton, a revelation of the contents of which might have caused serious scandal in the highest circles of society in the country.

Now, with this delicate commission out of the way, he had no other matters of a criminal nature to demand his immediate attention and only the prospect of

239

a few days shooting at the estate of Lord Fitherby for whom, as Holmes put it, he had at one time "performed a slight service." But that outing was still some two days in the future and meantime, nervous and ill-at-ease, he was putting in the time as best he could.

Just now he was engrossed in reading a book on mesmerism, a subject, along with others related to it, that had absorbed much of his interest for some time. At length, however, the book appeared no longer to hold his attention and he laid it down. Then, turning toward me as I was leafing over the sport pages of the daily to ascertain the latest standings in cricket, he pursued the subject.

"Did you ever stop to think what a large part thought control plays in the perpetration of crime?" he asked.

"Why, no," I replied absently. "Frankly, I haven't. Do you think it does?"

"No doubt about it. How otherwise do you explain the hoary hoax of a total stranger inducing some victim to go to a bank to draw out all of his life's savings as a 'proof of good faith' in order that the dupe may share in the division of a roll of money that he has seen the stranger 'find'?"

"I suppose that there is something in it," I said.

"Of course there is," he went on, "just as there must be something of the kind in every case where a smooth confidence man is involved. Which leads to another thought."

"What's that?" I asked.

"If the criminal can successfully exert some sort of hypnotic influence in the perpetration of a crime, why could he not, in somewhat the same way, misdirect the police in their efforts of detection after a crime is committed."

"Sounds like sheer nonsense to me," I said, and returned to my reading. But later I was to ponder these words of Holmes and wonder if, after all, there could be such a fantastic possibility. Now though, Holmes, evidently discouraged by my skeptical attitude, dropped the subject and sat gazing into space, apparently rapt in thought. But soon he was fidgeting in his chair; and shortly he got up, to pace back and forth, as restless as a new member of Parliament about to make his maiden speech.

I was about to protest against the thump-thump of his footsteps when I heard the sound of the postman at the entryway downstairs and almost immediately thereafter the tread of our landlady coming up the steps.

Tapping at our door, she wheezed, "Mr. Holmes, Mr. Holmes." Feeling somewhat piqued that it was always Holmes and never I that she addressed in such circumstances, my glance followed Holmes as he went to the door and opened it. "Yes, Mrs. Mullins?" he said.

"Here's a bit o' mail for you an' Mr. Harrington," she said, thrusting a batch of letters and circulars into his hands.

Thanking her, Holmes took the pieces of mail, handed me the two addressed to me, then sat down to examine the others. After an interval I heard him exclaim under his breath, then heard him say, "By Jove, Harrington, look at this!" extending a sheet of stationery that had obviously come out of an airmail envelope.

I took the sheet and read the message written on it. The letterhead read, "Office of Chief of Police, Akron, Ohio." The contents underneath it were brief almost to the point of curtness. After the usual superscription came the following: "Expect to fly to London to attend international meeting of law-enforcement officers, arriving on eighteenth. Right now am tied up here in case that threatens not only own career but safety and welfare of entire city. Though practically certain of criminals responsible, am afraid could never obtain conviction because of peculiar circumstances involved. Would like very much to consult you about matter if possible. Will try to telephone you for appointment immediately upon arrival. Urgently hope you can grant same. With best regards, Respectfully yours, Geo. H. Biggs."

"The writer seems pretty concerned, whoever he is."

"Concerned and obviously in a hurry. Either that, or he is a person with no nonsense. Note the total absence of all articles and a minimum of adjectives and adverbs. Reads more like a telegram than a letter. But what is he talking about and why apply to me?"

"Do you mean to say you don't know the writer?"

"Never heard of him as far as I recall, and the town or city of Akron means next to nothing to me. Seems to me that I remember vaguely that it is called the 'rubber capital' of the world, but outside of that I don't know a thing." And he shook his head perplexedly.

But in a moment he was meditatively saying, "Biggs? Biggs? I fancy I do have some recollection of the fellow. Have a feeling that he was here on a visit to England some years ago—a visit that was more or less professional. Let me see . . ." And he fell to musing again.

I remained silent, and shortly he nodded. "I remember now. I did meet him. A big, serious sort of chap— impressed me as very businesslike and efficient. Also downright earnest about his job. But he was not from Akron then. It was some other city. Some city with a name that ended with the syllable of 'town' or 'ville'—something like that. Humph . . . Ah, now I have it! Youngstown! That was the place. Well, evidently he has moved, though we don't know why. But we do know he's decidedly upset. By the way, what date is it?"

"The eighteenth."

"By Jove, you are right! Most likely Biggs is already in England. I confess I'm curious to learn what this is all about. 'Threatens the safety and welfare of the entire city.' Sounds a bit melodramatic, wouldn't you say? Let's hope we hear from him soon."

Yet we did not hear from him that day, and all the next day I was out. But when I returned to our quarters that evening, after a long day, I was informed by

242

Holmes that the police chief from the States had communicated with him by telephone that morning. "He said that he would be busy with meetings all day and had an important function later this evening that he had to attend, but that he would try to stop about half after seven on his way there."

"But it is past half after now."

"So it is," he agreed, glancing at the clock on the mantle. "In fact, it is nearer a quarter of the hour. However, I expect that he has only been delayed. Biggs does not impress me as one who would fail to keep an appointment." And hardly had he ceased speaking when we heard the street door below open and a heavy tread on the stairs. "Ah, I fancy that is our man now," Holmes continued, unable to keep a note of eagerness out of his voice.

The individual who now entered our room confirmed the picture created in my mind by the words of Holmes. He was a big man, at least six feet two inches tall, weighing fully sixteen stone. His well-rounded torso seemed to indicate an abundance of solid flesh rather than flabby fatness. It was surmounted by a large head with bold, rather heavy features. The effect of his whole person was one of unusual strength and seriousness of purpose. Just now he was dressed in obviously rented and too tight-fitting evening clothes and carrying an ordinary topcoat and slouch hat; but even this rather grotesque outfit was unable to detract seriously from his somewhat formidable appearance.

After greeting Holmes and being introduced to me, he accepted a chair, saying, "I am sorry to be late, Mr. Holmes. I usually make it a point to be on time. But I was held up and couldn't help it."

"Yes," said Holmes, "I see you came by bus and that you experienced a slight accident on the way."

"That's right," Biggs replied. "I intended to take a cab, but just as I stepped out of my hotel a Piccadilly bus came along and, remembering that it was the one that passed near your place, I jumped in. And—"

Then he suddenly broke off and stared at Holmes in incredulity. "But how did you know?"

"Elementary, my dear fellow. The bus stops at the corner half a block to the left of us. Between here and the corner is some construction work going on. I noticed this morning that there is a coating of lime and cement dust on the sidewalk there. And I observe that you have some of this dust on your shoes. Had you come by cab or private motorcar you would have parked nearer us and not walked half a block. Therefore, you came by bus."

"I see. But what of the accident that delayed us?"

Holmes smiled. "Why that, I confess, was sheer surmise. The bus is due at the corner at five and twenty after the hour. It now lacks only ten minutes of the hour. Even allowing for the few minutes it would take you to walk here from the corner, that would make the bus some twenty minutes late. Granted that it might sometimes be behind schedule, it is highly improbable that it would be as far behind as in this case except for some untoward circumstance. Hence the presumption of an accident. But as you made no mention of a mishap and as the delay was not unduly long, there is the further presumption that the accident was a minor one."

The big man looked at Holmes with an expression of admiration. "Right on all counts. And it does sound pretty simple the way you tell it. But it shows why you are considered a great detective. There aren't many who would have noticed my shoes or who would have gone on from there to figure things out the way you did, even if they had noticed them."

"Thank you." Holmes smiled. "But I fancy you will be wanting to get down to business. I gather that you are pressed for time."

"I *am* working on a pretty tight schedule," the other agreed. "There's a dinner at nine for all of us visiting firemen that the Lord Mayor is supposed to address. That's why I'm in this getup," he said, indicating his ill-fitting garb. "Didn't expect to go out in high society

244

and didn't bring any dress clothes. As you say, I'll have to cut it short and talk fast. But first, I'd like to call a cab to come for me in about twenty minutes."

I offered to make the call for him and went to the telephone. As I stood there, getting the call through, I could hear the two of them as they exchanged the customary personal remarks that pass between those who have met before but have been long separated. When I returned to my seat, Biggs was already launched on a recital of the circumstances that had prompted him to consult Holmes.

"You see, it was this way," he was saying. "Akron is what you might call in the United States a 'wide-open' town. I doubt if you have any places like it here in England, where your law-enforcement agencies and courts command more respect. Anyway, the city was in the grip of a sort of 'crime syndicate' bossed by a fellow by the name of Mantanelli. His specialty was slot machines, but he had had his hands in about everything: vice, liquor, dope—you name it. And apparently he had the police department and most of the courts in his hip pocket. Either that, or they were scared to death because he had a pretty good goon squad to take care of anyone who didn't toe the mark.

"But finally the decent citizens of the town got fed up and balked. Ran a reform candidate by the name of Brandon for mayor and a whole new slate of city officials, including prosecutor. And they got the people so stirred up that they finally turned the rascals out and elected a whole new ticket. Incidentally, that's where I came in. When the new setup went into office I was asked to come into the city to try to clean things up. At first I refused, but they kept sending letter after letter and finally sent a personal delegation of leading citizens to see me in Youngstown, where I was then heading up the police force, and they put things up to me in such a way that I couldn't well refuse.

"Well, Mantanelli didn't take it lying down. The very day after election he was quoted in the local paper, the *Akron Beacon Journal*, as saying that Brandon would never live to finish his term. And sure enough, after two months of lying low, Mantanelli and his hoods apparently struck back. Just thirteen days ago, one night about eleven-thirty, Brandon was shot down in cold blood as he was closing his garage door. What is more, we have just about conclusive evidence that it was a trigger man of Mantanelli's that did it."

"You have? Tell me about this evidence and how you succeeded in getting it," Holmes said.

"Well, we got it by plain luck," Biggs replied, "and not by any smart sleuthing on our part. It just happened that the killer, an ugly, vicious thug by the name of Scala, had a bad break. Evidently after shooting Brandon, who had just come home from a council meeting, the fellow ran back between two houses onto a street paralleling the one on which the mayor lived to make his getaway in a car that he had parked there.

"By the merest chance it happened that a man was out airing his dog at the time, and the dog had stopped by a tree. Scala, running out onto the street, tripped over the leash held by the dog's owner and fell onto the sidewalk. Surprised and mad as well as scared, I suppose, Scala looked up and swore at the owner; and, just as he did so, a car came along so that its lights hit him square in the face and the dog's owner got a good look at him. Not only that, but another man, who had just passed the spot a second before, heard the commotion, looked back, and also saw the killer's face as the car lights lit it up.

"Scala has got the kind of face you don't forget if you've once seen it—a thin-lipped, sneering mug with a mean, cruel look made all the worse by a bad scar near the corner of his mouth. The fellow's picture has been in the paper and he is pretty generally known as one of Mantanelli's mob. You can get some idea of what he looks like when I tell you that he's nicknamed 'the Snarler.'

"But having his ugly face recognized wasn't the worst. When he fell, a revolver slipped out of his hip pocket, slid across the walk, and landed at the dog owner's feet. We have it in our possession now. It has a peculiar, jagged mark on the handle, and we have a man who will swear that he once saw Scala with such a gun. When the gun bumped against his foot, the dog owner almost automatically leaned over and picked it up.

"Well, to go on, the fellow jumped up almost as soon as he fell and, without stopping to pick up the gun, made for the getaway car that he had parked in a shadow about half a block down the street, and racketed away. The witnesses both noticed that he limped as he ran, as if he had hurt himself when he fell.

"And that's not all. We arrested Scala on suspicion and found that he was still lame. Then, when we made him pull up his pant leg, we found a bad bruise and abrasion on his knee. And there's more! We asked him how he got hurt and he claimed that he had bumped it against a chest that he had in his room; but when we looked at his room—a cubbyhole of a place in a crummy rooming house in a shabby part of town—we found that there was no chest there. Not only that, but we did find a pair of pants with a three-cornered tear in one knee. The fellow isn't very smart and can't think fast enough to lie convincingly.

"Well, that's about it," the police chief ended. "As you can see, it's about as open-and-shut a case as you can get without an actual witness to the shooting."

"Yes, I would say it was," Holmes assented. "Then what's the problem?"

"Just this. Scala wasn't there."

"Wasn't there!"

"He wasn't anywhere near the scene of the shooting at the time that it occurred, and therefore could not possibly have been the killer. In other words, he has what looks like an unbreakable alibi."

"But any crook can prove an alibi. All it takes is a couple of obliging friends and enough money to buy their testimony."

The police chief shook his head. "I know, but this is not that kind of alibi. Scala and Mantanelli not only have the obliging friends to say that they were in Cleveland until midnight that night, but they also have three apparently disinterested witnesses who will swear that they saw Mantanelli and Scala in a car on their way from Cleveland to Akron between midnight and two A.M.—none of them, as far as we know now, friends of either Scala or Mantanelli. In fact, I'd almost swear that two of them, at least, are square and honest—good solid citizens who couldn't be bribed."

"Three of them? You mean people in another car who saw and recognized them?" Holmes queried.

"No, not as simple as that. Workers in three different service stations where Mantanelli and Scala stopped in Mantanelli's car. Their evidence is clear and explicit. They all clearly recognized Scala and are just as sure of themselves as are our witnesses—the man with the dog and the other man passing by."

"Humph!" grunted Holmes. "Sounds interesting. Suppose you go into more detail about this peculiarly pat alibi."

"Well, it seems that Mantanelli and Scala had a habit of driving to Cleveland on every other Thursday night for a poker party with some friends there. At one time or another they had stopped at all three of these gas stations, for oil or gas or whatnot, so that every one of the three attendants got to recognize them. And on the night of the murder, they stopped at each of the three—at the first one for gas and at the other two to put air in a leaky tire—all good, natural, legitimate reasons.

"The truth is, Mr. Holmes, we're stymied. We've got a clear-cut case and we're dead sure we're right, but we don't dare make an arrest or go before the grand jury. We could never get an indictment with the alibi they have, and we could never get a conviction if we did.

"And the pressure on us to do something is mighty heavy and getting heavier all the time. We don't dare reveal the evidence we have because of this alibi. Besides, we know that our witnesses would not be safe a minute if their names got out. We put a couple of plainclothesmen in the neighborhood where the shooting occurred, and one of them found Scala prowling around and made it pretty uncomfortable for him when he couldn't give a good reason for being there.

"The owner of the dog, luckily, had just moved into the neighborhood and was little known. For fear that some of Mantanelli's mob might try to locate him we told him to get rid of the dog as quietly as possible so that he would not be so likely to be identified if the hoods did inquire in the neighborhood about him.

"But we think that we may have one thing going for us. It's our guess that Scala hasn't told Mantanelli about his tripping over that leash because he doesn't want Mantanelli to know how he may have messed things up. If that's so, he's the only one that knows about the witnesses. More than likely, too, he doesn't know that the witnesses have come to us, as we have tried to keep the matter dark.

"But meantime we are taking an awful riding from the newspapers. If we don't solve this case and get a conviction, the whole city administration and the entire police department will have a black eye. Incidentally, I'll probably be given my walking papers. But worst of all, Mantanelli and his mob will be more sure of themselves than ever. There will be a complete breakdown of law and order and there won't be any such thing as decency or safety in the whole city. We've simply got to do something about this alibi or we're sunk."

"Yes, I can see it's a serious situation," Holmes nodded. "Do you mind if I ask a few questions?"

"Not at all. If I can give you any information that will help you to figure this thing out, I'll be the happiest man on earth."

"I see. Well, first, are these two witnesses of yours absolutely positive of their identification?"

"Absolutely. Even this claim of Scala's alibi hasn't made them change their story. They're dead sure they are right and they only want a chance to tell it in court if it'll bring the Snarler to justice and maybe help to get Mantanelli himself."

"Good. Now, these trips that Mantanelli and his killer made to Cleveland—you say that they were every other Thursday night?"

"Yes."

"And what evenings has your city council been meeting?"

"What—why, they have been meeting every other Thursday night, too. Ordinarily they would be meeting but once a month, but with a new regime in and so much to do . . . Say, wait a minute! Do you think there is any connection between the timing of these trips of Mantanelli and Scala and the council meetings?"

Holmes replied, "I think there is a very close connection," as Biggs stared at him with a puzzled expression. Then he went on. "Now, about these three petrol-station attendants—I assume that the stations are not all located right in the city of Akron?"

"No, they aren't. One is at a place called Steele's Corners, about five miles north of Akron, one at Northfield, midway between Akron and Cleveland, and the third in the south end of Cleveland near the outskirts of the city. Incidentally, Cleveland is some thirty to thirty-five miles north of Akron."

"And yet you say that even though none of these three presumably lived in Akron, all of them readily recognized this fellow Scala, even at night, sitting in a car?"

"That's right."

"Most interesting," ejaculated Holmes, rubbing his hands together. "Most interesting, indeed. Possibly there was something about this fellow that made it easy to identify him—or, at least, for them to think they did. Some peculiarity of dress for instance. Did he, by any chance, customarily wear some particular article of apparel that was unusual—something rather conspicuous, let us say?"

"Why, that's a funny thing, now that you ask it," Biggs answered. "He was an inconspicuous dresser. Practically always wore a suit of a dull grey color or an overcoat or topcoat of similar shade. But he did have a habit lately of wearing a hat with a loud band on it. Red and yellow, I think it was. You could spot it a mile."

"And when did he start wearing this hat? Could it have been three or four months ago?"

"Three or four months? Why, yes it was—just about. About the time Brandon took office, or a little before. But how—"

But Holmes interrupted him. "Another thing. Was this Scala the taciturn type? Not much given to talking?"

"He sure was. A surly kind of individual. Could hardly get a word out of him. But you sound as if you knew the fellow! Are you a kind of mind reader or something, Mr. Holmes?"

Holmes smiled. "Just an interested criminologist with an inquiring mind. And now, just a few more questions."

"Yes, sir."

"Does this fellow Scala have a twin brother, by any chance?"

"If he does, I never heard of it."

"Well, it might be worth looking into, although I do not expect such to be the case. Still, it pays to pursue all avenues of inquiry. And that suggests something else. Is Mantanelli particularly interested in the theater? Could he have a tie-up with some actor?"

"Do you mean could he have had someone made up to impersonate Scala? The answer is that we don't think so. We thought of that angle and looked into it as thoroughly as we could. We couldn't find any such tie-up. And we doubt if Mantanelli would take a chance on letting some outsider into any such shenanigans as that. So we think that's definitely out." Biggs spoke with a considerable degree of positiveness.

Holmes nodded and stroked his chin thoughtfully. "I rather thought that would be your answer. Which appears to leave but one possibility, unless your witnesses are mistaken."

. "I'm sure they're not," Biggs said in the same positive tone.

Just then we heard a loud rapping at the street door and I went downstairs to find, waiting at the entrance, a cabby who said that he had just come in answer to our call. I told him that his passenger would be ready shortly and went back to inform Biggs of the cabby's arrival.

"Great governor!" he exclaimed in answer to my news. "Is that clock right?"—glancing at the timepiece on the mantle.

"Why, yes, I fancy it is," Holmes said.

"Then I'm late and I'll have to be getting out of here. I meant to get away at a quarter after, and it's already eight twenty-five. Don't like to leave so abruptly, but with the Lord Mayor and all . . . Anyway, it was good of you to listen to my troubles, Mr. Holmes," he said, rising and extending his hand to Holmes as we got up, too. "And I'm pleased to have met you, Mr. Harrington," he added, taking my hand in turn.

Holmes said, "It's too bad you have to go so soon. I would have liked time for a more extended visit. But I *have* enjoyed discussion of your rather unusual case."

"It's unusual, all right," Biggs said wryly, shucking into his topcoat. "I wish that's all it was. And, as I said, it was good of you to give me the time to hear about it. I wish that you would mull it over and maybe you can come up with some sort of explanation."

"But I already have an explanation," Holmes said, smiling.

"You can't be serious!" Biggs cried.

"I was never more serious in my life, my dear fellow. Of course, I could be mistaken, and, in any event, it is going to take a great deal of investigation on your part to prove my theory right.

"The band on the hat is really the key to the whole matter, I would say," he continued. "Incidentally, I would suggest, among other things, that you make inquiry to see if there is some employee in one of the department stores in your city with whom Mantanelli may have made contact."

"Department store? Don't you mean hat store?"

"Not at all. But let me see you to your cab. On the way I'll try to explain myself more fully," said Holmes, taking Biggs's arm and walking out with him.

It must have been another ten minutes before Holmes came back. I assumed that he had been occupied not only in outlining his theory of this most peculiar case but in suggesting what investigation should be made to substantiate it. He volunteered nothing regarding their conversation on his return, and I knew better than to ask him. He would tell me in his own good time if he wished me to know.

Merely muttering, "Remarkable how simple it is to delude the human mind," he picked up the book on mesmerism and resumed his reading.

Time passed and I began to wonder if I would hear any more about this case of the puzzling alibi. If Holmes received any further word from the big police chief in far-off America, it came when I was out and he never mentioned it.

Then one day, out of a clear sky, he asked, "How would you like to make a little jaunt to the States?"

"The States?" I exclaimed.

"Why not?" he asked. "It's an interesting country and I have always had a fancy to see it. Its big cities—New York, Chicago, Los Angeles—must be among the foremost in modern equipment and methods for crime detection. And, of course, there are its great scenic attractions—Niagara Falls, Yellowstone Park, the Grand Canyon. We really ought to go sometime. And if we are ever to do it, why not now?"

Why not, indeed? We had no compelling ties of business or family to keep us from going. "Well, I said, "it's a new idea. Still—"

"I intend going about getting a passport and having the necessary inoculations at once," said Holmes decidedly. "And I suggest that you do the same. There's no knowing when we might find it advisable to take off."

He said nothing about the intriguing murder case, but I suspected that it had something to do with this sudden eagerness to visit America. Not that he was at all insular in his outlook; he had, indeed, always been decidedly cosmopolitan in his interests; but never before had he expressed a desire to venture so far afield.

As for myself, I had never contemplated such a journey, but the prospect of seeing this great and fabulous country across the Atlantic did appeal to me, and, as Holmes had said, when would there be a better time to go? So, wondering more or less what it was all about, but under the spell of Holmes's suppressed enthusiasm, I went about completing procedures necessary to our leaving the country.

There followed a period of inaction when I chafed with curiosity and impatience while Holmes went serenely about his business as if a trip to the land of our onetime colonies was the one thing farthest from his mind.

Then one morning, when I was late in getting away from our diggings, there came a letter to Holmes from Biggs enclosing a check for five hundred dollars. The letter, which he handed to me, was as terse as the one originally sent by the police chief about the Akron murder case. It briefly thanked Holmes for his services, apologized that the check was not larger, and said that investigation had tended to confirm Holmes's theory of the Akron murder with its bewildering alibi. It further stated that Scala had been taken into custody, charged and indicted with first-degree murder, and that his trial would probably begin within a fortnight. It ended by saying, "Wish you could attend trial to see your theory vindicated, but suppose this impossible. Warmest regards, G. Biggs."

"Surprising that we should get this letter right now," Holmes remarked with a straight face. "But it might be interesting to drop in on this trial, don't you think?

What do you say we hurry up our preparations for our visit to the States a bit, get reservations to fly over about next week. Do you think you could make it?"

I said I thought I could and set about making final arrangements for the journey at once. I had left the staff of the London *Times* some time since and was now doing free-lance writing. Moreover, as soon as Holmes had proposed the trip to America I had looked into the possibility of writing some articles about the country for one of our periodicals and had made a tentative arrangement to do so for the *Strand Magazine*. Now I had only to confirm this agreement, complete some last-minute details, and I was ready. So it was that just a week from the day of the receipt of Biggs's letter we were in New York. Then, after two days in that fascinating city, we were in Cleveland, where Holmes, in accordance with preconceived plans, visited a cousin, Mycroft Holmes. The day before the trial was to open we were in Akron.

Holmes had written Biggs of our coming, and on the morning of our arrival he dropped in to see us at the Mayflower, the city's leading hotel, where he had booked rooms for us. His delight at seeing Holmes was almost touching.

"I am so glad you could get here, Mr. Holmes," he exclaimed after greeting us. "Thanks to you, we have real hope of getting Scala and nailing his boss, Mantanelli, at last. And now that you are here you may be able to make some valuable suggestions as to the conduct of the trial."

Holmes smiled quietly. "Thank you, but I think you exaggerate my part in the matter. I'm sure that you would have come to the same conclusion as I did, once you had time to analyze the circumstances more fully. As for the conduct of the trial, I am quite content to leave it in the hands of the counsel. But I would be interested to know what the lawyers involved are like."

"They're both capable, if that's what you mean,"

Biggs said, "Though they are as different, for the most part, as they could well be. Scala's lawyer is an old reprobate, about sixty-five years old, by the name of Pollock. A typical criminal lawyer with a shady reputation. Fairly tall, around six feet, with a paunch like a watermelon. Partly bald, with a fringe of yellowish-grey hair around his dome. Has a long, heavy face with good-sized nose, a big mouth with what you call mobile lips, and sagging dewlaps like an old hound dog. Has a kind of shopworn appearance with a hint of whiskey huskiness in a rich, mellow voice that he uses for all it's worth.

"He's a good deal of an actor and dresses the part: old-time cutaway coat, figured vest, and striped trousers, and a pair of eyeglasses on a black silk cord that he keeps taking off and putting on and twirling dramatically. You might be inclined to write him off as a caricature, but you'd make a mistake. He knows all the tricks and how to play 'em. Usually he can get a jury to eat out of his hand. He's a regular showman and they like it—a sort of combination of Daniel Webster, evangelistic preacher, and medicine-show man."

"He sounds dangerous," Holmes commented. "How about the prosecutor?"

"The chief prosecutor, Halloway himself, is going to try the case, there is so much at stake. He's tall, too, taller than Pollock—probably six feet, two. But otherwise, he's just about the opposite of Pollock in every way. Some thirty-eight years old, dresses in quiet business suit, is more than just good-looking, with clean-cut features and trim, dark hair. Everything about him is neat and conservative. He's low-spoken, with a serious, straightforward manner, and has no tricks—at least none that are apparent. Handles witnesses, even those for the opposing side, in a pleasant, polite way. But don't let him fool you, either. He has a mind like a steel trap, and a knack of letting lying witnesses hang themselves before they know it."

"Sounds as if it could be quite a legal battle—or

perhaps one might better say a battle of wits," Holmes observed.

"Yes, it could be quite a show," Biggs agreed, "only it's really too serious a business to be called a show."

At this point I ventured to speak up. "You've told us about the opposing counsel; what's the judge like?" I asked.

Biggs answered, "Straight as a gun barrel. Oh, he'll lean over backward to protect the rights of the accused, but we like it that way."

"But why?" I blurted.

"Well, if he makes mistakes in his rulings against Pollock, we can't get a new trial because you can't put a man twice in jeopardy. But if he makes mistakes in his rulings against the prosecutor, Pollock *can* get a new trial—and we don't want any such mistakes."

"I see," I said.

Needless to say, the impending trial had the entire city all agog. From the moment of Scala's arrest it had been the leading topic of conversation. Partisans on both sides, the law-abiding on the one hand and the lawless on the other, were intensely interested, and there was a demand, particularly on the part of the better citizens as well as those merely seeking a thrill, that the case be given the utmost publicity. Many insisted that the proceedings be televised and others even went so far as to propose that loudspeakers be installed so that those unable to crowd into the courtroom might congregate outside the courthouse itself and listen to the conduct of the trial. But this nonsense the judge, a dignified man of severe aspect, promptly vetoed. Even so, on the day that the trial opened, not only was the courtroom packed but the corridors adjacent to it were jammed with a jostling, milling crowd of a highly varied character, including some of the most vicious-looking individuals it has ever been my misfortune to meet. Moreover, there was a large group of idlers and curiosity-seekers outside the courthouse, hanging about with that air of expectancy that people have on a circus-day morning. They, or others like them, were to

257

remain there throughout the entire trial, vainly listening, speculating, discussing, and arguing, and buttonholing everyone entering or leaving the building in an effort to glean the slightest scrap of information about the trial's progress.

Seats, of course, were at a premium, but thanks to Biggs, who felt that he owed a deep debt of gratitude to Holmes, I had a seat at the press table and Holmes was accorded a place beside the family of the murdered mayor.

I will not attempt to give a detailed report of this famous trial, but only enough of it so that the readers of these memoirs may appreciate the vital part that Holmes's analysis played in the final outcome. Anyone wishing a fuller account may find it by turning to the columns of any metropolitan daily; for the proceedings were reported at length in every big-city newspaper in the States, and, to a lesser extent, in those of England and the Continent as well.

Interest in the case was intense, not only because the fate of an important city appeared to be in jeopardy, but also because people were at a loss to understand how a prosecutor could hope to convict an accused with such a seemingly invulnerable alibi. Mantanelli, with a view to its psychological effect upon people in general and hence upon a prospective jury, had seen to it that the Akron newspapers and those in adjoining communities had given full publicity to Scala's alleged ride with him from Cleveland at the time that the murder of the Akron mayor was committed. The result was that almost everyone who could read knew about the notorious alibi, and many were inclined to think the prosecutor utterly foolhardy in undertaking a trial under such circumstances. The matter was viewed almost as a sporting event by the less serious-minded. Book was made on the nature of the verdict, and the odds were reported to be some seven to one in favor of the defendant's acquittal.

As might be expected, there was the utmost maneuvering on the part of the opposing counsel in the seating of a jury, and it took an entire day and a half before a full panel was obtained. Then, following the opening statements of the prosecution and defense, there was considerable routine testimony regarding the time and place of the shooting, the discovery of the victim's body, and similar details.

Finally, on the third day, there was called to the stand the first witness to impart really exciting drama to this trial that was to have so much drama before it was over. This witness was the dog owner, who gave his name as Daniel Bowman and his address as a house number some block and a half from the scene of the shooting. He was a man in his middle fifties, somewhat short and stocky, with a rather stodgy appearance but an earnest, sincere manner. As he sat in the witness chair, it was plain that he was nervous if not downright frightened; and no wonder, with so many evil-looking faces of Mantanelli's henchmen fixed threateningly upon him. His face was pasty white and his voice low. Time and again he had to be exhorted to speak louder. I could not but admire his hardihood in testifying as he did with the cold, reptilian eyes of the Snarler glowering menacingly at him from under hooded lids.

Bowman's direct testimony agreed in substance with the information that Biggs had given us on his visit to our chambers on Baker Street months before, including the dropping of Scala's gun on the sidewalk and his own recovery of it.

This would seem to be the first intimation that Pollock had of the existence of such weapon, and he appeared to give an all-but-imperceptible start as he glanced sidewise at the poker-faced Scala. But if this were true, he quickly recovered his poise, and gave no other indication that he was at all disturbed by this unexpected revelation.

I was sitting not too far from the notorious Mantanelli and saw him glare venomously at the scurvy defendant, who obviously had revealed nothing of the gun episode to his hoodlum boss.

At length Halloway was finished with his direct examination and Pollock took over. First he arose and stared at the witness for a long interval while he dangled the familiar eyeglasses with impressive deliberation. Finally he spoke.

"Mr. Bowman?" he growled in intimidating tone.

"Yes, sir."

"Mr. Daniel Bowman?"

"That's right, sir."

"Well, *Mister* Bowman"—and his emphasis on the word "mister" made it sound like a slur—"I suppose you have been well coached by the prosecuting attorney?"

Not knowing what to say, Bowman said nothing.

"Well, have you?" Pollock barked.

"Mr. Halloway talked to me, sir."

"And he coached you, didn't he?"

"Well, I suppose you might say so. To some extent, yes."

"Exactly. And just why didn't you say so in the first place, *Mister* Bowman?"

After some further badgering, he said, "You state that you had never seen the defendant before you caught a fleeting glimpse of his face in the headlights of a car. And yet you were able to identify him upon the instant and without question. Is that correct?"

"Yes, sir."

"Oh, you did, did you? And just how could you be so sure that it was Mr. Scala?"

"I had seen his picture in the newspaper—in the *Akron Beacon Journal.*"

"Oh, you had seen his picture in the newspaper!" Pollock's tone was scathingly sarcastic. "And how many times had you seen Mr. Scala's picture in the newspaper?"

"Once."

"Only once?"

"That's right."

"Well, well, gentlemen of the jury, we have here a veritable wonder man—a paragon of ocular ability."

Then, turning to the witness, he said, "You had seen the defendant's picture, a blurred——"

"I object," Halloway quietly interposed. "There is no evidence that the picture in question was blurred."

"Objection sustained," ruled the judge.

"Thank you, your honor," Pollock said with a half-bow. "I withdraw the term 'blurred,' which my honorable colleague in the practice of the law finds so objectionable. I have no desire to wound Mr. Halloway's delicate sensibilities, though I have yet to find a newspaper picture that is not blurred—*Mister* Bowman, you say you saw the picture of the defendant on the rough page of a newspaper in newsprint just once, only once, and then you got a flash of a face for a fraction of a second *at night,* by the light of a passing car traveling perhaps thirty, perhaps as high as forty or fifty miles an hour, and yet you immediately and unmistakably recognized it as that of the defendant. Quite a feat, *Mister* Bowman."—and again he slurringly emphasized the "mister" as he glared balefully at the witness and swung the gold-rimmed eyeglasses fiercely to and fro.

After several more questions in the same vein he wound up his bullying cross-examination as follows: "Now, *Mister* Bowman, let me ask you this, since you are such a student of the newspapers. Did you or did you not read in the newspaper the fact that Mr. Scala was not at the deceased's residence nor at his garage nor on any part of the deceased's premises at the time of this deplorable shooting, but was miles away, riding in an automobile as he had every legitimate reason and moral right to be? Did you or didn't you read that?"

"Something like that, yes, sir. I read that he claimed to be in a car."

"Exactly. Not only claimed, but was. Now——"

"I object," said prosecutor Halloway. "Learned counsel for the defendant says the defendant *was* in an automobile, but there has been no evidence introduced that such was the case."

"Objection sustained. Counsel for the defense will

please confine himself to the facts as they appear in the evidence."

Pollock made a deferential nod to the judge. "Very well, Your Honor. No offense intended . . . And now, *Mister* Bowman, answer me truthfully—remember you are under oath and there is a severe penalty for the crime of perjury—did you not have the faintest shadow of a doubt that you might be mistaken as to the identity of this face that you saw partially lit up for the merest fraction of an instant in the blackness of the night, and didn't you wonder that that face was not, after all, the face of the defendant, as you have now testified here—didn't you have some such doubt, *Mister* Bowman?"

"Why—why yes, I did for a little time."

"I did not ask you for how long you had this doubt, *Mister* Bowman—whether it was for a day or a week or a month. I merely asked you whether you did or not. Did you or didn't you? Yes or no."

"Yes."

"I thought so. Now a few more questions, *Mister* Bowman, about this mysterious gun that you say slid from the defendant's pocket to land so conveniently at your feet so that you could comfortably pick it up. That was a most opportune occurrence, wouldn't you say?"

"I . . . I guess I don't understand what you mean," said Bowman, obviously embarrassed.

"Ah, the gentleman says he guesses he doesn't know what I mean. I don't wonder, *Mister* Bowman."

"I object," said Halloway sharply.

"What is your objection, Mr. Prosecutor?" the judge asked.

"I object to counsel's constant browbeating of the witness and to his gratuitous comments on the witness's testimony."

"The Court thinks your point is well taken," said the judge. "Counsel for the defense will hereafter refrain from intimidating the witness and reserve any comments he may have to make upon the witness's testimony until his final summing up of the evidence before the jury."

"Very well," replied Pollock. "I will be only too glad to comply with Your Honor's request. Far be it from me to violate the strictures of legal procedure, let alone transgress the canons of good taste. I have only one or two more interrogatories to address to this witness. First I will rephrase my last question. I ask you once again, *Mister* Bowman, doesn't it strike you as a most remarkable circumstance that this alleged gun should slide exactly at your feet in such a convenient position for you to pick it up?"

"I . . . I hadn't thought about it. All I know is that it just did, that's all."

"Ah, all you know—"

Halloway was instantly on his feet again.

"Your Honor, if you please—"

"Very well, Mr. Prosecutor," the judge interrupted. Then turning to Pollock, he said, "I hope, Mr. Pollock, that it will not be necessary to admonish you again."

"I defer to the Court's wishes," said the old humbug with a courtly bow. Then, addressing Bowman once more, he asked, "Did *you* ever own a gun, *Mister* Bowman?"

"Well, no. I never did."

Pollock started to say, "Well, well, he never—" Then he caught himself and said. "That is all, *Mister* Bowman," in a tone that somehow seemed to imply that the witness's testimony was of no consequence, anyway.

Then Halloway arose leisurely in an unruffled manner, stating that he had a few questions in redirect examination.

"Now, Mr. Bowman," he said in a quiet tone, calculated to sooth the thoroughly disturbed Bowman, "Mr. Pollock asked you if you had been coached by me and you said that you had. But he did not ask about the character of that coaching. Please tell the jury exactly what I said to you about your conduct on the stand, as near as you can recall."

"You told me to make my answers as responsive to the questions as I could, not to volunteer any information beyond what was asked, and to tell the exact truth at all times."

"Very good. Mr. Pollock has also questioned you about a picture of the defendant that you saw in the newspaper, and he took pains to intimate that this picture was blurred and indistinct. As a matter of fact, was that true? Was the picture clear or not?"

"As far as I could tell, it was quite clear."

"And for the benefit of the members of the jury who may themselves have seen that picture, what was the date of the *Akron Beacon Journal* in which it appeared?"

"The thirteenth of last November."

"And how do you remember that that was the date?"

"Well, it was just two days after the robbing of the Wadsworth bank, and defendant's picture—"

"Never mind. You have answered the question. Now, one thing further. Mr. Pollock made a good deal of the fact that you had some fleeting doubt as to the identity of the man who tripped over your dog's leash after you read the report in the paper that the defendant was allegedly somewhere else at the time of this murder and not at the scene of the crime. Now that you have seen the defendant here in court, do you still have any such doubt?"

"No, sir."

"In other words, you are sure that his is the face of the man who tripped over your dog's leash after running out from the direction of the murdered man's backyard, and then ran limping away?"

"Yes, sir, I am sure."

"Another thing. Mr. Pollock made much of the fact that you were able to remember the face of the defendant after seeing it but once in the newspaper. Why do you remember it so well?"

"Why? Why, because it impressed me so, I guess."

"And why did it impress you so?"

"I . . . I'd rather not say."

"I'm sorry, Mr. Bowman, but you are under oath. I'm afraid that I will have to insist on your answer. Why did the picture of the defendant's face impress you so strongly?"

"Be—because it was so . . . so terrible."

"Terrible?"

"Yes, it . . . it's the kind of face that scares you, sir. It sort of . . . gives you the creeps."

"And are you scared now?"

"Yes. Yes, I guess I am, sir."

The witness's pallor and all-but-trembling voice gave ample evidence of his fear, and I could not but think that his steadfast adherence to his identification of the defendant under the circumstances must impress the jury with his complete sincerity.

The next witness that Halloway called was quite a different person than the stodgy, frightened Bowman. Though stocky, he was taller than Bowman and some ten years younger. Not only that, but whereas Bowman had seemed apprehensive and almost reluctant to testify, this second witness, who gave his name as Steve Ravich, was self-possessed and seemingly eager to give his testimony. Indeed, it was he who had originally gone to the police and it was through him that the more timid Bowman had been drawn into the case. Now, for fear that they might suffer violence at the hands of some of Mantanelli's gangsters, both witnesses were being held in the protective custody of the state.

In direct testimony, Ravich said that on the evening of the murder he had been going south on the east side of the street, where Bowman was airing his dog, on his way to a corner drugstore to get some headache tablets for his wife. He further testified that he had just passed Bowman when he heard the running footsteps of Scala and turned around in time to see the Snarler trip over the dog's leash. Scala's hat had been jarred to the back of his head by the fall and Ravich, who had then been about twenty feet away, had got a clear view of the fellow's face when the lights of a northbound car shone

265

full upon it. He had seen the Snarler look up at Bowman and growl, "What the hell do you think yer doin'," then scramble immediately up and run limping away, for a distance of some fifty yards, to a car into which he had climbed and been driven away. His identification of Scala was definite and clear.

Following this direct testimony he was subjected to a grueling cross-examination by Pollock. The defense lawyer stood up and glared at him silently for a long moment, then rapped: "You and Bowman talked this over together, didn't you?"

"We talked it over, yes."

"And you fixed it up between you that the men you saw that night—if, as a matter of fact, you saw anybody—was the defendant. Isn't that right?"

"No, we didn't fix up anything. There was nothing to fix."

"Now, just a minute, Ravich. Your friend Bowman just got through giving some sort of story about taking his dog out for an evening stroll and about Mr. Scala's falling over the dog's leash and—"

"Mr. Bowman isn't a friend of mine. He's just an acquaintance. I never saw—"

"That'll do!" Pollock thundered, holding up a soft, flabby hand and advancing threateningly toward the witness. "You'll speak when you are spoken to. Your friend—"

"I object," broke in Halloway. "The witness has just said that Mr. Bowman was not a friend, merely an acquaintance."

"Objection sustained. Counsel will please endeavor to confine himself to the facts."

"Very well, Your Honor," Pollock said, then turned back to the witness. "Your acknowledged acquaintance Bowman comes here with a story of somehow identifying a man tripping over his dog's leash in the dead of night as Mr. Scala, and you come here with the same story. Isn't that right?"

"It isn't a story, it's a fact."

266

"Let's not quibble. You *are* saying that it was Mr. Scala, aren't you?"

"I'm saying it was the Snarler, yes."

"So you did talk it over with Bowman and the two of you did decide—"

"We didn't decide. We just agreed."

"Decide or agree—it's much the same, isn't it, Ravich?"

"Maybe to you it is. But not to me. The facts decided us. We agreed on the facts."

"Oh!" Pollock's voice dripped with sarcasm. "So you are an expert in the science of semantics, are you, Ravich? Well, let me ask you this. Did you or didn't you read in the newspaper that Mr. Scala was miles away from the point where you and your acquaintance Bowman so glibly say you saw him on the night of this regrettable shooting. Miles away in an automobile proceeding on his lawful way as he had every right to do. Did you or didn't you read that?"

"Yes, I read that he claimed to be in a car."

"And you still say that it was Mr. Scala that you saw by the headlights of a rapidly passing car in the dark of the night?"

"Yes. But the car *wasn't* going fast."

"But even after reading the news account in the paper, you in your omniscience never had the slightest doubt that the man you claim to have seen was Mr. Scala?"

"That's right."

"And just how does it happen that you know so much more than the newspaper reporters, Ravich. Tell us that."

"Because I know about Mantanelli. And I wouldn't put any trick past him to put something over."

"Oh, you wouldn't?" Pollock fairly bellowed. "You, a nobody, come here and malign Mr. Mantanelli, a capable, successful business man. As a matter of fact, you aren't as successful as Mr. Mantanelli, are you, Ravich, and you don't like him, do you?"

"No, I certainly don't."

"And you don't like Mr. Scala, either, do you?"

"No."

"You've got it in for him, haven't you? And you would say anything against him to have him found guilty of this dastardly murder, wouldn't you?"

"As long as it was true, yes."

"I didn't ask you to qualify your answer. I asked you whether you would or you wouldn't. Now just answer the question—yes or no?"

"What is the question, please?"

"Wouldn't you say anything to try to pin this killing on the defendant—yes or no."

"No—not unless it was true."

Pollock turned toward the judge with a great show of righteous indignation. "*If* the Court please, we have here a self-willed, recalcitrant witness, a witness who is bound and determined to evade a direct answer. I ask that he be admonished—"

"Very well, Mr. Pollock," said the judge, turning gravely toward Ravich. "The witness will take pains hereafter to make his answers as responsive as possible to counsel's questions and not volunteer anything beyond such response."

"Thank you, Your Honor," said Pollock, all but bowing from the hips. "Now, Ravich, how many times have you been arrested?"

"Once."

"And wasn't that for threatening Mr. Scala with a revolver?"

"I chased him and two other thugs out of my place of business, if that's what you mean."

"Thugs? Let me warn you, Ravich, to be careful of your language. Remember, you are in a court of law, and the courts of the United States are worthy of respect, even if you don't think so. Now, listen carefully, Ravich. You pulled a gun on Mr. Scala and you were arrested, weren't you?"

"Yes."

"And what's more, you were found guilty of assault

with a dangerous weapon, weren't you? You can't deny that, can you, Ravich?"

"No, I can't. The judge was a stooge of Man—"

Brandishing the gold-rimmed eyeglasses, Pollock turned toward the bench. "Your Honor, I *beg* of you—"

"Quite so, Mr. Pollock." And, turning toward Ravich, the judge said, "The witness will refrain from any further outbursts. Otherwise the Court will find it necessary to find him in contempt."

"Thank you, Your Honor, thank you very much." And Pollock turned toward Ravich with a gesture of contempt. "That will be all. You can get off the stand."

But Halloway was on his feet. "I'm sorry, Mr. Pollock, but I'm afraid I have a few questions in redirect examination. I'm sure you won't object to having one or two things cleared up a little."

"Oh, no, not at all."

"Very well. Mr. Ravich, Mr. Pollock went to considerable pains to give the impression that you and Mr. Bowman were friends of long standing and had entered into collusion to identify the defendant as the one you saw run from the direction of Mayor Brandon's backyard on the night that the mayor was murdered. Now, for the benefit of the jury, will you tell when you first saw Mr. Bowman?"

"At that time. On the night of the murder."

"And how many times have you seen him since?"

"Twice."

"And when was that?"

"Once at your office about six weeks ago, and today."

"And when did you first find out his name?"

"At your office."

"Thank you. I think that that disposes of the matter. Now, another thing. You said that you do not like Mr. Mantanelli. Why don't you like him?"

"Because one of his guys came to my business place and tried to force a slot machine on me."

"I object!" shouted Pollock, pounding the counsel table.

The judge looked at him inquiringly. "Yes, Mr. Pollock? What is your objection?"

"I object to the witness's saying that one of Mr. Mantanelli's 'guys,' as he calls them, tried to force a slot machine on him. How does he know that this guy that he talks about was from Mr. Mantanelli? And I object to the word 'force.' This is a free country—nobody can force anybody to do anything."

"Your point is well taken, Mr. Pollock. The witness's answer will be stricken from the record and the jury is instructed to disregard same. Now, Mr. Prosecutor, if you care to repeat your question, perhaps Mr. Ravich can give us a more acceptable answer."

Halloway repeated the question and Ravich replied that a man whom he thought came from Mantanelli had come to his place of business and tried to leave a slot machine there.

Again Pollock thundered an objection. "If Your Honor please, there is no evidence whatever that this so-called guy who supposedly tried to force a slot machine on the witness came from Mr. Mantanelli. The witness merely thinks he did."

"Quite right, Mr. Pollock. But you yourself brought out the fact that the witness dislikes Mr. Mantanelli. You opened the door. Now it is the opinion of the Court that Mr. Halloway has a right to have the witness explain the cause of his dislike. The witness may be mistaken in his presumption, and the cause of his dislike may not be valid; nevertheless, it does furnish an explanation for that dislike."

Pollock grunted. "Very well. I ask the stenographer to note an exception to the Court's ruling."

"You may proceed, Mr. Prosecutor," said the judge, turning toward Halloway.

Thereupon Halloway asked Ravich to explain further about the attempted slot machine transaction. Ravich then explained that his visitor had proposed that such machine be installed in Ravich's place of business on the condition that the title to same remain in what he called "the company," that a man from "the company" would call each week, unlock the machine, remove its proceeds, and count them in the presence of Ravich, then give Ravich a certain percentage of what he called the "take" and keep the rest for "the company."

"And what happened when you refused this fellow's proposition?"

"He said, 'Don't think you can get away with this, Buster. You'll be hearing from us later,' and left."

"And tell us what occurred after that."

"Well, a couple of days later Scala and two hoo—two other fellows came into my place."

"And what followed? Did they ask you to buy anything?"

"No, they didn't say a word—just started toward me. One of 'em was wearing brass knuckles. I got scared, pulled a gun from under the counter, and told them to get out. Later a cop come around and arrested me for it."

After Ravich left the stand, Halloway summoned as a witness a ballistic expert to present in evidence the gun in question and to testify that the bullets found in the dead mayor's body had been fired from that particular gun.

When he finished his testimony, Pollock stood up with deliberation, twirled his eyeglasses dramatically until he had the full attention of all in the room, cleared his throat, and said, "Inasmuch as the defense will show conclusively that the accused could not possibly have fired the fatal shots that are the subject of this lamentable litigation, I will not take the honorable Court's time to cross-examine this witness."

Halloway then called to the stand one of the two police officers who had visited Scala's shabby room to arrest him and examine his belongings. The officer told of finding a pair of the defendant's trousers with a hole ripped in the left knee, and of finding that the same knee of the defendant bore an abrasion that was still red and ugly-looking two days after the shooting.

"And what explanation did the defendant give for the injury to his knee?" the prosecutor asked.

"He said that he had bumped it against a piece of furniture in his room at night when he got up in the dark. Then when we told him that there was no piece of furniture that he could have bumped into that would cause such an injury, he said that he had had a big 'sort of chest' in one corner but he had given it away to a friend. When we asked him what the friend's name was, he said 'Bill Smith.' When we asked where Bill lived, he said he wasn't sure because he had since moved."

"I see," commented Halloway drily. "And are those the torn trousers you spoke of?"—pointing to a pair which the officer had in his hands, a pair, grey in color, rather badly worn, with a pair of horrible gaudy braces still attached to them.

Upon the officer replying in the affirmative, the sorry exhibit was made part of the record.

When the officer ceased testifying, Pollock waved him airily off the stand with a nonchalant "No questions."

Then Halloway called the second officer, whereupon Pollock asked, "Is this witness to give merely corroborative testimony?" And upon being told that such was the case, he said offhandedly, "Defense will be glad to stipulate to such fact and save cluttering up the record."

This brought the state's case to a conclusion and, as it was rather late in the day, the judge adjourned proceedings until the next morning. It seemed to me that the prosecution had made an exceedingly convincing case, and that evening when Holmes and I were sitting around a restaurant table with police chief Biggs, and the prosecutor and his assistant, I was surprised at Biggs's somber tone as he said, "But you haven't heard the defense yet, and there's no discounting the ability of that old show-off, Pollock."

272

"That's true," agreed the assistant prosecutor, a man named Madden. "But he can't perform miracles. And, thanks to Mr. Holmes, I think that we can knock their story of an alibi into a cocked hat. And I don't think Pollock helped himself any today. I thought he rather overplayed his hand several times."

"I think you're right," Halloway agreed. "And I felt that, luckily for us, we managed to get a pretty serious-minded jury that is not too greatly impressed by the old goat's histrionic antics. There's only one thing that worries me."

"What's that?" Holmes asked.

"Whether the jury has the courage to find the Snarler guilty."

"The courage?"

"Yes. You have no conception of the grip that Mantanelli and his thugs have on this city. He has almost the entire population thoroughly cowed. If anyone dares to oppose him, he is beaten up, tortured, or killed. Or, maybe even worse, some member of his family is made a victim of the mob.

"My hardest job will be to work up the members of the jury to such a pitch of moral indignation and defiance that they will dare to find the defendant guilty. I've got to make them realize that this is their one great chance to rescue Akron from the stranglehold of Mantanelli and his hoodlums so that it will be a safe place for themselves and their families. I have to drive it home that Scala had no motive for killing Brandon but blood money—blood money that came from Mantanelli. And I've got to make them see that if they find Scala guilty, we can get Mantanelli himself."

The next morning when court opened, Pollock filed the routine motion to dismiss the case for want of sufficient evidence to show his client guilty, and when this was refused, he proceeded to put on testimony for the defense.

The first witness he called was Mantanelli himself.

He testified that on the night of the murder he had driven to Cleveland with Scala as he did every other Thursday night. He further testified that on these occasions it was the custom for him to go to the house of a friend by the name of Cargola, where he, with three or four others, would play cards while Scala went about entertainment of his own. This program had been followed, as usual, on the night of the killing until about midnight, when Scala had telephoned that he was ready to leave Cleveland, whereupon Mantanelli had left Cargola's to pick Scala up and they had ridden together back to Akron, arriving there about two A.M.

At the end of Mantanelli's direct testimony, Halloway got up and said, "Mr. Mantanelli, you say that it was your custom to go to Cleveland for these poker sessions with your friends twice a month. Is that correct?"

"That's right." There was almost a smirk on the crime boss's face.

"And these always occurred on the first and third Thursdays of the month. Is that right?"

"That's right."

Then, suddenly, Halloway said, "That's all. I have no further questions to ask this witness." When he left the stand I thought that Mantanelli seemed nonplussed and the jury appeared puzzled and not a little curious that the cross-examination should end so abruptly with only two questions.

Mantanelli was followed on the stand by Cargola, who substantiated what Mantanelli had said about the biweekly card-playing and the other evidence presented by the slot-machine king. When he ended, Halloway seemed preoccupied with some papers before him and appeared not to notice when he was about to leave the stand.

"Does the prosecutor wish to cross-examine this witness?" the judge asked.

At the question Halloway seemed to rouse. "Why, not just now, Your Honor. It is barely possible that I may recall him later if the court will permit me to reserve that right."

It was all very offhand, but I wondered if he were as indifferent as he seemed or if he had some trick of strategy to play. From a covert glance that Pollock gave Mantanelli, I thought perhaps he was wondering the same.

When Cargola left the stand, Pollock put on a third witness, who testified to being present at the poker party on the night of the murder and corroborated what had previously been said. Halloway dismissed him without any cross-examination whatever, and when Pollock was about to bring forward a fourth witness the prosecutor said, "May I ask if the purpose of this witness's testifying is solely to corroborate the evidence given by the previous witnesses?" When Pollock stated that it was, Halloway asked how many more of such witnesses he proposed to introduce. When Pollock replied that there were two others, Halloway addressed the judge. "If the Court please, the proposed testimony appears to be merely cumulative. The prosecution is willing to stipulate as to the nature of such testimony and dispense with the witnesses' taking the stand in order to save the Court's time."

This was agreed to, and again Pollock and Mantanelli seemed mystified that Halloway should make such a concession, and the jury seemed piqued and perplexed. Why should the prosecutor appear to make it so easy for the defendant to build up his ominous alibi? I couldn't understand it.

At this point there followed the first apparently disinterested witness for the defense, the attendant of the service station in the southern end of Cleveland where Mantanelli with his mysterious passenger had stopped for petrol that fatal night, just before leaving the city. The man, who gave his name as Andrew Zilch, was a sober-faced fellow of something over middle age. Responding to the purring tones of the warmvoiced Pollock, who addressed him familiarly as "Andy," Zilch told of Mantanelli's having stopped there on two or three previous occasions and of stopping on the night of the killing shortly after midnight. On each occasion, including the night of the murder, he had been accompanied by Scala.

Addressing him deferentially as "Mr. Zilch," instead of by his first name, and questioning him in courteous, conciliatory tones, Halloway took over the cross-examination.

"And how did you know that the two passengers in the car were Mr. Mantanelli and the defendant?" he asked.

"Oh, I had seen them two or three times before."

"But how did you know them the first time they stopped?"

"How—? Well now, let me see. Oh, I remember. They was driving—that is, Mr. Mantanelli was driving this big, shiny Cadillac with his initials on it, and I said, 'That's a fine-looking car you've got, sir.' An' he said 'Thanks,' or something like that, an' then he said, 'By the way, my name is Mantanelli—Vince Mantanelli—I live in Akron. An' this is my friend, Mike Scala.' I remember in particular because he give me a dollar tip, sayin' it was jus' fer luck."

"I see. Do you get many dollar tips, Mr. Zilch?"

"No, sir. In fact, this is the only one I ever got, as I remember."

"And did Mr. Mantanelli give you a tip the other times that he stopped?"

"Well, yes, in a way. That is, no matter what the bill was, he always says to me, 'Keep the change.' "

"And how much gas did he get on the night of March fifth, the night of the killing of Mayor Brandon in Akron?"

"Why, he got either three or four gallons. I remember thinkin' it wasn't much."

"So, with only about thirty-five miles to go, he had a tank almost full of gasoline when he stopped. Is that correct?"

"Why, yes. Yes, he did."

276

"You say that he bought three or four gallons of gasoline. How much was it a gallon?"

"Thirty-four cents."

"And how did he pay for it?"

"He give me two dollar bills."

"And told you to keep the change?"

"That's right. I remember 'cause it come to purty near a dollar."

"I see. Now, Mr. Zilch, didn't it strike you as a little peculiar that Mr. Mantanelli should take the trouble to introduce himself and his passenger and that he should stop so often at your service station and always take pains to tip so—"

"Object! Object!" shouted Pollock, working the silk cord of his eyeglasses up and down like a meat-chopper. "It makes no difference what the witness thought. The question—"

"Very good, Mr. Pollock," the judge said. "Objection sustained."

"I withdraw the question, Your Honor. Now, Mr. Zilch, I will put it to you in another way. Have you ever had anyone—anyone before, entirely unknown to you—introduce himself and those with him when he stopped at your service station?"

"Well, now that you mention it, I don't know as I ever have."

"And have you ever had anyone tip you as liberally as Mr. Mantanelli?"

"Why, no, not as I remember. In fact, I never had anyone tip at all unless it was fer somethin' special like puttin' air in the tires. That is, unless it was only a few cents change an' they was in a hurry an' didn't wait."

"I understand. And how long would you say that you had worked at a service station?"

"How long? Well, about fifteen years, I guess."

"Thank you, Mr. Zilch. Now, something else. You say that Mr. Mantanelli introduced himself and the defendant the first time he stopped at your station. How long ago was that? Eight or nine months?"

"Why, just about, sir, as near as I can remember. Right around the first of the year."

"In other words, about the time that Mayor Brandon took office?"

"Yes, sir."

"And Mr. Mantanelli? Was he always rather chatty when he stopped?"

"That's right."

"And how about the defendant? Did he talk any?"

"Not to amount to anythin'. Sort o' grunted when he was first introduced. After that I don't remember his ever opening his mouth."

"How about the night of March fifth, or the early morning of the sixth?"

"No, he didn't say anythin'."

"And he didn't get out of the car?"

"No, he just set there."

"And how was he dressed?"

"Didn't notice in particular. Same as always, I guess. Dark grey suit—somethin' like that. Course there was his hat."

"His hat?"

"Yes, he always wore this hat with a red and yellow band. Almost like a trademark, it was."

"And that was one reason you knew or thought you knew it was the defendant?"

"Why, yes, it was."

The witness was plainly nervous, but he gave his testimony in a straightforward manner and there seemed to be no reason to doubt that he was telling the truth. It made me wonder more than ever how the prosecutor could hope to break the killer's alibi.

The next witness was an attendant at the service station in Northfield, about midway between Cleveland and Akron. He was an alert young fellow by the name of Johnny Logan, and except for saying that Mantanelli had stopped to have air put into a leaky tire, his testimony was much the same as that given by the preceding witness, even to the facts that Mantanelli had first stopped there with Scala about the first of the year, that he had taken occasion to make known both himself and his passenger, and had always been liberal in tips.

Halloway's cross-examination followed substantially the same lines as his questioning of Zilch, and nothing that the young fellow said seemed in the least questionable. The validity of the baffling alibi seemed to grow stronger and stronger.

But then came the third witness, the attendant at the service station at Steele's Corners, only some three miles north of Akron. He was a slick-appearing fellow, some thirty to thirty-five years of age, who gave his name as Richard Simon, and to me there was something about him that did not quite ring true. Somehow he seemed a little too glib, his answers a little too pat. At this station, too, according to the witness, Mantanelli had stopped to have air put in the faulty tire, which presumably still leaked. The testimony of the fellow was similar to that of Zilch and Logan except that he said that at his station the defendant did not remain silent in the car but exchanged greetings with the witness and got out of the auto to go to the rest room.

When Halloway took over cross-examination, his manner, at the beginning, was just as mild and polite as had been his questioning of the witnesses who had gone before. Then, in a gentle, offhand way, he said, "You said your name was Richard Simon?"

"That's right."

"Richard? And do they sometimes call you 'Rickey'?"

"Why . . . why, yes, I guess they do."

"And your last name? Do you spell Simon S-I-M-O-N or is there an E on the end of it?"

"Why—er—either way. It don't make much difference."

"Isn't that because your real name is Enrico or Ricci Simone?"

"Well, maybe it is. But I got a right to change it, haven't I?"

"Certainly, Mr. Simone. You have a right to call

279

yourself anything you like. I am just curious to know when you made this change of name. When was it?"

"I don't remember exactly?"

"Don't remember? Wasn't it about the time you got the job at the gas station at Steele's Corners, and wasn't that about the first of last December, a month or so after Mr. Brandon, the murdered mayor, was elected to office?"

"I don't remember."

"You appear to have a very erratic memory, Mr. Simone. A short time ago you didn't appear to have any trouble recalling every little detail of Mr. Mantanelli's stopping at your service station nearly nine months ago although, presumably, you have had thousands of motorists stop there since. Let's test this convenient memory of yours a little further. Do you recall how many times you have been arrested, Mr. Simone?"

"I don't have to answer that. I refuse to answer on the ground that it might in—in— Anyway, it's against the constitution."

"And you are a great respecter of the constitution. I assure you, Mr. Simone, the fact that you have previously been arrested cannot possibly incriminate you—it can only reflect on the character of your veracity and the credibility of your testimony. Now, how many times have you been arrested?"

Simone pulled at his collar, squirmed uncomfortably, and looked at the judge.

"Just answer the question if you can," said the judge impassively.

Simone looked sullenly at Halloway, then mumbled, "I don't remember. Maybe a couple o' times."

"I'm afraid this memory of yours is misleading, Mr. Simone. Wasn't it nearer seven or eight times?"

"I don't remember."

"Then perhaps I should refresh your memory through the court records. I have here Docket 407 of the Criminal Court Records of Summit County. On page 73 there is an entry that says that one Enrico Simone, otherwise known as Ricci Simone, was found guilty of armed robbery on November second, 1957. Do you recall that, Mr. Simone?"

Then, ruthlessly, Halloway referred to docket after docket to recite convictions ranging from robbery to assault and extortion. When the prosecutor had finished, Simone left the stand a thoroughly discredited witness. I wondered why Mantanelli had taken the chance to call such a fellow as a witness when he had two other perfectly good witnesses to the defendant's alibi. There must be a reason.

When Simone was finally dismissed, Pollock announced that the defense had no further evidence to present and rested his case. Halloway promptly arose and said, "If the Court please, the prosecution would like to present some rebuttal testimony."

"Rebuttal testimony?"

"Yes, Your Honor. We propose to present evidence that this so-called alibi of the defendant is entirely fabricated, a diabolical hoax, cleverly conceived and fiendishly ex—"

But Pollock was on his feet, windmilling the ever-evident eyeglasses on the end of their black cord and bellowing, "Your Honor, Your Honor, *if* you please, I protest—"

The judge pounded with his gavel and said, "Very well, Mr. Pollock . . . Mr. Halloway, you will have ample opportunity at the conclusion of the evidence to comment on same. In the meantime you will kindly refrain from doing so. The jury is instructed to ignore remarks of counsel and give its consideration solely to the evidence. Mr. Prosecutor, you may proceed with your rebuttal testimony."

The witness that Halloway now called was a soberly impressive man, somewhat under middle age, with a calm, businesslike manner. He gave his name as William Rowland and his address as a house number in Rochester, New York. His responses to the prosecutor's questions were clear and incisive.

"What is your occupation, Mr. Rowland?" Halloway asked.

"I am sales manager for the Superior Mannikin Company."

Mannikin Company! Now it was explained: this fantastic alibi of the crime boss Mantanelli and his paid killer, the Snarler. There had been no one in the big, shiny Cadillac with Mantanelli on that trip from Cleveland to Akron on the night of the brutal murder of the Akron mayor—there had been only a dummy, a dummy that looked like Scala, a dummy with the readily recognizable hat, a dummy that had never moved and never spoken!

Now it was crystal clear how Mantanelli had arranged the brazen alibi from the very beginning, planning from the very moment of his election how the newly elected mayor would be killed and how his killer would go free. Now it was altogether plain why Mantanelli had made those biweekly trips to Cleveland and why they had coincided with the nights of the Akron City Council meetings, meetings that the mayor would attend, meetings that would last until eleven or twelve o'clock at night and would thus get him home around midnight. Now it was obvious why Mantanelli had made himself and Scala familiar to Zilch and Logan, why he had gone out of his way to chat with them and tip them and foster their goodwill. Now it was obvious, too, why the Snarler had always worn the hat with the gaudy red and yellow band and had cultivated that habit of sullen silence. Most obvious of all was the fact that the witness Simone had been planted at the Service Station at Steele's Corners so that he would testify, as the other two service station attendants had not, that on the night of the murder the mannikin had moved and talked. Yes, now the coolly calculated, cold-blooded character of the insolent alibi was all too apparent.

Upon questioning from Halloway, sales manager Rowland testified that a man calling himself Joseph Marvel had come to the Superior Mannikin office, saying he was from Canton and belonged to an amateur dramatic group calling themselves the "Canton Thespians." Explaining that the members of this organization were well-to-do individuals to whom the matter of expense was of little consequence and giving a plausible story about a mystery show they wished to stage, the fellow had brought with him the cast of a face with a scar by the left lower corner of the mouth and had asked that a sitting figure of certain dimensions with this ugly, scar-blemished face be constructed and sent to an address in Canton where the Canton Thespians supposedly had their headquarters.

Then Halloway put on evidence showing how the police, following one difficult clue after another, had finally ferreted out the facts. Investigation had first revealed that there were no Joe Marvel and no Canton Thespians in that city. It had further shown that the address given by the alleged Marvel as the dramatic group's headquarters was an empty storeroom in a dubious part of the city that had been rented for a brief two months by a fellow going under the name of Pete Mendoza. This Mendoza, at first, had proved as elusive as the mysterious Marvel, until police had shown mug shots to the landlord of the storeroom, when it was discovered that the so-called Mendoza was a former slot-machine salesman of Mantanelli's, now living in Youngstown and masquerading under a false name. Then, following every lead and figuring that Mantanelli would try to get someone locally unknown to secure the lifelike dummy, they had finally found out that the fellow calling himself Marvel was a hood of plausible appearance and ready tongue imported from Pittsburgh. It had been an intricate, involved web that had taken a long time to untangle, but at last it had been done.

Further incriminating evidence was given by two policemen who had systematically combed the dumps of the city of Akron until they had unearthed the fragments of a shattered dummy, one of these fragments showing the end of a telltale scar on what had been part of the mannikin's jaw.

But there was yet one final telling stroke—a stroke,

as I later learned, that had been suggested by Holmes himself. This was the presentation as a last damning exhibit of an almost exact replica of the lifelike dummy, as testified to by Mr. Rowland, complete with a duplicate of the rakish snap-brim hat of the vicious Scala, with its familiar raucous red and yellow band.

That did it. The outcome of the trial was no longer in doubt. Furious at Mantanelli for the undertaking of the perpetration of such a hoax, and fuming with frustration in the face of defeat, Pollock might declaim and storm and bellow and wave the magic-making eyeglasses like a sorcerer trying to cast a spell, but it was all to no avail. The sneering Snarler was doomed. I felt sure that Halloway did not need to worry about the courage of the jury. In the face of such spectacular evidence, they would not dare to find him *not* guilty.

After the trial, Holmes and I separated, he to go on to the West Coast and I to turn back to Niagara Falls, then through the part of the States known as New England, and finally to New York to board ship for home.

After I got back to London I received a letter from Holmes telling me that he had had one of Biggs's terse notes informing him that when the Snarler came before the judge for sentencing he ratted and gave full information implicating Mantanelli in the Akron murder and insuring the downfall of that arrogant tyrant and his petty kingdom.

At length, too, Holmes was back in England, and on the night of his return our talk inevitably turned to the dramatic trial and the destruction of the preposterous alibi.

"But how did you guess in the first place that the figure in the car with Mantanelli was a dummy?" I asked.

"Simply because it couldn't be anything else. When you have had to reject all other answers to an enigma and there is but a single one left, that is the one that you have to accept, no matter how improbable it may seem. Besides, I recalled reading an account in the American periodical called the *Reader's Digest* of a woman crossing the continent all alone in a car with a mannikin in the seat beside her for protection. At the time it occurred to me that if such a figure could be used to forestall a crime, it might be used to conceal one."

"I see. One other question."

"Yes?"

"Why did you suggest that Biggs try to find out if Mantanelli had any contacts with the employees of a department store?"

"Ah, that? That, I must confess, my dear fellow, was something of a shot in the dark. I said to myself, 'If I wanted to find out how to get hold of a mannikin, where would I go?' Why, to the most familiar place I knew of where such things were used—to a shop that displayed such figures in its show windows—and to a fellow like Mantanelli this would suggest a department store.

"As it happened, this was an intuition that paid off. Following my suggestion, Biggs found out that there was an employee in the receiving department of the M. O'Neil Co., one of Akron's leading department stores, who was intimate with one of Mantanelli's hoods. By the exercise of a little ingenuity, the police learned through the employee that this hood had made inquiries as to where the M. O'Neil Company purchased its show-window figures.

"From then on it was just a matter of time until the police searched out all the facts. In the investigation of crime you are almost bound to succeed if you know what you are after and just keep at it long enough."

"Well," I exclaimed, "it all sounds logical as you tell it! And at first it seemed completely baffling. With that everlasting reading of yours about mesmerism and hypnotism, you had me thinking that the whole thing involved some kind of thought control."

"But it did," he said.

"It did!" I stared at him, amazed.

"Why, my dear fellow, what is it but thought control when you convince people that they are seeing something that isn't there?"

"Humph, I suppose you're right," I grunted.

BESTSELLERS

☐ ALWAYS IS NOT FOREVER—Van Slyke	04271-0	$2.25
☐ KISS—R. Duncan	04112-9	$1.75
☐ TIM—C. McCullough	08545-2	$1.75
☐ MIDNIGHT EXPRESS—B. Hayes with W. Hoffer	04302-4	$2.25
☐ A BRIDGE TOO FAR—Cornelius Ryan	08373-5	$2.50
☐ CHILD OF THE MORNING—Paulene Gedge	04227-3	$2.25
☐ A CORONARY EVENT —Michael Halberstam, M.D. & Stephan Lesher	04213-3	$1.95
☐ DO BLACK PATENT LEATHER SHOES REALLY REFLECT UP?—John R. Powers	08490-1	$1.75
☐ EARTHLY POSSESSIONS—Anne Tyler	04214-1	$1.95
☐ THE FURY—John Farris	08620-3	$2.50
☐ THE HEART LISTENS—Helen Van Slyke	08520-7	$1.95
☐ TO KILL A MOCKINGBIRD—Harper Lee	08376-X	$1.95
☐ THE LAST BATTLE—Cornelius Ryan	08381-6	$2.25
☐ THE LAST CATHOLIC IN AMERICA —J. R. Powers	08528-2	$1.75
☐ THE LONGEST DAY—Cornelius Ryan	08380-8	$1.95
☐ MARINA TOWER—Charles Beardsley	04198-6	$1.95
☐ THE MIXED BLESSING—Helen Van Slyke	08491-X	$1.95
☐ MY HEART TURNS BACK—Oliver B. Patton	04241-9	$2.25
☐ SKIN DEEP—Susan Hufford	04258-3	$1.95
☐ SWEET GOLDEN SUN—Parris Afton Bonds	04226-5	$1.95

Buy them at your local bookstore or use this handy coupon for ordering:

POPULAR LIBRARY
P.O. Box C730, 524 Myrtle Ave., Pratt Station, Brooklyn, N.Y. 11205

Please send me the books I have checked above. Orders for less than 5 books must include 75¢ for the first book and 25¢ for each additional book to cover mailing and handling. I enclose $_____ in check or money order.

Name_____

Address_____

City_____State/Zip_____

Please allow 4 to 5 weeks for delivery.

HISTORY • BIOGRAPHY
• POPULAR CULTURE

Outstanding Non-Fiction Titles

THE THIRTEENTH TRIBE 0-445-04242-7 $2.25
by Arthur Koestler

This book by a world-famous author proves that the true ancestors of Western Jewry were not Semites but Khazar warriors. "Clear and convincing."—*Newsweek*

KISS 0-445-04112-9 $1.75
by Robert Duncan

They wear seven-inch platform heels and lurid, Halloween makeup. They are the rock group that America loves to hate. They are KISS. And this is their incredible story. Illustrated with photographs.

WHERE ARE THEY NOW? 0-445-04264-8 $1.75
Yesterday's Sports Heroes Today
by Phil Berger

They were the champs, and the sluggers. They made and broke the records, drew and held the crowds, earned and lost the money. Here are 50 sports greats and what happened to them after the applause died down. Illustrated with photographs.

ROBERT ALTMAN 0-445-04262-1 $2.25
American Innovator
by Judith M. Kass

Some love him, some hate him. But no one ignores the contribution of director Robert Altman to the art of American film. From *Mash* to *Nashville* and *Three Women*, Altman's films are technically outrageous, artistically stunning. Here is the first book to take an in-depth look at this provocative and ambitious filmmaker. Illustrated with photographs.

Buy them at your local bookstores or use this handy coupon for ordering: